The

RISE

of

LIGHT

ALSO BY OLIVIA HAWKER

The Ragged Edge of Night
One for the Blackbird, One for the Crow

The
RISE
of
LIGHT

A Novel

OLIVIA HAWKER

LAKE UNION
PUBLISHING

Published by Lake Union Publishing, Seattle

www.apub.com

Amazon, the Amazon logo, and Lake Union Publishing are trademarks of Amazon.com, Inc., or its affiliates.

ISBN-13: 9781542022453 (hardcover)
ISBN-10: 1542022452 (hardcover)
ISBN-13: 9781542017954 (paperback)
ISBN-10: 1542017955 (paperback)

Cover design by Rex Bonomelli

Printed in the United States of America

First Edition

The
RISE
of
LIGHT

1

THE HOLY GHOST

June 1, 1975

It was the first Sunday of the month, which meant Fast and Testimony. Tamsin was stuck in the Rigby family pew, sandwiched between her eldest brother, Aran, to her left, and the twins, Ondi and Brig, to her right. The twins had recently turned nineteen, so they were taut with anticipation, expecting to receive their calls to missionary work. Ondi and Brig were dreaming already of the places they would go, the new lands that would open eager arms, desperate for salvation. Ondi was actually shivering. Tamsin could feel it, a vibration running all through her brother, as if his soul (whatever a soul was) couldn't bear to keep still, even though his body remained calm and reverent, his back erect and his arms folded in the prescribed posture of sanctity.

The ward deacons—boys of twelve and thirteen years—were making their way down the aisles with the sacrament trays. Tamsin watched as the tray of broken-up white bread was passed from hand to hand among her cousins and aunts and uncles at the far end of the pew.

She never could watch the proceedings of a sacrament meeting without a pang of guilt. Her parents had dreamed of completely filling that pew with their children, a veritable army of Rigbys, all Gad and Arletta's breeding. But Tamsin had been the last of their children, born seventeen years ago. Her mother, Arletta, had had some mysterious difficulty while pregnant with the twins, the nature of which Tamsin had never understood, for Arletta refused to speak of it. The doctor had warned her not to attempt further pregnancies, but Gad, Tamsin's father, had insisted that the Lord knew better than any two-bit doctor with a fancy medical degree. He had prayed, and God had told him to get his wife with child again, as quickly as possible, and the blessings of Abraham would be his: children numerous as the stars.

The doctor had proved wiser than God, in the end—a fact that had stuck with Tamsin all her life. Arletta had almost lost Tamsin in the womb, and after her birth—Cesarean section—they'd had to take Arletta's uterus, too. There would be no more children for Gad Rigby. Only these four, which couldn't help but disappoint when you'd been promised the stars in the sky. Tamsin had always suspected that Gad blamed her in some vague yet permanent way. She was a wound in the Rigby body that could never be healed, a lasting reminder of Gad's failure to do what Mormon men do: be fruitful and multiply.

The sacrament tray came closer. Tamsin's younger cousins tried to sneak a few extra pieces of bread since it was fast day and they were hungry. Everybody in the whole church was hungry, except for Tamsin. She had spent the morning upstairs in her bedroom, because she'd gotten her period and had managed to convince her mother that she felt too sick to come down for family prayer. But she didn't really feel much worse than any other day. She'd sat cross-legged at the foot of her bed, listening to records on the old player Aran had given her when he'd bought a nicer turntable for himself. Tamsin's player had a set of big plastic headphones that could block out all the sounds of her home—Arletta singing in a wandering, warbly voice while she did whatever it was she did on Sunday mornings, and Brig and Ondi arguing in the hall, and her father yelling at Aran from his shop. All the noise of life was muffled by the music, and the music was nothing like her life. Whenever Aran went to the city, out to Idaho Falls, he brought new music back for Tamsin, but he didn't give her the records till they were alone, because no one else would approve of a girl listening to that stuff—David Bowie and Blue Öyster Cult and the Rolling Stones, Jimi Hendrix—worldly music, which meant it was music that made you think thoughts as big as the world. Tamsin hid the new records inside old sleeves that used to hold the Osmonds and recordings of the Tabernacle Choir, but she and Aran had long since taken those saccharine old records out to the unbuilt lots at the edge of town and flung them like Frisbees, betting on who could send Donny and Marie sailing farthest into the weeds. The music was just one of the secrets Tamsin and Aran shared. In fact, the music was the smallest of their secrets. Nothing made Tamsin feel more sure of herself than knowing a thing almost no one else knew, no one in the world.

That morning, she'd been up in her room with those heavy head-phones shutting out the world, replacing it with Neil Young. She'd wondered what it would be like to cross the ocean in search of one particular heart, the right kind of heart. Tamsin had often imagined leaving in search of something she couldn't define, but she had never seen an ocean before—not with her own eyes, not standing right there on its shore.

All the while as she'd thought of this, Tamsin had eaten saltines and Snack Mate cheese straight from the can. That was why she wasn't hungry, even though it was Fast Sunday. She kept the crackers and cheese in a shoebox under her bed, especially for the first Sunday of every month, because she didn't believe in fasting or bearing testimony. There were a lot of things Tamsin didn't believe in.

Arletta took her piece of bread and placed it piously on her tongue, then took the handle of the tray from Tamsin's uncle and swung it toward Brig. But Arletta wasn't watching Brig as he went through the motions of the sacrament. Instead, she stared past the twins, straight at Tamsin.

Tamsin had the uncomfortable, twitchy feeling that her mother knew she'd eaten on Fast Sunday and, to make matters worse, had spent the morning listening to worldly music. Her face started to get hot, but she told herself not to be stupid. There was no way Arletta could have known, not really. She met her mother's eye and smiled softly—just enough of a smile to look sweet and complacent, not enough to look irreverent.

Arletta jerked her head up toward the front of the chapel, a gesture so small only a mother's own child could notice. Tamsin was careful not to let her smile slip or to look away till her mother looked away first. Arletta expected her to get up there in front of the whole ward and bear her testimony. It was what good girls were supposed to do, eventually, at some point: proclaim before the whole community their unshakable faith in the church and prophet, their certainty that all of this was true. Some kids did it as young as eight years old. Some did it even younger, but always with their dads behind them, guiding what they should say. Tamsin had made it to seventeen without bearing testimony once. She didn't like the idea of baring anything in front of so many people. It had never seemed right to her, this public display of a thing that should have been private and sacred and honest, if it existed at all. There was only one person in all the world she could show herself to.

"People are going to notice, sooner or later." Arletta had said that the previous month, on the drive home from church, when yet again Tamsin's testimony had not been forthcoming. "Everyone will wonder where your faith is. You'll never find a husband if the whole town thinks you don't believe."

Ondi ate his bread, took the tray from Brig, and passed the sacrament to Tamsin. For a moment, she considered handing the tray to Aran without taking any bread for herself. After all, she didn't believe; she had no testimony. What right did she have to sit there, listening while others spoke of their faith and shed hot tears of passion? (There was always somebody crying during testimony. Usually they all cried, even the men.) But she could still feel her mother watching. Her father was watching now, too, and there was a heightened tension about Gad Rigby today. She could feel it in the way her brother Aran shrank away from him, leaning subtly into Tamsin's shoulder. Gad was looking for a reason to snap. Like some old junkyard dog. If she didn't play the role of the obedient daughter, there'd be hell to pay, no doubt. And Tamsin didn't know where she would go, how she would live, if she didn't carry on as the sweet, the complacent, the perfect Mormon girl.

She ate her bread. Then she took the handle of the tray and passed it to Aran. He took his bread, too, and put it in his mouth. As he held the tray for Gad, Aran kicked Tamsin lightly on the ankle. It didn't hurt. In fact, it made Tamsin smile—a genuine smile this time. That was the way they had, Tamsin and Aran, the special, silent communication that said, *Neither of us wants to be here, but here we are, all the same. Might as well make the best of it.*

After the bread came the water, delivered in tiny plastic cups that rattled when the congregation dropped them back into the trays. And then it was time for the bearing of testimonies.

One after another, the congregants went to the front of the chapel and stepped up to the microphone, and Tamsin stifled her yawns and tried her best to sit still with her arms folded, and tried not to think about the cramps in her back or whether she was bleeding through her pad and all over the skirt of her dress. Everybody who went up to that microphone recited the same words they all said, always, every time, Fast Sunday after Fast Sunday. *I'd like to bear my testimony. I know this church is true.* It was like they'd all rehearsed it, like they were reading from cue cards. Like they were afraid of what might happen if they deviated even a little from the script. *I'd like to bear my testimony. I know this church is true. I know Joseph Smith was a prophet; I know Joseph Fielding Smith is a prophet today.*

I'd like to bear my testimony.

I know this church is true.

The tears, the sobs, the wavering voices. All this was supposed to be a manifestation of the Holy Ghost. Tamsin never doubted that the congregants were swept up by genuine emotion. But it was the thrill, she supposed, of standing up in front of a group of like-minded people and proclaiming yourself one of them. The thrill and the excitement; the terror, for some of them, of putting one's self on display. She knew that feeling well enough.

This couldn't be the true fire of divine inspiration. If such a being as the Holy Ghost existed, it must be more original than this. Surely divine inspiration didn't make you do the same tired thing everybody else had done a thousand times before.

Through the hours of rote recitations, Tamsin bumped Aran's ankle with her foot or jabbed him surreptitiously with her elbow, or felt the lean of his weight against her shoulder, and read in that minute change of his posture his exasperation and resignation, and the intrinsic humor of it all, the way they each felt so thoroughly trapped and yet there were no bars on their cage. They could leave, in theory, at any time, but they never did—not even Aran, who was twenty-three now and a man by anybody's reckoning. That was the funny part, the strange part: how they both just *stayed*. As if they expected that something would be different this month, this Sunday, this any-day-of-the-week. Nothing was ever different. Not here.

She watched her brother from the corner of her eye, the way his lips pressed together, his fists tightened where they rested on his knees. She wondered what Aran would do and what he would make of himself if he ever left the town. He would cross the ocean, Tamsin knew. That was Aran for you—big in a way that had nothing to do with physical stature or the way other men saw him. His bigness was all on the inside, but Tamsin could see it. Aran would find ocean after ocean and cross them and never be afraid of what waited on a distant shore.

Sometimes Tamsin watched Aran when he didn't know he was being watched. And then she loved him most of all, because in the moments when he thought himself alone, something lifted from him—a weight or a darkness, the deliberate confinement he carefully maintained when he could feel the world's eyes upon him. Then, in the half acre out back of the sign shop, or in the green shade beside an irrigation ditch, under an abstracted willow, his limbs would go slack and his shoulders would loosen. His back would curve as he settled into the silence, and there would come over his face a certain expression Tamsin couldn't define. His eyes would be closed, always. His mouth would fall open, just a little, as if he had to taste the world. And his brows would draw together, and the corners of his eyes go tense, and he would look both hungry and ecstatic, simultaneously overfilled and emptied of everything, even sense, even hope, even self.

That month's testimony meeting was an especially zealous one. Tamsin couldn't pretend any longer that she was transfixed by every speaker. She allowed her attention to wander around the chapel. Now and then, one of her school friends, who were seated with their families in the other pews, saw her looking and smiled. She stared hard at Lauresa, who'd been a freshman that school year but had been in Tamsin's junior English class because she was so smart. Lauresa felt Tamsin looking and glanced over. Tamsin crossed her eyes and held the expression. She knew Lauresa was doing the same. They'd done it all through the school year, whenever their teacher's lectures had grown too boring to bear. The object was to face one another with crossed eyes until one or the other couldn't take the absurdity any longer and started to laugh. It was a dangerous game to play in church, especially during Fast and Testimony, and doubly so because Gad and Arletta were both ready to snap the head off one of their children, or all four. But Tamsin wouldn't be the one who cracked up first. She was certain of that.

Aran nudged her hard with his elbow. Tamsin felt a little guilty then for clowning around. She left Lauresa to hold in her giggles and looked the other way, down past the far end of the Rigby pew to where the Jepson family always sat. Old Russ Jepson was there with his plump, white-haired wife, and Sandy was back in town—Russ's granddaughter. Sandy had moved away years ago with her parents and all her siblings because her dad had taken some important job engineering airplanes out in a big city on the West Coast, but Sandy had always come back to Rexburg every summer because she loved her grandparents that much. Or because she liked the town that much, though Tamsin couldn't understand why anyone would willingly return to Rexburg when they had a city to explore. But Sandy was a nice girl—always had been. She was nineteen, like Brig and Ondi. Tamsin had assumed Sandy would give up on Rexburg now that she was an adult. But there she undeniably was, watching the testimonies with rapt and shining eyes.

Even more interesting than Sandy was the girl who sat beside her. Tamsin had never seen her before, and in a town the size of Rexburg, there was no one who could escape notice. She must have been an outsider—come over from Sandy's new city, Tamsin supposed, for she was seated right beside Sandy, shoulder to shoulder like a friend. The newcomer was Sandy's age, too, with a sharp nose and black hair cut into a long, tousled shag, and though she faced the podium, her eyes flicked around the chapel, lighting on the backs of heads, the piano woman slumped on her bench, the placard above the altar displaying the numbers of the day's chosen hymns. The stranger was both reverently still and restless. Tamsin was transfixed by the mystery of the dark-haired girl, the contradiction.

The man who'd been speaking finished his testimony and made his way back to his pew, dabbing at his eyes with a handkerchief. The bishop shifted in the foremost pew, on the verge of standing to call the meeting to a close, but then Aran rose, so suddenly that Tamsin jumped in her seat. He slid past their father and walked up the aisle. The space beside Tamsin felt conspicuously, dangerously empty. The wood of the pew still held warmth from Aran's body, but he seemed so dreadfully and finally gone, as if he'd died, as if he'd never existed. Across the void where Aran once had been, Gad went tense—a tight, fierce energy Tamsin didn't understand but recognized. Gad knotted up that way whenever Aran did anything on his own.

Aran approached the microphone, opened his mouth to speak. By chance, his eyes found the Jepson pew and he paused, slack and stunned. For a moment, Tamsin thought he was staring at Sandy, but then she understood that Aran was caught up by the dark-haired stranger with the restless eyes. Then he recovered himself and tipped the microphone up to catch his voice. The mic squealed in the weary silence.

"Brothers and sisters," Aran said, "I'm grateful for this opportunity to stand before you today and share my thoughts on the church and what it has meant to me."

He spoke so smoothly, with such self-assurance—something he'd learned how to do on his mission, Tamsin guessed. He'd been sent to New York City, which had excited Aran and infuriated Gad, because New York was about as worldly and secular a place as you could find, and Gad was sure that meant Satan was going to get his claws into his eldest son and change Aran forever. Tamsin had endured the mission in a state of constant low-grade pain, like having a headache that wouldn't subside for two years. Aran was the only Rigby who understood her, who even tried to understand. Doing without Aran had felt like doing without half of her body or a hemisphere of her brain. The few letters and postcards he'd been permitted to send had sustained Tamsin through the most difficult years of her life so far.

Aran said, "I have a good family, a righteous family that nurtures and upholds me, and I hope I make them proud. I have the best examples in my mother and father of the kind of woman I want to marry someday and the kind of man I want to be. I have opportunities . . ."

Aran faltered there. The microphone whined again, a tinny, panicked sound. Tamsin thought of the shack at the edge of the wheat field, all the things it contained, the small beauties of the world—the sanctuary Aran had made for himself, the secret he allowed only Tamsin to share.

He said, "I have opportunities many other people in the world lack. I'm grateful for the blessings the church has brought me. I'm grateful that I was born into this church and have only known goodness and righteousness from the time I was a baby."

Don't say it, Tamsin thought. *Not you.*

But he did say it. Her brother—who was so different from the rest, spectacularly different from everybody else in Rexburg, which might as well have been the whole world as far as any Rigby was concerned—he said what they all said.

"I'd like to bear my testimony before you all today. I know this church is true. I know Joseph Smith was a prophet of God. I know his teachings lead to happiness."

Aran didn't look happy. His eyes were distant, not with the holy transport that usually carried speakers on Fast Sunday, but with something that looked very much like sadness.

"I say these things in the name of Jesus Christ," Aran said. "Amen."

Amen, the congregation answered—even Tamsin. There were no bars on the cage, but a good girl always stayed.

2

Interior Portrait

Aran never kept his radio turned up loud when he was in the shack at the edge of the wheat field. Mainly because the reception was terrible, and he found it distracting. He'd just get into the flow of a painting, he'd sense exactly which way the light ought to fall across the canvas or identify the perfect place to drop in a hard edge or that compelling play of warm color against cool, and then the music would turn to static and he'd be pulled right out of the moment. He'd have to start over, feeling out the work, doubting the painting before it had really begun.

But he also kept the radio low so he could hear if someone was coming. He didn't like the thought that anyone could find the shack and the things it contained. Especially, no one ought to come upon the shack while Aran was absorbed in his painting. There wasn't much worse than being caught unawares.

The wheat field and the old disused shack were almost a mile outside Rexburg, which meant they were three miles, maybe more, from home and Gad's sign shop, where Aran was supposed to be working part time. He did work there, in fairness. He put in the twenty-five hours per week his father expected, and sometimes more. But he avoided the shop whenever Gad was present. Now that Aran was a man, with a mission behind him and the whole nine yards, Gad could say little about his comings and goings. As long as he finished the work his father left for him to do and kept the family business running smoothly, there was little anyone could say against Aran Rigby. But folks would talk about Aran no matter what he did. That was a lesson he'd learned years ago.

Above the faint hiss of the radio and the forced cheerful chatter of the DJs, above the sounds of the wheat field sighing, the distant highway, Aran could hear his kid sister, Tamsin, whistling at the edge of the field. She did the special pattern that was theirs alone—a short, rising note, then a fall. Aran whistled the response. A moment later, Tamsin stood in the doorway, blinking. Even though the shack's windows let in plenty of light, it was painfully bright outside with the sky so open above you and the earth so dry and pale brown, even in June. It took a while for your eyes to adjust to the interior. Tamsin leaned against the door frame, waiting for Aran to say something. He didn't. He liked to get on her nerves by keeping quiet. That was what big brothers were supposed to do. It was funny, the way she rolled her eyes when she started to feel a little flustered. And anyhow, Aran thought women did enough keeping quiet and waiting for men to speak. Or at least women kept too quiet out here in Idaho. He had met all kinds of other women in New York, but his mission seemed a very long time in the past—decades gone by, rather than a couple of years.

Tamsin kicked something across the floor—a pebble or a chip of wood. She was wearing the striped culottes she'd made the week before, even though their mother said they weren't modest enough for a Sunday. She must have left the house when no one was looking.

"Aren't you coming home tonight?" Tamsin said.

"It isn't late."

Aran returned to his painting. He had set up a still life days ago on a small table beside one of the windows—bunches of coreopsis in an old blue pitcher. He had to work on the painting every day, this precise time in the afternoon, an hour or so before sunset, because the light was consistent. The coreopsis were withering, petals falling fast. He didn't have many more days to finish.

Tamsin said, "Sunset pretty soon."

Aran shrugged.

"You'll come back home, though, won't you?"

There was such urgency in her voice that Aran stuck his brush in the can of turpentine and looked at her again. There was a flush on Tamsin's cheeks and a smudge under one eye, as if she'd wiped her face with the back of a dirty hand.

"Tam, when have I ever not come home before? Besides when I was on my mission—that doesn't count."

"I don't know. You were just different today. In church."

Aran sighed. He'd known Tamsin wouldn't like it, if he got up and did the testimony thing. He hadn't liked it much, either. But he had to do something, he had to try to make things work—this life, the doubts that soured his insides. Or maybe it wasn't doubt inside him so much as it was longing. What kind of longing, Aran couldn't say. There was a restlessness in his soul, a feeling of being incomplete, a feeling that he would always be incomplete because completion was a cruel, hard lie. He didn't know what to make of it. He had hoped that standing up in front of the whole ward and saying the things that seemed to comfort and reassure everyone else would comfort and reassure him, too. Instead, he'd left the podium shaking.

He had expected to find purpose and resolve at the testimony meeting. But all he could think about were the petals dropping off his coreopsis flowers and how quickly time ran, how day by day, the still life was changing and soon it would be too degraded, too transformed, for him to paint it from life any longer. He would need to take photos and then wait to get them developed, and photos weren't the same. He was losing minutes and light. There were other things a proper man was supposed to think about, he knew, but that was what it all came down to for Aran: minutes and light.

"Why was Dad so ticked off at you today?" Tamsin said.

"You noticed."

"He was all stiff and red around you."

"He's always that way, with me."

"More today than usual. What happened?"

"You know Grandpa is sick," Aran said. "I think it's weighing on Dad's mind."

"No, this is something different. Grandpa has been sick for months, but Dad seemed grouchier than ever. Something really set him off."

Aran sighed. He looked at his canvas so Tamsin couldn't see his face. He didn't want Tamsin to hate their father. He didn't want himself to hate Gad, either.

The radio murmured in the silence—a newscaster talking about the dam that was being built upriver, the lawsuits some environmental group had filed to stop construction. *It's a travesty,* someone was saying, the words crackling through static. *It's a perversion of nature.*

Finally, Aran said, "Dad's upset because I wouldn't ask Judy Kimball for a date."

"Judy Kimball," Tamsin blurted, "the bishop's daughter?"

"I know. It's ridiculous. Even if Judy said yes—which she wouldn't—Bishop Kimball wouldn't let me within a hundred yards of his daughter. Not with all the stories this town likes to tell. And her brother would beat me to a pulp if the bishop didn't get me first."

"Which brother?" Tamsin said. "Joel?"

"It doesn't matter. Any of them. All of them. Yes, Joel most of all. Joel has heard the stories about me, I guarantee it."

"It isn't fair," Tamsin said. "None of the rumors are true. It's all a bunch of lies—stupid lies and slander."

He looked at her from the corner of his eye. Her gangly shape in the brightness of the door, the light pouring in around her, thinning and lengthening her form. That was the most he could bear to look at Tamsin just then. Rexburg did love to talk about Aran, but not all the stories were untrue. Or at least, they weren't entirely false. There was a fragment of truth inside, a small and shameful pit at the center of a rotting fruit. He couldn't bear it, that Tamsin should ever know just how all those rumors got started.

"You know Judy never goes to Singles Ward," Aran said, "since her father is the bishop and all the Kimballs stick together like glue. Dad heard through the grapevine that she isn't engaged, so he started in on me—'That Judy Kimball is a fine-looking girl,' and all that. I could see where he was heading, and I put my foot down before he got carried away with the idea. Can you imagine how this town would blow up if Gad Rigby's black-sheep son took the bishop's daughter to the drive-in?"

"Carnage."

"Dad tried to convince me to at least take Judy out on a group date. A group date! With who?"

"With whom," Tamsin corrected.

Aran ignored her. "He thinks I have friends. He thinks the other guys my age would be eager to pal around with me. He doesn't seem to realize—"

"He knows," Tamsin said. "He just pretends it isn't true, that you're not an outcast. He wants it all to be different, and he thinks somehow if he pretends hard enough, then everything will change."

"He blew up at me when I said no," Aran said.

"Of course he did."

"But, my heck, I'm sparing poor Judy the embarrassment. Imagine how she'd feel if I asked her for a date."

"You don't know that." Tamsin sounded offended on Aran's behalf. He didn't need to look at her again to know that she had pulled herself up in that way she had, a sudden vertical strength that always made her seem ten times bigger than anyone else, immovable as a mountain. "Maybe Judy thinks you're cute. Maybe she wants to stick it to her boring old dad. You don't know that she'd be embarrassed. You don't know unless you try."

Aran added a few more petals to the canvas. "Whose side are you on, anyway?"

"Yours, you big dummy. The problem is that you aren't on your own side. You don't give yourself a chance."

"Come on, Tam. No girl in this town would agree to go out with me unless she was a total stranger and hadn't heard the rumors at all."

Tamsin said nothing for a long moment. She didn't even shuffle her feet on the dusty floor. Aran knew then that she was thinking, remembering, running the day's testimony meeting over in her mind, playing back the moment when Aran had stood at the podium and looked out into the congregation and stopped. The black-haired girl in the Jepson pew. His face went hot, and he gripped his paintbrush so hard, it was useless in his hand. He had given himself away. Tamsin knew what he was thinking about. She always could tell.

"That new girl." Tamsin was crossing the shed now, coming to stand close beside him. "The one with the dark hair. With Sandy's family."

Aran rinsed his brush and beat the bristles on the leg of his homemade easel. Droplets of turpentine scattered in the air. The turpentine smelled harsh and compelling, like the feverfew plants that had naturalized all around the Rigby home. Those little white flowers had escaped, Aran's mother had told him once, from a pioneer garden left over from the days when Rigby ancestors had settled the Snake River Valley, a testament to the family's roots—deep, deep roots in dry, stony soil.

He said, "She's a friend of Sandy Jepson's—that new girl. Just arrived in town. She and Sandy are going to Ricks College in the fall."

"You know all about her."

"Her name is Linda."

Tamsin was staring at him, expectant and maybe a little amused.

Aran felt the need to explain himself. "Brig and Ondi told me about her. You know they've always run with Sandy's crowd during the summers, when she's back in town."

"You asked Brig and Ondi who she was." She was grinning at him now, teasing. "You like her."

"Cool it, will you? I don't even know her."

That was true, yet the new girl had still caught Aran's attention. Chapel and congregation and bare white cheerless walls had all seemed to recede before his eyes, everything fading and dissolving, retreating to some trivial point on a misty horizon, and even the podium under his hands had felt like air. The stranger had stared back at him, narrowing her eyes in a brief expression of suspicion or judgment. And he had felt himself pulled toward her, falling forward, tipping into the girl's compelling gravity.

"You might have had a chance with that stranger," Tamsin said, "if you hadn't borne your testimony."

"How do you know she didn't like it? Just because you didn't like me bearing testimony, that doesn't mean—"

"You didn't like to do it, either," Tamsin said.

Aran made no answer. She was right, as usual.

Tamsin said, "If you had to bear your testimony at all, why didn't you use your own words? Why did you say what everyone expected you to say?"

"For once, I wanted to try being the kind of man everyone expects me to be."

She smiled at him. Then she laughed, which lifted a little of the self-loathing from Aran's back.

She said, "You aren't the man everyone expects, and that's a good thing."

"According to you."

"Well, I'm your only sister, so my opinion ought to matter a lot more than anyone else's."

She was joking, but Aran couldn't go along with her game. He took up his palette knife, mixing just the right shade of yellow to capture the low, late sunlight on the drooping petals. He said, "Dad is never going to be satisfied with me. Doesn't matter how hard I work in the shop or how many testimonies I bear."

"It would help if you'd work during normal hours. Like, in the daylight. You only work nocturnally."

"Where'd you learn that word?"

"I'm smart," Tamsin said, frowning. "You wouldn't notice, 'cause all you ever do is make fun of me."

"I know you're smart, Tam. You're the smartest sister I have."

"I'm serious," she said, emphatic, almost stamping her foot. "Dad thinks it's weird that you only work at night. It makes him feel suspicious about you."

"I'm doing other things in the daytime."

"You're painting in the daytime. Out here in your shed."

"Exactly."

"Why can't you paint signs during the day and come out here at night?"

"No light. There isn't any electricity here, and anyway, it's not the same, painting under electric lights."

"How would you know it's not the same?"

"I've painted at home before, you know."

Tamsin hadn't known. Aran could tell from the way she stared. It almost made him feel like laughing, just knowing he'd finally surprised Tamsin with something.

"Look." He nodded toward a whole collection of Masonite panels propped up against one of the walls: the paintings that had dried over the preceding weeks.

Tamsin went to the paintings and knelt right there on the dirty floor. She began looking through the panels, one at a time. She paused over each piece, taking in Aran's work. It always gave him a sick, sinking feeling, to watch her looking at his paintings, because he felt like nothing was good enough to be seen.

Finally, Tamsin came to the piece Aran especially wanted her to see. It was, of all things, a simple interior portrait of the upstairs bathroom of the Rigby home. Aran didn't know why he'd painted it in the first place. Something about all that blue had caught his attention. It had been afternoon, and the sun had traveled to the other side of the house, so the eastern gable had been all quiet and shadow. No one had been at home, except for Aran. The air had been so still it had almost felt like a person, like the solitude had made itself into a body and had come up to stand very close beside him, and the difficulty that always seemed to plague him had lifted. He'd gone to his bedroom and taken one of the panels from under his bed along with the little pochade box he'd made from scraps of old signs. He'd sat on the floor in the hallway so the perspective was skewed, and he'd sketched it all in, colors and form, and then the door to the family car had slammed out in the driveway, so he'd put it all away again and had to finish the painting later, from memory, in his secret studio.

"Oh my God," Tamsin said. "It's perfect, Aran."

"It's all right."

"You should frame this, hang it up at home."

"No! Are you kidding?" Sweat sprang up under his arms at the mere suggestion. He couldn't bear the thought of his father walking past that portrait—past any painting Aran had made—and judging it the way he judged everything: harshly.

"Dad hasn't seen your paintings, Aran. If you'd only show him—"

"No." He said it with finality—maybe too much finality. Tamsin gave a little sniff, as if she were holding back tears, and Aran instantly felt like a monster. "I'm sorry. I didn't mean to be like that. It's just that Dad wouldn't understand if I showed him. He thinks this sort of painting is a waste of time. He thinks it's . . . girly somehow. I don't know."

"What's wrong with being a girl?" Tamsin said.

"Nothing, according to me, but lots, according to Dad. He can't ever see my paintings and you can't tell him, got it? He wouldn't understand. He'd make me give it up."

"You're twenty-three now. Dad can't make you do anything." Tamsin sounded uncertain, not even halfway convinced.

Aran only shrugged. They both knew Gad Rigby could make any of his children do any damn thing he pleased.

"Dad wants me a certain way," Aran said, returning to the coreopsis. "I want to make him happy, you know I do, but I just can't. So it's better if he never finds out about—" Aran waved his hand at the shack's interior.

"Same old, same old." She sounded a little sly, cajoling.

Aran knew what was coming next. His chest tightened.

She said, "Can't tell anyone anything."

"Tamsin—"

She flipped through a few more panels and pulled out another, just the one Aran knew she would find next. She held it up, facing out. The painting confronted Aran like an accusation. He couldn't look at it directly, and he damn sure couldn't look at his sister just then.

She said, "When are you going to finish this one?"

Aran lifted his eyes to the panel for as long as he could stand. It was mostly dark, mostly shadow, save for the side-lit figure, a young feminine shape standing in the light—Tamsin, nude.

Aran said, "I don't know. When I have the time."

"You have plenty of time. You said it was a study and you'd make a bigger painting from it someday, a better painting."

"It is. I will."

Someday when he could understand this thing he and Tamsin did together. That day hadn't come yet. If only that one study existed, the whole mess might have been something Aran could live with, but there were at least a dozen more in the shed and more still hidden elsewhere, in places where Aran was sure his family would never find them.

Tamsin had started the whole thing a year ago when their father learned she'd gone on a date with a boy he hadn't approved of—Nick, an Armenian kid from one of the immigrant families that worked on the farms. The boy wasn't a Mormon, and wasn't American enough for Gad's liking, and Aran had never known which offense Gad had found the greater. He'd gone to Nick's house and threatened the kid and his father, and the next day, the boy had broken up with Tamsin and she'd been furious and red faced, shuddering with the need for revenge. She'd come out to the shack. Before Aran could stop her, before he'd even realized what she was doing, Tamsin had stripped off all her clothes and said, *This is me. This is mine. It doesn't belong to anyone else. I want you to show me, make me believe it. I can't believe it any other way.*

Aran remembered being horrified at the sight of her, pale and womanly, taut with a wiry, latent strength. He also remembered how quickly he'd responded. He should have told her to put her clothes on, get hold of herself, go back home—or take a walk if she couldn't stand to be at home. Instead, something loud and heavy had roared right through him, something that had felt alive and distinct from himself. He felt no desire for Tamsin; the very thought that he might desire her turned his stomach. But whatever it was had left his ears ringing, his heart pounding high and wild in his chest, and he'd done what the feeling, the roaring thing, had told him to do. He always did its bidding whenever it came thundering in. He'd put a fresh panel on his easel. His brush had moved rapidly, guided and controlled by a force that was both inside and outside of himself. In minutes, the underpainting was complete, and by the time the study itself was taking shape, Tamsin was calmer, breathing easily, staring hard at the wall of the shack with an expression of confidence Aran had never seen on her before.

After that first study, Tamsin had gotten dressed and returned home without a word, and Aran had sat for hours at the edge of the wheat field till twilight came, wondering what the hell he'd just done, whether it had been art or sin. When the day was almost over, Aran had gone back into his shack. A thin, diminishing light had come wilting in through a window, and by its faintness, he'd looked at the study, still on his easel. The study was only a precursor to a better, larger, more completed thing, yet Aran knew at once it was the finest work he'd ever created. He had captured not Tamsin's nakedness but the nakedness of her rage, every line of her body tense and expressive, even the flushed hot color of her skin lively and undeniable.

The work was so good it had frightened him. He'd wondered if he'd been possessed. This was nothing like he'd ever experienced before. The painting had made itself; Aran had been only the vehicle for its creation.

But then, weeks later, Tamsin had asked him to paint her nude again—God knew what fresh sorrow or injustice had moved her. Aran had told her no. She had stripped anyway, like the first time, and as before, that thundering thing had run up to Aran and shaken him to his bones, and he'd had no choice but to try to capture in form and color the thing he saw before him, the planes and shapes and bending of light that described Tamsin's potent power and her abiding powerlessness.

It happened again and again, and Aran's protestations became only words he knew he was expected to say. The truth was, he was eager to paint her now, because he knew by now that only she could draw from him this great gouting flame of brilliance. He worked diligently at his other paintings, the mundane subjects, the still lifes, the landscapes. He worked in his father's sign shop in the evenings and did that work well, too. But there was only one subject that could arc sweet fire between his heart and his spine. And he had long since begun craving it, wanting her posed before him even when she wasn't there.

Tamsin dragged a dusty old ladder-back chair closer to a window.

"No," Aran said weakly.

She pulled her shirt off over her head and tossed it onto the table beside the vase of coreopsis. Aran watched, defeated and glad to be, as she unhooked her bra and threw it, too. Then the culottes came off, her socks, her shoes, everything except her underwear. He supposed she had reasons of her own for leaving those on.

She sat on the chair, rested one arm on its back, turned her face toward the light. "This good?"

"Jesus," Aran muttered, taking the still life off his easel, fitting a blank gesso panel in its place. Then he looked at her—but she wasn't Tamsin anymore. She was a composition, a thing asking to be made and made whole, made original. He said, "Turn toward the light a little more, if you can. There."

Aran worked quickly and with absolute assurance. That was the way it happened, when they did this thing together. It was smooth and perfect and easy, like nothing else in his life ever was; he knew where to put each stroke, every slash of color. And all through that golden stir of easy perfection, he asked himself whether he was a sinner or worse, a deviant, a pervert. Even though it had nothing to do with desire, he still felt filthy and hated himself a little bit more because he loved something so terrible, because he needed this shameful thing so desperately.

When he was finished—the new study took only twenty minutes, if that—Tamsin dressed in silence. The habitual calm was on her now, a soft glow of renewal as if she had exorcised something deep and monstrous from her soul. Aran took the panel down. He leaned it against the shack wall, under the still life table where he wouldn't have to look at it, and secured his coreopsis painting on the easel.

When he turned to look at Tamsin, Aran found her watching him, patient and waiting, because she knew he wanted to say something.

"Why do we do this?" Aran said. "Why do we keep making things we can never show to anyone? I don't understand the point of it, Tam. No one can ever see these paintings. No one would understand." He felt the usual guilt building up inside him—or rising, at least, coming to the surface so easily because it was always there, barely hidden.

She said, "That's why we do it. Because no one will understand."

Aran turned away. He never should have come back to Idaho. He should have left from New York, or stayed there. He should have run off one day and never gone back to his companion or the other missionaries. Every day since his mission, Aran had thought about the museums he'd seen in New York, and the feeling of walking those streets at night, the feeling of streets in a big city, a real city, not like Idaho Falls. The day's heat breathing out of the sidewalks and the brick, the pink light of evening, a summer evening, and the smell of night's coolness coming down. The noise of those streets had been like the noise of a waterfall, never ending, but it brought a rush of excitement along with the sound, a sense of possibility. Sometimes in New York a thrill would come over him, sweeping up behind while he walked beside his mission companion to the next block of apartments. That electric jolt would hit him in the back first. Then it would wrap around him and his heart would beat harder and his whole body would go hot and he would see something that would strike him as beautiful because it was so simple and ordinary and impermanent—the color, for example, of a fire hydrant against all that gray, or the slender arm of a woman leaning out from a high window to flick the ash off her cigarette.

But instead of staying and painting everything he felt, Aran had come home to Rexburg when his mission was finally over. Back to the dry summers and the glare. That was what good Mormon boys did, after all, and Aran was determined to make himself that: a good man of the faith. Here, painting brought little joy or relief, for there was only one subject he truly wanted to paint, and that was all shot through with shame. If he could get away again, if he could turn his back on this town and his family, he might find another place that captured his heart the way New York had done. He might find some other subject that spoke to him the way Tamsin's nakedness did. And then he could forget all about the studies. He could be free from Tamsin, free from his father, free from guilt and sin. Everything he painted would be excellent; nothing would disappoint.

"The light is dying," Aran said. "I need to get back to work. I'll come home tonight, I promise, right after sunset."

"Don't do that again," Tamsin said.

"Do what?"

"Testimony."

"Why not?"

"Because you don't really mean it. And you shouldn't say things if you don't mean them."

She was gone after that, and Aran stood alone in the silence of the shack. Far out over the wheat field, a magpie called with a rising, questioning note. It sounded very distant and lonely. He returned to the still life. He laid the brush against the canvas and marked out a slender petal, a line of gold through the dark.

3

The Feeling Would Pass

When Gad heard the hiss of bike tires on the gravel driveway, he came out of his sign shop. It was almost sunset. The light was low and golden, lazy, and Tamsin was riding slowly through bands of shadow from the birch trees across the street. She pedaled from one side of the driveway to another, back and forth, wobbling a little from the lack of momentum. She glanced at Gad now and again from the corner of her eye, in no hurry to come down the drive because then she would have to speak to him. Gad knew he wasn't exactly fun to talk to, especially not for a teenage girl, but his job was to be a father, not a friend. He could outwait the girl. He folded his arms, watching her dink around out there in the driveway, the front wheel of her bike shivering. Tamsin jerked suddenly at the handlebars to keep herself from falling. She was wearing shorts, which was probably something Gad ought to get after her about, especially since this was a Sunday. Her legs in the long evening light were distinct—the bare skin bright below her knees, the shape of her calves patent and far too adult. She was strong and lean and wiry now, and it made him uncomfortable to recognize the woman emerging from the child, his child, his youngest and his only girl. Tamsin used to have short, pudgy legs and a round face and a sweet personality, though she had never been exactly biddable. And now she was taking a new shape, one he didn't recognize, and soon his youngest child would be grown up and married, off to handle her own life, and Gad would have to confront the fact that he was already getting old. He was forty-four. That was too young to be an old man.

All these realizations made him feel—what? He'd never been much good at naming his feelings. Whenever he tried, they all congested into one vague but persistent pressure like clogged sinuses, an annoyance, something to be forcibly extracted and tossed into a wastepaper basket, the sooner the better. The feeling would pass, the way all feelings did. Gad would go on with his evening and his life, go on holding this family together with his two hands.

Finally, Tamsin gave up her dawdling and pedaled down the driveway to the shop. "Hi," she said, not looking at him. She got off her bike and leaned it up against the pale-green corrugated metal of the shop's wall. There was a horsefly bite near one of her ankles, red welted with a spot of dried blood in the middle. One of her knees was skinned. That made Gad feel better, some, about his being so danged old all of a sudden, and Tamsin growing up. She wasn't all that grown up if she was still skinning her knees and running through the fields where the horseflies lived.

Tamsin tried to head for the house. Gad said, "Wait a minute."

She stopped and faced him, arms already folded across her chest, like his were.

"What are you doing wearing shorts on a Sunday?"

"They aren't shorts, they're culottes."

"Whatever they are, you shouldn't be showing so much skin. And don't back talk me, either, Tamsin DeLene."

She sucked in a deep breath, then let out a heavy sigh. It was better than rolling her eyes, which was what Gad knew she really wanted to do. Tamsin never could stand it when you used her first and middle name together. She said, "Do you really think God cares if my legs show on a Sunday?"

That force inside Gad pushed outward, the tangle of feelings, so many he couldn't sort them one from another: offense at her sass, anger that she was back talking him, and a shocked, still sadness way down in his middle—sadness over this persistent questioning manner the girl had, as if she might not believe in God after all, and if that was true, what waited for her, this youngest precious child of his, Gad's only daughter, his treasure? You couldn't lead a happy life if you didn't have the Lord on your side; everyone knew that. And after you died—

"Oh my heck," Tamsin said when she noticed how red Gad's face had become. "It's not that big a deal, Dad."

"The Lord cares very much," Gad said slowly, struggling to moderate his tone, "about your modesty. You aren't a little kid anymore. You need to be more careful about modesty."

"People wear shorts all the time and God doesn't, like, send clouds of locusts after them."

"Those people are worldly. You are not. I raised you better than that."

She smiled then. It was small, secretive, and her eyes had a curious enigmatic cast, as if she were looking inward on some landscape Gad could never see.

The kid was too smart for her own good, and too much for Gad's liking most of the time. But even when Tamsin infuriated him, which happened on a daily basis since she'd reached adolescence, there was still a part of him that was proud of her fierce intelligence. He had made her, this sharp-eyed, willful, wholly alive thing. Other girls in the church, other men's daughters, were meek and complacent. They were like Arletta, yielding, uncomplaining, the way a woman is supposed to be. Tamsin had been a handful since she was a tyke, questioning everything. It had been cute for a while, but now it was troublesome. There was no way in heck Tamsin would find a good man to marry her if she couldn't keep her mouth shut and do what the head of the household said. Gad had been too permissive all along, too charmed by her unique spark, and too sinfully proud of having sired a kid like her—so smart and capable. He should have kept her on a tighter leash from a younger age.

He said, "Modesty in the way you dress is a reflection of the modesty that's in your heart."

Now Tamsin couldn't stop herself from rolling her eyes.

"Appropriate clothes," Gad went on, "are an outward reflection of appropriate thoughts. If you're flaunting your body, then it means you'll do anything with your body, and no one will respect you. Is that what you want? Do you want to marry a man who doesn't respect you and treats you like dirt?"

"Who says I want to get married at all?" She muttered those words, almost too quiet for Gad to hear. But he did hear.

"Dang it, Tamsin, I'm only trying to protect you. Don't you know that? I'm trying to keep you safe and set you up for a good, happy life. I'm your father; I don't want anything bad to happen to you. And it's time you started taking your future seriously. You're growing up fast. You're old enough to date now, not that I think you're mature enough to go out on your own—not after that stunt you pulled with the Armenian boy. But you will be dating one of these days, when you can demonstrate self-control."

"I can control myself just fine." Tamsin said it so levelly that it struck Gad as an immediate and undeniable truth. It was the truest thing he'd ever heard. The frank, inescapable fact of Tamsin's prodigious self-possession made him question, for one wild moment, everything he thought he knew. None of his own beliefs sat upon his soul with this same immovable certainty.

"Where's Aran?" Gad asked, just for a change of subject.

Tamsin looked down. She kicked a pebble out of the grass, back into the driveway. "I don't know."

"I've got work for him to do. Big lettering project. It needs to be finished by Wednesday."

"Maybe he's out walking."

"Why would he be out walking when there's work to be done here?"

"Not today," Tamsin said, smiling again in that covert fashion. "It's a Sunday."

Gad felt the pressure rising. He knew his face was turning red. He hated it when his face gave away his feelings to everybody else, while he still couldn't fathom his own emotions, not at all. He said, "I can show him what to do, though, so he can start first thing tomorrow." When Tamsin still said nothing, just went on toeing the grass, Gad said, "All right, get inside. Go see if you can be any use to your mother."

Tamsin turned at once and strode toward the house, briskly, as if she couldn't wait to get away from him.

Gad stared down the driveway to the road. A flatbed truck rumbled past loaded with bales of hay. Somewhere closer to the heart of town, a dog was barking, a high, repetitive yip, but far enough away that it wasn't a nuisance. The low light caught the dust kicked up by the hay truck; for a moment the driveway was swallowed in slow eddies of gold, glittering dust, and the even monotone of the barking dog was like a funny little spell cast over the fading day. The sound and the light pulled Gad back through the years, to when he was a kid playing with his many brothers and sisters down that same long driveway or sitting in the grass with a clipboard full of typing paper and a few pencils, drawing while the others chased each other around and around. And his mother had come out onto the step to call them in for supper; his mother who had always been so happy and serene, so warm, not like Arletta, who was distant all the time now—and had been, if Gad was honest, almost from the start, since long before Tamsin came along and took her ability to bear more children. His mother was happy with a big family. His father was proud and respected throughout the whole community; Rexburg looked up to Gad's father, the very best of the lauded Rigbys. What greater blessing, what better indicator of a man's worth in the eyes of the Lord, than an abundant family? And here Gad was with only four children, and no chance for more. And Tamsin was flaunting her bare legs and making noise about never getting married. And Aran . . . well.

Gad went to the door of his shop and picked a long stem of grass from an especially tenacious clump that grew next to the metal wall. He leaned there in the last vestiges of sunshine, sucking on the grass stem, prodding between his teeth. The light and those thick bands of shadow across the driveway certainly were pretty. So were the birches, pale trunks picking up the gold of evening, drooping catkins bobbing at the ends of their branches. Gad narrowed his eyes and watched the road instead of the trees. He felt it was wrong somehow to appreciate the beauty of the world too much. That was why he didn't allow himself to draw anymore. At least, he only resorted to sketching and scribbling when he was in such turmoil that the choice came down to picking up a pencil or doing something more drastic and unforgivable. It was weak and feminine to goggle at nature; it betrayed a lack of mastery over Creation. Adam was made to subdue the earth, to have dominion and lordship over everything upon it. Not to draw or paint like some woman.

If Gad couldn't exert his lordship by fathering a large and righteous family, at least he could run a good business. He was the most sought-after sign maker from Jackson Hole to Idaho Falls. That was something, wasn't it? And if he took too much pride in his success, he expected the Lord would forgive him that one small sin. After all, a man has to feel good about something in this life, or what's the point of living?

If only Aran would step up and take the business seriously, so Gad could be sure his legacy would continue even after his death. Damn that kid. Twenty-three years old and rudderless. And dreamy, and just about useless as far as Gad could see. Aran had been a good little thing when he was small, but the adolescent years had made him quiet and thoughtful—the way no natural boy was supposed to be. Gad had hoped Aran's mission would shape him up. Instead, he'd come home from New York ten times worse, full of worldly ideas and sullen silence. He'd even begun dressing like a city freak, faded jeans with wide legs and those loud paisley shirts; goodness knew where Aran found them. His hair was almost down to his shoulders these days, and he was growing a beard. It was embarrassing to sit next to Aran in church, looking like that. What must everyone think? And he still wasn't married. Wouldn't even ask any girls out for dates. What was wrong with Judy Kimball, that Aran should turn her down without even trying? A bishop's daughter would make a fine wife, and marriage with the Kimballs would lend Gad's branch of the Rigby clan some of the esteem they lacked because of their skimpy numbers. Yet Aran refused.

Four children, one of them too smart for her own good, and one a black sheep through and through. Gad would give Aran a piece of his mind as soon as he dragged himself home from wherever he'd been all afternoon. This wasn't the way a man was supposed to live. Aran would be made to see that, one way or another, for his own sake as much as for Gad's.

4

SONS OF PERDITION

The summer Aran was twelve, he felt grown up, and it wasn't till years later, after the world had kicked him around some and bruised him around the edges, that he came to understand just how young twelve really was. But the days were hot and long and there were cicadas that year, metallic in the grass. Later, he tried to remember what had drawn him out to the fields and canals, the banks where the air was lazy from the smell of heat and sluggish water. He thought it must have been the cicadas. That year, the sound those insects made was the biggest thing in all the world. The buzzing surrounded you and penetrated every moment and thought, and it was maddening, the way you heard the insects everywhere but never caught a glimpse of one, not ever. So that must have been why he'd ventured into the fields, and then he'd gotten distracted, he supposed, and stayed away from home too long, much later than he should have done.

Tamsin had followed Aran that Saturday. She was six, and Aran had long since learned it was no use trying to make her stay away if she wanted to tag along. She always insisted on following Aran. He didn't try very hard to make her stay. Aran and his friends, the other boys his age, had just been raised to deacons in the church, and the bishop had admonished them all to be good men now and look after their families. All the same, Aran knew his friends thought it looked funny when he came to the park to play ball and there was Tamsin, running along a few paces behind, her face smudged with dirt and one of her red-gold pigtails unraveling. It didn't matter whether they'd been charged to look after their families, the other boys still poked fun at Aran for allowing his kid sister to follow him like a duckling after its mother.

Aran bore their mockery with good humor. The truth was, he liked having Tamsin along on his adventures. She was funny, for one thing, and wanted to know everything about everything, so Aran could teach her everything he knew about the world and he could make up stories about the things he didn't know, and Tamsin would drink it all in, wide eyed and still, which made Aran feel as big as Goliath. Most of all, though, Aran could get away with a lot more when Tamsin was beside him. Their father's anger never came down too harshly on Tamsin. Because she was so young, or because she was a girl—Aran was never certain which—Gad would let their most unruly moments slide. He would shake his head fondly at Tamsin and call her a little scamp and send her on her way, and give Aran nothing worse than a small, silent frown that said he ought to set a better example for his sister and the twins, especially now that he was a deacon. This was nothing like the scolding Aran got when he acted on his own. Gad's full-force dressing down would leave Aran shaken for days, sick to his stomach with a lingering, unwelcome pressure. The pressure and the sickness got worse whenever his father looked at him with that accustomed expression, a cold, narrow stare of such distaste, Aran was sure his father hated him, actually hated him right to his core. After he grew up a little and realized how young twelve was, Aran figured out that the nauseating pressure was called shame.

That summer, cicada season, Aran and Tamsin went out into the fields a few blocks down the road to hunt for the bugs and find out once and for all what they looked like. Aran asked Brig and Ondi if they wanted to come along, but Ondi said no because Dad had said they could have ice cream that afternoon, and in his eight-year-old literal way, he didn't understand that the ice cream would still be there when they got back from hunting cicadas. And Brig planted his feet and went along with Ondi, because that was what Brig had always done.

So Aran had led Tamsin down the road and off into the tall grass, and they'd chased the whirring sounds of the insects and the brief flashes of movement, sun on glassine wings—and finally, hours later, they managed to catch one, a fat black thing with bulging gray eyes. It was the size of Aran's thumb, and it had a face, angular and armored, like the faces of invading robots in his comic books, and it scared him to look at it, let alone touch it. But he held the cicada down low so Tamsin could examine it, and he prayed it wouldn't bite his fingers while she leaned in close to stare.

After a few seconds, the cicada started to twitch, then to vibrate its abdomen against those magnificent and terrible wings. The sound was high and desperate, like a scream. Aran felt a surge of pity for the little creature, and a mysterious, powerful loathing for himself—the ease with which he'd held the bug, the fat, cold thrill of knowing he could crush it if he chose. He put the cicada up against a tuft of grass and opened his fingers. It crawled a few inches away, vibrated its body once more, then spread its wings and flew off in the direction of the river.

"Why did you let it go?" Tamsin said.

"Because it was scared," Aran answered.

"So?"

Aran crouched so he could look at Tamsin, right in her eyes. "We shouldn't scare little things. It isn't right."

"Why not?"

"Do you like to be scared?" Aran said.

She thought about it for a minute, turning to see where the cicada had flown to. She was quiet and sober in the way that meant she was thinking about what Aran had told her, really thinking. Finally, she answered, "No."

Only then did Aran notice the color of the light, how low the sun was riding in the sky. It was late afternoon—maybe past supper already. He took Tamsin's hand. She didn't want to leave the field and go back home, but Aran was starting to get worried. He didn't have a watch and couldn't guess what time it was, but he had that unpleasant feeling inside, a certainty that his parents would be angry—Gad especially. Gad most of all.

By the time they got to the edge of the field, Aran knew he was in trouble deep. Gad was there at the end of the block, where the newest house had just been built and the neighborhood gave way abruptly to weeds and scrub willows and the shallow slope leading down to the river. Gad was shading his eyes with his hand, peering the other direction, back up the street like maybe he expected to see Aran and Tamsin playing in someone's backyard. He wasn't alone. Sheriff Hatch was there, with one hand on Gad's shoulder as if he was trying to keep him calm, and over by the newest house, Aran could see a police car parked behind Gad's flatbed truck.

"There they are," the sheriff said.

Gad turned quickly. He gave a wordless cry when he saw his children. Aran never knew whether it was an angry sound or a glad one. But when he marched up to Aran, the stiffness in his gait was all rage, and Aran knew he was going to catch it bad that night.

"I told you they'd turn up, safe and sound," the sheriff said.

"Thanks, Brother Hatch. They're both in one piece, so I'll take it from here."

Gad swept Tamsin up in his arms and stood there in silence while Sheriff Hatch got into his car and drove away, waving out the window like everything was all right. Aran knew everything wasn't all right.

"Get in the truck," Gad said when they were alone again.

Aran got in the truck. The seat was hot from the late sun; the air inside felt too thick to breathe. Gad put Tamsin on the bench seat between himself and Aran and slammed his own door hard and started the engine. He pulled away from the curb with an energy that said he was mad enough to scorch.

"Do you know what time it is?" Gad said.

Aran shook his head.

"Do you have any idea how upset your mother is?"

"No," Aran said, because he knew it was what Gad wanted him to say. He had a pretty good idea how upset his mother was, and it made a lump come up into this throat. He never liked to hurt his mother's feelings.

"She's at home with the boys. She was worried sick about you both. We looked for you for hours. We had to call the police just to find you."

Aran thought that wasn't fair. Sheriff Hatch hadn't had a thing to do with their reappearance.

"What were you thinking, running off that way?"

"We didn't run off," Aran said. "We only went out into the fields to look for cicadas."

"Tamsin could have fallen into the river. She could have drowned."

"I wouldn't drowned," Tamsin said.

Gad hushed her gently, patting her knee, but when he spoke to Aran again, he was just as mad as before. "You're almost a grown man now. You've got the responsibilities of a deacon; you hold the Aaronic priesthood. You are supposed to behave like a man who's worthy of these honors, worthy of serving his Lord."

"I am worthy." Aran's protestation sounded weak, too high pitched.

"Where is the responsibility?" Gad pounded the steering wheel on that last word. It made Aran's heart leap in a shameful, fragile way, and made Tamsin sniff like she was about to cry. He and Tamsin looked at each other. She had an angry frown, but she wasn't mad at Aran. He knew that. She never got mad at him—not over something like this.

Gad said, "I've told you before that you need to live up to certain expectations. You can't fall short. You can't afford to fall short; no one can. I've told you repeatedly to tell your mother or me if you're going off somewhere, especially if Tamsin is with you, so we won't have to worry."

"I forgot," Aran said.

"You're too old for forgetting! You can't make that excuse anymore; not now that you hold the priesthood. It isn't forgetfulness anymore. It's plain disobedience. It's Satan's influence. You're an unruly child."

Aran folded his arms tight across his body, which felt very small and young under his own hands, not at all like the body of a man who could bear the burdens of priesthood. He looked out the truck's window, blinking so he wouldn't cry.

"I'm tired of your disobedience," Gad said. "Sick of it. You know what'll happen to you if you don't cultivate a spirit of obedience. You'll be cast into Outer Darkness. Is that what you want? To spend eternity beyond the reach of the Lord's love?"

Gad paused as if waiting for Aran to make some response.

"No," Aran said feebly, confused.

"You have certain obligations," Gad said. "That's what it means to hold the priesthood. You're expected to act in accordance with the laws of the Lord. It's your job to uphold righteousness. It's your job to remember your responsibilities. Above all else, it's your job to obey the will of the Father. There is no path to goodness that doesn't run through Him. If you don't obey the Father's will, you'll be named a son of perdition in the afterlife. You'll be thrown beyond the reach of Heaven. Your soul will be sent so far into the darkness that not even the Lord can reach you. Do you think I want that for my son? Do you?"

They had pulled up the long drive to the house by then, and Arletta came out the kitchen door and saw Aran and Tamsin both in the truck and wept into her hands, her whole body wilting with relief.

"Outer Darkness," Gad said, pounding the steering wheel again for emphasis.

Tamsin burrowed against Aran's side, whimpering.

"You're scaring her," Aran protested.

"Good. Everyone should be scared of crossing the Lord. Everyone should be scared of disobeying the Father."

Aran opened his door and got out while the truck was still rolling to a stop. He pulled Tamsin out before Gad had cut the engine and set her on her feet so she could run to their mother.

Gad was around the truck and at Aran's side before he could flinch away. He seized Aran by the back of his shirt. His nails scratched the nape of Aran's neck as he made a fist to hold him.

"You received the Holy Ghost when you were baptized," Gad said, low and cold, close beside Aran's ear. "What does Scripture say about the Holy Ghost and Outer Darkness?"

Aran struggled to remember. His throat had gone dry. "All sins will be forgiven, except any sin against the Holy Ghost."

"That's right. And what is disobedience?"

Aran leaned, trying to pull away from Gad. "Sin against the Holy Ghost?" He asked it as a question, because he wasn't at all sure the Bible or the Book of Mormon listed disobedience among the unforgivable sins. But he supposed Gad knew Scripture better than he did. At any rate, Gad wouldn't have asked if he hadn't wanted that answer. Aran guessed all sin was some form of disobedience, if you looked at it from the right angle. Maybe that made disobedience every kind of sin.

Gad noted Aran's attempts to cringe away. He pulled Aran closer. Aran could hear his mother crying and kissing Tamsin on her cheeks and the boys crying, too, everyone talking at once. Aran wanted nothing more than to let his tears fall along with everyone else, but he knew that would only provoke his father to a greater, more piercing rage. Over the sound of his family weeping, Gad's voice came slipping in, eclipsing all the rest of Aran's thoughts, the way it always did.

"Outer Darkness. Beyond even the Father's love. Never able to reach Him, never able to repent, trapped in an endless blackness where you're alone, entirely alone forever, and no love or mercy ever comes for you. Can you imagine what that must feel like?"

That night, after all the crying had stopped and Arletta had reheated supper and everyone had eaten a dish of ice cream just like Brig and Ondi had been promised, Aran went up to his room and tried to read his comic books. But all he could do was stare out the window. The cicadas hadn't stopped calling. He could still feel the place on the back of his neck where Gad had accidentally scratched him. He thought maybe there was no real difference between gods and fathers. It was almost ten o'clock, and the deep ruddy glow of sunset had faded to cool blue, and soon all the light would be gone from the sky and night would extend all around him. There was a dreadful longing inside him, a hollowness that went somehow beyond the mere limits of the flesh, a void bigger than his twelve-year-old body, bigger than the house, the fields, the night itself. Aran felt as if everything around him that was solid and real—all the dim, small things in his bedroom, and the birch trees at the end of the drive, and the sound of the cicadas that went on and on—all of it was poised to fall into the deep black pit of his longing, the place that should have been filled by his father's love. It frightened him, this sudden realization that an absence could be bigger and therefore more real than all the things he could see and hear and touch.

He sat very still beside his window, listening to the insects as they called. He watched darkness fall firm and binding across the land.

5

Lessons

When the first Sunday of the month was over, Linda and Sandy left their rented duplex on West Fourth South and prowled through the red evening toward the park. Linda had suggested the walk as she'd driven home from Sandy's grandparents' house, where the whole Jepson family had gathered to break their fast on a big supper of roast beef and baked potatoes. After an entire day without food, the rich, heavy meal sat like a rock in Linda's stomach. Or maybe it was only anxiety that weighed her down. Linda hadn't been able to shake a persistent thrum of worry since she and Sandy had arrived in Rexburg a few days before. Even the bustle of settling into their new home couldn't drive back the unease. Something had left her restless, whether it was fear or just the roast beef, and she was glad for the movement, the fresh air, the feeling of going somewhere.

"My family sure took to you," Sandy said. "All my aunts and uncles and cousins thought you were swell. And Grandma told me she thinks you're a real well-behaved girl. That's the best compliment you can get from her."

Linda laughed. "Gee, thanks. I liked your family, too."

Linda had long since fallen in love with Sandy's parents and siblings in Seattle. The Jepsons had seemed like a bulwark to Linda, their bright and noisy home a sanctuary from the grim, cold reality of her own family life. It came as no surprise that the Rexburg branch of the family was every bit as warm as the Jepsons back home had been.

"Your grandma is a great cook," Linda said, "but I think she fed me a little too well. It's a good thing I didn't try to put my jeans on when we got home. I'd have split a seam for sure."

"Don't let anyone catch you wearing jeans on a Sunday."

"Not even after church?"

"No way—especially not on Fast Sunday. You could get away with it in Seattle, but folks are more traditional out here."

They both still wore the same clothes they'd put on that morning. Linda's white blouse with crocheted collar and dark, ankle-length skirt made her feel dislodged, unmoored from linear time, as if she were drifting rather hazily between pioneer days and the modern era. She couldn't find her feet in either world. Sandy, for her part, was perfectly at home in a prairie dress of sweet blue gingham. Her golden hair was cut in the pageboy style, rolled at the edges—a thing Linda's hair would never do, not even if she'd wanted it to. Sandy's little upturned nose and freckles and big, bright, innocent eyes all fit so perfectly in Rexburg. She looked as if she'd risen up out of some farmer's field, grown there like a damn potato.

Back in Seattle, Linda had thought Sandy's carefully polished, conservative style intentionally quaint, maybe even ironic—mod, ten years too late. All the Mormon girls at their high school had been the same—the boys, too. It hadn't struck Linda till now, when she'd seen Sandy moving as naturally through Rexburg as a bird in flight, that the Mormon kids in Seattle hadn't been making a fashion statement. Modest and rigidly controlled was *who they were*. This was what their religion expected of them—what Linda's new religion expected of her. She was suddenly self-conscious of her shag hair, though no one but

Sandy could see her. The neighborhood was still, all the families inside, clearing away the dishes from their own hearty suppers and listening to the children's prayers before bedtime. She longed for her high-waisted jeans, the knit tops she wore because they clung to her breasts and she liked that, enjoyed looking young and lush and desirable.

"Now that I've done my family duty and gone to church with the whole clan," Sandy said, "we can ditch that ward and go to Singles instead."

"Singles?" Linda echoed.

"Sure. Don't you know about Singles Ward? There was one back in our stake in Seattle, but I don't think Singles Ward is as popular there as it is out here. Everyone who's young and unattached goes to Singles Ward. It's the best way to find dates."

"Sounds like a meat market," Linda said.

"It is"—Sandy chuckled—"but it's a lot of fun, too. The girls are real nice. You'll see. They're always organizing dances and game nights and sometimes we all go out to the drive-in theater together and watch a movie with all of us packed in the back of a couple of pickup trucks. It's a blast, Linda. You'll like the Singles gang, and they'll like you, too."

"If you're going, then I'm going. You can't leave me all alone on Sundays."

That was how this all had started—Linda's crazy, impulsive decision to move to Rexburg. *If you're going, I'm going.* Sandy had told her she planned to attend Ricks College in the fall, all the way out in Eastern Idaho, and Linda had said at once, "I'm coming, too." Seattle held very little for her now. Her parents' divorce had finally, officially concluded. Her mother had long since thrown herself into her jobs, a distraction from the wreckage of her home. Linda's father, who'd been receding from the picture for years, had succeeded in vanishing at last. She had no roots left to tear up from her native soil. It had been easy, painless, almost amusing to tell Sandy she would come to Idaho, too.

Linda hadn't even considered that she might have made a mistake till she and Sandy had almost reached the town of Rexburg. They left Seattle at five that morning, hoping to cover the whole distance to Eastern Idaho in one shot. It was almost eight o'clock at night when Linda's Beetle chugged up a gentle slope—not much of a rise above the flat rangeland, but enough to tax the engine after a long day's drive. Almost an hour had passed since they'd left the interstate for a two-lane stretch of highway that led, straight as an arrow, to nothing. The flatness of the land struck Linda with a particular significance she couldn't quite decode. The world was flat, unvaried, except for the odd gully cutting steep and black through endless tracts of wasteland, which were supposed to pass for cattle ranges. It was late May, so the land to either side of the highway was green and flushed with new growth, but all the plants clung together in wiry thickets, tiny oases amid a wrack of black stone and bare earth. Behind all that frantic green, Linda could make out a persistent dull buff waiting to emerge—the natural hue of the land. Once hotter weather set in, the grass, the ground, all that monotonous sagebrush would turn the same color: dry.

The landscape came as a shocking change from what Linda had known all her life—the cool, wet shade of evergreens, the morning mist coming up off Puget Sound, even in summer. In that moment, at the top of the rise, Linda missed Seattle with a sudden ferocity that took her aback and left something cold and relentless in her chest. Where were the high hills she had known, their fertile green color, the smell of salt water and stranded kelp on a foggy morning? That first evening in Idaho lay heavy over a wide, mute land, the sunset a weight flattening everything into one featureless insignificance, the shallow domes of little hills merging with the tracts of the gullies. The sky was so vast and so many colors that Linda felt it crushing down on her, and she was wildly convinced that she couldn't breathe. She pulled her car to the side of the highway. She needed, then, to stand, to know that she could still hold herself upright.

"What are you doing?" Sandy was reading a magazine in the passenger seat, but she sat up and looked around when Linda pulled over.

"I have to pee."

Linda cut the engine and reached behind her seat for the roll of emergency toilet paper, then got out of her Beetle with Sandy calling through the rolled-up window, "Can't you hold it? We're almost to Rexburg."

Linda looked out over the rangeland, all the way out to that bright hillock of cloud on the horizon, but she didn't see anything that might pass for a college town. How could they be almost to Rexburg? Here and there, some vast rectangles of uniform color lay spread along the contours of the land—farms, fields. Sandy had told her this was potato country; the dry climate and volcanic soil produced the best potatoes in the world. Sandy had spent all her summers in Idaho. She could go on long rhapsodic tears about the virtues of potato country. Linda couldn't imagine anything more boring than potatoes. She didn't even like french fries. Wheat country and corn country sounded about a hundred times more thrilling than potato country, by her estimation. At least she could imagine what might be hiding in a cornfield. She could see everything plainly in Eastern Idaho from that rise above the highway. What secrets could a life out here contain? Pale dots among the potato farms indicated barns and silos and the houses where farmers lived. Serpentine lines of a deeper, more definite green marked the paths of small creeks. There was a flash and glitter of water, a switchback arm of the Snake River peeking through stunted trees. She made out one small cluster of dusty white beyond the river, nestled against the flank of some flat-topped geological something or other, a ridge or plateau. *That must be a tiny village,* Linda thought. A gathering of feed stores, a gas station, maybe a small dusty tavern, a post office. *All the way out there.*

She walked into the scrub, just a few paces. Normally, she would find a rock or a bush to hide behind, but she'd seen no other vehicle on the highway for miles. She'd finish and pull her pants back up long before anyone but Sandy caught a glimpse of her bare ass. Linda picked a spot between two clumps of sagebrush and skinned down her jeans.

Sandy got out of the Beetle then, slamming the passenger door. "I can't believe you're doing that right here. We're almost to town."

"Couldn't wait. Emergency."

Sandy went on talking while she stretched her back and legs. "Isn't a bathroom at a restaurant better? Or at the hotel?"

"Who knows what kind of hotel we might find tonight. It's already so late. Maybe all the rooms are booked up."

"In Rexburg?"

Linda shrugged at her friend from down there in the sagebrush. "Peeing in nature might be preferable."

"You'll get a tick if you aren't careful," Sandy said. "Ticks are bad enough as it is, but really, Linda, you could end up with a tick in a truly unfortunate place."

"If I do, you get to pick it off me."

"You don't pick ticks off. It doesn't work that way. It's much worse, much grosser." Sandy laughed, shaking her head, while Linda tossed her toilet paper out into the scrub and hiked up her pants. "It's going to be wild watching you try to adapt to living all the way out here."

"What's that supposed to mean?"

"It's just that you're so *city*. And Rexburg is . . . well . . ." Sandy made a sweeping gesture, taking in everything, the endless flat emptiness of the world, the unsurprising potato fields, all that nothing.

"You think I can't do it."

"I think Rexburg is going to be a bit of a culture shock for you, that's all."

"You're a city girl, too," Linda said.

"I've had the benefit of spending my summers out here. I know what to expect. I know how to get along and blend in."

"It's not like I'm a Martian."

"You might as well be."

46

"Well, thank goodness I'll have you to teach me. What are friends for?"

Linda felt a little better for stretching her legs and relieving herself—stronger, less out of her depth. She went back to the driver's side but paused there, leaning against the door, listening to the engine faintly ticking as she stared over the land.

"Where is Rexburg, anyway?" she asked. "You said we're almost there, but I don't see any city. And you can make out everything from up here—as much as there is to see."

Sandy pointed to the cluster of white at the base of the plateau, the patch Linda had imagined was some farmers' village. "Right there. That's Rexburg."

"Are you kidding me? That place isn't big enough to be a college town."

"It's Ricks College," Sandy answered wryly, "not Yale."

"Holy shit," Linda muttered.

"If you're going to fit in—I mean in Rexburg and in the church—you've got to clean up your language. That's lesson number one in being a proper Mormon girl."

Lesson number one. Plenty more lessons followed as Linda and Sandy hunted down their duplex, paid the first month's rent, and began settling in. Sandy was really putting the "saint" in Latter-Day Saint, gently correcting Linda whenever she got a little too *city* for comfort, endlessly explaining the whys and wherefores of modesty, meekness, moderation. Sandy's patience seemed to have no limits. So Linda wasn't exactly thrilled about this Singles Ward, this meat market, but she did trust her best friend. What was the point of having a best friend if you couldn't trust her? If Sandy really thought Singles Ward was the place to be, then Linda was determined to give it a fair shot.

They turned a final corner. Porter Park lay before them. The park took up an entire city block, a huge sward watered aggressively into year-round green, patchworked here and there with tennis courts, a swimming pool, an ancient carousel. The brass poles rising from the horses' backs reflected the evening light. A walking path surrounded the park, and the path was shaded by ranks of weeping birches with wide white boles and leaves that never stopped shivering. Linda and Sandy crossed the street and set out along the footpath. The light between the birch trees had faded into dusky purple. The little brown mourning doves that were everywhere in Idaho had settled for the night in the tops of the trees. Linda could hear them purring and rustling overhead.

"I just know you're going to be a big hit at Singles Ward," Sandy said. "The other girls are going to take to you right away."

"I'm not so sure about that. You were right when you told me I might as well be a Martian. Remember?"

"Oh, Linda, don't be such a downer. You haven't been in town a week. You have to give Rexburg a chance."

"I just wish I knew someone other than you."

"You'll meet plenty of interesting people. Not only at church—there's school to look forward to in the fall."

Everyone Linda had encountered in Rexburg had struck her as interesting, though she would have bet money it wasn't the kind of "interesting" Sandy had meant. The people here were kind enough, but there was a curious sameness to them all, which only served to heighten the thrill of anxiety Linda had felt since her arrival. Polite, smiling, blandly dressed, the citizens of the town were not unlike the land that surrounded it—unvaried and dry. The one exception she had noted had been the young man who'd borne his testimony that afternoon—the last congregant to speak at the podium. He'd worn a shirt and tie and neatly pressed slacks like all the other men, but his dark hair had been almost long, not quite brushing his shoulders. And he'd had a beard. Not an extravagant one, to be sure; the reddish hairs had been neatly trimmed close to his cheeks and chin. It never would have passed for a beard among the burnouts and freaks who roamed the streets of Seattle, but it made a startling contrast to the meticulously clean-shaven men of Rexburg.

"Speaking of interesting people," Linda said, "who was that guy at testimony? The last one who spoke."

"That was Aran Rigby," Sandy said gravely, "and he's not interesting."

"He looked pretty interesting to me."

"Stay away from him. I'm serious."

Linda laughed uneasily. "Why, is he a murderer?"

"He might as well be. Aran is no good. Everybody knows it. My cousins all went to high school with him, and you wouldn't believe the stories I've heard. Drugs, stealing, all kinds of trouble with the law."

"Does he come from a bad home?"

"No—that's the really crazy part. Aran's parents have been picture-perfect Saints all their lives, but he still turned out to be a bad apple."

Linda struggled to contain a smile. "I have a very hard time picturing anyone in this town using drugs."

"He wasn't using," Sandy said. "He was selling."

"I also have a very hard time picturing anyone in this town buying drugs."

"There are plenty of no-gooders around here. Not any church members, I guess, but out on the edge of town and up by St. Anthony, that's where all the farmworkers live. If they aren't Mormons, you can't be sure of them. Humans are sinful creatures. We need the church to guide us, and if we don't have the church, well . . ." Sandy shrugged.

Linda still couldn't make herself believe it was true. She didn't know this Aran Rigby from Adam, but he had seemed as humble and sincere as any of the other people who'd gone up to the podium to bear their testimonies. And he had looked at her before he'd spoken—looked right into her eyes for a long moment, and his eyes had been gentle and startled, somehow compelling.

"But has anyone actually seen him committing crimes?" Linda persisted. "Maybe it's all rumor."

"Joel saw him selling drugs once," Sandy said, "out on the edge of town, just like I said, to the farmworkers' kids. You know Joel wouldn't lie. He's a bishop's son. And he sure as heck wouldn't lie to me, of all people."

Linda had already met Joel Kimball, who was twenty-one and freshly returned from a mission in France. Sandy had enlisted Joel to help move some of the furniture around in their new duplex. It had been clear from the way Sandy had looked at him, and the way she'd giggled whenever Joel had spoken to her, that she'd had a crush on him for years. Linda even suspected that Joel had more to do with Sandy's summertime visits to Rexburg than her grandparents and cousins had. For her part, Linda hadn't seen much difference between Joel and the rest of the young men in town—trim, clean cut, blond haired. But he had been helpful, generous with this time and his muscles, and Sandy evidently trusted his opinion.

"There are other stories about Aran," Sandy went on. "Some people have seen him worshipping the Devil."

Linda laughed so hard and so suddenly, it came out sounding like a goose's honk.

"It's true," Sandy insisted.

"Did Joel see that, too?"

"No, but one of my cousin's friends saw Aran Rigby down by the river holding his arms up to the moon like he was worshipping it."

"The moon isn't the Devil."

"Well, the moon isn't God, either, so what's the difference?"

"Come on, Sandy, that's a little too out there, wouldn't you say? No one worships the Devil."

"Some people must."

"Well, if anybody in the whole world actually worships the Devil, then I guarantee you, no one does it down by the river where anyone else can see. Sounds like rumors to me, and some pretty unbelievable rumors, at that."

"Maybe the Devil-worship stuff is only a story," Sandy conceded, "but I do believe Joel. He saw Aran selling drugs."

They reached the far end of the park. Twilight had pulled most of the color from the town. The flat expanse of grass and the night sky were the same deep blue. The old carousel had faded into darkness, and the swimming pool behind its chain-link fence reflected a nearby streetlight, a long, low ripple of gold.

The girls paused on the corner, under the whispering birches. Linda tried one last time to make sense of what Sandy had told her.

"He went on a mission. He bore his testimony."

"Who?" Sandy said.

"Aran Rigby. Shouldn't that be good enough for everyone in this town? If he made some mistakes in the past, maybe he has repented now."

"You can't get mixed up with someone like him. Here's another lesson you've got to learn if you want to make a good start in Rexburg: stay away from Aran Rigby. Even if only half the stories about him are true—and even if there's only a little bit of truth inside that half—then he's nothing but trouble, and no sensible girl would get involved with that sort of guy."

Linda let the subject drop. They talked of simpler things on the way back home—what it would be like at Singles Ward next Sunday, and where Linda ought to look the next morning for a summer job, and how nice Joel's smile was. He did have a nice smile. But all the while, as they moved in and out of the orange circles cast by the streetlights, Linda kept thinking about the last man who had given his testimony. The way he'd paused there at the podium and looked right at her, into her, as if he'd been startled by the difference, as if he'd been glad to see that Linda wasn't like the rest.

When they were home again, Sandy ran a bath, and Linda took off the hateful long skirt and the white shirt with its restrictive collar and left them in a heap on her bedroom floor. She found her favorite pajamas in a half-unpacked box and put them on and sat cross-legged on her narrow bed with the phone in front of her, its cord stretched to the limit from the hall outside her room. She took a deep breath. Then another. She picked up the receiver and dialed her mother's number.

When her mother answered, Linda said "Hi" with a cheer she was afraid might sound forced.

"How are things going out there?" Her mother sounded rather short and distracted, but she always sounded that way.

"Great. We found a neat little duplex a couple blocks from campus. I'll be able to walk to my classes in the fall."

"And is your friend treating you well?"

"Of course she is. You know Sandy, Mom. She's the best." Linda wasn't sure her mother really did know much about Sandy. Had Sandy and her mom ever met? Linda couldn't recall if they had.

"Did you go to church today?" her mother asked dryly.

"It's Sunday, so . . . yes."

A long sigh on the line. Linda could see her mother now, pressing her forehead with the tips of her fingers as if Linda was giving her a headache, as if the whole damn world was giving her a headache. "I don't know about this, Linda, I just don't know."

"Mom, it's fine."

"These *Mormons*."

"They're nice people."

"But they aren't your kind of people."

What did her mother think Linda's kind of people were? The kind who fight all the time and shove each other into walls and slap each other and scream about how much they hate one another? The kind of people who put their daughter through years of hell while they bicker in court over a dragged-out divorce? Maybe the kind of people who work so much, they're never around to talk to. Those kinds of people.

"You don't know me as well as you think," Linda said patiently.

"Like hell I don't. I'm your mother. I thought you'd give up this Mormon thing once you were out of high school, but there you are, hundreds of miles away, thinking you're going to get a good education at some crazy religious college."

"Well, I didn't give up the Mormon thing, so I guess you don't know me as well as you thought."

"Linda, don't talk to your mother that way."

What was she going to do, Linda thought wryly, slap her?

"I'm one of them now, so you're just going to have to get used to it. And I'm a grown adult. I can make my own decisions."

She could hear her mother huffing on the line, a hard, bitter laugh.

"Listen, Mom. I don't want to fight with you."

"I know. I don't want to fight, either. I just want to make sure you're okay."

"I am. I'm fine. Everything is fine."

Linda wasn't sure that was true.

After she and her mother made smaller, lighter talk and finally said goodbye, Linda dialed her dad's number, too. She hadn't spoken to him in weeks, since well before she'd decided to move to Rexburg. She thought her dad might like to know where she was, what she was doing, that she was getting on with life, building a future of her own. Linda was certain she had dialed the number correctly, but the phone rang and rang. Her dad never picked up the line.

6

Sky Holes

Aran kept his word to Tamsin. He arrived home from the shack at the edge of the wheat field just after darkness fell, which at that time of the summer was close to nine p.m. The field crickets were still calling as he came up the long drive, and the light above the shop's door was a sphere of mellow softness, cut through with the rapid black tracks of poplar moths. It would have been a nice sight, a welcoming sight, if not for the hard, dark bulk of his father leaned up against the metal wall of the building, waiting for him.

Aran sighed and stuffed his hands in the pockets of his corduroy trousers. He went right up to Gad. There was no use pretending he hadn't seen him.

Gad had chewed a stem of grass down to nothing, just a couple inches of bent, soggy green. He spat the stem out into the darkness and looked Aran up and down. "Where have you been?"

"Out walking."

"Walking, all these hours since supper? Where?"

"Nowhere in particular. Around."

Gad's jaw worked at his anger and disappointment. Aran could see the muscle in his temple twitching. But when Gad spoke, his voice was even and calm, almost gentle. "What are you hiding from me, son?"

"I'm not hiding anything." Aran looked away when he said it, off toward the house where the lamp was burning in Tamsin's room, green through her gauze curtain.

"Don't give me that. I can tell you're keeping something from me." Gad's pique was rising already. He never could keep it under control, not for long. "A father can tell when there's something wrong with his son."

"There's nothing wrong with me." Aran knew that wasn't true. "You're worrying over nothing, Dad."

"Why shouldn't I be worried? Don't I have every right to be worried, isn't worried what any good father would be with a son like you?"

Aran looked down at his feet. He waited.

"Your mother and I have been beside ourselves with worry for you, son, since you were a teenager. And now you're a grown man still hanging on to us—"

"That's not fair. You're the one who's been insisting I learn the sign business so I can take over for you someday."

Gad ignored Aran's protest and pushed on. Like a liturgy, he recited each of Aran's failings. It was always his favorite refrain. "There were rumors about you when you were younger, you know, stories all over town that said you were involved in sinful things, things I won't even mention."

Weakly, Aran said, "None of the stories are true."

"I'd thought your mission would put the rumors to rest and change you for the better—"

"You didn't want me to go to New York."

"—But here you still are, like some damn boat drifting down the river, no steering, no power, no destination."

Aran clenched his jaw, just the way his father did. Gad had already picked out a destination for the vessel of Aran's life. All this talk was nonsense, an endless grievance Gad never tired of airing. Aran had long since grown sick of hearing it. He had been made to listen all his life. But whenever he tried to tell his father to drop it, let it go, something stole the voice right out of his throat. He never could make himself speak against his father—not forcefully. A good son respected his father, listened to him, learned from him. Aran had always tried to be a good son, but there was no such thing as "good enough" for Gad Rigby.

"Twenty-three, and not married," Gad said. "Don't even have a steady girl. And now this nonsense with refusing to ask Judy Kimball on a date, when you know she isn't engaged to anyone. You refused! What am I supposed to make of that? What's anyone supposed to make of it? That long hair of yours, that beard, those hippie clothes you wear. I'll tell you what people will make of it: they'll think you're some kind of queer."

Aran rolled his eyes. "Come on." Silently, he prayed—because he couldn't think of anything else to do just then, anything other than sock his dad in the jaw, which wouldn't have solved a damn thing. *Heavenly Father, give me strength right now. Give me wisdom. Don't let me lose my cool all over my old man.*

Something stilled inside Aran's chest. Maybe it was only the weight of shame settling into him, or maybe for once the Lord had actually answered a prayer. Wherever that moment of clarity came from, Aran was grateful. He remembered his testimony that afternoon, how it had felt to try—really try—to be the kind of man he was supposed to be. He found the will to try again. He resolved to accept his father's rebuke because, after all, a father was supposed to guide his children. The Lord was supposed to grant fathers the wisdom to shepherd their children rightly.

Even as he felt that brief swell of inspiration, a contrary thought rose up in Aran's mind, a kind of internal smirk like an unseen devil on his shoulder, whispering in his ear. *The Lord has put all kinds of things into your heart, Aran, that have no business being there.* He glanced again at Tamsin's window.

No, Aran decided, while Gad ranted on. He could conquer this. He could set everything to rights. It was never too late to save a sinner; no door to redemption was closed for good. He could commit right now to being the kind of man he'd told the whole congregation he was: righteous, grateful to his family, dedicated to God's purpose, with no stain upon his soul. It had to start now, with the will to obey his father and forge peace between them.

Aran forced himself to speak mildly. "What is it you want from me, Dad? Just tell me, and I'll do it."

"I want you to work harder," Gad said at once. "Take the sign business seriously—my business. *Your* business, someday, when I've retired. Work alongside me like a proper son. Show me you actually care about this thing I've made, the work you'll inherit from me someday."

"All right. Whatever you say."

Gad softened a little. He said, "You've got a real talent for sign making, son. You're good at the work. I'm happy with the work you do for me—I'm even proud of it."

"You are?"

Gad laid a hand on Aran's shoulder. The intimacy of that touch seemed to surprise Gad at least as much as it did Aran. "Of course. You've got a good eye, a real good hand. It's just . . . strange that you'll only work at night." He smiled tentatively. "Like some dang vampire."

Aran tried a little laugh. It made Gad's smile go wider.

"I'll work with you in the day," Aran said. "First thing tomorrow."

"Well, that would be great." Gad withdrew his hand from Aran's shoulder and looked down at the clump of grass beside the door as if he was thinking of pulling another stem, just to distract himself from that unexpected moment of connection. "I'll look forward to it. I'm sure we'll get heaps done if we're pulling together. Probably get through the backlog of orders before the week is up." Gad shifted on his feet, suspicious of Aran's quickness to capitulate. The moths went on spinning around them.

"And," Gad said, "you need to ask a girl on a date."

"Dad—"

"Even if it isn't the bishop's daughter."

Aran sighed. He nodded, which wasn't the same thing as agreeing.

"We'd best get inside," Gad said. "Getting late, and we'll have plenty of work tomorrow."

He started for the house. Aran followed a few paces behind. He thought that was where Gad wanted him to be, back there, trailing wherever he led.

~

Aran kept his word to his father, too, and toiled beside him in the shop all week, bearing Gad's barks of correction and the sharp sideways dart of his eyes, carrying the weight of Gad's judgment till Aran's stomach went sour. At least the hours were mercifully short. Today, they had finished two orders in record time, and Gad declared that they could bug off early, enjoy a little hard-earned recreation.

Aran didn't go back to his shed at the edge of the wheat field. By now, the still life was long past saving, the flowers wilted and dry. Instead, he took a long, rambling stroll through town, north past the hospital, through the buzzing yellow heat of late afternoon, till he left the town behind. He crossed a canal on a little wooden footbridge and kept going toward the Teton River.

As he walked, he asked himself just how he felt now that he'd done a week in Gad's company, under Gad's control. He didn't like the work of painting signs, but he didn't exactly dislike the work, either, and he held out some hope that in forcing himself to cooperate with his father, he could train himself. He could shape his heart and mind, find some love for the business Gad wanted so desperately to hand to Aran like a wrapped parcel, like some grand gift. But the idea that he might ever come to love the work of sign making, even by force of will, filled him with a sadness deep enough to drown in. Sign making wasn't his passion. It wasn't his calling. If he could love the business merely for his father's sake, he would love it. But Aran wasn't even sure he loved Gad for Gad's sake.

Aran came at last to the bank of the river. He stood watching the water move, ripples over submerged stones. Above the endless hiss of the water came the noise of leaves in wind. The trees and the river in its switchback course, and the steady but gentle wind, seemed more permanent and eternal than Earth itself, as if all of Creation had been formed around this place and this moment. In the shallow margins, the water slowed, and there, in the place where Aran stood transfixed and listening, everything smelled of a heavy green lentor. He breathed it in deeply. The ripples moved, arrows in the sun. Flat rocks lay in the shallows at his feet. He plucked one from the water and a glacial cold bit into his hand. He turned the rock over, looking down at the polished wet surface as if he might scry with it, as if he could read his future there. But he saw nothing except the glare of the afternoon and speckled stone below the glare.

Aran withdrew to a stand of cottonwoods and the shade below their branches. He sat and watched the water moving for a while. There were half-formed, half-blinding questions rustling inside him, and no answers came. After a while, he lay back on the earth, and the tall grass rose up into his periphery and roots and chips of stone dug into his shoulders and scalp.

There was no passion in sign making. That was the problem. Now, inverted, looking up to the branches and the sky, Aran could see his trouble clearly. No passion in the signs, in that shop. There were so many longings inside him, so many things he wanted to say to the world, though he couldn't understand why he felt compelled to say anything at all. Was he wasting his time and his life when he painted the small, mundane magics he had seen, the visions of beauty the world had granted? What difference could his art make?

It ought to matter. It ought to make a difference, that one ordinary man had seen and felt something beautiful in a commonplace world—something revealed in a flash of insight to him alone. It should matter that he might be able to make someone else feel that stir of awe, too. The things he painted were bright patches of revelation surrounded by flat, black negative spaces where all possibility had gone into hiding. His paintings were captures, like the click of a camera's shutter, of seconds in time when he'd had something—elation, astonishment—because at every other moment, he had nothing. He considered the books he'd read and loved. The music that spoke to his soul. And he realized that all of it, the really great stuff, was about a thing not had, a longing, the emptiness and ache.

Aran lay there under the cottonwood trees with the wind moving the branches and the branches moving the sky, the jagged rips of blue showing between the cool dark shadows of limbs and leaves. Sky holes, painters called them, and Aran had figured out how to add them into a painting, slashing blue into the green and brown of a formless thing so it took shape all at once and became a tree. All these longings inside of him, great wide-open rents, the voids he couldn't see into and couldn't describe. The empty parts were the greatest substance of self. There was no way to define himself, except by what he lacked. At least now, in this brief moment, he longed for nothing other than what he had: the earth hard and comforting under his back, and the grass rising up all around him, and the sound of the river close by, whispering.

7

It Won't Take You Anywhere

After he had his lunch, Gad returned to the sign shop and found it abandoned, as he'd known he would. He'd told Aran they could bug off early, but he'd still hoped his son would remain. He stood for a long while in the stillness. Over by the table saw, flecks of dust revolved on a lazy current of air, glittering in a shallow angle of light from the nearest window. The radio was off. No more of that staticky fuzz Aran liked to listen to while he worked, undercut by broken bars of music, or what passed for music these days. The intensity of the silence unsettled Gad. It felt not peaceful but accusatory.

The latest order was complete. Gad and Aran had finished the sign in record time, and now it lay flat in the center of the swept concrete floor, drying. Gad stood over it, assessing the work. *Jepson's Feed, Pocatello, Since 1928.* The lettering arced perfectly across the nine-foot-wide panel, goldenrod words on a hunter-green field. Aran had used an old-fashioned script style, evoking a simpler time. It was a fine piece of work. The boy certainly had a steady hand, a natural instinct for color and composition. His brushwork left nothing to be desired. One day, Aran would understand—he would realize why Gad had pushed him so hard in the direction of the family business. He would finally comprehend why the business wasn't Rigby, Sign Maker, but Rigby & Son.

Aran had loved drawing and painting since he'd been a small boy. Gad had watched that passion growing in his eldest son, year after year. Sign making was a good outlet for an artist's skills—steady, reliable work, not enough to get rich on but enough to support a family. That was all any man could ask of his profession. That was all any right-minded man should hope for.

Why, then, did Gad so often feel this blunt dissatisfaction with his own life? In the stillness, he looked down at the new sign. Despite its objective quality, the sight still made Gad want to spit. Not because Aran had made it. Gad felt the same way almost every time he finished a job. Most days, he couldn't shake a small, lingering suspicion that he was misusing something trusted to him, something of great rarity and value.

A small, mocking thing muttered in his head. *You know why you feel this way. You know why no sign will be good enough.*

He went to the big metal drafting desk in the shop's far corner, sat down, unlocked the bottom drawer. His old sketchbooks were hidden there—years' worth of sketches, decades' worth, along with the pencil box he'd made in shop class his senior year of high school, when he'd been the star of the football team and his mission had been just around the corner and he'd felt as if every possible avenue were opening before him. Back then, every path led to a bright and worthy future.

Gad fished behind the hanging files and found his old pencil box. He brushed a callused thumb over its lid. He had burned the eagle design into the wood freehand. He could still remember the shop teacher watching over his shoulder as he'd handled the pyrography pen with the same natural ease with which he'd handled a pencil or a brush. The shop teacher had praised Gad's steadiness, his eye for realistic rendering, the fine detail in every feather. Gad had felt faintly embarrassed over his teacher's acclaim, and hungry for more at the same time, for by that age, his father had sat him down and looked him in the eye and told him squarely the way it was, the way it was going to be.

This art thing, Gad—it won't take you anywhere. There's no money in it. You need a sensible job. You aren't a boy anymore, or you won't be a boy much longer. This art stuff—it's for women. Girls. I expect you to live up to the covenant you've made with Heaven. No more of these girly interests. It's long past time you started acting like a man.

What did it matter if the world called to him with endless arrays of color and light? The things of the world were not of Heaven, and all that existed here on Earth would soon pass away. A man kept his eyes on the great rewards to come, the blessings he'd been promised in the hereafter. A man minded his obligations to God, to the church, and to his family, in that order.

He opened the pencil box, prodded through stubs of graphite and vine charcoal sticks that left black traces on his fingers. He asked himself, as he'd done a thousand times before, why he kept these old and useless things.

Gad plunged his hand into the drawer again, took hold of the first sketchbook he touched. When he pulled it out, he saw that it was the oldest one—not his first sketchbook by any means, but the earliest one he'd kept.

Gad leaned in his desk chair. The backrest was a little loose and it squealed under his weight. Slowly, he paged through the old sketches. That book must have dated from the middle of high school all the way through the months after he'd returned from his mission. There was a two-year void in the work while he'd been off serving the Lord in Finland, but he'd taken up drawing again when he'd come home to Rexburg—secretly, of course, for fear his dad would find out and scold him. Gad looked at the old drawings of the neighborhood, the long driveway outside and the birches at its end—the trees had been much smaller in those days. Cattle in the fields, the distant Teton peaks, the burger restaurant in town where Gad and his friends had assembled every Saturday night.

Months and years passed too swiftly as Gad went through the old sketchbook. He could see his artwork evolving with every turn of the page. The drawings had grown more expressive as Gad had fallen more deeply in love with the world. "Love"—no. That was the wrong word. He had lusted after worldly things, and his dissatisfaction, his desire for more than he'd been given, was nothing any man ought to be proud of. He especially had no cause for pride now, at his age, with wisdom and priesthood on his side.

He turned another page and there was Arletta in profile—a girl of eighteen, bright and fresh, the pencil lines blurred only a little by the twenty-two years that had passed since Gad had drawn the portrait. The sight arrested Gad. Arletta's hair was swept back from her temples and slicked over the crown of her head, gathered in abundant curls like a fistful of peonies. Her nose was sharp and impudent, and it caught at Gad's heart, exactly the way it used to catch him decades ago. She was laughing in the portrait, mouth wide and sincere, eyes shining like they never shone anymore, with a hunger for living. Gad had almost forgotten Arletta had ever looked that way.

He raised his eyes from the sketchbook. Through the shop's window, he could see Arletta, her shape distorted by a flaw in the glass, sitting on the kitchen stoop with a white plastic bucket between her knees. A neighbor had brought over a bushel of peas from their garden, and Arletta was shelling them, letting the peas fall into the bucket. Even through the warped glass, Gad could tell Arletta's expression was vacant, or distant—gone from here, the way she'd been for most of their marriage.

He remembered the autumn night, October, at the stake's harvest dance, when he'd asked Arletta Haynie if she would marry him. And she'd said yes, which Gad could hardly believe—the prettiest girl in the whole town had said yes to him. Gad couldn't wait to break the news to his family. Just back from his mission, he was already stepping boldly into the next phase of his life. His mother and father would be proud.

A door slammed. Instinctively, Gad slapped the cover of the sketchbook closed, stuffed it and the pencil box back inside the drawer, and closed the drawer with his foot. He didn't know what he was afraid of. He only knew he never intended for anyone to see those old drawings. Or the newer ones in more recent books, or the panels he'd painted and stuffed into the drawer and never looked at again. His scalp was still prickling when he realized it had only been Tamsin coming outside. She stormed down the kitchen steps dressed as usual in an inappropriate fashion—a sleeveless top that was much too tight fitting, another pair of shorts that left her white legs exposed.

Brig came out into the yard after her. Tamsin rounded on her brother before Brig could speak a word. "I don't want to hear it!" the girl shouted. "You aren't my dad!"

"You know Dad will be after you if he sees you," Brig shouted back. "And if he hears you've been going around town looking like that, he'll be real mad, Tamsin. I'm only trying to spare you."

"Oh, how gallant," Tamsin said. "Why don't you do the world a favor and go sit and spin?"

That was enough for Gad. Loud as the girl was yelping, the neighbors were sure to hear. He headed for the shop door, but before he could step outside, Aran had already materialized from wherever he'd been hiding. Brig and Tamsin had butted up against one another, nose to nose. The girl probably would have taken a swing at Brig, but Aran stepped calmly between them. His mouth was moving, but he spoke too quietly for Gad to hear.

Gad watched through the half-open window as Aran gently pushed Brig and Tamsin apart. Tamsin folded her arms, turned her face away, petulant and offended. Brig was nodding in response to whatever Aran had told him. Brig wore a thoughtful expression. He raised a half-hearted protest. "She can't dress that way. It isn't right." Aran spoke to him again, put an arm around his shoulder. A moment later, Brig sighed and said to Tamsin, "Sorry." He went back inside the house without any more fuss.

Next, Aran took Tamsin by the shoulders, held her at arm's length while he spoke to her. Whatever he told her seemed to cheer her up some. She kicked her feet in the grass and listened to Aran's words, then flashed him a smile that was maybe grateful or maybe mischievous—Gad couldn't say. When Aran let go of her shoulders, Tamsin ran around the back of the house and vanished in the green shade, bare legs flashing.

Gad knew he should have been grateful to Aran for throwing water on the fire and sparing some of the family's dignity. Instead, he felt personally offended. No one in the family could calm Tamsin's fits of temper half as well as Aran, and those fits were becoming more frequent as Tamsin waded deeper into adolescence. She sided with Aran in all things, listened to his advice and guidance as she never listened to her own father. Of late, Gad had begun to have a vague, rather panicky notion that Tamsin and Aran were conspiring against him—in what way, he didn't know. Gad had submitted to the will of the Lord, had made himself a steadfast provider. He had sacrificed his dream in favor of stability. And yet he couldn't even control his teenage daughter. He couldn't even stop his own children from fighting.

Gad blinked. Aran was headed for the shop, shaking his head fondly as if the fight were all in a day's routine. Gad arranged his expression into perfect neutrality as the shop door opened.

"It's almost three thirty," Aran said. "We've got to get downtown and take pictures of Orton's Café."

Gad inhaled sharply through his nose and glanced at the calendar on his desk. Sure enough, the day was circled in black marker, yet Gad had forgotten all about the appointment at Orton's. He'd told Aran to take off work early. The boy could lead Gad's family better than he could himself, and now here he was running Gad's business with a steadier hand.

Gad pulled the truck keys from his pocket, climbed inside the cab. The camera was waiting on the bench seat. No doubt Aran had put it there.

Gad cranked over the engine and began backing down the drive before Aran could reach the passenger door.

"Wait," Aran called. "Don't you want me to come with you?"

Gad didn't answer. He didn't look at his son, either, as he maneuvered the long drive and pulled onto the street. He kept his eyes on Arletta. She hadn't looked up from her work, not once, not even while Tamsin had been hollering. She ran her thumb down the length of a pod and the peas fell into her bucket like small, secret jewels.

When Gad returned, the boys were outside—the twins, the good ones—at the far end of the yard, throwing a baseball back and forth in the afternoon light. The ball was so new and white that it seemed to trail itself like a ghost through the reddening sky. Arcs of its bright and evident self seared into Gad's vision as it crossed from Brig to Ondi and back again, over the old, rusted oil drum where Gad burned his scraps from the shop.

Gad could tell his boys were feeling pensive and dissatisfied. They always threw the ball that way whenever something got either of them down. He walked from his truck with his hands in his pockets, out to the edge of the property, never taking his eyes off his boys. Crickets made their metallic sounds in the long grass on the other side of the fence, the lot that had been empty for as long as Gad could remember. The slap of the ball hitting the boys' gloves was a comforting sound. The air smelled rich and mineral from the irrigation canals that cut through this end of the town.

He watched the twins for a long time. Ondi's form was elegant and sure; his throwing arm whipped with unconscious ease. Brig seemed to have a strange foreknowledge of where the ball would be, even before Ondi threw it. He never missed a catch, not once, not even when Ondi tried to challenge him. He could tell by their small, pinched frowns and the hardness of their eyes that something was eating at both of them.

After a while, Gad said, "All right, boys, pack it in. How about you tell your old man what's bothering you?"

Ondi caught Brig's return throw and stood for a moment tossing the ball up in the air, catching it in his palm, smack, smack. He couldn't meet Gad's eye.

"Is it about your missions?" Gad guessed.

Ondi sighed and punched the ball into his glove. "It feels like we've been waiting forever, Dad, and we still haven't gotten the call."

"Heck, you boys only just turned nineteen."

"Which is the age when we're supposed to get called for our missions," Brig fired back.

Gad smiled in what he hoped was a reassuring way. "The call comes later sometimes. It's different for everyone."

He knew these consolations must sound weak to his boys. Truth to tell, they sounded weak to Gad, too. Mission calls were sometimes delayed, but typically only when a young man's bishop felt the kid was struggling spiritually—wrestling with the specters of lust and rebellion, those commonplace demons that seemed to possess every young fellow who stood on the precipice of manhood. But such delays seldom came to the oldest and most important families of the church. The bishopric was usually cognizant of how it would look for the son of a bulwark clan to be held back while his peers were sent forth in service to God. The Rigbys had been pillars of the community since Rexburg was only a few homesteaders' cabins in the nineteenth century. But then, Gad reflected bitterly, the rest of the Rigby men had fulfilled their directive to be fruitful and multiply. He had fallen somewhat short of glory in the Lord's estimation. He supposed he couldn't expect the bishopric to look on him or his boys with more favor than Heaven did.

He said, "You're both good boys—good men. You've always kept your noses clean and been diligent in service to the church and the community."

"Gee, Dad," Brig muttered, "you sound like a filmstrip."

"Well, it's true. You've worked hard to raise the money for your missions . . ."

Gad trailed off. Maybe the ward leadership thought two missions at once would pose too great a financial burden on Gad's household. He clenched his jaw to keep himself from cussing. He wasn't a rich man with a house up on the Bench, but he had always provided for his family's needs. And his business was something to be proud of, even if it hadn't made him a millionaire. He would have a talk with Bishop Kimball about this. If Kimball had put off interviewing the boys and passing their papers along for the mission call—if the bishop thought he was doing something noble, sparing Gad from penury—he'd set him straight in a hurry.

Gad coughed into his fist, hoping it excused the pause. To deflect the boys from thoughts of money, he said, "Are you sure both your hearts are free from sin? Maybe you've done something to stay the Lord's hand."

Ondi made a little huffing sound, a sigh of annoyance, and went back to tossing his baseball in the air.

Brig said, "What the heck are you talking about, Dad?"

"Sometimes fellows of your age fall into temptation."

"Come on; not us."

Ondi muttered, "We aren't the Rigbys who've been out sinning."

Brig said, "Aran is ruining everything for the rest of us, like always."

"Aran has done his best lately to stay out of trouble," Gad said. "Anyway, I don't think you'd be held back from your missions because of your brother's failings. Bishop Kimball is a fair, righteous man. He does the Lord's will, and the Lord is never unjust."

The truth was, Gad didn't have the least idea whether Kimball might be watching the whole family, not just the twins. And if anything was preventing the boys' calls from coming, Aran was the most likely culprit. But Gad wasn't about to cast doubt on the righteousness of his bishop. Not in front of his boys.

Ondi tossed the ball again. "I'm telling you, Aran is the reason. We're the ones who're paying for his sins."

The sun was glaring through the poplars right into Ondi's eyes. He missed his catch, hissing in frustration as the ball rolled over the short grass.

"We'd best get inside for supper," Gad said quietly. "There's no point staying out all night."

"Will you talk to the bishop, Dad?" Brig asked. "If Kimball really is punishing us for Aran's bad reputation, then it isn't fair. Someone has to make Kimball see."

"You should pray to set your minds at ease," Gad said. "Bishop Kimball isn't holding your brother's wrongs against you. I can promise you that. But I'll talk to him and find out if there's anything either of you can do to improve the situation. You have my word on that."

8

City Girl

The manager of the ice cream shop looked down at Linda's application. "Well, uh . . ." He pushed the application a little to one side with his finger, as if he were afraid of what it might do to him. "I'll give you a call if we have an opening that might be right for you, Ms. Duff."

Linda slumped back in her chair. She was sitting with the manager at a small table in one corner of the shop. The noise of the shop went on around her—sappy 1950s music playing over the sound system, kids clamoring at their mothers for a double scoop, the repetitive metallic *ching* of the cash register. It all made her feel depressed, as if the cheerful atmosphere of the shop were mocking her on purpose.

"You aren't going to hire me, are you?"

"Now, now," the man said, flushing, "I didn't say that."

"You've got a Help Wanted sign in the window and here I am, looking for work, but you still won't hire me. Why not?"

The manager glanced uneasily toward the counter. "It's just that you're a bit . . . out of place. It's nothing personal. I'm only concerned about how my customers will take to you."

Linda could have screamed. She had borrowed one of Sandy's long skirts for the interview and had worn a loose-fitting, long-sleeved prairie blouse. She'd thought she had suitably disguised herself as a Rexburg regular, that she could blend right in. But it was a small town. Everyone knew everybody else on sight, so of course any resident could peg Linda as an outsider with a single glance. She had thought Rexburg a welcoming place, but days spent searching for a job had disabused her of that notion. No one would hire her because no one would trust her, and no one would trust her because she was a city girl.

Linda fought down an urge to throw a little sass at the manager—some snide comment about not putting signs in your shop window if you didn't really mean it. But if she showed the least bit of attitude, news would quickly spread to other businesses. Linda would do herself no favors by antagonizing the men who interviewed her. At least this guy had bothered with an interview. Most of her applications had met with no response.

She pushed back her chair, forcing a smile. "Thanks for your time. I appreciate it."

The man seemed relieved that she was going.

She left the ice cream parlor and stalked down the block to where she'd parked her car. The day was bright, a white glare hanging over everything, so she kept her eyes lowered to the pavement. She didn't want to look at the town, anyway. Never in her life had she felt more discouraged. She had lived in Rexburg just over a week now. When it came to finding work, her luck seemed to get more rotten by the day. If she didn't find steady work well before fall semester started, she would have to return to Seattle in defeat.

I can't, she told herself, and knew it was true. *I can't go back. I've waited all my life to escape the mess of my family, and now I've finally gotten out.*

A low red flash caught Linda's attention. She slowed, halted, blinking through the day's glare at the graffiti scrawled along the bottom edge of the nearest building. *The Dam Is Bull Crap.* The red letters were crowded together just above the sidewalk, almost blending in with the brick on which they'd been painted. She thought the vandal must have been from one of the immigrant families at the edge of town, the Lao and Mexican kids whose families worked the farms. Then Linda discarded that idea. She gave a reluctant laugh. This was the most Mormon-looking graffiti she could imagine—tentative, selfconscious, trying its best to be unobtrusive even while it rebelled. The culprit was most certainly Rexburgian to the core. She wondered who had done it—which kid she might have seen in church, all buttoned up to his neck with his shoes polished, his hair neat as a pin, hands folded reverently in his lap, and any day but Sunday, he was lashing out at his folks and his bishop and the whole damn town in the only way he knew how, with environmentalist graffiti carefully placed where almost nobody would actually see it.

With a sudden chill, Linda thought, *Everyone in town will think I did it. They'll never suspect one of their own children. They'll think it was the outsider.*

Maybe the graffiti was why no one would hire her. She pressed on, long skirt swinging around her ankles.

As she came upon her car, Linda was jolted back by a sudden blind collision. With her eyes fixed to the sidewalk and narrowed against the glare, she'd run right into a man who'd been coming from the opposite direction. Linda staggered, trying to regain her balance and her dignity.

"Sorry," she said, looking up in a panic. "I'm sorry."

The man was stocky, florid, with dark hair at his temples and the beginning of a bald spot shining at his crown. He carried a camera in his hands. He looked at Linda with surprise, which quickly turned to open scorn. "Why don't you watch where you're going?"

His spiteful attitude was more than Linda could take. Was the whole damn world set against her? "I could say the same thing to you, mister."

"Excuse me?"

The man took a slow step toward her. The gesture was meant to be intimidating, and Linda knew it. She didn't budge. In fact, she leaned toward him, daring him to come closer, but all the while, her heart pounded. The memory of her father was near and entirely too vivid. She could feel him looming over her, his raised fist ready to strike if she opened her mouth, if she said anything in defense of her mother.

When Linda spoke, her voice was steady. "You heard me. Watch where you're going. You don't own the world, you know."

The man huffed. It was a laugh of sorts, though one without amusement. "You aren't from around here, clearly."

"What's that supposed to mean?"

"A whelp like you doesn't know her place."

She could feel the pulse beating in her throat. "Listen, mister, I've had enough of the Rexburg high-and-mighty act for one day, so why don't you keep on walking?"

"Why don't you?"

"Because you're taking up the whole sidewalk."

The man smiled grimly. "You know how I can tell you aren't from around here, young lady?"

"I really don't care, Jack."

He kept talking anyway. "A proper woman knows her place. A proper woman would never speak to anyone so rudely, especially not a priesthood holder."

Maybe it was only the immediacy of her memories, the sudden undeniable intrusion of her parents into her thoughts. Surely it was her mother's scorn that flashed up, a combustion inside her. These Mormons, these men with their self-importance, their lack of regard for a woman's worth.

"A priesthood holder?" Linda sneered. "Well, whoopee, aren't you something."

He recoiled with a grimace, as if Linda had said something truly offensive. Then he hurried past and got into his truck, an old-fashioned flatbed with a white cab. The door was painted with a business insignia: *Rigby & Son, Sign Makers Since 1952.* She got into her own car, slammed the door, and drove off as quickly as she could, burning with a terrible consciousness of the scene she had caused, the rumors she had started, the mess she had made.

As she drove home, Linda tried to calm her nerves with a few deep breaths. Any tense encounter with a man rattled her more badly than she liked to admit. Angry men always put her in mind of her father, and she often found that she couldn't keep tears from her eyes, even when she was more furious than frightened. The tears came now. Linda blinked to clear her vision and swore under her breath, scolding herself for the weakness. The town was flat and small around her; the very look of the place depressed her. Linda shoved that feeling aside, too, and by the time she parked at the curb outside the duplex, she was calm again, if not happy.

Inside, she found Sandy howling in the kitchen. A pot of chicken noodle soup had boiled over and Sandy was fanning the air with a kitchen towel, trying to chase the smoke out through the window screen before their hair-trigger fire alarm could go off.

Linda opened the patio door, then kicked off her shoes, which had been rubbing the backs of her heels, anyway, ever since that disastrous interview.

"Jeez, Sandy. You're the only girl I know who can burn a can of Campbell's."

"I know," Sandy moaned. "I'm hopeless."

Linda pulled the pan off the burner and set it in the sink. "What were you doing, anyway?"

"Watching TV. *The Young and the Restless* was on. I get so wrapped up in that show, I can't help it."

Linda made no attempt to curb her temper. "You're going to burn the house down if you aren't careful."

"All right, give it a rest." Sandy noticed, then, the redness of Linda's eyes, the tension in her shoulders. "What's the matter? You're upset about something, and it isn't my bad cooking."

"I'm sorry. I shouldn't have snapped at you."

"No, really, Lin. Tell me what's wrong. You look like you've been crying."

"I have been." Linda started to cry again. It surprised and disgusted her, how suddenly she lost control, how forcefully the sobs took her. She covered her face with her hands and wept for a long time, standing there with the kitchen linoleum cold under her feet and the smell of burned soup all around her. Sandy hugged her. It reminded Linda of the way Sandy's mom used to hold her when she cried.

"I'm never going to fit in here," Linda choked out.

"I guess your interview didn't go well."

"No one's going to hire me, because no one will trust me. Everybody knows I'm a stranger."

"Rexburg isn't easy to break into," Sandy said.

"I knew it'd be hard to get my start here, but I didn't think it would be like this. I can't even count how many jobs I've applied for. I'm getting nowhere. If I don't find work soon, I won't be able to go to school."

Sandy led her to the sofa, sat her down, and switched off the television.

"My money is going to run out before much longer," Linda went on. "I thought for sure I'd be able to find work as a waitress or in a department store or *something*. But everyone treats me like I'm a leper. I can't go back to Seattle, I just *can't*."

"Why can't you? Don't get me wrong—of course I want you here with me. You're my best friend. But would it really be so bad if you had to go home for a while?"

"Yes! Don't you get it? There isn't any *home* to go back to." Another wave of desperation took her. Linda wept and coughed and wiped tears on her sleeve, but they just kept coming, more all the time. She had never felt so far beyond her own control. "My family isn't even a family anymore. And my mom doesn't have the money to support me, even though she works all the time. She doesn't earn enough. I have to make it on my own. I have to stand on my own two feet. That's why I came all the way out here with you. To the middle of nowhere."

They shared a feeble laugh. That helped Linda some, just knowing that Sandy was on her side. She breathed deeply, like she'd done in her car, and after a minute, the tears slowed. She could talk without sobbing.

"You know," Linda said, "when I first joined the church, my mom thought it was kooky. She thought it was a phase I was going through."

"Becoming a Jesus freak?" Sandy guessed.

"Something like that. She figured I'd grow out of it."

Sandy smiled wryly. "I'm not sure you ever grew into it. But there's no shame in going back to Seattle if you need to. You don't have to live with your mom. I'm sure my parents would take you in till you find a job and get on your feet."

"No," Linda said. "I used to escape to your house all the time, when things got too depressing at my own house. I'm twenty now. I can't go running to someone else's home the way I used to."

"My mom and dad never resented you. They were always happy to let you stay as long as you wanted."

"I know." Tears again—this time from gratitude, which felt a whole lot better than crying from impotent rage. "Your parents are the reason why I'm here. Your home was really a sanctuary to me. I can't tell you how crazy things got at my house sometimes. And sometimes the loneliness and silence were worse than the fighting. Your parents were like guardian angels to me. They're the reason I joined the church, why I'm determined to go to school here, why I have to live here and make myself a part of this world. I want what you had, growing up. It's too late for me to have had it as a kid, but I can have it now. Can't I?"

"Have what?"

"A happy home. A real family. A strong marriage, if I ever meet someone worth marrying. I want my chance. All those times I came to stay at your house, do you know what I learned there? That the church makes happy families. This is my chance. If I go back to Seattle, I might not get another opportunity to make the kind of family I want."

Sandy leaned back on the sofa, staring at the blank TV. She was chewing the inside of her cheek, which Linda knew meant she was thinking of the best way to say something unpleasant.

Linda couldn't take the silence any longer. "What?" she demanded.

Sandy went on chewing a few moments longer. Finally, she said, slowly and with ostentatious care, "I'm not sure that's the secret to happiness, Linda. Religion, I mean. I don't think this church or any other can make families whole . . . though I know our church tries. But there are broken families everywhere, and sad families, and families that probably had no business coming together in the first place. I think maybe it's the luck of the draw, whether we get good parents or lousy parents or just plain indifferent ones."

Linda stared at the empty television screen. She had never considered that before. And it seemed impossible, that she hadn't thought of such a thing. Her blind faith in the church seemed so stupid as to be comical. All at once she was nakedly aware of her age, how young and inexperienced twenty was, how vulnerable.

"I think," Sandy went on, "whether a family is good or bad depends on the people who lead it. I don't think any church can give you a perfect blueprint for happiness. We have to make our own happiness, with our own strength and our own free will. That's what I believe."

"Well, something has to be my blueprint." Linda knew she sounded petulant. She didn't care just then. "How am I supposed to make a good life without any examples to follow?"

"You have to follow where your heart leads," Sandy said, smiling, as if it were all that simple. "Listen to the Holy Ghost. He'll guide you."

Linda slouched into the cushions, groaning. She'd heard all about the Holy Ghost since her earliest days in the church, but she still had no idea what the hell it was supposed to be. Some feeling in the pit of your stomach. Linda had all kinds of feelings, and often when she followed where they led, she ended up nowhere any sane person wanted to be.

"What else is eating you?" Sandy said.

"Nothing."

"Are you sure?"

Linda sighed. "Some jerk I ran into after the interview. Literally ran into him, because I wasn't watching where I was going, but neither was he. The guy got all huffy and yelled at me, told me I should respect a priesthood holder."

"Welcome to Rexburg," Sandy muttered. She sat up a little. "Who was it?"

"How should I know?"

"Describe him. Everybody knows everybody here. Small town, you know."

"Why should I describe him? Are you planning to toilet paper his house?"

"That's not a bad idea."

Linda laughed despite her distress. "Listen to yourself. There's a bit of the city girl in you, too, I guess." Sandy was still waiting. "He was broad," Linda said, "with dark hair, but he was getting older, going a little bald. I think he was in his forties. He drove a white truck. Something about sign making on the truck's door."

"Ugh," Sandy said at once. "Rigby."

"That was the name on his truck. Wow, you really do know everyone in this town."

"All of Rexburg is aware of the Rigbys—that branch of the family in particular. Remember that no-good guy I told you about, the one you saw on Fast Sunday?"

"Aran," Linda said.

"That was his dad you met. Gad Rigby."

"You told me Aran's parents were both good people."

"They are."

"If you ask me, his dad is a grade-A jerk."

"Well," Sandy said, "I suppose Gad Rigby is all the proof you need that the church doesn't automatically make perfect families. Gad has a short fuse, I'll admit, but he's as righteous as they come. Technically, anyway. Always pays his tithe, according to what people say. Not that I really listen to gossip, of course."

"Of course," Linda said, half smiling.

"He raised his family in the church, served his mission and Aran served his. And his wife, Arletta, is always first in line to organize or work for the Relief Society. They've both followed the righteous path without putting a foot wrong. But their firstborn son still ended up the black sheep of the town, and Gad, as you saw for yourself, is a miserable, crummy little man who would just as soon bite you as look at you. The Rigbys make my point: the church doesn't guarantee happiness. Maybe you have to make your own happiness within the church."

"What about you?" Linda said. "Are you happy here, now, away from your parents and the home you knew?"

Sandy pressed her lips together, thinking hard about the question before answering. "Sometimes I feel pretty homesick. I think it'll be better once school starts and I'm busier. We'll both be too busy then to mope around thinking about how much our lives have changed."

"But are you happy? Can you see yourself living in this town forever?"

"Gosh, Linda"—Sandy laughed—"I'm not going to stay in Rexburg forever. You and I are both city girls at heart. I'm only here for college, and once I've gotten Joel to marry me, I'm going to convince him that we should move away. Denver, maybe, or even Salt Lake would be nice. I might convince him we should go back to Seattle, so I can be near my parents. But I couldn't live here for good. This town is too traditional, even for me."

Sandy sat up again, slapping her palms against her knees with an air of getting down to business. "I know what'll cheer you up. I'll call some of my friends and we'll have a jamboree. You'll meet them all on Sunday anyway, when we start at Singles Ward, but there's no reason why you shouldn't get to know them now. They're a real nice bunch. They'll make you feel right at home."

"What exactly is a jamboree in the context of rural Idaho?" Linda asked cautiously.

"We go out into the pastures and throw potatoes at cows."

"Ha."

"We'll drive out to the sand dunes and watch the boys race their dune buggies. Or we can get everyone together for a hot dog roast down at one of the parks." Sandy put her arm around Linda, pulled her into a sideways hug. "I know my friends, and I know you. If you don't want to go back to Seattle, you need a job. And if you want to get a job, you're going to have to start building a good reputation here in Rexburg. What better place to start than with my friends?"

Inside Linda's stomach, a sudden upwelling of hope collided with a dreadful, dragging certainty that she was about to make a fool of herself. Very likely, she'd say or do something that would harpoon her final chances in this town and sink her altogether. But she couldn't sit at home crying.

"All right," she said. "I'll do it. Call up your friends." *And if there's a God in Heaven, get me through this, one way or another.*

9

INSIDE THE SPLIT

The evenings in Idaho seemed to last forever. That was one thing Linda had noticed already: the way the light rose above the flat, dry land, or mellowed and settled in deep-golden hues and lingered, making every leaf and blade of grass stand out with a poignant significance till sunset finally came, and that was a long, slow unrolling, too, like the sky was savoring its colors. Sunset was still a couple of hours away, though, as Linda and Sandy headed west out of town.

"I'm nervous," Linda said, not for the first time.

"Will you relax? Honestly. You act like my friends are a bunch of ogres. They're no different from all the kids we knew back in Seattle."

"It's not that. I'm just—"

"Afraid you won't fit in," Sandy said. "I know. You've said it a hundred times already."

"I'm sorry."

"Shush," Sandy said, "and trust me. I know the older generations are set in their ways, but the kids out here are all right. Besides"—Sandy bumped Linda's arm with her elbow—"I heard Lee Christiansen is coming."

Linda glanced at her friend. Was that name supposed to ring a bell?

"He's LaMara's neighbor," Sandy said. "LaMara is one of my cousins. She told me Lee is back from his mission, so I told her to invite him to our little get-together. He's cute—really cute."

"Oh my God." Linda caught herself, corrected. "Oh my gosh, Sandy. You're trying to set me up!"

"There's no harm in getting to know a few nice guys. And Lee is as nice as they come."

Linda had already been feeling self-conscious about the way she was dressed. The news that Sandy was trying to fix her up on a date only made her worry more about her clothing. She wore her old stovepipe jeans, because she didn't have anything else in her closet that might suit a hot dog roast on a riverbank, but all the long-sleeved blouses she owned were too stiff and dressy for the occasion. She'd thrown on an old checked flannel shirt, buttoning it to her neck. She'd left the shirt untucked, too, so it hung down over her backside. She felt ridiculous, like she was wearing a burlap sack, but she hoped the outfit would read as suitably modest—especially now that she had a returned missionary to impress, on top of everything else.

"Take the next turnoff," Sandy said, "right after we've crossed the bridge."

Linda left the two-lane highway for a long dirt drive. The road cut through a stand of poplars toward a silver-blue flash of river.

"Everyone will be here," Sandy said. "My cousins and their friends, and my mom's friends' daughters, and I know they've invited plenty of boys, too, besides just Lee, so if he's not your type, you can have your pick of the others."

"Have my pick? I can't even get hired at the ice cream shop."

Sandy made a snoring sound. Linda was supposed to take it as a signal that her constant protestations were a real drag and a bore.

"Now listen," Sandy said, "if LaMara comes across a little short, don't take it personally. She doesn't mean to be rude; she's like that with everybody. I just don't want you to think—"

Sandy cut off abruptly as Linda hit the brakes, staring up at the park's sign, a huge arch of rustic wooden planks. The name was painted in bright goldenrod letters: *Beaver Dick Park*.

"Oh my God," Linda blurted. She immediately added "Sorry," but then she began to laugh again, hunched over the steering wheel.

"For goodness' sake," Sandy said.

Linda went on laughing. Cackling, really, and snorting, which was unforgivable, but she couldn't help herself. All day long, anxiety had been building inside her like a swelling boil. She couldn't withstand the pressure any longer. Something had to give. She was grateful she'd found something to laugh over; it was better than crying.

"Come on, Linda; you're acting like a twelve-year-old."

She gasped, fanning her face till she had herself more or less under control. "You can't tell me you don't think that's hilarious."

"It's a little funny, I guess, but it really was the guy's name."

"Really. Beaver Dick."

"He was a fur trapper."

"I'll bet he was."

Sandy rolled her eyes. "The gang's waiting for us at the fire pits."

The road looped around a central grassy area supplied with a pair of bizarre log sculptures, massive stick figures vaguely in the shape of horses or giraffes. Maybe, Linda thought, the sculptures were supposed to represent moose. She'd heard horror stories about moose since her arrival in Rexburg. She wondered how frightened of moose she really ought to be. They seemed a ridiculous, cobbled-together sort of animal, not the kind of creature who could do real harm. Closer to the river, at least a dozen cars were parked near a picnic shelter. Someone had already started a fire in a brick pit; a column of sparks burst into the air, and a pack of girls leaped back, squealing. Guys in sweater vests were shuttling from the cars to the picnic shelter, carrying coolers and grocery bags. One of them noticed Linda's Beetle and waved.

A moment later, as Linda pulled into a parking space, the girls were flocking around.

Linda and Sandy got out of the car.

"Look out," one of the guys called from the fire pit, "it's the babes from the big city!"

Sandy put an arm around Linda's shoulders. "Everyone, meet Linda Duff. We were good friends back in Seattle, and she came all the way out here to go to Ricks in the fall. Isn't that fantastic? We've been roomies ever since. Linda, this is . . . Well, I can't introduce everybody all at once, but you'll get to know the whole gang tonight."

"Thanks," Linda said. "It's really great to be here at Beaver Dick Park."

She looked around the group for some sign that she wasn't alone in her amusement, but the whole crowd stared back at her with blank, polite smiles. It stunned her for a moment, how earnestly squeaky clean the whole lot of them were, how innocent. Something inside her recoiled, wary of such a guarded existence. She checked that impulse as soon as it arose. Wasn't this the very life she wanted for her future children—gentle and protected, their souls preserved, held safe against the hard edges of the outside world? She tossed her hair, smiling at them all, and pretended she hadn't said a thing. It was all a matter of perspective, she decided. She could find their naivete weird, or she could find it charming and sweet. They were giving her a chance, after all, when no one else in Rexburg would.

Linda reached into the back seat for her guitar case.

"Hey," one of the girls said, "you play guitar?"

"I do."

"She's really good at it, too," Sandy added.

Linda shrugged. "I'm all right."

"She's just being modest," Sandy said. "Linda's a real whiz when it comes to music."

One of Sandy's friends came forward and linked arms with Linda. "Gosh, you just have to join the Relief Society at the Singles Ward. We're trying to put together a music group for the Young Women's programs across the whole stake. You'd be a big help. We only have a piano player now. We've been talking about finding someone who can play guitar."

"Oh," Linda said. "I'll think about it."

Maybe Sandy was right. Maybe the way into Rexburg society lay with these young women and men. They certainly weren't hesitating to welcome Linda in. If she could convince them she belonged among them after all—if she could convince herself—then word would spread through the town. Surely a few doors would open.

The girls pulled Linda toward the fire pit, chattering as if they'd been friends for years. They flung their names at Linda, faster than she could catch them all. And the boys were perfect gentlemen, passing around old coat hangers, helping the girls untwist the wires and shape the hangers into skewers for roasting.

When the cookout was well underway, Sandy slipped off to one of the coolers, where a guy with square glasses was dishing up potato salad. Linda watched as Sandy leaned close to him, talking. The young man looked up, caught Linda staring straight at him, and glanced away again, piling even more potato salad onto his paper plate as if he were flustered and couldn't think what else to do. *Oh, God,* Linda thought, *here we go.* Sandy was already leading him by the arm, back to Linda's side.

Sandy said, "I want you to meet Lee Christiansen. He lives next door to my cousin LaMara. You met her already. Lee's dad is the first counselor to our ward's bishop."

Lee put out his hand to shake.

Linda took it automatically. "Wow," she said. "First counselor. That's really something." She had no idea what it meant and was uncomfortably aware that she ought to know. She had been a member of the church for a few years now, after all.

"We're all so glad you're here," Lee said. "I'll be going to Ricks in the fall, too, now that I'm back from my mission. Maybe we'll have some classes together."

He had the same hairstyle all the other men had: carefully trimmed, parted on one side, combed to shining perfection. At the collar of his sweater vest, Linda could see the knot of a necktie. She thought, *Who wears a tie to a hot dog roast?* Combined with his prominent glasses, the tie gave Lee the air of a nascent accountant or an actuary just emerging from its pupal case. He wasn't her type, not by a long shot, but there was something charming about his unashamedly nerdy appearance. And he was just as nice as Sandy had promised he would be.

She invited Lee to sit beside her while they roasted their hot dogs, more to keep Sandy off her back than for any other reason, but she found she enjoyed their conversation. Lee asked her plenty of questions about Seattle, how she liked Rexburg so far, what she was most looking forward to in the fall semester. If his sense of humor didn't follow the same path as Linda's, at least he was quick with a joke. She found his stories about his recent mission to Argentina intriguing. He had a knack for describing the land and the people in a way that held her interest, and the love he'd developed for Argentinian culture seemed genuine. So what if he didn't set her heart on fire? She could see herself going on a few dates with the guy. Maybe kissing him, too.

True sunset came at last, painting the sky with a brilliant wash of red. The water flared carmine between the poplars. By then, everyone had eaten their fill. The crowd began to break up into smaller groups— clusters of four or five, though a few couples walked along the riverbank, stealing the chance for private conversation. Sandy was among them. She had invited Joel, of course, and clearly intended to make the most of the sunset, holding Joel's hand as they moved toward the water.

Lee cleared his throat. "Would—uh—would you like to go for a walk, Linda?"

She gave a little shrug and stood up. "It's a nice night. We might as well."

They passed the parking area and walked across the grassy expanse to where the stick-horse sculptures loomed, thin and gray, like a suggestion of ghosts or gargoyles. Linda felt drawn to those strange shapes, those effigies, and didn't understand why. Lee seemed content to follow wherever she led, chattering about Argentina all the while.

When they reached the sculptures, Linda ran her hands over the wood. So many people had touched it—for years, for decades—that the surface was polished smooth as glass. She leaned against one leg of the horse and looked up at its belly, a single beam, a bone-thin, emaciated Trojan thing. Her eye followed a fissure in the wood, a dark crack like a line of ink drawn down the length of a page.

"There are so many great statues of horses in Argentina," Lee said. "They're in just about every public park. Well—horses and riders. Generals, you know. They're really into their military history. I'm hoping to become a historian myself. Maybe a professor."

Linda made some small noise of interest. It wasn't that she didn't care about what Lee was saying. She wanted to hear his stories. But her eye was still following the crack in the wood, back and forth along the horse's belly. She wondered about the darkness inside the split, the lack of light at the heart of the beam.

"I'm really looking forward to fall semester," Lee said. "I'll be taking a military history course with Professor Young. He's the best history teacher the school has. Came up from BYU last year, but I missed out on his course this spring, since I didn't get back from my mission till April. But I've been working as an assistant in the history department. Hopefully that will set me up for a good mentorship with Professor Young."

"I won't be able to go to school at all," Linda admitted, "unless I can find a summer job. I need the money for tuition. And rent."

"There are plenty of shops hiring this time of year."

Linda tried to smile. It didn't go well. "No one's hiring me, though. I think I've applied to every shop in town. No luck. Too much of an outsider, I guess."

Lee glanced back toward the fire, then down to the riverbank, furtive for reasons Linda couldn't understand. He said in a low voice, "There is one place I bet will hire you. They won't care that you're from the big city, believe me. Actually, they'll probably count it in your favor."

"Really? Who?"

"The Idaho Environmental Council." He sounded half-ashamed, as if he'd said *The Office for Punching Grandmas* or *The Federal Bureau of Puppy Kicking*. "They've been at the campus for a couple weeks now, trying to hire kids to do wildlife surveys in the valley. Not many people will sign on with them, though. Everyone knows the IEC is only in Rexburg so they can try to find some excuse to stop the dam."

"This dam! It's all I hear people talk about."

"The whole town is tied up in knots over it—the whole region, really. It'll benefit the farmers, and without farmers we wouldn't have Rexburg at all. We wouldn't have anything out here. I don't see what all the arguing is about. If the dam keeps the farms going, then that's all that matters. Besides, the thing is practically finished by now. It's pointless to try to stop its construction."

Linda slouched again into the horse's leg.

"But that's no reason why you shouldn't take the job," Lee said quickly. "A paycheck's a paycheck, right? And it might be kind of fun, walking around in the fields counting birds or snakes or whatever you'd be doing."

"You know," Linda said, "you're the first guy I've met who has actually encouraged me to take a job. Sandy's grandpa and her uncles seemed to think the smartest thing I could do would be to find a man to marry me as quickly as possible and forget all about working. I suppose they think I ought to forget about school, too."

Lee chuckled. There was something rueful in the sound, something self-aware, which made Linda like him all the more. "Folks around here are pretty old fashioned," he said. "I don't see any good reason why women shouldn't work and go to school if that's what they really want. There's nothing in the Scriptures against it. Nothing that says a woman can't be a wife and mother *and* have a job, all at the same time."

Linda took him by the arm so suddenly, he flinched in surprise. She pulled him to her and kissed him before she could ask herself why she was doing it—but the whys came the moment their lips touched. This was experimental, she told herself. She had to kiss him in order to know whether she could go through with this—any of this—with Lee or another man like him, and all the men were like Lee, all the same if you looked under the ties and the glasses to see what was inside their hearts. There was something attractive about him, something comforting and wholesome that made Linda want to get closer, like a fire on a fall day. She warmed to him more the longer the kiss lasted. She thought triumphantly, *I can do this. I can make it happen. I can marry a nice Mormon guy and make myself into a real, true-believing member of this church, and my life doesn't have to turn out the way my mother's life did. I can have something better.*

Lee stepped back into the twilight. Gently, he pushed Linda's hands down to her sides. She realized she'd been touching his chest, trying to work her fingers in under his sweater vest to get at his tie or maybe the bare skin under his shirt.

"Whoa," Lee said, "hang on."

"What? What's wrong?"

He answered quickly enough. "Nothing's wrong. Honestly, I think you're great, Linda. You're beautiful and fun and I've had the best time getting to know you tonight."

She swallowed. Her throat was burning. "But?"

"But I want to make sure we're doing this for the right reasons."

She was aware suddenly of the mosquitoes spinning all around him—around them both—and an itch on her ankle that was almost fiery. Far in the distance, she could hear the others laughing. Linda wasn't sure whether Lee was really as pale as he seemed just then, or whether it was a trick of the failing light, the sideways glow and the long shadows from the river.

She said, "I want to do it. Isn't that a right enough reason?"

Lee didn't come any closer. Linda felt as if a chasm had opened between them, as if she had taken the fabric of the world in her hands and ripped it, pulling the two of them apart forever. And maybe, just like that, in one thoughtless moment, she had torn a gap between herself and all the rest of Rexburg, too. She'd never known she had such power, to tear the world into pieces. It sickened and terrified her.

"I'm sorry," she said. "I'm sorry. I should have known—"

"Hey, don't worry about it. We all make mistakes."

Someone called from the fire pit, *Yoo-hoo!*

Lee glanced over his shoulder. He did it quickly, which made Linda think he was grateful for an excuse not to look at her anymore. "They're getting out the marshmallows," he said. "And they're waving at us. I think they want you to play your guitar."

"You won't tell anyone, will you? I don't know what came over me. I'm not usually . . . like that." Which wasn't true. But she had to make it true, out here.

"Of course I won't tell," Lee said. "It's no one's business, except ours."

By the time Linda and Lee returned to the fire pit, the whole crowd had reassembled. The boys were chanting for music, jostling each other, trying to whip one another's legs with the charred roasting wires. Linda took her guitar from its case, though her hands were so numb she didn't know if she could play. She couldn't look anyone in the eye, especially not Sandy or Lee.

Everyone shouted out requests. "I Wanna Hold Your Hand" and "I Got You Babe" and "Hey, Mr. Taxi," all the saccharine songs Linda had never bothered to learn but might be able to strum out if she could recall the chord progressions.

Her hands began to move along the fretboard, strumming as if by their own will. She fell into a pattern of chords, but it wasn't anything the crowd had requested. It was the song that wanted to come to her then—the one by Simon and Garfunkel about the bus trip, the young couple caught in a cramped and determined kind of love, with pies and cigarettes in their pockets. It was melancholy and it made her ache in a way that pushed back all the rest of her pain. By the time she was a few bars in, the group had fallen silent. Linda shut her eyes so she wouldn't have to see them, not any of them. All she could see was the firelight moving on the wrong side of her eyelids. All she could hear was her own voice singing, and the lyrics, the lost longing hunger at the heart of the words.

When the song ended, the last chord hung silver and prolonged above the gathering. Everyone was so silent, Linda could still feel the strings of her guitar vibrating, a light tactile buzz against her arm like a current of electricity, moving, moving.

She opened her eyes and found the group staring back at her. Linda didn't know how to take their wide-eyed, poignant attention. Hadn't they liked the song? She had always thought herself a decent enough singer, but maybe out here in Idaho she couldn't pass muster in that respect, either, not even when it came to campfire stuff.

"Well," she said, a little defensively, "you wanted some music, so there you go."

She reached up to wipe one eye with her knuckles, and only then realized she'd been crying all through the singing.

10

LIGHT TO SEE

Aran paged slowly through the books he'd checked out of the city library earlier that day. All the books were about George Inness, or at least the Barbizon school, but there were only three—everything he'd been able to find on the subject. Inness was a great ranter, it seemed, which was surprising in an artist whose subjects had always struck Aran as pacific and serene. Inness's cantankerous nature would have made Aran laugh, if not for the scorn he'd felt for figure painting. For nudes.

There were saving moments, certain passages when the artist turned away from moral diatribes. Titian and Correggio, according to the journalist who had interviewed Inness, led the soul away from penitence to dwell on the religiously fruitless: a pretty face, a flush of color, the confounding complexity of emotion.

"I want to ask the moralist if he is going to create Heaven by his morality," Inness answered. "If he intends to create spiritual states by means of moral ideas. The world is full of sensuous beauty. Would you destroy it? Why did God create it? Could the human spirit rise unless it had power through the body of gratifying passion?"

At that moment, Aran's record ended, so he put a torn scrap of paper in the pages of his library book and took off his headphones and stood up to find another record to play. His room was filled with a soft, warm light, an Inness kind of light. Sunset was bleeding through the birches outside, a low flare fragmented by branches and leaves into splintered gold. The house was silent, except for a far-off muffled rise and fall of tin conversation, the nightly news. He could hear the rhythmic leather slap of a ball against a glove. He moved closer to the window and looked down into the yard, and there were Brig and Ondi, past the end of the sign shop, tossing their baseball back and forth in the dying light.

Aran watched his brothers for a while. They were loose limbed and free, because no one was looking, as far as they knew. They had abandoned the rigid control they usually showed around their father. They were smiling, laughing while they played. It made Aran think of the time they'd taken their Boy Scout tents and gone camping, just the three of them, out past Atomic City, right along the edge of Craters of the Moon National Monument. The twins had been thirteen that summer, and Aran seventeen, half-terrified because it was all up to him, keeping his little brothers safe in an alien wasteland of sagebrush and black lava chasms. The twins had been spindly things, scabbed at knee and elbow. They had seemed to Aran very fragile and small. The sight of them, new in the world and surrounded by all that sharp, barren rock, had made him perilously aware of his own youth, his lack of strength and wisdom. But as soon as they'd found a campsite near a swift, shallow creek and put up their tents, Aran had forgotten all his worries. Brig and Ondi were different boys out there in the wide world, beyond the reach of Gad's hand. Soon Aran was joining them in the cool, dark fissures of the earth. They were army men in the trenches. They threw chips of basalt for grenades. And when they climbed in and out of their hiding places, they cut themselves on the jagged rocks—even Aran was cut and bleeding—but it didn't matter. The blood and bruises bound the three of them together.

He couldn't tolerate the feeling of being inside, under his father's roof. He left the bedroom and paused at the head of the stairs, listening, hoping Gad wasn't down there in the kitchen, hoping he could slip outdoors unnoticed. Gad had been in a spiteful mood all day long. Supper had been a study in silence—Gad eating with fixed determination, never making eye contact with anyone, not even Arletta, and no one spoke a word because that was the way Gad wanted it when one of his moods came over him.

The kitchen was empty. The television in the den was playing the opening song to some game show, a bright clangor of sound, loud enough to cover Aran's footsteps. He dodged out the kitchen door. Outside, the air still held the day's heat, and it mingled with a damp scent from the irrigation canals on the northern end of town. The drowsy smell and the slow, lingering light gave a feeling of density to the evening. Aran felt as if he walked through something more solid than air, as if reality had mustered a flagging energy to condense itself around him and impress upon him the significance of everything he saw. The ball rose and hung in the air between Brig and Ondi. For one strange heartbeat, it seemed as if nothing could fall. The law of gravity had excused itself because of the heat and the thickness, and the moment was suspended like the ball was suspended, unnatural and high. Then it dropped again and Ondi caught it with a quick, efficient flick of his hand.

"Hey," Aran said.

Ondi didn't look at Aran when he threw the ball back to Brig, but he said "Hey" in a neutral tone, so Aran knew the twins weren't angry. Not angry at him, anyway.

"Dad still giving the silent treatment?" Brig spoke as levelly as Ondi had. Aran knew it upset the twins when Gad got into one of his moods.

It upset the whole family. That was the point. The twins always tried their damnedest not to rock the boat. They hated Gad's punishing moods so viscerally that they'd been trying to make themselves perfect from about age ten. Aran had always wanted to tell them there was no point in striving for perfection. The ideal son could never exist, as far as Gad was concerned.

He said, "I don't know. I've been avoiding the old man since supper."

Brig grunted in answer, threw the ball back to Ondi.

"Listen, Brig," Aran said, "I'm sorry I got after you today when you and Tamsin were arguing."

"It's okay," Brig said. "You were right, anyway. We can't control Tamsin, she has to make her own decisions. It's just that—"

"We're worried about her," Ondi said. "She's so . . . different. From how she used to be."

Aran tried to hold back a smile and failed. Tamsin had always been exactly as rebellious as she was now. Aran had seen the independent streak in her almost from the time she could talk—Tamsin had never hidden anything from him. Now she was revealing her true self to everybody else. That was the only difference.

He said, "She's growing up. She'll always be our little sister, but she isn't a baby anymore. We have to let her make some mistakes on her own without protecting her too much from harm. That's the only way anybody learns."

"She's going to get herself into real trouble," Ondi said, "dressing the way she does. You can't blame us for wanting to protect our sister from *that* kind of danger, Aran. One mistake and her whole life could be ruined."

"Tamsin isn't dressing scandalously." Aran hoped he sounded more patient than he felt. "Believe me. I saw women dressed far less modestly in New York."

That changed the course of their thoughts.

"When do you think we'll get our calls for our missions?" Brig asked.

"Heck, I don't know. You guys just turned nineteen. You sure are eager for it, both of you."

"Why shouldn't we be?" Ondi said. "We've been looking forward to it since you left for New York, Aran. Brig and me, we thought it was just about the coolest thing you could imagine, having our big brother off on a mission."

"You did?" Aran couldn't help smiling, though there was more than a little sadness in his heart just then. If his brothers knew what he'd done on his mission, how little he'd devoted himself to the cause, it would shatter their high opinions. They could never look at their big brother the same way again.

"I guess you could say we were inspired," Brig said. "Die-hard dedicated to the cause, from that point on."

Ondi made a small sound, a grim laugh cut short. "Not like Dad would allow us to opt out of missionary work, whether we wanted to or not."

"You do want to, though," Aran said, "don't you? I mean, it isn't something you should tackle unless you're really sure."

Brig looked at him like he was crazy. "Of course we do. What kind of man doesn't want to serve his mission?"

"I only mean," Aran said carefully, "it isn't all fun and games."

In fact, nothing about the actual mission had been particularly enjoyable. All the enjoyment had come from shirking his duties to God. Even the startling clarity those two years had brought to Aran's life struck him as traumatic. He had taken a Greyhound to Salt Lake City, then spent an exhausting and intense week at the old Lafayette School being drilled in the fine art of proselytizing. He'd lived in a crowded dormitory with a few dozen other clean-cut, bright-eyed young men headed for English-speaking cities around the world. He'd been assigned to another young man his own age, his first mission companion, and they had never left one another's sides, except to shower or use the bathroom. When they weren't being lectured or tested by one of the church apostles, they were serving in the temple downtown—which, Aran had to admit, was a beautiful building, its white rooms glowing with light, permeated by an air of the sacred and mysterious. The teachers had run the new missionaries so hard that by the time Aran was on his plane to New York City, all he'd wanted to do was sleep for days. For months, if he could manage it. And he'd had it lucky. The young men who'd been assigned to European and South American and Asian missions were in for three solid months of language classes in Provo, on top of daily training in how to convert the wayward and save lost souls.

"We don't expect it to be fun," Brig said. "We expect it to be hard work."

"Rewarding work," Ondi added.

"Well, I'm glad you've got your heads screwed on straight."

Aran was waffling and he knew it. He hoped his misgiving didn't show in his eyes. The last thing he wanted to do was tarnish the shine on his brothers' dreams. The twins were so certain these missions would amount to the great works of their lives—yet for Aran, his assignment to New York had been the genesis of his present troubles. His father had feared that New York City would make Aran worldly, and it had. Aran and New York had conspired together. He had allowed the city to strip him of all his righteous armor. Never in his life had Aran imagined Satan could do his work so easily, with so little effort, but by the time his mission was half over, Aran wasn't sure he believed in Satan anymore. At least, not the way his father believed. The Adversary was supposed to hold dominion over foul and evil things. But everything Gad called "worldly" now struck Aran as beautiful and true.

When he returned home to Rexburg—both heartbroken and relieved—Aran wasn't sure where he stood on matters of religion. He still felt God was real. But he wasn't sure God had gotten everything right. It was nothing he could explain to his father. He couldn't even explain it to himself, not in any way that satisfied. He sure as hell didn't want to talk about it with his brothers, not now, when they were wide eyed with anticipation.

"You all right?" Ondi said.

Aran pulled himself up straight. He'd been staring into the tall grass at the edge of the yard, just on the other side of the cyclone fence. The sunset had almost faded. A blue twilight was coming down through the tops of the birches and the cottonwoods.

"Yeah," Aran said. "Lost in my thoughts for a minute."

"Well," Ondi said, "you're the returned missionary. Give us your best advice, man to man."

"You don't need any wisdom from me. Not that I have much to give, anyway. You've both got purity of faith. That's the most important thing."

It was true. Brig and Ondi believed with their whole hearts. No shadow occluded the world, not for them. The light of righteousness fell on every vista, illuminated their every path. Aran wanted that confidence so desperately, the wanting almost made him shake. Perfect faith was what his father had always expected him to have, and Aran had never delivered.

"There's still a little light in the sky," Brig said. "Go get your glove."

Aran smiled. "I don't know where my glove is. It's been so long since I've played catch with anybody. The light will be gone by the time I find it."

"I'll tell Tamsin I'm sorry," Brig said, tossing the ball again, "as soon as I see her. *Really* tell her sorry, like I mean it."

"Thanks, Brig. She'll appreciate that. You're a good man."

Aran went back up to his bedroom and found a wool sweater in his closet, draped it over his arm. He didn't need it just yet, but he would, because he knew this would be the kind of night when he stayed out rambling by the river or out in the cattle pastures for hours after dark, till the moon had set and the first faint suggestion of a new day had begun to color the horizon. Then he drove out of town and between the fields as the light left the sky and the moon glided slow and indifferent from behind the foothills.

After a while—an hour maybe, who could tell?—Aran realized he'd pulled down the long dirt road that led to the park on the river. His headlights fell on the wooden horses, the skeletal sculptures that had always unnerved him since he'd been a little boy. He thought the park was as good a place to walk as any other, though by that time of night, the mosquitoes would be a misery. He pulled into the parking area and saw that some kind of party was just breaking up, men and women of his own age gathering coolers and plastic cups, dumping water on a fire in one of the brick pits. Probably a crowd from Singles Ward. They often went out for hot dog roasts or to the drive-in theater packed in the beds of pickup trucks. Their outings always looked like fun to Aran, but he was never invited along. He knew he wouldn't be invited even if he could somehow convince himself to attend church at Singles Ward.

He put on the sweater and got out of his car and headed at once for the river with his hands shoved into his pockets, but he hadn't gone more than a few feet when he heard a man calling to him from the edge of the milling crowd. Aran glanced over his shoulder. Then he cursed under his breath. It was Joel Kimball calling, the bishop's son. Joel was the last person Aran wanted to see that night, or any other.

"Hold up, Aran."

Joel came jogging over the dark grass. He put out his hand to shake. Aran didn't take it.

"I don't want trouble, Joel. That's not why I'm here."

"Why are you here, then?"

"Not to talk to you. I didn't even know you'd be here. I came to the river so I could be alone."

"You're pretty good at being alone." Joel laughed as if he'd made a pleasant joke, as if this were a conversation between friends. "We were having a little get-together. No big deal, you know."

"Great. I'll leave you to it."

Aran turned away. Joel put a hand on his shoulder to stop him. Instantly, Aran whipped around.

"Don't touch me."

He knocked Joel's hand away, harder than he'd meant to. But it had felt good, to strike out at him. Joel skittered back a few feet.

"Take it easy," Joel said. "Listen, if you want to make some money—"

"I don't."

"My friend over in Idaho Falls has more grass to sell. Plenty."

"I'm not doing it. Get lost."

"You used to sell grass all the time."

It hadn't been all the time. It had been once, and only out of desperation, only to fund his mission. None of it had been worth the hassle—not selling the grass, not the missionary work, not coming home to Rexburg.

"Beat it," Aran said. "I told you I don't want trouble."

"It's no trouble, buddy."

"I'm not your buddy."

"Why don't you relax?" Joel said, grinning. "Your reputation is already shot. You can't make it worse by earning a little cash."

Aran lunged at him. He couldn't have stopped himself, even if he'd wanted to, and he didn't want to stop. He wanted to pound that little bastard, break all the perfect white teeth out of his missionary smile. He settled for a hard shove, right in the center of Joel's chest. He felt a quick stab of gratification at the fear in Joel's eyes as he went staggering back into the dark, arms windmilling.

"Joel!" a woman cried.

Then the whole pack from Singles Ward were running toward them, absorbing Joel into their midst. Aran could see their hard faces, their disapproving eyes, all around him in the dark.

He'd gone and done it. What an idiot he was. Picking a fight with the bishop's son wouldn't do a damn thing to mend his reputation. By morning, the story would be all over town: Aran Rigby had assaulted Joel Kimball, emerging from the darkness to attack like some demon out of Hell.

Aran backed away from the crowd, let them lead Joel off toward the parking lot. Every suspicious glance over their shoulders felt like a punch to his gut.

You've only got yourself to blame. A man ought to have more control over his feelings.

The party disassembled rapidly. Everyone piled into their cars, eager now to get away from Aran. He could see some of the girls whispering behind their hands, cutting their eyes at him. The coldness in those girls made him want to spit or howl.

A dark-haired girl, carrying a guitar case, broke from the group and headed toward an orange Beetle. Joel's headlights caught the stranger as she crossed the parking lot. The plaid pattern of her shirt leaped out of the darkness. For one flashing moment, Aran could see her profile, the sharpness of her nose, the long, shaggy fringe of her hair, as if they were the only things in the world worth seeing. It was the stranger, the girl from the Jepson pew at church. She turned, isolated against the night, and looked at Aran—looked at him squarely, which no one else dared to do anymore. He expected her to duck her head and hurry away, avoiding his eyes like the other girls did. Instead, she stood and watched him while the headlights of the other cars swam and pooled around her. Aran stared back. Night ate the vision one piece at a time as the cars pulled away and the headlights receded, but the new girl kept on looking at Aran till there was no more light left to see by.

11

SATELLITES

That night, when all the light had drained away—even the low, lingering summer trace of blue—Tamsin went out into the yard to look up at the stars. She found her brother Brig already standing there. Brig had turned his face up to the sky, watching, and Tamsin stood in his proximity, not close enough that anyone could say she was next to him, but near enough for conversation. It was cold, as nights were always cold in the high, dry valleys and the black volcanic waste. They both wrapped their arms around their bodies, waiting for the other to speak.

"I'm sorry," Brig said, not looking at Tamsin, "for being such a jerk today."

"It's all right."

"I'm only worried about you. And Ondi—he's worried, too. And Aran."

"Aran is worried about me?"

"Of course, Tam. We're your brothers. It's our job to look after you."

"Did Aran say he was worried?"

Brig didn't answer the question. He said, "The world is a dangerous place for girls. We only want to protect you."

"I know," she said. "But you don't have to be afraid. I'm smarter than you think."

"I know you're smart. That's not what I'm talking about."

For a minute, Tamsin wanted to ask him, demand of him, what exactly he was talking about. She didn't think he could name it. She didn't think he understood his own possessiveness, his compulsion to defend her from imaginary dangers. None of her brothers knew exactly what they were shielding her from, nor did Gad understand. They did it by instinct or habit, long habit that went all the way back to the pioneer days and maybe centuries before. It had always been there, this male desire to cover up her body, to call it sinful, the very origin of sin. There was more fear in it than love—a superstitious dread.

She would have challenged Brig on that point, made him confront his own fixation, but she didn't want to undo what Aran had done. He had calmed Brig down, forged a peace among them all, and now here Brig was apologizing, which was an event rare enough to count as some sort of divine phenomenon. Better not to disturb that peace. Truces were rare events among the Rigbys.

"I learned a new word the other day," she said. "Thaumaturgy."

Brig laughed and glanced at her. "What?"

"It means 'performing miracles.'"

"Have you been reading the dictionary again?"

"I don't read it from cover to cover. I just flip through it to find new ideas."

He gave her an affectionate look, which made her a little angry because it implied that she was young and therefore stupid, or at least it implied that he still considered her to be a fragile and dangerous thing, requiring the stewardship of someone wiser. Brig was only two years her senior, and even then, Ondi had been born first.

He said, "What are you going to do with all these new ideas you find?"

"I don't know," Tamsin answered. "Anything I want, I guess."

He looked at the sky again. Then he pointed. "Look, it's a satellite. Can you see it moving?"

Tamsin watched a tiny white star traveling west to east amid all those fixed points of light. It was going fast. She said, "How do you know it's a satellite and not an alien spaceship?"

Brig just laughed again. After a minute, he said, "I'm getting cold. We'd better go back inside."

"You go. I'm not cold yet." Which wasn't true; she was freezing. "I'll come in after a few minutes. Don't worry about me."

Brig hesitated.

"Go," she said. "Nothing is going to hurt me out here in the backyard. Unless that really is an alien ship and they're coming to take me away."

Brig went back to the house. Tamsin wrapped her arms tightly around herself and shrank down into her sweater. The stars overhead were white as ice and seemed impossibly far, farther than stellar distance, which was also something she'd read about recently, not in the dictionary but at the library—a place, she knew, where no teenage girl ought to spend her summer vacation. The stars were so far off, they might as well not exist in Tamsin's reality at all.

This idea Brig had, that women had to be protected from themselves. Everyone else in Rexburg felt that way, too. In fact, Tamsin had never met anyone who thought differently. Even Aran felt that way. She could tell because whenever they painted together, the shame came off him and Tamsin could feel it striking her own body and rolling through her, a hot, prickling wave, though she let it move on, never allowed it to settle inside.

This was a wonder in the world. Where did ideas come from? Not from the dictionary—not only from there. The insidious origin of all Tamsin's strange thoughts must have been in the little things Aran gave her—the records she hid inside Donny and Marie sleeves, the dog-eared paperbacks that Aran found goodness knew where and slipped to

Tamsin when no one else was looking. That was why her father feared and hated worldly things. Tamsin understood it all now. The world was much bigger than Rexburg. The world was nothing any man could control.

~

Tamsin stayed out there in the chilly night for more than an hour, counting the satellites and circling herself with orbits of ideas. And inside, the light in the den was dim and the television was off because Gad had gone to bed. His favorite armchair was vacant, but there was still a sense of him in the room, where Arletta sat very still at her piano, touching the cool, smooth keys. She had an urge to play. How shocking it would be, to rain a bright arpeggio down like a hailstorm on the silence of the night. Her fingers moved up and down the ivory in unconscious unison, but she never depressed the keys. The imagined music filled all her blank spaces; she walked along the edge of daring, but never could bring herself to leap. She felt the empty place inside where once her womb had been. She felt a thousand other voids where other critical things had been taken away. She was more space now than substance. She wondered if she had allowed the taking, had been complicit in all this emptiness. Or if everything had been swept away before she'd had a chance to notice.

Upstairs, the twins had brushed their teeth and gotten into their beds, and Brig was still cold from being out there in the night, and they both lay awake, unspeaking, in a room they continued to share even though they were grown men now. Brig thought his conversation with Tamsin had gone all wrong, but he couldn't put his finger on how. He had a vague impression that she had outwitted him by saying very little, and the notion made him feel restless, so he kept turning over and kicking his feet and generally making a rustle with his sheets and blankets, which caused Ondi to sigh across the room in exasperation.

Ondi wanted silence so he could think about girls, which was the subject that usually preoccupied him at night, just before he fell asleep. He figured it was all right to think about girls, as long as he didn't do anything other than think. If not for Brig's kicking and thrashing, he would have been imagining what they looked like with all their clothes off—the girls he'd known in his final year of high school, the cheerleaders who'd talked to him on the sidelines during the football games when, in the biting fall air that was sterilized and magnified by the halogen lights above the field, he had sworn he could smell the girls' perfume over the mud and his teammates' sweat. The smell came back to haunt him in times like these.

He remembered Melissa Magleby laughing at one of his jokes while he waited on the bench. He remembered the way she'd lifted her shoulders, which had made her breasts press against the sweater she wore, Madison Bobcats in red and gray. He felt a peculiar, enthralling dread at the memory. And at the thought of her body uncovered. She would uncover her body for Ondi alone to see, that collection of mysterious parts that so controlled his thoughts at night, even the mere supposition of what she might look like under that sweater could keep him awake for hours. He might convince Melissa to marry him. He might convince her to wait for him while he was on his mission. What was all this torment for, if not a sign that he was destined to marry the cheerleader?

Downstairs, in the master bedroom, Gad had just fallen asleep. There was no rest in sleep that night. There hadn't been rest for years, if truth be known. Gad never talked about it to anyone, not even Arletta—the dreams that left him dull eyed and hollowed out by morning. When he slept, all his complaints and frustrations materialized, became wretched monsters with long, jerking limbs and calculated movements. They took human form; they surrounded him so he couldn't escape. Sometimes these shades came to him in Tamsin's guise, but fifteen feet tall, twenty, towering with all her skin exposed, and then he was painfully conscious of his smallness, the everyday weakness of his hands. Sometimes it was Arletta, with vacant eyes and a meaningless smile, and she didn't listen to Gad at all, no matter whether he shouted commands at her or pleaded with her to leave him alone, no matter if he wept in fear. It was always a woman, though—the grim, soft-bodied dream figure, and she always possessed a hunger that Gad couldn't begin to understand or wouldn't allow himself to investigate. The hungry ghosts crowded in around him and he could feel their need, their voices rising like the waters of a flood. By morning, Gad would wake with his heart pounding; he would lie in bed breathing deep till he was sure the dreams hadn't consumed him and his body was still his own.

At the park, which had been abandoned now for a good long time, Aran stood at the edge of the river. The earth there was soft and yielding. He sank into it a little, felt the silt and mud hold his feet to the ground as if the land itself were trying to reclaim him. He thought of Adam in the Garden, shaped out of mud. *For you are dust, and to dust you will return.* There was a moon in the sky and a moon in the water—rippled by the current, fragmented, yet unmistakably lunar. Between water and sky, an impossible separation.

In thinking of Adam and the Garden, he remembered his seminary lessons from when he was a boy. Mosiah, fourth chapter, maybe third. He couldn't recall the number of the verse, but he remembered the words—or the gist of the words, anyway. *Man must become as a child, submissive, meek, willing to submit to all things which the Lord sees fit to inflict upon him, even as a child submits to his father.*

Such a terrible pain struck him then. He swayed where he stood, and it was only the firmness of the mud around his feet that kept him upright. The river seemed to edge closer. The toes of his sneakers were almost in the water, as if the current were reaching, trying to pull him in. The moon was a crescent in the sky and so was the moon in the water. It made him think of Joel Kimball's smile and the girls whispering behind their hands, and that lone woman, the stranger, watching him, watching. He would have taken hold of both moons and pulled them together and made them into one, if he'd had the strength to do it. But he was powerless to make anything whole, or so he thought that night. He thought that night—he really believed—that he'd been bred powerless, made that way to suit some lone God's purpose, and he told himself a man could never change his nature.

Back at the duplex, Linda and Sandy got out of the Beetle and walked up the path to their door. But Linda stopped well short, and Sandy was forced to wait for her, hugging herself, hopping from one foot to the other because of the cold.

"That was Aran at the park," Linda said.

"What? Who?"

"The guy with the beard. The one who pulled up in the Charger when we were cleaning up. The one who shoved Joel."

"You don't like him, do you?" Sandy was plaintive, maybe alarmed.

"I don't know. He still seems pretty interesting to me."

"I told you he's trouble. You saw for yourself tonight. I can't believe the nerve of that guy, appearing out of nowhere when he wasn't invited to our party, and pushing Joel around. You'll stay away from Aran if you've got half a brain—far away."

Linda shifted her guitar case from one hand to another. She looked up at the stars, because she didn't want Sandy to see her face just then.

"What did you think of Lee?" Sandy said. "Did you like him?"

"Of course I did." It wasn't a lie. Lee had been pleasant enough company. If Linda hadn't kissed him, she'd have had no cause to squirm now, thinking about him.

"It's freezing," Sandy said. "Let's get inside."

"You go ahead. I'll be in soon."

Sandy shrugged, found her house keys in her handbag, and let herself in. A moment later, the porch light came on. Linda turned her back to the duplex so the light wouldn't blind her. She looked up at the night sky again. The moon was a crescent, white and aloof, and in the dark places between the stars, there were satellites moving, moving.

12

The Language That Suits

Aran turned his back the moment he was finished with the study. Tamsin's chair scraped as she rose and stepped away from the shack's small window, its plane of yellow light. He could hear her clothing whispering while she dressed. This was the way it always happened. He couldn't look at her while she was dressing. She was no longer a representation then but a solid fact, and his sister, and a sin beyond his ability to describe. He kept his eyes on the study: A nude young woman sitting and facing the viewer with a kind of frank, challenging directness, her legs extended somewhat before her, crossed at the ankles, one heel pressed against the dusty floor. Her hands rested comfortably in her lap, and her back was very straight and sure. Tamsin's eyes hadn't left Aran's face while he'd painted. Every time he'd looked up from the canvas, she had been staring right back at him with a patient self-possession that had felt at times like mockery, or an accusation.

The study was a good one. It gave Aran that characteristic thrill that came to him now and again, when a painting spoke in a voice he could hear. A certain warmth in the pit of his stomach, a trembling awe—not awe at himself, but at the great mysterious force that had brought the painting to him, causing it to proceed from his ordinary hand. This study was one of the very best, in fact—clear, certain, vivid in its mood. It was among the best he'd ever made of Tamsin, which meant it was the best he'd made of any subject, because he never could paint half so well as he did when he painted her. Nothing else felt as real.

She stood beside him, dressed now, and looked at the study for a beat of silence.

"What are you going to do with it?" Tamsin said.

"I don't know."

"What are you going to do with any of the paintings you've made of me? There must be—what—two dozen now, at least."

Aran shrugged. Tamsin knew their predicament, the necessity of silence.

She said, "You'll do something with the other paintings, won't you?"

"Tamsin, you know I can't show anyone these . . . these studies." He didn't know what else to call them.

"I'm not talking about the nudes, dummy. I mean the flowers you've painted, and the landscapes and the pastures."

Aran didn't answer.

"Jeez, Aran. Why do you paint at all if you aren't going to show your work to the world? What's the point?"

"I don't know that, either," he said. "I'm not sure there is a point. I only know I have to do it."

"You ought to be an artist," Tamsin said. "I mean, your job. Your profession."

Aran gave a small, bitter laugh. "Impossible."

"Why? Just because Dad doesn't want you to do it?"

Aran turned away. "Dad is right. You can't support a family by selling paintings. It isn't reliable, and that makes it useless. For a man's purposes." Those were Gad's words, which Aran had heard a hundred times at least, ever since he'd been a boy. He thought if he said those words himself, he might come to believe them. Then he could finally give this up—the shack, the secrecy, this compulsion to capture Tamsin's bright essence.

She said, "Art isn't useless."

"What is the use, then? What purpose does it serve?"

"Are you quizzing me?"

"No," he said, laughing a little, "I'm only curious what you think."

Tamsin frowned again, her freckled brow tense. She looked at the study, almost scowled at it, as if it were hiding some cryptic definition under the layers of paint. "The purpose," she said, "is to make people see. To force them to see the things they don't want to see. The things they pretend don't exist."

"Interesting," Aran said.

"Now you tell me yours."

"My what?"

"Your definition. What's the point of all this? Why do you keep coming out here?"

"I think the purpose is to make people feel things they can't bring themselves to feel any other way."

They were both quiet again. A car murmured out on the road and faded into the distance.

Tamsin said, "Dad can't make you feel anything you don't want to feel. He can't force you to do anything you don't want to do."

"He can't force *you*." Aran said it to the panel on his easel, not to the Tamsin who stood there beside him. "All my life, Dad has been making me feel and do whatever he wants."

"Lately," Tamsin said, "it almost seems like Dad doesn't want to be happy, not with anything. Or maybe he's been that way all our lives, but we've only now grown up enough to notice."

"Well, I'm damn sure Dad doesn't want to be happy with me. Haven't you ever noticed how hard he comes down on me? Much harder than he cracks down on the rest of you. Brig and Ondi skate by and stay on his good side—"

"Only because they've given in," Tamsin said. "They gave in long ago, when we were still all little kids."

"They figured out it's easier to do whatever Dad says and be whoever he wants them to be." Aran paused, drew a long breath. "They were right, I guess. Their lives are easier because of it. And you get cut a lot of slack because you're a girl."

"I do not," Tamsin said. "What a stupid thing to say."

"It's true."

"No, it isn't. You don't see the way he comes down on me, because I'm a girl and you aren't. You don't get it, how hard it is to put up with Dad. How hard it is to just *be*."

Aran held his tongue. He had upset her, though he'd never meant to hurt her feelings.

"If you don't believe me," Tamsin said, "just ask yourself what Dad would think if I told him I wanted to go to college."

"You do?" Aran was surprised and pleased.

Her cheeks flushed. "I've wanted to go for a long time now."

"That's great, Tamsin. Why haven't you said anything about it?"

"How do you think Dad will react when I finally break the news?"

Aran could feel his smile fading.

"Exactly," Tamsin said. "You get it now. There's no way he'd allow it. He wouldn't see the point in sending me to school. The only life he can imagine for me is marrying some moron, sooner rather than later, and then cranking out a whole litter of babies. Why should he pay for me to get an education when the only thing I'll ever need to know is how to cook dinner or change a diaper?"

Aran didn't bother to contradict her. Tamsin was right. He could practically hear their father ranting in those exact words, his face going red as he shook his finger, scolding Tamsin to be the right kind of woman.

He said, "I think you'd do great at college, for whatever my opinion is worth."

"It isn't worth much," she answered sadly, "unless you've got enough money hidden away somewhere to pay my tuition."

"I don't have a penny," Aran said.

"I don't, either, and fat chance I can earn it on my own. Dad would have a stroke if I got a job. But I'll figure out some way to do it. There has to be a way." She lifted her chin, a defiant angle, and held Aran's eyes for a moment, testing him, prodding to learn whether it was safe to say more. "Do you know what I'll study, when I get into college?"

Aran shook his head.

"Environmental science."

He failed to understand the significance of her confession. When he didn't react, Tamsin tossed her red-gold hair impatiently over one shoulder.

"I'd be an ecologist," she said. "That's the biggest reason of all why I haven't told Dad I want to go to college. You know how he feels about environmentalists and hippies and city freaks. He'd lose his mind if he knew I was one of them."

"Are you?" Aran stifled a smile. "One of them, a hippie freak?"

She narrowed her eyes, suspicious. "I don't know. Maybe I am. I've read *Silent Spring*. I've read lots of books about the environment. This dam, Aran, the one upriver—I'm telling you, it's a disaster waiting to happen. It'll ruin the trout runs and mess up all the migratory birds, and it'll cause more problems with irrigation than it can ever solve."

"Don't let Dad hear you talking about the dam. He'd lose his mind."

"I know." She smiled, and Aran understood in that moment why Tamsin was so drawn to these ideas—ecology, college. It was more about getting their father's goat than any true passion of the heart. Then again, maybe asserting herself over Gad's insidious power was the passion of Tamsin's heart.

"Sometimes," Aran said, "I think Dad wants me to be a kid forever. He doesn't want me to grow up and become my own man, because he likes having someone beholden to him—someone who will do whatever he says, become anything he tells them to be."

"Then don't," Tamsin said. "Don't give him that power. Take it all away. Decide for yourself what you want to be. Go out and make the kind of life you want to live. You're twenty-three, Aran, for God's sake. You aren't still a kid, like me."

Tears stung him. He couldn't even find voice enough to scold Tamsin for taking the Lord's name in vain. Aran blinked and left his easel, walked to the other side of the shack and looked down at all the panels drying in their rows, so Tamsin wouldn't see that he'd just about broken, just about cried. When he was sure of his voice again, he said, "That's not something I can do."

"Bullshit."

"You shouldn't talk that way."

"Oh, shut up."

"I'm not like you," he said, defensive. "You understand who you are. You know that you can make something of yourself. I've never even been myself."

"What's that supposed to mean?"

"I'm trying to explain it to you. I've spent a lot of time thinking about this stuff. It isn't easy to put into words." He didn't even think he could put it into not-words. How could you paint a shame so great, a void so encompassing?

"All right." Tamsin sounded contrite and gentle, but Aran still couldn't look at her. "I'm listening."

"I don't know who I am." He glanced at her. "Not without Dad for context. I've spent my whole life trying to make him love me."

"This wouldn't make Dad love either one of us," Tamsin said, nodding toward the easel. She was half smiling, proud of the fact, pleased that their painting sessions would destroy Gad if he knew about them. Then she burst out suddenly, "God, what a hypocrite!"

"Who, Dad?"

"Yes, Dad. He's an artist himself, Aran."

"Signs don't count as art—not in his estimation."

"I'm not talking about the signs." Tamsin looked over her shoulder, as if worried someone might sneak up on their shack and overhear. "I mean, Dad is an *artist*. Like you. I've snooped around his shop when he was away. There's a drawer in his desk full of old sketchbooks, even a few small paintings—watercolors, I think. I picked the lock once and had a look. He's pretty good. Not as good as you, but better than your average hobby painter."

Aran stared at his sister. He was aware that his mouth had fallen open, but he seemed unable to close it.

Tamsin looked at him for a long moment, assessing the depth of his shock, weighing the impact her words had made. At length, she said, "I'm only myself because I've decided to be. I'll tell Dad that I want to go to college. You'll see. I'll make him face the facts about me, that I'm my own person, that he can't control me forever, no matter what he thinks. I'll tell him, I swear it, when the time is right. I'll stand my ground. And maybe by then, you'll believe that you can tell him who you really are, too."

Tamsin left the shack. Aran watched her pass over its threshold, into the brightness of the day. Framed by the open door, she lifted the kickstand on her bike, mounted it, pedaled away down the long dirt lane, rapidly, and in a matter of seconds she was lost in the afternoon glare.

What a hypocrite, she had said. Sketchbooks in a drawer.

Aran remembered a Friday afternoon. He must have been thirteen. Gad caught him drawing in his room again and took the sketchbook right from his hands, and a tin can full of pencils. Then he opened the drawers of Aran's dresser and took all those books, too, five or six in all—a year's worth of practice. Aran shouted for Gad to give it all back, but Gad ignored him. He watched from his bedroom window as Gad took all his artwork into his shop. But his mother left the house, too. Arletta got into the family car and drove away while Aran was still leaning from his bedroom window, crying, pleading with his father to bring back his sketchbooks, he'd be good, he'd do what he wanted if only his dad would give him back his art. Gad went on ignoring him as perfectly as if Aran had never been born. That was the thing that always got to Aran—the way Gad could turn him into a cipher merely by pretending he couldn't see him or hear him. There was nothing more terrifying, no punishment greater than being thrown suddenly into nonexistence.

An hour later, Aran stopped crying and was huddled on his bed, stomach cramped, head hazy with a miserable half sleep. The door to his bedroom creaked open timidly. His mother stood on the threshold. She held a flat paper sack against her chest, and she slipped inside and shut the door behind her without a word.

Aran sat up, sniffling, and Arletta perched on the edge of his bed, hardly denting the mattress. She was as insubstantial as Aran. She reached into the bag and took out a brand-new sketchbook and a good graphite pencil, all black, shiny along its smooth barrel.

"I got these for you," Arletta said, "in town."

Aran opened the book to its first blank page. The paper was bright white, faintly textured like pebbles at the bottom of the irrigation canals.

"I'm proud of you," his mother said, softly, so no one else could hear. "You're good at drawing. You're good at feeling. I'm proud of that, too."

Aran waited, clutching the graphite pencil in his hand, unsure whether he ought to draw right then and there for his mother. He felt a tension of expectation and thought perhaps she wanted to see what he could do. But after a moment, he understood that the tension was from words unsaid. Arletta had been trying to tell him something important, but hadn't known how to say it.

"I was a good piano player when I was younger," she said. "When I was your age. I was really quite good. I wanted to make a life out of it. I wanted to go and play for the opera house in Salt Lake City."

She kissed him on his forehead then and stood up as lightly as she'd sat down, leaving the rest unspoken. She started for his door, but Aran stopped her.

"You're still good at playing the piano," he told his mother. "I always thought so."

13

FAR OUT

Tamsin rode her bike through town in the warm sloping light of early evening. It was a Sunday, and most families were well into the supper hour, so the streets were quiet, all the kids inside washing up, moms pulling roasts and casseroles from their ovens. Arletta always fed the family early on Sundays, as soon as they got home from church, and today Tamsin had eaten quickly and excused herself from the table, and her father had let her go with an indulgent little smile because lately she had taken special care to be meek and modest and not tick him off too badly. She had to keep Gad complacent till she figured out how to pay her way into school. The effort of being good was starting to wear her down.

There were still a couple hours of daylight left. Tamsin could enjoy some time to herself, far from Gad's possessive stare. She leaned her bike against one of the birches that encircled the park and took her old backpack from the basket between the handlebars. Then she wandered out into the expanse of grass and reached into the pack for the old lap blanket and her latest paperback. She spread the blanket and sat down. The low sun fell warm and gentle on her face. The park was almost entirely empty, save for a handful of college boys far across the field. They were throwing an orange Frisbee around their loose circle, shouting and chasing after it when the disc glided too far. They seemed very distant and small, their movements slow, their voices insignificant.

Tamsin lay on her back and opened the book against the sky. It was a science fiction novel about some duke and his lover, and their son who put his hand into a burning box in order to prove his humanity. The story was dense. Tamsin couldn't make much sense of it, but Aran had given her the novel because, he'd said, she was interested in ecology. She couldn't see what the story had to do with ecology—not yet, anyway—but she always persevered through anything Aran gave her, all the books and records and magazines, the mimeographed copies of poetry collections that he picked up at the college library when he visited to look through their books on art history. Tamsin didn't always like the things Aran gave her, but they made her think. Anyway, she figured it was better to read at the park than at home. Gad would be on her case if he saw her reading a novel. He would grill her about the book's contents till all the fun had gone out of reading. Gad didn't object to science fiction in particular, but he was especially vigilant about "wholesome" things, admonishing Tamsin not to fill her head with dangerous or distracting ideas. Tamsin didn't want to dryly evaluate whether the themes in her novels were suitable for a young lady's developing mind. She just wanted to get lost in a good story.

She could well understand what Aran had meant the last time she'd talked to him alone, in the shack after their latest painting was finished. It was impossible to make Gad happy. No one could even make Gad mildly content. The endless work of trying to please him was enough to wear you down, and Aran had been under that grindstone far longer than Tamsin had. Was it possible she might get stuck, the way Aran was, in their father's rut? Was it possible that she, too, could become so eroded by Gad's endless friction that she could no longer be certain whether she was a whole person or only a fragment pretending to be whole?

She cast that fear aside the moment it arose. The biggest difference between herself and Aran was that she was no longer interested in trying to impress the old man. Just one more year—that was all she had to put up with. One more year of Gad's ceaseless criticism, his rabid policing of her every move, her every word, the length of her hems. Then she'd be eighteen, free to go wherever she pleased, free to leave this town behind for good if she wanted. She could leave her family and the church. She definitely wanted to leave the church—that was already decided.

I'll fly to another planet, if I can get there, Tamsin thought, turning another page.

All the stories she'd read and the albums she'd listened to crowded into her head at once. Each seemed ripe and sweet with potential—the other lives they described, an endless array of new realities that might become her own, if she could make up her mind what to do with herself next, when the waiting was over and she was old enough to choose her life on her own terms. College was the one clear idea in a vast, disordered clamor of possibility. She would go to college and learn how to be an ecologist, and an environmentalist. Where she might study ecology, she hadn't figured out just yet. It would be nice, though, to find a school in another state. She would like to get away, someplace far from Idaho. Maybe she could win a scholarship. Then she wouldn't need Gad's cooperation at all.

Gradually, Tamsin became aware of movement and shadow, nearer than the Frisbee game. She blinked and turned her head on the blanket, watching as a dark-haired young woman spread her own blanket on the grass, some fifteen or twenty feet away. The dark-haired girl settled cross-legged with a book in her hands. Tamsin lowered her arms till the paperback rested on her chest. She stared at the newcomer. Tamsin had seen her before—Fast Sunday, in fact, a few weeks ago—but more recently still. That very day, during Sunday school, the teenage girls of the Laurels and Mia Maids classes had gathered in the gymnasium for a special presentation. A group of singers had come from the Singles

Ward, all women, doing their best to look as hip as they could manage in their church clothes. They had cooked up new lyrics to popular songs, made all the songs about being in love with Jesus and waiting for marriage and having a pure heart. Tamsin had thought the whole display unforgivably corny, but the guitar player had stood out to her. Tamsin had recognized her as the out-of-towner who'd sat in the Jepson pew the day Aran had borne his testimony. With her shag hair and ironic smile, the guitar player hadn't been trying to be cool—she was cool by nature. All the modest clothing and butchered lyrics in the world couldn't hide her spirit.

Tamsin sat up so quickly, she felt a little dizzy. The dark-haired girl went on minding her own business, absorbed in her book. Tamsin wanted to talk to her more desperately than she had wanted anything before. Something about that girl's style spoke of a world beyond Rexburg—the choppy tousle of her hair, the way her T-shirt clung to her body. Tamsin was desperate to know what she was reading. It had to be a book like the ones Aran found, rich with the flavors of a greater reality.

"Hey," Tamsin called, before she could think better of it.

The other girl looked up, startled, and glanced around, trying to discern whether Tamsin had yelled for someone else. But the park was empty, except for the Frisbee players, and they were far away.

Tamsin's cheeks were burning, but she'd already hollered, so there was nothing for it but to start a real conversation. She called, "What are you reading?"

The stranger answered with obvious hesitation. "*Pilgrim at Tinker Creek.*"

"Oh," Tamsin said, as if she'd heard of the book already, though she hadn't, not at all. She held up her own paperback. "*Dune.*"

She thought that would be the end of it. They could both go back to their reading, and Tamsin could pretend she'd never opened her mouth. But the girl sat up straighter. "That's one of my favorites. Are you a big reader?"

"I guess," Tamsin answered.

The stranger moved to one side of her blanket. "Come on over."

"Really?"

"Yeah. I haven't talked to another book person since I came to this town."

Tamsin stood up slowly and walked across the grass. Her legs were shaking. "I don't know if you can really call me a book person," she admitted, shy now. "I like reading, but I haven't read very many books. Not yet."

"Sit down. Make yourself at home. I won't bite, I promise."

"I think I know you," Tamsin said, settling on the other side of the stranger's blanket.

"No one knows me."

"Well, I recognize you. You came to our ward today. You played the guitar."

She threw back her head and laughed—loudly, wildly, as if she were setting loose something that had been trapped inside for a long time. "Guilty as charged," the stranger finally said. "I feel like I should apologize for inflicting that torture on you. None of it was my idea, I swear."

"It was pretty ridiculous."

"I know. I tried to convince the other girls from Singles Ward that they were going a little too far. I knew we'd come off like a bunch of goons."

"If it makes you feel any better, I'm pretty sure I was the only one who thought it was corny. Everyone else ate it up."

"That's worse, somehow. I'm Linda Duff, by the way."

"Tamsin Rigby."

"Cool name."

"Thanks." No one had ever called Tamsin's name cool before.

"Rigby," Linda said. "That sounds familiar."

"To you and everyone else. The Rigbys have been here for a thousand years, more or less."

"Is your dad the guy with the white truck? The sign maker?" Linda affected a casual air, toying with her paperback, riffling its pages.

"How did you know?"

"Lucky guess."

Linda chewed on her lower lip, turning her attention to the Frisbee game. The players' voices carried through the warm, yellow distance, lazy, isolated, rising just above the murmur of a breeze through the birches.

After a pause, Linda said a little too offhandedly, "I think I met your brother a couple weeks ago. Or I saw him, anyway. Aran, right?"

Tamsin was surprised. Aran hadn't mentioned anything about meeting a girl. "Where did you meet him? How?"

"At the park on the river. We all had a party. I suppose you can call it a party."

"Aran went to a party?" Tamsin didn't know whether it was more shocking that Aran had attended a party, or that he'd been invited to one.

"No," Linda said. "He came down to the river by himself. I noticed him, that's all."

"Where did you come from, anyway? You mentioned you're new in town, and I haven't seen you much before today."

"I stick out, don't I?" Linda didn't sound pleased about it. "Is it the way I dress?"

"Partly. But I like your outfit; it's neat."

"The dress I wore to church today, for that cheeseball concert—I borrowed it from my roommate, and she's Rexburg to the core. I still looked like an outsider, though, didn't I?"

"Rexburg doesn't sit well on you."

"Guess I'd better try harder if I want to fit in."

"Why would you want to fit in here?"

"I'm going to the college this fall, so I've got to blend in a little bit. In the right ways, you know."

"Going to college," Tamsin said. "So you're looking for a husband? That's why all the girls go to Ricks."

She expected Linda to laugh again, the way she'd done when Tamsin had commented on the music, but Linda was sober, almost melancholy.

"I guess I am looking for a husband. Not right away, but eventually." Linda watched the Frisbee players again, then muttered, "God, listen to me. Going to college just so I can get married. Betty Friedan would shit herself."

Tamsin burst out laughing.

"Sorry," Linda said. "I've got a blue tongue. I forget to keep it in my head sometimes."

"Are you a member of the church? I mean, I've seen you at church a couple times now, but you don't look much like the other girls. You don't talk like them, either."

"Technically, I'm a member. Got baptized back home while I was still in high school. Though the way I talk, I think the church would rather not have me."

"I don't mind the way you talk. I kind of like it."

"You're the only one."

"So where are you from? You never told me."

"Seattle."

Tamsin supposed she ought to have known. This girl was friends with Sandy Jepson, after all. But Sandy had always run with the twins' crowd, not with Tamsin's. She said, "Where's that?"

"You don't know where Seattle is?" Linda didn't sound condescending—only amazed, and maybe a little delighted, as if she'd discovered an entire civilization untouched by the wider world. "It's in Washington. To the west."

"I knew that. I just didn't remember. What's it like? It's a big city, right? Why did you leave? You couldn't pay me to leave a real city and come to a nowheresville like Rexburg. I wouldn't do it for a million bucks."

Tamsin had always heard that cities were terrible places, brimming with every sort of corruption—crime, broken families, communists lining the gutters, felled into shameful stupor by drugs. And loose women committing whoredoms. She had been to Salt Lake, of course, but that place was different, according to her father. Salt Lake was a stronghold of Latter-Day Saints. At the heart of the city stood the greatest temple in the faith and the silver-domed Tabernacle where the glorious choir raised their songs of praise up to Heaven. Gad often waxed rapturous about the fine and righteous features of Salt Lake City, but apart from its size, Tamsin had always found it unappealing. Salt Lake was just Rexburg at a larger scale. She'd always harbored a secret desire to witness firsthand the sins of more worldly places. She tried to imagine Seattle, the genesis of this mysterious stranger in her tight T-shirt, but all she could picture were the bleak scapes of noir films, like the ones she and Aran watched late at night on the TV set in the den, rotating the rabbit ears to pick up a clearer picture. In her mind, Seattle was a warren of tall buildings and heavy shadows, and its music was the wail of sirens and saxophones, punctuated by bursts of gunfire and the screams of terrorized women. The whole idea was thrilling.

"Seattle is all right," Linda said. "I don't think you can really call it a big city, though I guess compared to Rexburg it's gargantuan. I didn't leave because I was trying to get away from Seattle. I left to get away from my family—what's left of it."

"And you came here, of all places?"

"For the college. A nice LDS college where I can meet a nice LDS guy and start a nice family. But now that I'm here, I've got a new problem on my hands. I can't blend in, no matter how hard I try. And if I can't pass muster in Rexburg, there isn't much hope for my future."

"Not if the only future you want is to get married. It seems like there ought to be more things a girl can do with her life, though, besides finding a husband and having babies."

"There are heaps more things a girl can do." Linda sounded distracted now, distant. "But what I want most is a good family. I think I deserve it, now that I'm an adult. I never got to have a real family when I was a kid."

I never had a real family when I was a kid, either, Tamsin thought. She didn't say it aloud. She didn't want Linda to think her callous or dismissive. "I'm going to college," she said.

"Where, at Ricks?" Linda cast her book aside, wrapped her arms around her knees. "Are you starting this fall? Maybe we'll have classes together."

"I'm not going yet. I still have one more year of high school. But after that, I want to go to college. Not to Ricks, though. I want to live in a bigger place and do bigger things." She glanced uneasily at the Frisbee game, though the boys were all too far away to hear. "I want to become an ecologist."

"Far out." Linda perked up suddenly. "I just landed a job with the Idaho Environmental Council."

"No kidding? You're into protecting the environment, too?"

Linda laughed. "I'm into paying my bills. It was the only job I could find, to tell you the truth—and I understand it'll make me public enemy number one around here."

"Everyone in this town just loves that dam," Tamsin said darkly.

"I didn't have much choice but to take the job, since no one else would hire me. Without a job, I wouldn't have made it through school, not even the first semester. But now that I'm finally working, I think it's pretty keen. I get to walk around in the fields counting birds and plants and making observations on nature. And the more I think about nature, the more important my job seems. So who knows—maybe I'll become an ecologist, after all. Maybe you and I have something in common."

"I'd give anything for a job like that."

"You should apply. The IEC is looking for more workers."

"My dad would fall over dead. His daughter working at any job would be bad enough, but working for a bunch of environmentalists? He'd have a heart attack for sure. But if I had a job," Tamsin said, "you know what I'd do? I'd buy my own car. I have my license, but there's never any chance to drive on my own. Someone in my family always has to use one of our cars for something or other. I'm lucky if I get to make a trip to Broulim's once a month because my mom forgot to buy toilet paper."

"You like to drive?" Linda said.

"I like to go places."

Linda stood up, tucked her book under one arm, and brushed the seat of her jeans. "Come on. I have a car. Let's go for a joyride."

"Are you serious?"

"Just me and you. Go get your stuff."

"I came here on my bike," Tamsin said.

"Leave it. No one in this town would steal a bike. No one would dare."

A few minutes later, Tamsin had her pack on her shoulders and she and Linda were leaving the park side by side, as if they'd known each other for years. Tamsin had a floating, flying sensation, as if she were getting away with some sort of mischief. She had friends, of course, when the school year was on. But as she'd gotten older, Tamsin had found she had little in common with the girls from school. They were all too focused on boys and dances for Tamsin's liking, and when she'd started dating Nick, most of her friends had been shocked or saddened—actually crying, in a few cases—as if Tamsin had done something unforgivable. Since the Nick incident, Tamsin hadn't missed her friends much. She'd been content to keep to herself all summer long, too. But now, beside this mature and sophisticated outsider, Tamsin decided there were some benefits to friendship, after all. Not that she could call herself Linda's friend; they'd only just met. But she had a sense that they would become real friends, with time. Probably Gad would freak out over that, too, like he'd done over Nick.

Linda stopped walking next to an orange Beetle. "This is me." She pulled a key ring from the pocket of her jeans and tossed it to Tamsin. "You're driving."

They threw their blankets and books into the back seat, and Tamsin fired up the engine. It took her several tries to get the hang of the clutch. The Beetle lurched and sputtered up the street, and stalled a time or two, and all the while, Tamsin and Linda laughed till they were both crying. Once Tamsin had control, they cruised away from the park. Linda fiddled with the radio, trying to tune in something other than the AM talk station that broadcast out of Rexburg. Fragments of music broke through the static.

"Reception is better up on the Bench," Tamsin said.

"Let's go, then."

They passed the college campus. Linda stared at the tidy collection of buildings and watered lawns with an incisive squint. She had dark eyes and a way of narrowing them that made Tamsin feel as if she were cutting the world open, as if sight were a deft tool that Linda could wield at will, with more finesse than anyone Tamsin knew except maybe for Aran. But Aran's way of seeing was gentle, accepting, while Linda's was efficient and sharp. She was flaying the world with her eyes, stripping away everything extraneous till only the bones were left, and there was nothing behind which to hide.

As they climbed toward the summit, the radio crackled and whined. A song lifted out of the noise, bright and clear. They rolled down their windows, and Tamsin drove as fast as she dared, the wind whipping their long hair together, Linda's black and Tamsin's red gold. They sang along, whatever words they knew, and laughed when they didn't know the words at all, and Tamsin had never had so much fun with a girl before, never allowed herself this joyful abandon.

"There's the water tower," Linda said. "Whenever I see that thing, it makes me think of the fighting machine from *The War of the Worlds*. You know, the tripod."

"I've never read *The War of the Worlds*. Anyway, the tower has four legs, not three."

"Humor me. There are no water towers where I'm from—at least, none that stick out like this one does. Maybe we've got too many trees in Seattle, so all the tripods hide, and you don't know they're looking at you. You can't miss the tower out here, can you? I feel like it's watching me, whenever I come up onto the Bench. Like I can't hide from its eye."

"Nothing can hide from the water tower. Up there, you can see everything in this town."

"You've been to the top?"

"Not the top, exactly. There's a walkway that goes all around the base of the tank. Want to climb up and see for yourself?"

"Won't we get caught?"

"No one from Utilities is around right now. It's a Sunday. Anyway, it's almost seven thirty."

Tamsin found the track that led to the base of the tower. She pulled the Beetle off the road. It rocked and bounced and kicked up a cloud of dust, which rose in the rear-view mirror to obscure the world behind. The tower's steel legs were bolted to an enormous cement pad, its lip protruding only an inch or two above bare earth. She maneuvered Linda's Beetle up onto the cement, close to one of the legs, and cut the engine.

"We'll have to climb onto the roof of your car," Tamsin said. "It's smaller than my mom's car, so we might have to jump to catch the lowest rung of the ladder."

"Your mom's car?"

"That's how I got up before." Tamsin reached into the back seat, snagged her pack by one of its straps, and pulled it onto her lap. She could hear the spray can rattling in the bottom of her bag. "Right at the start of the summer, I came up here with some red paint and had a little fun."

"It was you," Linda said. "I've seen the graffiti in town. Red paint on the bricks, 'Down with the Dam' and all that."

Tamsin shrugged.

"We probably shouldn't do this." Linda spoke with a certain lilt to her voice that said she wanted to do it anyway.

Tamsin got out of the car and slung the pack on her shoulders. "Okay if I climb up onto the roof?"

"I guess so."

Linda got out, too. She watched as Tamsin hiked herself onto the hood, then scrambled on hands and feet up the slope of the windshield. The lowering sun was bright in Tamsin's eyes; the drifting dust made her want to sneeze. She rose up on her toes, reaching for the ladder. It was only a couple inches beyond her fingertips. She gave a little experimental hop and brushed the metal. The car rocked when she landed. A harder jump, and she caught the ladder with both hands, swung her body, braced her feet against the tower's leg.

"Holy shit," Linda said.

Tamsin walked her feet up the pitted blue surface. Soon she had enough purchase to reach up for another rung, then another. She groped for the ladder with her foot and found it.

"See," she called down, "it's easy."

"I don't know. It seems dangerous."

"The view is worth it. I promise."

Before long, Tamsin was halfway up the ladder and Linda wasn't far below, shrieking with laughter and fear as she climbed. Tamsin reached the metal grate of the walkway. She paused to catch her breath and shake the trembling from her limbs, then bent to help Linda pull herself onto the platform. Linda was panting. Beads of sweat glittered at her temple. But when she stood and looked out over the railing, her eyes widened, and Tamsin smiled. Rexburg and the whole Snake River

Valley swept out below them. Night was an hour away; the light slanted rosy and mellow across the land. The town was like a child's toys left in the dust. Everything within Rexburg's boundaries seemed insignificant from up there. The land was vast and endless, summer dry, except for the green veins where the cottonwoods hugged the river—green and river blue branching and flowing, meandering out toward the pale band of the sand dunes and distant Menan Butte, where the college's white *R* had turned bright pink in anticipation of sunset.

"Look." Linda pointed.

Tamsin turned to see. Far across the valley, at the northwestern horizon, something bright and golden was rising into the sky. Her first instinct was to recoil in dread—a hard, sudden, familiar fear, bred into her as it was bred into everyone in that place—a certainty that the End Times had come. That terrible, stately ascending light could only be the Lord coming back to cleanse the world with fire. The next moment, Tamsin reminded herself that she didn't believe in the Lord anyway, which meant she didn't believe in the End of Days. In another rapid heartbeat or two, she realized it was only the moon rising, but such a moon as she had never seen before—huge, deliberate, so close she almost thought she could hear the old-hawser creak of its motion.

"You were right," Linda said. "The view was worth it."

"I'd climb up here every Sunday if I could, but my parents would flip if I took the car for something like this." She turned her back on the valley and the moon, squinting at the surface of the water tank, which was glaring in the late afternoon light. "Look, you can see where they covered over my graffiti. The white doesn't match."

Tamsin took the pack off her shoulders and delved inside for her spray paint. She popped the top off the can with practiced ease and shook it, eyeing the surface. Before she could think better, she had sprayed a tall blood-red *F* onto the curve of the tank. Then she paused. She could feel Linda's sharp eyes on her, waiting, judging. The paint beaded and ran and lost its sheen as it dried. The acrid smell of lacquer and propellant hung in the air. Tamsin didn't know whether Linda would think it cool or crass if she continued with the word. She swallowed hard, not looking at her new friend, then added a curve to the *F*, transforming it to a *P*. She wrote the rest of her slogan quickly: *Protect the Valley*.

"That's good," Linda said.

Tamsin dropped the can back into her pack. She and Linda leaned their forearms on the steel railing, a posture that would have come off as casual if they hadn't been some hundred feet up in the air.

"Why go to all this trouble—I mean, climbing up here and risking getting caught—when you already know everyone in town wants that dam and loves it?" Linda said.

Tamsin shrugged. "I don't know. I guess I'm just mad."

"About what?"

Tamsin didn't know how to answer. She'd spent so long filled up by a mute, nameless anger that she didn't think it was possible to explain. The feeling had been with her almost as long as she could remember—a thick, stifled pain. She had never examined it before, not much, and now, turning some calm inner eye upon her rage, she couldn't pick out any single feature. She was mad about . . . everything. And she couldn't imagine why everyone around her wasn't seething in exactly the same way.

At length, she said, "I guess my life isn't what I want it to be."

"Neither is mine. I suppose that's why I came to Rexburg. I'm trying to make the kind of life I want instead of the kind of life fate gave me."

"Fate," Tamsin said, amused, "or God?"

"It's all the same thing, as far as I'm concerned."

Tamsin flushed. She had harbored similar thoughts before—constantly, if she was honest. But she'd never heard anyone talk that way, as if God didn't exist or, if He did, was more or less insignificant. Not even Aran talked that way.

She said, "You're trying to make a life you want by marrying some regular old boring man?"

"It must sound crazy to you. You've lived in Rexburg all your life, right? But the Molly Mormon game looks pretty appealing from where I sit. My family was . . . not so great. My dad was mean, and drunk half the time, and when my mom could finally leave him, he vanished anyway. It was just me and my mom for the last few years, till I was old enough to get out on my own. Even then, Mom was so tired from working all the time that she wasn't really there, you know? She was just . . . angry. Bitter. That was all I got from her, it was all she had left at the end of the day."

"That's sad," Tamsin said.

"My friend Sandy—her family was nothing like mine. Sandy's house was this amazing place where everybody loved each other even if they didn't always get along. I could feel how happy their home was the second I walked through the door. It was like heaven to me. I spent as much time at Sandy's place as I could get away with. It's a wonder her parents didn't get sick of me and make me leave, but they practically treated me like I was one of their own kids."

"I always liked the Jepsons," Tamsin said. "It was too bad when they moved to Seattle."

"After a while," Linda said, "I realized it was the Jepsons' faith that held them together so strongly—not just Sandy's parents but her brothers and sisters, too. I knew I wanted that for myself. I knew I had to make my life as peaceful and sweet as theirs was. So I got baptized and joined their church when I was seventeen, and when Sandy decided to come out here to Ricks College, I came with her."

Tamsin was staring at Linda now, furrowing her brow.

"What?" Linda said.

"I'm trying to wrap my head around it. You think it's the church that made the Jepsons so happy?"

"Why wouldn't it be the church?"

"My family has been in the faith since the pioneers first came to this valley. But we aren't like the Jepsons—not at all. In fact, I'd say we're exactly the opposite, and that's on a good day. The Rigbys might have been in Rexburg since the town was founded, but we aren't a normal family. We don't have a happy home."

Linda didn't say anything to that. She kept her eyes on the rising moon. There was a paleness to her features now that made Tamsin feel a little guilty, like maybe she'd struck some unfair blow, though she hadn't meant to hurt Linda. She had only meant to tell the truth.

"I'm sorry," Tamsin said, "if I upset you."

"It's not your fault. It's just . . . Sandy told me something similar, that it isn't the church that makes good families. I didn't want to believe her. I still don't. I don't want to believe you. This is all I've got to hold on to. It's the choice I made, you know?"

"And now you've got to see it through."

"Yeah. That's right."

"I'm sure you'll do better than my family has done. You're smart, and . . . and not from here. That has to give you some advantage. You won't pick a dud for a husband, some grouchy old drunk like your dad. You'll do better. You can tell what people are like just by looking at them."

Linda gave her an amused smile. "I can?"

A wind came up from the valley floor, sharp with a smell of sage. It blew the dust into Tamsin's eyes and stole her breath away. When the gust had gone, she blinked the water from her eyes and found that Linda was still looking at her, sober and steady.

"Tell me about your brother," Linda said.

"Aran?"

Tamsin felt starkly exposed. Solid ground was very far below. She would have moved toward the ladder and started climbing down, but Linda had fixed her in place with the terrible perceptivity of her eyes.

She felt as if she had revealed too much already—had shown more than she'd known she'd been hiding.

"Tell me," Linda said. "I've heard certain things about him."

Tamsin relaxed a little. Linda was only talking about the rumors, those miserable untrue stories that had followed Aran for years.

"I bet," Tamsin said, "you've heard he's a druggie. You've probably heard he's a Devil worshipper, too. That's my favorite rumor—the stupidest of all. You know why they say that about him? Because his hair is long. That's it. That's the whole reason why."

Linda's mouth twitched. Tamsin realized she was holding back another smile. It made her somewhat less imposing. "Your brother's hair isn't long."

"It's long compared to every other man's hair. Haven't you noticed?"

"I don't get it. Why does everyone say those things?" Linda asked.

"Everyone wants the stories to be real. But wanting doesn't make a story true. Believing doesn't make it true, either."

"What would anyone have to gain by spreading lies about your brother?"

All the passion came roaring up inside Tamsin then. It was never far below the surface. She rounded on Linda, all but shouting. "They need someone to point fingers at, so they'll feel better about themselves, about all the thoughts they're trying so hard to suppress, all the things they want to do but don't dare try. They need someone to scare their kids with. 'Be careful, or you'll end up like Aran Rigby.' You know what I think? I think the whole town hates Aran because he won't go along. He won't become what everyone says he has to be. It makes them crazy and mean with jealousy, 'cause they all want to be who they really are, too. Aran is the only one who has the guts to do it. And now here you are, trying so hard to become a part of Rexburg that you're all set to believe the rumors. But you don't know Aran. You have no idea who he is or what's inside his heart."

Linda said nothing for a long moment. She watched Tamsin steadily. Her eyes softened, the tightness of her mouth relaxed a little. "You really love your brother. I can tell."

"He's the best person I know, the best person in the world."

"Why is he the best?"

Tamsin thought about that. The silence was only broken by a few whips of wind and the far-off calling of a magpie. Finally, she said, "Because he sees everything for what it is. He sees the whole world, and he's honest with himself about what the world is. No one else is honest, not that way. I think the only thing Aran can't see clearly is himself."

"No one ever sees themselves perfectly," Linda said. "No one understands their own mind."

"I do."

Linda watched her again—that cutting, efficient gaze—and made no answer.

Tamsin said, "Why are you being so friendly with me, anyway?"

"Am I being friendly? I think I've just made you mad."

"You caught me off guard, that's all. I'm not mad anymore. I'm used to people saying terrible things about Aran—that's nothing new. But I don't get you, Linda. You're older than me—"

"Not by much. How old are you, anyway?"

"Seventeen."

"We're only three years apart. That's nothing, in the grand scheme of things."

"I still have a year of high school left, and you'll be at the college in the fall. We might as well be from different planets."

"I think maybe we are from different planets." Linda spoke so quietly that Tamsin wasn't sure she was meant to hear. Louder, Linda said, "I like you. That's why I'm being friendly. You're the first real person I've met in Rexburg, except for Sandy, and now she's all hung up on some guy, trying to get him to propose to her, and she isn't like herself at all anymore. But you're still you. You aren't hiding anything from me."

Tamsin stared over the valley, the sunset bleeding low across the earth, the moon rolling fat and orange from the edge of the world. "Don't be so sure I'm not hiding anything."

"Whatever you may be keeping secret, at least I can tell you're exactly who you seem to be."

"That's true," Tamsin said, placid now, grateful that Linda had seen.

"I guess that's why I like you. And it doesn't bother me that I'm a few years older. I still think we should be friends."

Tamsin nodded. She thought it must mean something, really mean something, if this self-possessed city woman could like her and call her a friend. Maybe it meant she could survive out there beyond Rexburg, past the luminous horizon. Assuming she could find a way to get there.

14

WHITE LADDER

The truth of it was, the rumors about Aran weren't entirely unfounded. He took great pains to conceal that reality from his family, especially from his mother and sister. But when the nights were long and he tossed in his bed, when he asked himself the same unanswerable question—why was he still there, why, under Gad's roof and his hard, callused thumb?—the truth came back to him. It wouldn't let him rest.

As a kid, Aran worked—like all boys worked in his town—to save money for his mission. He was a wiry boy with sun-reddened arms, mowing lawns and pulling weeds from old ladies' flower beds. He put the quarters he earned in a big Mason jar in his bedroom, and whenever the jar was filled, he sorted the coins into paper rolls. It always amazed and disgusted him, how heavy those coins felt, how quickly they filled the jar, yet they were worth so little once he'd packaged them in their tidy paper skins.

When he got a little older, he lucked into a rare opening as a paperboy. In the crisp light of early morning—air damp with dew, smelling of a coming frost—Aran would ride his bike through several Rexburg neighborhoods, chucking newspapers onto front steps. The new job required him to wake even earlier than he'd had to get up for seminary.

He would have skipped seminary if he could have gotten away with it, but by that time he'd been ordained a teacher in the church, the second step of his priesthood, and how would it have looked if he'd failed to keep up with his religious studies? Between the paper route, his early-morning Scripture classes, and a full day of schooling, Aran was left with a constant wobble in his limbs and a dullness to his thoughts, which he would have attributed to lack of sleep if he'd had the energy to sit and think about it. Now that he had his paper route, the money added up faster. He was earning a steadier wage than he'd ever done mowing lawns.

The trouble started just before Aran turned fifteen. That was the spring his dad took him to Salt Lake City one Saturday on a business trip of some kind, the exact nature of which Aran could no longer remember, if he had ever known. The only thing he recalled from that trip was the record store where he'd whiled away the time. Gad was engaged with a client or a paint supplier across the street, and Aran, being almost a grown man in his own right, was allowed to look after himself while his father conducted business. He went into the record shop on a whim, without any real idea of what he was looking for, but he soon found himself entranced by the great wooden bins of vinyl in their cardboard sleeves.

The shop was run by a man with hair as long as a woman's, limp and stringy, pale brown, and his loose plaid shirt smelled of some exotic spice that Aran couldn't name. The shopkeeper sure didn't look like a Mormon. The turntable behind his counter was hooked up to a couple of speakers hung high on the walls, and the whole space was filled with a simple, plaintive sound like nothing Aran had ever heard, nothing he'd imagined music could be—a man's loose, unschooled voice and one persistent guitar. The song told of a white ladder, a dead pony, a woman on fire. Aran was suspended in the moment, standing yet feeling as if he were hanging above the earth. He stared up at one of the speakers. A certain clear, sharp intensity of feeling went right through him, almost like pain, but it was sweet—oddly sweet. In a dim and hazy, fish-swimming way, he realized that music was kin to some of the paintings he'd seen in the art books at the library. It was vivid like the paintings, and honest, and it made him burn inside and made his throat feel tight with tears. The song, Aran felt, was telling the story of his life. Not life as he had known it so far, at age fourteen, but life as it must be someday, a long imminent slide, and he was horrified and hypnotized and instantly, entirely, helplessly in love with the sound.

"Not bad, eh, kid?" the shopkeeper said.

"What is this?" Aran asked him.

"You've never heard Bob Dylan before?"

When he got back to Rexburg, Aran figured out how to wrap aluminum foil around the antenna of his radio so he could pick up the faint transmission of the rock station out of Idaho Falls. That tided him over till the summer of his sixteenth year, but by then, his hunger for music had grown to a gnawing, insistent pain. He couldn't be satisfied by the radio any longer. After his paper route was finished, Aran would take a little money from his Mason jar or from the shoebox under his bed where his rolled quarters lay neat as sardines in a tin, and buy bus tickets to Idaho Falls—and there he would hunt through the two small record stores and the junk shops and every yard sale he could find, searching for more music. He didn't often find good records at the yard sales—too much of the usual church-approved stuff, safe and saccharine, nothing like what he craved. But now and again, he'd come across some dusty trove of jazz albums or ancient bluegrass recordings. Those old records hissed and popped under the needle but still struck him with the same beautiful pang of longing that Dylan could effect. He carried his treasures home carefully, concealed in a backpack, and Gad never knew what kind of sprawling ideas Aran was cultivating, not till it was too late to rein him in.

By the time he was sixteen, Aran was also itching for something better than the simple paper pads and school pencils with which he'd been drawing. It wasn't hard to convince himself that he could dip into his mission funds to buy art supplies, too. He had a car by the end of that autumn, a rusted old Crosley station wagon that he'd beaten back into shape in the school's auto shop, and he didn't think twice about driving out to Idaho Falls to try out a new kind of paint—those nice tins of watercolors like candies in a box, or the miniature tubes of gouache that dried down to a papery whisper on his panels. By then, of course, Aran knew full well that Gad didn't approve of his drawing, and if Gad didn't like drawing, then Aran was dang sure he wouldn't approve of painting. So he kept those excursions a secret, too, as well as the paintings he made. But Aran didn't stop. He could have stopped his own heart from beating more easily, with less trouble and hurt. He never quite made a painting that felt the way the best music made him feel, like his body was shot through with fire, like there were eyes on the inside of him and all the eyes had opened at once. But now and then, he came close.

The new self he'd discovered inside came out to face the rest of the world, one sliver at a time. He let his hair grow just a bit longer than the other boys' hair, and he was big enough that Gad had a hard time forcing him down to the barbershop to get it cut. Instead of the plain polo shirts and pressed slacks the other boys wore, Aran put on the clothes he found at yard sales, loud shirts and wide-legged pants; goodness knew where those rags had come from, or how they'd found their way to Idaho Falls. At first, Aran liked being the rebel in his school. It gave him a cachet no other kid in town could touch, a faint whiff of danger that appealed to him, a certain notoriety. But as the end of high school approached, the boys in his classes started talking about their missions, and the girls began to go out on dates to the burger joint or, if you were lucky, the drive-in theater, but never with Aran, who no one's father approved of. He stopped feeling cool and began to feel lonely. His dad was impatient, angry that Aran didn't have any dates. Gad assumed Aran wasn't interested in the dances hosted by the high school and the various church wards scattered around town, and he was shaken with fear over what it might mean, that his eldest son didn't want to dance with girls. It wasn't that Aran lacked the interest. He just knew better than to go to a dance where no girls wanted to be seen with him. Aran retreated into the fields with his sketchbooks and his little cakes of watercolors. There was refuge in art, in the great wide open. Gad couldn't find him out there.

Arletta knew about the paintings, of course. Arletta was safe. Aran knew his mother would never mention the paintings to Gad—and whenever Gad was out of town, delivering a new sign in Pocatello or Jackson Hole, Aran shared his paintings with his mother, just to see the light come into her eyes, where normally no light could be found. In those still, easy hours, he would approach Arletta almost shyly and show her what he'd made. It was the same thing he'd done as a small boy, opening his hand to reveal a caterpillar he'd caught under the birch trees or a flower he'd found growing up from the lawn. When Arletta looked through his small, hasty watercolors, she smiled. Better still, something fierce and defiant hardened her face. Aran wished he had the courage to give a painting to his mother, but where would she keep it? If Gad came across a strange picture framed on the wall or hidden in a drawer, he would ask where it had come from, and then both Aran and Arletta would be forced to explain. They would both face the consequences— hours of shouting, berating, demands to know why Aran couldn't be a proper man like any other good and righteous fellow in Rexburg. It was better for everyone if his art remained a secret.

Soon he was eighteen and his mission was around the corner. One day he opened the box under his bed and found it empty, or near enough to empty as made no real difference. Aran sat stunned on his bedroom floor. All those years of work, all the hours of lost sleep, gone just like that. He knew he should have been angry at himself for blowing through all that money. But his life had color now for the first time in my memory. He couldn't regret the only things he loved.

He comforted himself with the possibility that he might not be called to a mission after all. He'd heard the stories about himself, rumors that he'd fallen in with Devil worshippers or had long since broken the strict sobriety code known as the Word of Wisdom. No doubt Bishop Kimball had heard those stories, too, and wouldn't recommend Aran for missionary work, not till he'd spent years repenting. But just after his nineteenth birthday, Bishop Kimball sat Aran down for his interview, and shortly after, the letter came. Maybe Kimball, alone of all the souls in Rexburg, didn't believe the wild stories about Aran's sins. More likely, the Rigby name was too important in the complex web of small-town society, and the bishop thought it riskier to delay Aran's mission than to recommend him.

"New York City," Gad said, scowling at the letter. "It's damn near an insult. Pit of degradation—that's all New York is."

"I don't have to go if you don't want me roaming around New York," Aran said hopefully. "We can find some excuse—"

"Like hell. No son of mine will fail to serve his mission."

Aran had known his father would say as much. He also knew he was powerless to put his foot down and refuse to undertake the mission. It was the thing he hated most in himself, that frailty before his father.

Of course, it was out of the question that Aran should confess to spending all his mission money on art supplies and records. He had no choice but to try to raise the $2,000 all over again—in a matter of weeks instead of years.

Aran never knew how Joel Kimball, the bishop's son, came to learn of his financial difficulty. Maybe Joel merely guessed he would be hard up for money and took a chance. Maybe Joel had no idea Aran was hurting for a quick buck, but believed the rumors so strongly, he assumed Aran would be a ready mark. The reason never mattered. All that mattered was what came after.

Joel approached Aran casually one afternoon while he was filling his gas tank at the Circle K.

"Say, Aran. How would you like to make some fast money? I'm talking real good money, too, not pocket change."

Aran was so surprised and relieved, he let go of the gas pump. Some of the fuel sprayed down the side of his Crosley before he could get control of the nozzle.

"Yes," he said, never asking what the job was. "Absolutely. I'll do it."

He had some idea that the job would involve physical labor—painting houses, maybe, or hauling furniture for a moving company.

Joel gave him a few vague details. He had a friend in Idaho Falls who had something he needed to get rid of. If Aran could sell it, he could keep a cut of the profits. Twenty percent. It was a good deal.

A roaring filled Aran's ears. He'd seen enough movies and read enough books to guess what Joel was talking about, that buttoned-up bishop's son, the golden boy of Rexburg. But damn if he didn't need the money.

"How soon can I get paid?" Aran asked.

"Depends on how fast you can sell it," Joel said. "It's not so hard. I've done it a few times. The pay is pretty good."

"You've done it here?"

"Sure." Joel scuffed his shoes against the pavement, as if they were discussing a football game or the latest movie, something of no real consequence. "You have to go out to the trailer parks at the edge of town, or up to St. Anthony. Hit the immigrants who work on the farms. None of them are members of the church; they never talk to anyone who's a member. It's perfectly safe that way. No one will find out."

Aran made the drive out to Idaho Falls that evening and met Joel's friend just where he said he could find him. He stashed a few plastic-wrapped bundles of grass under his car seats and drove away again, blinking to keep the tears from his eyes. He could smell the grass faintly through the plastic, acrid and accusatory. He told himself he was only doing what everyone already expected him to do, living up to his image, the son of perdition. It didn't make him feel any better. Somehow it made him feel ten times worse, to give in, to become what they all expected him to be.

Despite Joel's advice, Aran couldn't bring himself to sell the stuff anywhere near Rexburg. The mere thought made him feel ponderously sinful, as if he would poison a well of some exquisite purity. He told his family he was going on a solo camping trip to think and pray alone before he committed himself to his mission. He spent a few days drifting between Pocatello and Malad, even wandered all the way out to Twin Falls, selling off the grass a little at a time, sleeping in roadside hotels, waking each morning with his eyes gritty and painful and a hard knot of shame in his gut.

He still had more than half the grass to get rid of, though, and the days were speeding by. His mission was almost upon him. Then he recalled an ad he'd seen some years before in an art magazine. There was a conclave of artists who gathered each year at Jackson Hole, just across the Wyoming border. They took over one of the ski resorts, which were no use to anyone without the winter snows, and passed the summer painting and doing who knew what else together, whatever artists did.

He set out for Jackson, stopping only once, in the town of Blackfoot, to eat his first filling meal in days at a truck-stop diner. He called his mother, let her know he was still alive, still in conversation with the Lord. Then he pressed on to Wyoming, pursued by the shadow of anxiety. He figured that transporting drugs across state lines must somehow transcend illegality. Surely it reached whole new realms of criminal offense. He didn't know which he feared worse: his father or the law. But he managed to descend the steep mountain pass into Jackson Hole without any sheriffs on his tail, and by nightfall, he found the ski resort turned artists' commune and blended into the culture of the place more easily than he had anticipated.

Aran spent six days living in those cabins, under the tall pines with the air summer-still and golden between their trunks. By day, he joined the artists on short hikes up into the mountains where they painted en plein air. He hadn't intended to bring his small block of watercolor paper and his old pochade box, but he found them both in the bottom of his duffel bag, so he was able to pass for one of them, an artist with real intent, real purpose, a right to be there at the summer commune. Between paintings, he talked to the others—middle-aged men with tangled beards, women with sun-tanned skin and wide mouths who let their armpit hair grow. Young fellows with haunted eyes who would bolt upright in their cots at night, shouting with memories of the war. He didn't meet a single person who was a bit like him, not a bit like his family or his hometown. They had come from Philadelphia, Toronto, Phoenix, San Francisco, Florida. There was even a married couple from Ireland and a thin, quiet boy from Japan who only knew a few phrases in English. They were worldly—of the world, the kind of people he'd been raised to fear or pity, the kind of people he would soon be tasked with converting to his religion in order to save their souls. None of them needed saving. It was Aran who was taken in and embraced by that community, Aran who was given succor and patience and a place beside the fire.

Word got around that he had plenty of grass to sell, and by the end of his six days, the whole load was gone. Aran had done the math. His 20 percent cut would give him more than enough cash to see him through his mission. What was more precious to him by then were the paintings he'd created in the hot, dry shade under the pines, beside his new friends, that ragtag family to which he knew he belonged.

I could stay, he told himself. *If I never went home, never called my mother again, never took the money back to Idaho Falls, no one would know what became of me.*

They would all think he'd been eaten by a bear or had walked off a cliff somewhere in the high, dark labyrinth of the Rocky Mountains. There was no real reason to go home—not now that he'd found a new way of living.

But even as he told himself these comforting lies, he could already feel Rexburg and his father and the great strong arm of the church pulling him back. Whatever those six days of freedom had meant to Aran, the drive to win his father's approval meant far more. Or controlled him more, at any rate.

He drove back to Idaho Falls with a fat roll of cash, more money than he'd ever imagined holding in his hands. It seemed like more money than had ever existed in the world, an amount that made him giddy and sick all at once. He made Joel's friend count out his 20 percent three times, just to be certain every penny was there. Then he returned home, shaking, with the windows rolled down to pull in the clean, sage-laden air.

It was only those ten days. That was the worst—that was all he ever did, and only because he couldn't admit the truth, that all the money for his mission was gone.

It'll be all right, Aran told himself, while the wind of the highway pulled the breath right out of his lungs. *I've got all the money I need now. I can go on my mission and Dad will never know what I did. I can go on my mission and Dad will be proud once I'm home, once I'm a real man in his eyes, finally, finally. God, please let it be true.*

But of course, by now anyone could see that it hadn't worked out the way Aran had hoped. Nothing had worked out. Nothing at all.

15

COMPANIONS

When he reached New York City, Aran was assigned to a new companion, Dean, a senior missionary who had already been spreading the word of the gospel for more than a year. They weren't allowed to use one another's first names, not even in private conversation. Aran referred to his companion as Elder Udall, and Aran became Elder Rigby, which raised a disorienting wall of formality between them. The distance felt stiff, artificial. They were supposed to remain within one another's sight at all times, and yet they were anonymous, or close to it. Aran often felt as if he were living and working with a ghost. He wondered sometimes whether anyone else could see Elder Udall. He wondered whether Elder Udall really saw him.

From his first day in the city, Aran sensed the vastness and variety of the world, the great irreligious clamor of sins and ideas and infinite beauties that Gad had always cautioned his children to avoid. Side by side, Aran and his companion walked the long, gray, stinking streets of New York and he felt, with every step, the tight thing woven around his heart loosening and fraying. Rexburg was very far away. And his family was far away; all of Gad's impatient expectations were thousands of miles behind him. It startled Aran, how quickly the bonds of expectation were slipping from his spirit. He had committed to the church's purpose for two years of his life—agreed to have no friend but Elder Udall, whom the church had assigned to him, agreed to communicate with his family only by letter, except for phone calls on Christmas and Mother's Day. He had agreed not to touch a woman, not even to come within arm's reach of a woman for the duration of his mission. These were not promises that anyone could make lightly. Aran had made them with the fullness of his heart. And yet the city was already picking at the threads of his faith. New York—huge and thick with humidity, blaring with terrible noise, with a reek like sweat and piss and fouler things—was transcendent in its beauty and its ugliness. It was the most honest thing Aran had encountered, a city more powerful than God.

Aran didn't know what he ought to call these treacherous thoughts. "Doubt" didn't seem like the right word. He didn't doubt whether God existed—he merely felt as if God were far away, farther even than Heaven, than the stars, than infinity. He felt as if everything were beneath God's notice, especially one nineteen-year-old man sweating through his short-sleeved white shirt in the swelter of New York. Why would the Lord of all Creation bother looking into the heart of a mere human being? Aran never paused to think about the sins and aspirations of the ants scurrying across the pavement. It all seemed so trite and foolish, the mission, the church, this urgency to save wayward souls. He figured if he ever voiced these thoughts to his companion, Elder Udall would tell him it was Satan working against him. Aran had learned in his training classes that Satan prowled with special emphasis for missionaries. Men caught up in the holiest work of their lives were like sweet fruits for the Adversary to pluck, real prizes worth the effort of winning. But why would Satan be nearer or more interested than a dim and distant God?

At least sheer amazement was enough to keep Aran working toward his mission's goals. His private ideas on divinity and damnation had turned out rather ambiguous, but if he continued sharing the gospel, he could remain in New York for two whole years. So he kept his private musings to himself and kept his hair trimmed and his face shaved clean, and gave his companion no reason to suspect he was anything but the ideal dedicated missionary.

That was why Aran felt such a numb shock when Elder Udall was the first to break the rules.

They'd been heading up Forty-Ninth in Woodside, toward a cluster of public housing high-rises, when Elder Udall stopped walking. The day was hot, the air heavy. Aran's head was pounding, his thoughts moving too slowly. It took several strides for him to realize that he was walking alone, and his companion was no longer by his side. Aran paused, turned, saw Elder Udall standing and looking up at the brick high-rises with a slack face and a quiet air of desperation.

He went back to his companion, patted Elder Udall on the shoulder, then the back. He asked if he was okay.

Elder Udall drew a deep breath and frowned. His eyes focused. He looked at Aran directly then, and Aran could tell he had reached a decision.

"Fuck it," Elder Udall said.

Aran's brows arched up so high, he thought they would climb right off his face. He laughed, startled and halfway delighted by his companion's language. It was that laugh that encouraged Elder Udall to say more.

"First of all," he said, thrusting his hands in his pockets and turning to face Aran squarely, "I want you to stop calling me Elder. My name is Dean."

A stillness of significance came over both of them. This was a thing not done. Elder Udall—Dean—was breaking the rules and doing it quite deliberately.

Aran decided to meet him halfway. "Then you have to call me Aran," he said.

"I've been on this mission for more than a year now," Dean said, "but I don't know why I'm here. I thought I knew at the beginning. And then when it got harder to know, I figured I'd find my true purpose if I stuck it out and served faithfully. But I haven't found a thing—not a single thing. And I don't know how I ended up here in the first place. That's what I think is eating at me. How could they have called me for this mission when I wasn't worthy of serving? Shouldn't God and His apostles know the difference between a sinner and a Saint?"

"I've wondered the same thing about myself," Aran confessed.

"I have a girlfriend back home in Provo. Lisa. She's sweet, and I love her, I really do. I'm going to marry her when I get home. But you know, we've gone all the way. A lot." Dean chuckled again, uneasily. "I mean, *a lot*. And when I did my interview, and they asked me if I had any unconfessed sins, I just told them no. Easy as that. I lied about how much I'd been sinning, and no one called me out on it, because no one knew. You see what I mean?"

Aran saw. "I wasn't exactly worthy for this mission, either, but nobody seemed to realize it."

"What are we doing, man? What's the point?"

"We're here," Aran said. "Maybe there's some reason why we're here, even if it isn't the reason we expected at the start."

After that strange, unprovoked rush of frankness, Aran and Dean found it easier every day. They left their apartment each morning looking like devout Mormon men, with their collars fastened high in defiance of the muggy Northeast climate and their holy books clutched in their hands. But by the time they'd rounded the corner, their name tags and black ties were stuffed in their pockets and their white shirts were unfastened down to the sternum to let in a breeze, and they never minded if their temple garments showed, because they looked just like the undershirts all the other men in the city displayed, damp with summer sweat.

That was how Aran passed the better part of two years: in disguise. He and Dean knocked on enough doors to keep their mission president happy—he was an easygoing fellow anyway, fuzzy about milestones and goals. They taught a handful of lessons to interested parties, even dunked two new converts apiece. But by keeping themselves barely active enough to avoid drawing attention, Aran and Dean managed to buy themselves considerable free time. And even after Dean's mission was finished and he went back home to Provo, Aran kept it up with his next companion, and the next. He was the senior missionary by then. It was easy to corrupt the new ones. All he had to do was tell them, as Dean had told him, what a bust his interview had been, what a joke. And all the other companions' stories came pouring out, predictable as a sunrise, and Aran led them all into the heart of the city, laughing and free.

Those first months had been the best, though. Dean was a real friend. He and Aran spent their unobserved hours wisely and well. They visited bookshops with entire rows of literature—books that would have been thrown on a bonfire back home. They slipped out in the evenings and took the train to Greenwich Village to listen to the poetry slams. They found their way into basement clubs where bands thrashed and screamed, and the audiences danced like they were trying to hurt each other. One evening while they were headed back to their apartment, fishing their ties from their pockets, a Puerto Rican with a lilting voice hooked them both by the arms and pulled them into a back-alley warehouse, in which they found a pageant in progress. Majestic dark-skinned men wearing high heels and makeup and sequined dresses strutted and posed before a table of judges. That pageant pulled Aran outside his body, beyond a place of comprehension. All that had existed in that moment was the startling, subversive beauty all around him, an elegance and power so great it made him feel vast and hollow inside.

And of course, there were the museums. He brought Dean to the Whitney and took in the small gallery of Wyeths. Dean lost patience and wandered off to find some lunch, but Aran stared at one painting in particular for minutes—for hours, as far as he could tell. A crow lying dead in a field. The beak slightly open, the honest, uncomposed curves of horizon and sky. The dry weeds splayed, the mobile white seedpods, a bird's scaly foot, curled. It wasn't only the Whitney. There were dozens of museums. He could have spent every day of those two years exploring their galleries; he still wouldn't have seen every painting and sculpture. Aran dragged Dean to the museums as often as Dean would agree to go, and there he gorged himself on a feast of fat things till his spirit was full. And even after he felt drowsy and sated, he kept on looking, studying, till the art had crowded everything else from his awareness.

Now and again, Aran and Dean—and later, Aran's other companions—succumbed to attacks of guilt. The waves came upon them suddenly, like those delayed blasts of wind that follow in the wake of trucks on the highway, sudden slaps of remorse. In those moments they would leave their ties on and preach to anyone who would listen, talking about the gospel so earnestly they sometimes made themselves weep. But when they were finally expelled from their puzzled hosts' apartments, they collapsed on one another's shoulders, laughing. Once, they laughed so hard that Dean gagged in an alley and almost threw up.

Dean's mission came to an end before Aran's was half-finished. On their last evening as companions, they ate hot dogs at Coney Island and leaned on the metal railing of the promenade, watching the couples walk hand in hand along the beach.

"Are you going to marry Lisa when you get home?" Aran asked.

"If she still wants me," Dean said.

"Why wouldn't she want you?"

"I haven't exactly been the ideal missionary."

"Do you think she'll find out?"

"I'll tell her," Dean said, calm and decided. "She deserves to know. What will you do? You've got more than a year left. You'll be the senior companion now."

"Strapped to some wide-eyed kid who still believes," Aran said.

"Don't you still believe? In anything?"

Aran smiled. "Do you?"

Dean wrinkled the paper from his hot dog and tossed it in a trash can. "Let's get back to the apartment," he said. "We should pray together, like good missionaries do."

16

LITTLE GIRL IN A BLUE ARMCHAIR

In the same month of the same year, just as Aran first arrived in New York and the city began pulling him further from his faith, a girl on the other side of the continent was being drawn steadily toward it.

Linda was sixteen when her mother finally filed for divorce. By that time, Linda couldn't feel anything other than a dull sense of inevitability. All the years of her childhood had already been wasted—first in denial that anything was wrong with her family, then with the many years she'd spent in desperation trying to stop her mother and father from fighting: the bargaining, the pleading, the crying that never got her anywhere and sometimes only seemed to make matters worse, inflaming her father's rage and expanding the cold distance her mother put between herself and the world, her daughter included. Linda wasn't out of high school yet and she was already tired, ready for it all to be finished, ready for the world to break apart.

Her father moved out, to where exactly, Linda never learned—she only had his phone number. Her mother threw herself into work at the drugstore—behind the cosmetics counter—and then, when the drugstore job wasn't enough to make ends meet, she began typing transcripts for the neighborhood pediatrician. The house felt menacing in its quiet.

Linda had thought the house would feel peaceful with no one inside but herself. Maybe it would finally feel like a home. Instead, the stillness and the unlit rooms, the muffled silence between the walls, seemed to emphasize with brutal force how empty the place had always been. She couldn't spend the summer by herself, sprawled on the carpet with the television on, sound turned all the way down, while she stared up at the ceiling. And so she began riding buses through the city, visiting one museum after another.

It wasn't that Linda was crazy about art—not yet. But the silence of the museums was contemplative rather than hostile, and no one tried to talk to her there. She didn't have to explain herself to anyone. She could walk and think and stare for hours at the old historic artifacts, the sculptures, the paintings. Looking at the exhibits was better than lingering in her house where there was nothing to see and nothing to feel. After a few weeks of escaping to the Seattle Art Museum, the Burke, the Frye, Linda was less a visitor and more an inhabitant. She began to feel like a specter haunting the halls, tracing her own footsteps from one painting to the next. The repetition did not depress her. On the contrary, Linda found she could wring new experiences from the paintings and sculptures every time she saw them. There were no emotions left for her anywhere else, but each work of art carried feelings inside. In the austere silence, she learned how to drink honey from the cup of art. It was a sweetness she craved more the more she tasted it.

Sometimes she would pass whole hours with her eyes fixed on a single object—an old marble bust or some nineteenth-century portrait with cool light and soft edges in an antique frame. On those days, she found that a single work, one old relic in a whole collection of wonders, could reach out and take hold of her as if it bore a secret meant for her especially, as if it had been waiting decades or centuries for Linda to appear. Those were the most melancholy of all her days, yet somehow she loved those moments best. Once, she kept returning to the Mary Cassatt, the little dark-haired girl limp and listless in a turquoise chair, a girl with no childhood at all. And there was another painting, Chardin, *Still Life with Dead Hare*, all brown shadows and drooping form. She stared at that one so long, her back started to ache, but she couldn't move, couldn't leave the painting alone. It had punched holes clean through Linda's spirit. All the sadness was running out. The rush of sorrow was a relief, more than anything else, and Linda asked herself why a girl of sixteen would be drawn to something like a painting of a dead rabbit instead of clothes or the Beatles or boys, all the things girls her age were expected to fall in love with. She thought perhaps there was something wrong with her. Then she felt certain there was something wrong, a deep and intrinsic flaw that would drag behind her all her life.

The day she spent staring at the Chardin was a Monday. She was walking home from the bus stop wondering what she would do about dinner, and wondering whether it would be worth it to take out books from the neighborhood library about French painters in the eighteenth century. She stopped, because something had made her stop, and stared dully ahead down the street. What had halted her? Something had cut into her thoughts and seized a small part of her consciousness. Linda hadn't the least idea what it was.

Then she heard the voice again. "Hey, Linda! Over here!"

Someone had called her name.

A few houses back, a girl with a blonde bob was leaning over a picket fence, waving. Linda blinked, rubbed her eyes, went toward the girl in a daze. As she came closer, she saw that it was Sandy Jepson, who'd had home ec and social studies with Linda that year in school. Sandy had always been friendly, though Linda couldn't have said back then that they were friends. Not yet.

"I saw you walking by," Sandy said, "and thought I'd say hello."

"Oh," Linda said. "Hi."

Sandy pressed her lips together. For a moment, her elfin face lost its sparkle. She seemed rather hesitant. "How are you doing?" Sandy asked the question delicately, as if Linda were a cancer patient.

"I'm okay. Why?"

"Well, I . . . I don't want to pry. But I've been worried about you. *We've* been worried—my family. You see, my parents heard about your parents splitting up, and . . . gosh, Linda, we all feel so bad about it. We wanted to make sure you're all right."

"Oh." Linda hadn't realized the divorce was the talk of the neighborhood.

"I shouldn't have said anything. I'm sorry, really, I am. It's none of my business. But I always thought you were nice in school, and I just wanted to tell you I'm here if you need anything. My whole family is here, if you or your mom need anything at all."

Linda glanced past Sandy toward her house. It was a big yellow Craftsman with a wraparound porch and a wreath of summer flowers on the door. Two thick clouds of daisies flanked the porch steps. The flowers and the wreath, the house itself, seemed to be smiling in just the way Sandy had always smiled at school, with a real inner joy, the kind of happiness that couldn't be faked.

The front door opened. Sandy's mother leaned out. "Come inside, sweetheart. We're about to start charades." Mrs. Jepson noticed Linda, pale faced and forlorn, on the other side of the fence. "Linda! My, how nice it is to see you."

"Hello, Mrs. Jepson."

"What are you doing this evening?"

"I was just on my way home from the art museum."

"What a smart way to spend your summer vacation." She cast a significant look at her daughter. "You could learn something from your friend, Sandy."

"Mom," Sandy said, "what if Linda joins us for Family Home Evening?"

"No," Linda said quickly, "I don't want to be a bother."

Mrs. Jepson beamed at her. "That's a lovely idea. You aren't any bother, Linda. Come in, come in."

Linda didn't remember passing through the gate or going up the walk with Sandy at her side. Before she knew it, she was climbing the steps between those mounds of daisies and Sandy was muttering beside her, "It's a religious thing. We spend every Monday night together, the whole family. I hope you don't mind a little bit of praying and Bible talk. There isn't much of that stuff, I promise. We mostly just play games and sing songs."

"I don't mind at all," Linda said. It seemed another prospect for silent observation, like the time she spent in the museums.

Inside, Sandy's five younger brothers and sisters had gathered on a rug in front of the fireplace. Their dad, a lanky, balding engineer with glasses and a big grin, was strumming chords on his guitar and trying to get his children to sing. They were more interested in the stranger who had just come through the door.

"This is my friend Linda," Sandy said, putting an arm around her shoulders. "She's going to play charades with us tonight."

Linda wondered whether Sandy had meant it, that they were friends. They had worked on a few school projects together, but that didn't seem like friendship, exactly. Nevertheless, she smiled and waved an awkward hello. Mrs. Jepson asked if she'd had supper yet. Linda admitted she hadn't—she had been at the Burke Museum all day—and before she knew it, Mrs. Jepson was handing her a plate of leftovers. Meatloaf and buttered corn, still warm, with a salad of green Jell-O, grated carrots, and raisins on the side.

"Come and eat in the living room with us," Sandy said. "The little kids aren't allowed to, but you and I are old enough to break a few rules."

The food was terrific. Linda told Mrs. Jepson so between bites. She realized she was eating like a starving wolf and made an effort to slow down. Mr. Jepson finally got the kids to sing a funny little song about an apricot tree in flower, how the white blossoms looked like popcorn, then another about a little stream turning the fields green. By that time, Linda had finished eating. Sandy took her plate to the kitchen.

"Thanks," Linda said. "That was really good. You're a great cook."

In response, Mrs. Jepson hugged her.

Linda didn't know what to do with herself when Mr. Jepson prayed. Sandy and her brothers and sisters all closed their eyes and bowed their heads, but Linda felt it would be disingenuous if she did the same. Instead, she kept her eyes on Mr. Jepson's guitar, which was leaning against his knee now, and she tried to recall the words to the song about the apricot tree till Mr. Jepson said "Amen" and the family echoed him. As soon as the prayer was finished, the little children jumped up, ready for their game, and Sandy's mother brought a tray of chocolate chip cookies from the kitchen.

Linda could scarcely believe how easy it was to fall into play—how naturally she took up the game, how all her self-conscious hesitation vanished in that environment of warmth and laughter. She joined in, giggling with Sandy, cheering for the little ones when they guessed correctly or when they stumped their parents. Vaguely, she was aware that a sixteen-year-old girl ought to be cooler than this. Yet the Jepsons had fed more than her stomach that night. She had been starving for happiness and harmony, and ease enough to let down her guard. She had never known such a feeling of comfort and familial love, not for as long as she could remember.

When the games were finished, Mr. Jepson prayed again, and this time Linda closed her eyes like the rest of them. Then Sandy walked with her down the block to her own quiet house.

"That was fun," Linda said.

Sandy shrugged. "It's a little cheesy, I know, but it's sort of a tradition."

"No, I mean it. I had a good time. Thanks for inviting me in. Your family is really nice." Her eyes began to burn then, so she half turned away, scuffing her feet on the pavement.

"Say, do you want to sleep over Thursday night?" Sandy asked. "My parents are going away for their anniversary so it's just me taking care of all those little monsters by myself."

"Your brothers and sisters aren't monsters. They're good kids."

"They're all right. But it'll be lots more fun looking after them if you're there, too."

Linda didn't need to think about it for long. She liked Sandy—her family, too. She nodded and smiled, and Sandy threw her arms around Linda and squeezed her hard before she turned back for her own house.

That Thursday sleepover marked the start of the closest friendship Linda had ever known. She and Sandy got along so well, Linda spent at least one night a week at the Jepson place. Linda was aware that Sandy's parents pitied her a little and were offering some small refuge from the turmoil of her own life. She was too grateful for their kindness to feel ashamed. As the divorce proceedings dragged out—and even pulled Linda herself into court to testify before the judge about her father's absence, the missing child support payments—the Jepson home became a rock of peace and stability. It mystified and fascinated Linda that any family could remain so easily together when her own was steadily breaking apart. Sometimes Mrs. Jepson would circle Linda with her soft arms and allow her to cry all over her shoulder when the tension or loneliness became too much to bear, and Mr. Jepson would discretely slip Linda a few extra bucks for school lunches or gas for her car. Linda couldn't remember the last time her own father had checked to see whether she had everything she needed. And though Sandy occasionally argued with her siblings, they were kind to each other more often than not.

Linda became a regular fixture at those Monday night gatherings, too, delighting in the games and songs, attempting to strum Mr. Jepson's guitar with limited success. She began to listen more attentively when Mr. Jepson read from the Bible or from his Book of Mormon. The Scripture was interesting, a curiosity like the cultural relics she found in the museums. Nothing he read ever moved Linda's soul, the way religion was rumored to move a person, but she had never responded that way to any prayer or incantation, any passage from a holy book. She figured her distinct lack of inner fire was a personal failing and kept it to herself. She didn't want to lose the Jepsons' respect, especially not Sandy's, who had become like a sister to Linda. When Mr. Jepson prayed, Linda bowed her head and closed her eyes and murmured "Amen" as if she meant it.

On a drizzling spring night just before Linda's seventeenth birthday, she was eating supper with her mother—a rare occasion, as her mother worked late most days. Linda seldom saw her anymore. They were having soup from a can and rolls that Linda had picked up from the grocery store, with margarine instead of butter. It was a far cry from Mrs. Jepson's cooking. Linda had spilled some of the soup on the range top, and now the whole house smelled like something burning. There were silences in the conversation, pauses where Linda could feel the distance between herself and her mother growing longer, wider, and the rain rattled against the panes. The street was black outside.

"You've been spending a lot of time with that Sandy girl," her mother said. "What do you do with that kid, anyway?"

Linda shrugged. She stirred her soup. "Nothing, really. Hang out."

Silence.

"She's a Mormon, you know," Linda's mother said. "Her whole family is."

"I know."

"Has she been trying to get you into that religion of hers?"

"We're just friends. Sandy isn't pushy."

A car moved slowly through the neighborhood. Its headlights reached through the window, pooled above the kitchen table, slid across the wall. The light vanished.

"I don't have much good to say about Mormons," her mother said.

Linda sat up straighter in her chair. If her mother didn't have much good to say, then Linda was more interested in Mormons than ever before.

Her mother went on relentlessly. "That religion isn't good to women, you know. Women aren't allowed any agency."

Linda shrugged again. She had already noticed how Mrs. Jepson never took the lead, never spoke too loudly or with much authority. She deferred all the time to her husband. Even Sandy never crossed her father's will. She wouldn't even roll her eyes behind her dad's back, or call him a drag or a square. But Sandy and Mrs. Jepson both seemed content, even happy—and Mr. Jepson was kind and generous and soft spoken, concerned for the well-being of everyone around him. He was unlike any other man Linda had known. What did it matter if Mrs. Jepson allowed her husband to take the lead?

"It's a kooky religion," Linda's mother said. "Prophets and Bibles buried in the ground and Jesus preaching to the Indians."

"It's no crazier than believing a man could walk on water," Linda said, "or a virgin could give birth to the Son of God."

"You're right." Her mother laughed. "It's all horseshit, if you ask me."

Linda hadn't asked.

The next time she went to Sandy's house, she told the Jepsons she wanted to become a Latter-Day Saint. They all surrounded her and hugged her, and Mrs. Jepson made cupcakes—actually baked them in celebration. There was a process, Linda was told. She had to be taught all about the church by missionaries, and of course, Mr. Jepson said, she could have the discussions in their home. There was no need to upset her mother by bringing missionaries back to Linda's place. He would talk to the bishop of their church the next day and make all the arrangements. All Linda had to do was show up.

The missionaries were two eager, awkward boys practically Linda's own age, and much of what they told her didn't make a lot of sense, but none of the details mattered—not the history of the church, nor the particulars of sin and salvation. The only thing that mattered to her was the happiness she had found in Sandy's home, and the unshakable strength of the Jepsons' marriage.

Linda didn't bother asking either of her parents to come to her baptism some six weeks later. She knew her mother would only scorn the idea, and her father wouldn't respond at all. But their absence didn't matter, either, any more than the doctrine had mattered. The entire Jepson family was there, along with most of the congregation that would be her church now, her new community. And when Linda, dressed in a heavy robe of white, walked down the steps into the waist-deep baptismal font, Sandy was smiling with tears in her eyes.

The missionary boy who had taught her gripped Linda by the wrist and prayed up to an abstract Heaven. Then he folded her arm against her chest and pushed her backward, under the water.

When she rose up, Linda felt no different—only wetter. She climbed the steps hastily and went back into the adjoining changing room. Through the walls, a piano played, and the congregation began to sing. Linda moved toward the bench where she had left her clothing. She passed a full-length mirror in a cheap gold frame. At the sight of her reflection, she stopped.

She hadn't realized the thick polyester robe would be transparent when wet. She had worn no undergarments into the baptismal font. No one had told her she must. Dripping, Linda stared at herself. She could see the outline of her nipples through the soaking fabric, the dark triangle of her pubic hair. Her first reaction was panic and shame. Had the whole congregation seen her nakedness? But no—she had left the font so quickly, and there had been such a thrash and churn of water and limbs. No one had seen. No one but her.

Linda stood there, looking at herself for a long time, allowing the music and even the chill to recede from her awareness. Through the purity of that white cloth, through its sturdy weave, she could see her true self looking back, unconcealed, unashamed.

"What are you doing, Linda?" Sandy had come into the changing room. "Get dressed, you goon! There's cake and punch in the reception hall, and Dad has a present for you."

Sandy helped her wring the worst of the water from her hair. Linda put on her own dress, and together they went out into the gymnasium, where the congregation was ready to welcome Linda as one of their own. Mrs. Jepson gave her a new copy of the Mormon Scriptures, embossed in one corner, her name in gold. Mr. Jepson gave her a guitar in a velvet-lined case.

"I don't know how to play," Linda said.

"That's all right." He patted her back. "I'll teach you how it's done."

The warmth that flooded into her then was, Linda thought, like the warmth of the Holy Ghost. The way a real surety of spirit was supposed to feel.

17

The Darkest Dark

Aran helped his father slide the last of the plywood panels into the bed of the truck. He tied an old green rope to one of the cargo hooks and tossed the bight over the panels. Gad caught the line, looped it under his own hook, and sent the rope flying back to Aran's side. It was early in the afternoon, a hot summer day, and the sun was in Aran's eyes. He missed his catch. The rope struck him on his cheek, stinging like a slap.

"Damn," Aran said, before he could think better.

"Watch your language." Gad came around the end of the truck bed, already puffed up and red in the face. "We're in public, for heaven's sake."

They were not in public, as far as Aran was concerned. The lumberyard where Gad purchased his panels was all the way out on the western edge of town. The yard was large enough that none of its workers could have heard Aran even if they'd been trying. The Mooseburger drive-in next door was blaring music through its tin-can speakers, lending a little atmosphere to the lunch rush in the parking lot. Aran and Gad were, if anything, even more alone in the lumberyard than they would have been in their own shop. Back home, there were neighbors to hear an argument or a cuss over the fence line.

"Relax, Dad. No one can hear me."

Gad took the rope from Aran's hands, none too gently, and secured the line himself. Then he tossed it over the panels again and went around to the other side. "That's not the point," Gad said. "You need to be more aware of the impression you make. Your lack of concern for how your behavior affects other people in this family is—"

"What are you talking about?" It was too much. Since the summer began, Aran had paid more attention to Gad's endless string of demands than he'd ever done before. Hadn't he worked meekly alongside his father for weeks now? Hadn't he taken special pains not to rock the boat, deferring to his father in all things, keeping peace between Tamsin and the twins? He had even borne his testimony—a public display of good behavior to mollify the neighbors and the church ward. When would Gad be satisfied? Not till Aran had a girlfriend, he supposed. The thought made him sick with anxiety.

The green rope gave a convulsive jerk; the panels settled against one another and creaked as Gad tightened the line, tied it off on the far side of the bed. Then he reappeared and stood very close to Aran, talking quietly.

"I'm having a conversation with Bishop Kimball later this afternoon. I aim to find out why the boys haven't been interviewed yet."

"For their missions?"

"Of course for their missions. What else?"

"What does that have to do with me?"

Gad drove a finger into Aran's chest. "Everything, I bet. There's no good reason why Brig and Ondi should be delayed like this—no good reason but you. These stories about you, circulating through town—"

"All lies."

Bitterly, Aran thought, *Why don't you ask Bishop Kimball about his own son, if you want to know who the real troublemaker is?* He never dreamed of saying those words aloud. The rumors had run unchecked through Rexburg so long, they were practically a part of the town's geography. The damage was already done.

"Well, something has to be holding the twins up," Gad said. "What else could it be, if not their brother's reputation?"

Aran answered as calmly as he could manage. He could feel his pulse pounding heavily in his throat. "Bishop Kimball wouldn't hold the twins back over rumors. No bishop would. For heaven's sake, Dad, the Lord doesn't play petty games."

"The Rigbys have been in this valley as long as Rexburg has existed. The bishop might delay an interview for other families, but not ours—not without good reason. None of your cousins have been delayed this long. My brother Delyle's youngest boy turned nineteen in April. He's already down in Provo for his training. There's no good reason to wait so long, unless Kimball feels the family itself—my family—is unworthy."

The pulse beat harder in Aran's neck. A frill of eerie light throbbed in time around the edges of his vision. Could Bishop Kimball know about the paintings—the things Aran and Tamsin did when no one else could see? Since his own missionary days, he had grown rather skeptical of the revelatory powers of the priesthood. But maybe he'd been wrong after all. Maybe the Lord had revealed to Kimball exactly what went on in that old, abandoned shack outside of town.

I've only ever painted her—just that. Painting isn't a sin. He didn't know whether he was justifying the whole mess to himself, or actually praying to God, asking in a roundabout way for absolution.

He drew a deep breath to steady himself. "I've been on my best behavior. Kimball has no cause to fault me. And if he is denying my brothers an opportunity because of something I've done, then he isn't being just or wise."

"Don't you dare talk about your bishop that way."

"Lay off me, can't you, old man? It doesn't matter what I do, it's never good enough for you, or for the bishop—not for anyone."

"This is exactly what I'm talking about." Gad's voice was rising right alongside Aran's. "You're always making a scene, drawing attention to yourself. It's unseemly."

"Why should I care? You never cut me any slack. It doesn't matter how good I am, how obedient or helpful or righteous—"

Gad laughed. "You, righteous?"

"What, do you think you've got a lock on holiness now, is that it? You think you're beyond sin? I could name all your spiritual failings—"

Gad butted up against him, chest to chest. "Be quiet. You're making a scene. You're making a fool of yourself, like you always do."

Aran glanced toward the Mooseburger parking lot. A crowd of young people from Singles Ward had gathered around their cars with milkshakes in paper cups and grease-spotted bags full of burgers and fries. They were staring at Aran, the whole lot of them. He could imagine the whispers, the fresh new rumors that would take flight today. *Aran Rigby cussed out his father. Aran doesn't obey the head of his family. Aran Rigby has the Devil in him, for sure.* It was all so pointless, so stupid, this prison cell the town had made for him. The bars of his cage were only idle words, yet there was no escaping. Public opinion had locked Aran inside, and now neither contrition nor propriety could set him free.

He stared back at his peers for a moment. Then he lifted both hands, first and pinkie fingers extended in the sign of the Devil's horns, and ran out his tongue so far, the tip met the hairs on his chin.

The Singles crowd burst into activity, circling around one another, holding up their hands to shield their mouths while they talked. The men in the group shook their heads, in sorrow or disgust, and the women cast wide-eyed, frightened looks in Aran's direction.

"For the love of all that's holy," Gad muttered.

Aran turned just in time to see his father climbing into the truck. Aran moved toward the passenger seat, but Gad had already cranked the engine over. He pulled away quickly, spitting up gravel and dust.

There was nothing Aran could do but stand there like a perfect idiot, watching his father drive away.

Now he would have to walk home, three miles or more through town. At least it would give him time to cool off, and think about what he ought to do next, how he could atone for this latest failing. The afternoon was hot. Aran was already sweating through his temple garments and his shirt. He risked another look at the Singles crowd, wondering for one foolish moment if he should ask one of them for a ride home.

Most of them were still muttering and flicking their eyes in Aran's direction. One, however, stood apart. Linda, the new girl in town, had drifted a few yards away from her friends. She watched Gad's white truck as it turned up West Fourth and headed back into town. The moment the truck vanished, she turned toward Aran. He didn't know what else to do, other than stay where he was, staring. A dry wind whipped the hair around her face—black hair, stark against her pale Irish skin. He recalled a certain principle of composition, one he used all the time without thought, as an instinct. The focal point of any painting is the place where two opposite elements meet: The warmest and coolest colors laid down side by side, the sharpest line among a blur of lost edges. Or the darkest dark beside the light. He should have been moving by then, walking away from the latest disaster he'd made. Instead, he only stood, transfixed by the focal point of that girl, the wind, the hair moving across her face.

A woman's voice called from the Mooseburger parking lot, high and afraid. "Linda, come back." That was the first Aran realized that the girl was walking toward him. She ignored whoever had called to her. She sucked on the straw in her milkshake, eyes smiling.

She came right up to Aran and stood there before him, so he couldn't leave now if he wanted to.

"Sorry," Aran said after a long, repentant pause.

"For what? That was funny, what you did just now."

"I shouldn't have. It was stupid."

"It was a scream. I think you just about made some of those kids lose their minds."

"Now everyone will talk even more. I shouldn't have let my old man get the better of me. This whole town already thinks I'm a Devil worshipper. I just gave them proof."

She sipped her milkshake again, then said, "I've heard."

"You've heard what?"

"That you're some kind of Satanist." She wrinkled her nose. It took Aran a moment to understand that she was making an ironic little smirk. He was fascinated by the freckles on her nose—slight, pale, almost not there at all.

He said, "You've heard that story, huh?"

"Yeah. But I don't believe it."

One of her friends called her again from the edge of the parking lot. She didn't move, just went on looking up at him, tilting the paper cup this way and that.

Aran swallowed hard. His throat was dry from the dust in the lumberyard, and fear of what he was about to do. He said, "You're Linda, right?"

"And you're Aran Rigby."

"My reputation precedes me."

"It does."

"Do you want to go out sometime?"

Her nose wrinkled again. "If you didn't ask me, I was going to ask you."

18

What Wins a Girl's Heart

Sandy really let Linda have it, all the way back to their duplex. "I told you, Linda, you can't get mixed up with Aran Rigby. What were you thinking, talking to him like he's an ordinary person?"

"He is an ordinary person."

"You know he's not. I told you everything Joel said about him. And you saw the way he was behaving. Who yells at their dad in public like that—or anywhere? Someone who's out of control, that's who. Someone who's dangerous. And that face he made at all of us . . . and that thing he did with his hands. You know what that means, don't you? I told you he's a Devil worshipper."

"His dad probably deserved it. Remember when that old bag of wind yelled at me, how upset I was? You admitted it yourself: Gad Rigby has a short fuse."

"That doesn't mean it's acceptable to get into a shouting match with your father. The head of the family is supposed to be respected."

Linda took the final turn before their duplex more sharply than she needed to. From the corner of her eye, she watched Sandy slide and jostle in the passenger seat. Linda pulled to the curb and cut the engine.

She didn't get out, though, till she felt a little calmer. Sandy wasn't trying to be a drag. She was only worried.

"Just stay away from Aran," Sandy said. "I don't want you to get hurt. Promise me."

Linda glanced again at her friend. "I promise I won't do anything that might get me hurt. Cross my heart and hope to die."

She hadn't promised she would stay away from Aran, which was why Linda felt no remorse that evening, slipping out of the duplex in jeans and a tight-fitted T-shirt while Sandy was in the shower. She'd left a note on the kitchen table: *Going for a drive. Might meet up with Lee for dinner. Don't worry if I'm not home by 9.*

She found Aran waiting at the west entrance to the college campus, exactly where he'd said they should meet. He was leaning against the trunk of his Charger, dressed in orange polyester pants and a loud shirt with lapels like a bat's wings. The shirt was open just far enough to show the neck of his white temple garments underneath. It surprised her, that this man still wore his garments—a constant reminder of the commitment he'd made to his faith. That only seemed more proof that Sandy and everyone else in town was wrong about Aran. If he were such a danger to society, if he'd truly been sin made flesh, surely he would have discarded his temple garments long ago.

She parked her car and said hello casually, as if a clandestine rendezvous with the local reprobate were ordinary as apple pie. Aran looked as nervous as Linda felt. He kept watching the neighborhood across the street, the tame little dun-colored homes with their tidy yards and picket fences. Children played in the driveways. An aging woman in a pink terry housecoat was watering her marigolds. No one was paying the least mind to Aran and Linda, but still Aran's eyes kept shifting up and down the street, wary as a hunted animal. Linda didn't mind. It gave her more opportunity to stare at him openly. There was no refinement in his features. He was coarse and reddened by the sun and wind—a farm boy, rustic, which made him even more a creature of this place, and made his status as an outsider seem more ridiculous still. The evening light clung to his beard, which was red, unlike his near-black hair. Even while he watched the neighborhood with obvious suspicion, his eyes had a heavy, almost sleepy expression. Linda liked that about him, the drawn-down blinds of his eyes, the way he didn't try to look as chipper and eager as everyone else in Rexburg.

When he was satisfied that no one was watching them, Aran said, "What do you want to do?"

"I haven't had dinner yet. Why don't we check out that Italian place on Main Street? We can go see a movie after. *Shampoo* is playing at the theater downtown."

Aran shifted uncomfortably. Linda realized in an instant it was a dumb idea. This was a Saturday night. Every restaurant and the movie theater would be packed with young people out on dates. None of them would have a kindly thought for Aran—and word would quickly get back to Sandy that Linda had been spotted going around town with the Devil worshipper.

"On second thought," she said, "let's just go for a walk. I've already seen *Shampoo*, anyway."

"You have?"

"That movie came out in February."

"We're a little behind the times here in Rexburg."

"I've noticed."

They set off down the street with the lowering sun at their backs. Their shadows stretched blue along the sidewalk.

"A walk isn't exactly the kind of date that wins a girl's heart," Aran said.

Linda kept her eyes fixed on the shadows. "Are you trying to win my heart?" She had meant the question to sound ironic, teasing—but she felt a little jump inside her chest. She said, "This will give us a chance to talk and get to know each other. We can't talk in a movie theater, not unless we want to get a bag of popcorn dumped on our heads. Anyway, now we've got plausible deniability. We're only going for a stroll. No one can accuse us of dating."

Aran glanced across the street again, cleared his throat. Linda followed his gaze. The woman who'd been watering her marigolds had straightened, the garden hose kinked tight in her hand. She followed them with narrowed eyes as they passed.

Aran said, "I guess you probably don't want word getting around town that you were out on a date with me."

"I thought you wouldn't want anyone knowing you'd gone out with me. I'm almost as much a subject of gossip as you are."

They looked at one another, then laughed.

"So," Aran said, "was it any good?"

"Was what good?"

"The movie."

"It was. I liked it. A bit heavy for the Rexburg crowd, I'd say. I was surprised to see it on the marquee here, even months too late. But the soundtrack—wow. Paul Simon did the score."

"I love him."

"Me, too. I've been half-terrified the Relief Society girls will ask me to rewrite the lyrics to 'Paranoia Blues.'"

Linda laughed again. Aran did not. She had put her foot in her mouth, all right. Probably the last thing Aran wanted to talk about was grass.

They turned a corner and headed into the downtown sector, such as it was. When they passed the post office, a fresh bit of Tamsin's handiwork caught Linda's attention: *Damn the Dam* in green letters, vivid on the dull brick. The slogan wasn't hidden along the bottom of the building, but was up at shoulder height, where anyone could see. Tamsin was getting bolder. Linda wondered when the kid found time for her vandalism. She must be sneaking out of the house in the middle of the night. Did Aran know his sister was behind the defacements?

Aran didn't seem to notice the graffiti. He said, "So you're the culprit behind those awful songs."

"Tamsin told you all about my crimes, I guess."

"You know my sister?"

"I've met her. We were both reading in the park last weekend and we started talking. She's a good kid."

"She is a good kid," Aran agreed, but there was something distant and unsettled in his voice, something almost like guilt.

"I thought you'd be upset that I'd met Tamsin," Linda said.

"Why would that upset me?"

"Did she tell you I work for the IEC?"

"The what?"

"The Idaho Environmental Council. I'm doing biological surveys in the Teton River floodplain. You know—gathering evidence against the dam."

Aran chuckled. "I don't care about that. And Tamsin is into that ecology stuff, too. I bet she thinks you're the coolest."

"She's the only one. You wouldn't believe some of the dirty looks I've caught since I started that job."

"Oh, I'd believe, all right."

They were passing the restaurants now. The smell of rich foods and frying oil made Linda's stomach growl. She didn't look in the windows of the cafés. She could feel the eyes on the other side of the glass, watching her, watching Aran. *We're only walking. Just out for a stroll.*

"I suppose you get it," Linda said, "how it feels to be an outsider. I guess you know better than anyone else."

"I'm not all the things they say I am," Aran muttered.

Linda looked up at him, sober now. "I know you're not."

The restaurants and the movie theater were already behind them. That was one good thing about a small town, Linda supposed: there wasn't much of it to wade through. But the two long shadows were still there, leading her and Aran down Main Street.

A few nights later, Linda went out with Aran again. She told him not to pick her up at the duplex but asked him to meet her instead outside the college, as they'd done before. Aran didn't ask why. No doubt, Linda thought, he already knew. She walked the two expansive blocks to the campus. Aran was waiting, the trunk of his Charger open. He was rummaging inside. Linda approached quietly. She wanted to observe him up close, see what he was like when he wasn't on his best behavior, trying to impress a girl. She wanted to see how his hands moved.

She peered past him into the darkness of the trunk space. Night was already well on its way, so most of the interior was too dark, but she could make out an old army pack with frayed webbing straps. Aran was fussing with its contents. Then Linda noticed something far more interesting lying flat on the floor of the trunk: an unframed painting, a landscape.

"Oh my God," Linda said.

Aran started violently, whirled to face her, his cheeks burning red. "You scared me!" He slammed the trunk shut.

"Wait. What was that?"

"Nothing. It was nothing."

"That painting—let me see it."

Aran looked at her with an expression she'd never seen on him before—almost hard, almost scowling, and yet too wounded for that.

"Please," Linda said. "Did you paint it? I really want to see."

He glanced around the neighborhood again, as he'd done the first time they'd met. Finally, he unlocked the trunk. The lid squealed open on its struts.

Linda leaned in, blinking into the shadows. There the painting lay, a river scene, loose and expressive. She could see now that it was clamped inside the wooden frame of an easel, its telescoping legs drawn in, folded into a compact mass. Linda lifted the whole contraption out into the fading light. The painting described a gentle curve of water, the fading green of early summer, a bright sky dancing with color, more colors than blue. It was a simple scene, and only a small panel, yet still it spoke to her. Still it transfixed her as all those works of art had done in the museums of her teenage years.

"Did you paint this?" She could scarcely speak louder than a whisper.

"Yeah," Aran said, sheepish, ashamed.

"It's good. It's really good."

He hesitated. "It is?"

Linda clicked her tongue, glancing at Aran with dismissive scorn. "Come on. You know it's good."

His face reddened again. "I don't really show my work to many people. No one, really, except my sister."

"Not even your mom and dad?"

"God, no. Especially not my dad. Well—I used to show my mom, when I was younger, but not anymore."

He paused again, while Linda went on poring over that landscape. The river bent with a strange harmony. She could feel it, a sympathetic upwelling in her chest.

Cautiously, Aran said, "Do you want to see more?"

He retrieved a plywood box from the depths of the trunk and opened it. Inside, several more panels were standing upright, separated by small wooden dividers that kept their wet surfaces from touching. Aran slid them out, one by one. Each was a landscape, a depiction of the plain, flat world around them, and yet each one hummed with vivid life. This was not the Idaho Linda had known these past weeks since her arrival in Rexburg. It wasn't even the Idaho she'd found on her workdays, wandering through the pastures and the lava heaves in heavy canvas pants and a reflective vest, tallying the animals and plants she found. Aran's paintings were a window looking out on a different reality. That other world was breathing. Its pulse was color and its form was light, and Linda thought she could fall in love with something so alive and real.

When she had examined the last of Aran's paintings, she looked up at him and realized for the first time that tears were standing in her eyes. "These are really good," she said levelly. "You're very talented."

He looked away. "Thanks."

"I mean it. You're different, Aran, from the rest of them. You're special."

"Everyone has their gifts." He cleared his throat, slipped the last panel back into the carrying case, and closed the trunk again. "So, what do you want to do tonight?"

"Let's go to the drive-in theater," Linda said.

"There will be other people there. Other couples. People from Singles Ward. They won't like to see you there with me."

"I don't care." Linda took his hand. It was rough, which surprised her—callused already, and dry, though he wasn't much older than she was. Linda said, "Let everyone see."

19

SMALL SINS

The Relief Society room at Singles Ward was almost empty. Linda was sorting through the dishes on the buffet table, trying to match up serving spoons with casseroles, while the rest of the girls chattered and pulled the crepe-paper streamers from the walls or untied bundles of balloons from the backs of chairs. Someone sucked helium from a balloon and started singing "We Meet Again as Sisters" in a high, squeaky voice. Everyone laughed, Linda included, though she felt as if she didn't have any right to laugh. Her amusement carried a different tone, an alien inflection. She bit her lip, trying to stop herself, and concentrated on the casserole dishes.

Rodella bustled up to the buffet table. The party had been in her honor; Rodella had been called to take over as president of the ward's Relief Society, since the prior president had married and would now attend church at her neighborhood ward. Rodella was already bursting with enthusiasm for the role.

"Linda," she said, "I'm so glad you haven't left yet. I wanted to talk to you about putting on another concert for the Young Women."

"Oh." Linda glanced around the room. Where was Sandy? They had to get away before Rodella could rope them into another musical disaster.

"I was thinking," Rodella said, "we could do an all-ABBA show. Rewrite the lyrics like we did last time. Some of their songs would be so easy to make more religious. 'He Is Your Brother' and 'She's My Kind of Girl.' I don't know what we can do with 'Waterloo,' but I'm sure you can come up with something. You're just swell with music."

"Thanks," Linda said. "That's really nice of you."

She was surprised to find that she meant it. She might not be enthusiastic about another session of lyrical butchery, but knowing she was appreciated—and was already considered an important part of Relief Society—gave her an unexpected pang of gratitude.

"Will you try it? See what you can come up with. There have to be all kinds of Scripture references you can fit into those songs. They're all so upbeat and fun; the girls in Young Women's will just flip."

"I don't have any ABBA records," Linda said.

"That's no trouble. I can lend you mine."

Sandy came into the classroom pushing a large rubber trash can on caster wheels. "Garbage day," she called. The cleanup crew flocked to her with paper plates and armfuls of rumpled streamers.

"There's Sandy," Linda said to Rodella. "I'd better get her back to our place. She has a doctor's appointment this afternoon and I don't want her to be late."

"I'll stop by tonight with the records," Rodella said.

Linda waved and hurried away with Sandy's empty casserole dish in her hands. Once she and Sandy were safely in the Beetle and on their way back to the duplex, Linda tried to suppress a laugh of pure relief, or maybe it was incredulity. Either way, it came out through her nose in a long, jagged snort.

"What?" Sandy said.

"I don't know. Everything is just so damn funny to me. Rodella wants me to write new lyrics to a bunch of ABBA songs so we can get up another hip yet moralizing concert for all the teenage girls in town."

"Oh, brother," Sandy said.

"My thoughts exactly. But I'm glad she thought of me to do it—really, I am. I feel like such a jerk for thinking it's a terrible idea. Rodella is so sweet and sincere, and she only wants to make the world a better place."

"By grafting Scripture onto ABBA?"

"I know." The treasonous humor was swelling inside Linda's chest. If she didn't let it out with one huge guffaw, it was going to stab right through her. She drew a deep breath, brought herself under control. "You know the worst part? I'm going to do it. Rodella's going to bring all her records over tonight, and I'm going to listen to them, even though I don't like ABBA at all, and I'm going to figure out how to make all the lyrics Jesus approved."

"I'm officially divorcing you as my roommate."

"I have to, Sandy! Do you have any idea how hard I've been working to fit in? And you know half the town is suspicious of me now that I'm working for the IEC. Rodella is president of our Relief Society. If she likes me, then everyone else will have to forgive me for my environmentalism and like me, too."

Sandy stared at Linda. "Everyone already likes you. Gosh, Linda, haven't you noticed?"

"I know all the girls at church like me. I mean, rationally I know it. But I still don't *feel* like I'm a part of this town. I can't explain it, not even to myself. I've lost sleep trying to figure out why this nagging feeling follows me everywhere, every day. All the girls are so nice to me—and the guys at church, too. But I still feel like there's an invisible wall between myself and them, like I can't get to where they are, I can't stand in the same place." All the humor had died away. Linda felt sober now, and grave. "It's something inside me, I guess—that wall. I'm holding myself back from the life you all have out here, the happiness you've found."

"That's nonsense," Sandy said gently.

Linda shook her head. She didn't know how to make her friend understand. She had examined that invisible barrier countless times. She knew its dimensions by now. She knew the strange hollow longing that opened up inside whenever she came close to the barrier. It was like a hunger in the pit of her soul, an emptiness pleading to be filled.

"I don't know what to do," Linda said.

"You need to pray about it."

That was Sandy's answer to every problem. Linda could admit to herself that she seldom found much comfort in prayer. Certainly, she'd never received any guidance. She wasn't even convinced there was anything out there listening. If God existed, she didn't think It bore much resemblance to the God all her church friends believed in. She did believe in harmony, though—in love, and a binding together of souls.

"I'm afraid to pray," Linda said. "What if God doesn't answer?"

"He always answers. But sometimes the answers aren't what we expect." Sandy shrugged. "Anyway, if for some reason God doesn't answer you—or if you aren't paying close enough attention to realize He has answered—then you'll still figure it out. I know you. You'll find a way to tear down that wall or climb over it. You're the smartest, toughest, most determined girl I've ever met."

"I am?"

"Don't you know how much I've always admired you?"

Linda couldn't say anything. She smiled, but it felt wobbly, like maybe she was about to cry.

"You make things happen in your life," Sandy said. "You don't sit around letting life happen to you. You've got drive and brains. And you're stubborn as a mule. That's the problem, if you ask me—you decided from day one that you weren't going to fit into Rexburg, and that's why you still *think* you don't have a place. It's all in your head.

But that's the way you've always been. Once you've decided to do a particular thing or *be* a certain way, all bets are off. You'll go on doing or being, whether it's a good idea or not."

Linda pulled to the curb outside their duplex. She let her head fall sideways against the window. "You're right. I'm the worst."

"For goodness' sake, stop feeling sorry for yourself, or I'll make you wash all the dishes alone tonight." Sandy held up the encrusted casserole. "Come on. Let's put on our bathing suits and sit in the backyard. I want a nice tan for Pioneer Day."

"All right." Linda got out of the car. "Don't let Rodella see you when she drops by. I told her you had a doctor's appointment this afternoon."

"Why did you do that?"

"I don't know. I guess I panicked. I had to get away from her and ABBA."

"Well, don't tell fibs." Sandy led the way to the front door. "That's probably why you're afraid to pray. Those little sins add up and weigh on your soul."

"Don't you ever sin, even a tiny bit?"

Sandy was fumbling with the house keys and the doorknob, balancing the casserole dish in her other hand, but she turned at once with an impish spark in her eye. "I may have done something a little naughty. A time or two."

"Give me all the details."

She wouldn't say a word till they were safely inside. Then she giggled. "With Joel."

"Did you go all the way?"

"Of course not! For heaven's sake, Linda, I'm saving it for marriage, obviously." She narrowed her eyes. "But we've parked, you know, up on the Bench. Only for kissing—I have my limits. And I know I probably shouldn't kiss Joel at all. It's dangerous. But he's so dreamy, I can't resist!"

Sandy flitted off to the kitchen. Linda could hear her running water in the sink. She called, "How are things going with Lee? Have you kissed him yet?"

"Not yet." It was another fib, but the lie was less mortifying than the truth.

"Not even once? Gosh, you've been going with him for weeks now."

The sink kept running. Linda's eyes lost their focus. She listened to the hiss of the water and felt everything pulling away from her, the town and the church and even Sandy receding beyond her reach, growing smaller, more hopelessly distant with every moment.

Finally, she said, "I'm not."

"You're not what?"

"Going with Lee."

The tap shut off. Sandy reemerged from the kitchen. "Why not? Don't you like him?"

"I do. He's terrific. And he's the one who told me to apply for my job—he's the reason why I have a job at all. Lee's great, but . . . I don't think I'm his type of girl."

"Of course you are." Sandy frowned. "Wait a minute. You've gone out on tons of dates recently. Who are you going with, if not Lee?"

"Don't be mad. I've been going with Aran Rigby."

Sandy's mouth fell open. She drew in a breath so long, Linda felt as if she ought to grab on to the back of the sofa, or risk being sucked right down into the pit of Sandy's astonishment.

"Linda! How could you?"

"It's fine," Linda insisted. "He's fine. Really. Aran has been a perfect gentleman every time we've gone out together."

"But everyone knows—"

"Nothing," Linda said, a little too forcefully. "No one in this town has the story right—I'm convinced of that. Aran is kind and smart and funny and incredibly talented, and . . . and I really like him, Sandy, a lot."

"Stories don't come out of nowhere. Aran has a reputation and there's a good reason for it. If you say he's been a gentleman so far, then I believe you, but it's only a matter of time before he shows his true nature."

"For Pete's sake. I've seen his true nature. Aran isn't the monster everyone thinks he is."

"How do you know that for sure? How many times have you been out with him?"

"A couple. I don't really know. It depends on how you define a date." She had gone out with Aran five times exactly and had enjoyed every minute of their time together.

"How you define a date," Sandy said. "What's that supposed to mean?"

"We don't do the things most couples do—restaurants and dances and all that. I don't think Aran likes to be in public, where everyone in town can see him." She added pointedly, "You know how people talk. But we did go to the drive-in theater once."

"That's the worst place you can go! All alone in a car with a man . . ."

"He only held my hand. Besides, we were watching *Jesus Christ Superstar*. You can't get into that kind of trouble while the savior of mankind is singing at you. It's a total mood killer."

"You should take this seriously."

"I am taking it seriously."

"This isn't the way to make a good start. No one trusts Aran, with good reason. If you think you've had a hard time making friends, just wait till everyone finds out you've been dating the local Devil worshipper."

"Come on," Linda said, chuckling a little. "You don't really believe that."

"I don't know what to believe. Some of the stories are pretty grim."

"What if there's no truth in the rumors at all—not even a particle? If that's the case, then you and everyone else have spent years maligning a good person, treating him like a leper."

"When stories are that consistent, there must be some truth at the core."

"Well, I don't know what to do. I like Aran more than any other guy I've met in this backward town."

"Rexburg isn't backward." Sandy had gone a little stiff, a little cold. "Listen, Linda—if you're serious about living a good life, and finding out what Heavenly Father wants for you, then you have to stay away from guys like Aran. God won't reveal your path if you don't have a pure heart. Don't you want that? Don't you want to find out where you belong and what kind of life you're meant to have?"

"I do," Linda said, quiet and sober.

Sandy pulled her into a hug. Linda didn't return the embrace—not because she didn't want to, but because her arms had grown heavy. She couldn't seem to lift them at all. Some great, monolithic weight was dragging at every part of her, crushing down on her heart.

"If you want to marry a good man," Sandy said, "then you have to be the kind of girl who can attract a good man. And that means no more running around with dangerous guys. Okay?"

"Okay," Linda said. "I promise."

Another lie.

20

A Perfect Eternity

Tamsin kept the oven mitts on her hands even after she'd pulled another tray of Arletta's Jell-O cookies from the oven. There was still paint under her nails from her most recent midnight foray into town, and she didn't want her mother to see. Arletta noticed more than her dull, smiling eyes let on, and Tamsin knew she would be made to explain the green stains around her cuticles. On nights when she found she couldn't sleep—when thoughts of college or other forms of escape crowded into her head and kept her alert and restless—she often left the house while the rest of the family slept, and rode down to Main Street on her bike with her backpack full of rattle cans. If she ever felt remorse over the vandalism, those twinges of guilt were fleeting. Now she only wondered at the silence of the town, why every wall in Rexburg wasn't covered with graffiti, why she was the only one venturing out with her spray cans and her indignation. There were enough frustrations and injustices to paint the whole place fury red.

Arletta handed a spatula to Tamsin. "Get those cookies off the pan and onto the cooling rack, quick."

The mitts made handling the spatula awkward, but Tamsin managed, scooping the cookies off the hot surface before they could suck up too much heat and go brown around the edges, which would ruin the effect of their cheerful coloration. Most of the cookies were pink, since they were intended for a baby shower the Relief Society was throwing the next day. Tamsin lined up all those perfect pink circles on the cooling rack and thought, *Lucky you, baby girl—about to be born into this place.*

She picked up one of the green cookies that had already cooled and bit into it. At once, Arletta rapped Tamsin across the knuckles with a wooden spoon, which didn't hurt since she was still wearing the oven mitts.

"Leave them alone or I won't have enough for all the shower guests," Arletta said.

"But I'm hungry."

Tamsin was not hungry. In fact, she was still stuffed from supper. She had eaten more heartily than she'd done in weeks, maybe because Gad hadn't been there. He'd called from Blackfoot to tell Arletta he'd been held up with a sign delivery and the family shouldn't wait on him. He would have warmed-up leftovers whenever he got home that evening. So it had just been Tamsin and her brothers and Arletta at the table, a quiet, peaceful assembly where everyone got along and nothing sat cold and hard in Tamsin's stomach. That suspended dread, the waiting for her father to blow up at someone—Aran, usually—made it impossible for Tamsin to eat more than half of what was on her plate.

Arletta filled another baking tray with cutouts and handed it to Tamsin. She slid the tray inside the oven, then paused for a moment with the door open so the heat could buffet her face.

"Don't let all the heat escape," Arletta said. "The cookies will bake unevenly if you do."

Tamsin closed the door, straightening slowly. It seemed significant that Arletta had used that word, "escape," since it had been so much on Tamsin's mind. Not for the first time that evening, she felt a question building and pressing inside, but didn't know how to ask it or whether it was wise to try. She wanted to say, *Mom, did you ever think of going to college?* Or maybe, *Do you think it would be a good idea if I went to a university after high school?* But she couldn't make the words come. She was half-afraid of what her mother would say—scold her, maybe, the way she knew Gad would scold if he found out.

She managed to approach the subject sideways, leaving an avenue for denial. A route for escape. "Mom, did you ever do something unexpected when you were my age?"

"Goodness," Arletta said. "Unexpected?"

"You know—something a little crazy. Or dangerous."

Arletta dropped her cookie cutter on the countertop, followed by the wooden spoon. She laughed—a surprisingly rich and lively sound, which made Tamsin realize how rarely she had heard her mother laugh. She turned from the stove and looked at Arletta, who wasn't watching Tamsin but standing with her back to her daughter and the kitchen, one hand on her hip, staring out the window into the blue night outside.

"Once," Arletta said, "when I was, oh, maybe your age, maybe a little younger, I went with all my girlfriends down to the river. The park, you know. I don't remember how we got there. Someone drove, I guess, one of the older girls. It was probably Dina Whitmer. Her dad had an old Ford Runabout with a pickup bed and she would borrow it sometimes and all us girls would pile in the back and roll around town."

"That's it?" Tamsin said. "You rode in the back of a pickup truck? That's the craziest thing you ever did?"

"No, goodness, no. That night at the river, I don't know what came over us. We all stripped down to nothing, naked as the day we were born, and jumped in the water. It was so cold. I remember the cold most of all—it felt like teeth biting into me, biting all over at once. We were laughing and screaming and raising a ruckus so loud I'm surprised they didn't hear us all the way over in town, and come to investigate, and find us all there buck naked like a bunch of I-don't-know-whats. Anyway, Francelle Magleby went out too far and got caught by the current."

"Francelle," Tamsin said, "the bishop's wife?"

"Yes, that's the one. She was crying and sputtering and getting pulled downstream and we could all tell she was in trouble. We figured she'd be sucked into the headgates at the canal and drowned, and then when they found her body, she'd be naked, and we would all have to confess to our sins."

Arletta went quiet again. Her hand fell from her hip. She turned, her face yellow in the kitchen light, yellow against the deep pang of blue outside the window.

"What happened?" Tamsin said.

"She caught a slack in the current, I guess, and managed to swim to shore. Lucky for her, and lucky for all of us, too."

Arletta went back to cutting the dough, placing each perfect circle carefully on a new baking sheet. Tamsin watched her mother fall back inward to the place where she usually dwelt, a self-contained, visceral world, its boundaries small and restrictive.

Tamsin wanted to ask more questions. About Arletta's childhood, what she dreamed of back then, if anything. She wanted to ask what it felt like to keep everything you wanted inside of you and never let any of it out for the world to see, for yourself to see. She wanted to ask what Arletta thought about the dam, the fragility of the valley, the migratory birds, the rare plants that lived out there among the lava crags, but what would she do if Arletta said she was in favor of the dam, and loved it as much as everyone else seemed to love it? What would Tamsin do then, once she knew Arletta had never been on her side? What would she think about her mother, when a mother was supposed to be a daughter's strongest ally?

"That cold," Arletta said quietly, still cutting the dough. "The way it went right into me and pulled me up out of myself. Made me feel like I was living ten lives at once. Like I was a thousand feet tall."

Tamsin slipped the oven mitt off her hand and took another cookie from the rack. Arletta looked up then, just in time to see Tamsin put it in her mouth.

"Enough cookies for you, miss."

"Come on."

"You're getting to the age now where you'll need to watch what you eat. As women get older, it gets harder every year to keep trim."

"So?"

"So you want to attract a good man, don't you?"

Tamsin stared at her mother. Then she put the other half of the cookie in her mouth.

"You're shaping your character right now," Arletta said, "at this age. Shaping your future. Now is your chance to make yourself into the right kind of girl who can marry a good man and have a happy life."

Tamsin was about to make some retort when she heard her father's truck coming up the drive. She busied herself with the oven instead, removing the tray of cookies, transferring them onto the rack. Gad's feet came down heavily on the kitchen step, and then the door squealed open and he said hello. He kissed Arletta on the cheek, then Tamsin. He smelled like the inside of his truck, like gasoline and dust and old leather.

"Look at you," Gad said, laying his hand briefly on Tamsin's head, "doing the baking like a good girl."

He headed toward the den, where his favorite chair was waiting, and the TV.

"I'll fix you a plate," Arletta called after him.

Tamsin watched her mother take the leftovers from the refrigerator and assemble everything on a plate. Pork chop—Arletta had saved the largest for Gad—a mountain of mashed potatoes with a spoonful of congealed gravy, a pile of green beans in Campbell's mushroom soup. Arletta slid the plate into the empty oven and left the door half-open, so long wavering streamers of heat rose up from its mouth and distorted the kitchen. She went back to cutting the cookies. Tamsin leaned against the counter and watched her mother, the quiet efficiency with which she kept house.

Presently, the timer dinged. Arletta took the oven mitts from Tamsin and pulled the plate out, set it on another plate that was cool to the touch. Tamsin thought Arletta would carry Gad's supper into the den, but instead she stood with her arms braced on the countertop, looking down at Gad's supper, leaning over it. The gravy had melted and run. The mushroom sauce around the green beans was bubbling. Tamsin looked from the plate to her mother, but there was no expression on Arletta's face, nothing in her eyes.

"Mom?"

Arletta didn't answer. She didn't give the least indication that she'd heard. But she did go to the cutlery drawer and take out a fork, so carefully it barely made a whisper. Then, as Tamsin watched open mouthed, Arletta began to eat Gad's food. She lifted mashed potatoes in great white mounds and stabbed the green beans on the tines of her fork and put them all into her mouth. She cut pieces off the tender pork chop, not even bothering with a knife, using only the edge of her fork. She went on eating till her stomach must have protested. Then she ate a few bites more, just to make a point. When she swallowed down the last forkful she could possibly hold, she looked down again and blinked as if startled.

"Get me the Wonder Bread," Arletta said.

Tamsin made a dash for the bread box, took out a few slices of bread, and buttered them liberally. Arletta set them on the plate to make it look a little fuller, then rearranged the mashed potatoes, the beans. She pushed the pork chop up against the potatoes so Gad wouldn't be able to tell where part had been cut away.

Slowly, Arletta lifted her face and looked at Tamsin. They held one another's eyes in silence. And when at last she carried the plate into the den and set it on Gad's TV tray, Arletta was smiling her usual placid smile. But Tamsin could still smell the pork fat in the kitchen.

~

That night, Gad found that he was still hungry, even after he tried to go to sleep. He slipped out of bed—Arletta was turned away from him, breathing in a low, steady rhythm—and went to the kitchen, which was empty and still at this hour. The room was spotless, because Arletta had always kept house with meticulous, almost ostentatious care, but the absence of her in that place felt stark and accusatory. Gad couldn't understand why. He flipped on the light. A sallow glow spilled all over the counters, the walls, ran down to the economical yet cheerless brown linoleum of the floor.

A sound came faintly from the rear of the house, the den—the piano striking a few pallid chords as if Arletta were there. But of course, she wasn't at her piano. She couldn't be. Arletta was sound asleep—Gad had just seen her. He shuddered; this was only the remnant of one of his dreams, those nightmares he had sometimes of Arletta stepping out of her place, Arletta being everywhere she wasn't meant to be, in places Gad never expected to find her—folded up and grinning inside the file drawer of his desk, or standing multiplied in the closet, a dozen of her all in a row like clothing on hangers, staring out at him blank and unseeing.

Just to prove to himself that he was a fool and there was nothing to be afraid of, Gad left the kitchen and walked through the dim house toward the den. It hadn't always been a den. Back when the kids had still been kids and the Rigbys had gathered on Monday nights for Family Home Evening, it had been their rumpus room, where they'd played board games and sang songs and put on skits with all the pomp of a Shakespearean company.

Those skits. It was all a skit, Gad sometimes thought—the Monday nights, the fiction of Family Home Evening, the play the Rigbys put on to convince themselves everything was all right, and they were a perfectly normal, perfectly loving family.

He padded through the quiet house, let the umber and solitude take him. The walls and floors seemed for one dizzy moment to elongate as he moved, so that he would be forced to walk forever through the corridor of his isolation. All the artifacts of his marriage huddled like ghosts in the periphery of his vision—the family portraits framed on the wall, the bookshelf with the Rigby copies of the Bible and the Book of Mormon, the sets of baby shoes preserved in bronze, displayed in a row on the sideboard. But the walk wasn't as long as he feared. He stood on the threshold of the den, which was empty and dark, exactly the way he'd known he would find it. The piano cover was down. Arletta was still in bed.

Gad breathed deep to dispel his fear. At the den's edge, he promised himself, he swore, the next life wouldn't be like this one, cramped and disordered. The Heaven Gad would make with his family would be one of laughter and joy, of love given ungrudgingly and gratefully received. In the life beyond, Gad would know how to be tender and kind. His family would understand then. They would surely know why Gad had never been a gentle soul here in this earthly realm.

His stomach growled. He remembered that he was hungry. He went back to the pantry, where Arletta sometimes kept a cake under glass. The shelves inside were packed with the fruits of his wife's labors— peaches and pears in glass jars, jams, dried beans, even rice and flour stored in the biggest jars, so neither mice nor insects could spoil the supply. A five-gallon bucket of raw honey sat below the shelves. It was the usual cache of necessities one might find in any true-believing family's home. The church had always stressed self-reliance and preparedness for disaster, for the ever-looming End of Days. Arletta had put enough food by to make any church leader happy, and the flawless organization of the emergency stores, like uniformed soldiers on a parade ground, gave Gad a welcome frisson of rightness and security. But he didn't see anything he could eat right away.

His eye fell on the little cupboard in the corner, the one that extended into a void under the stairs. There was no reason to suspect that a cake might be hiding in there, but Gad did notice that the cupboard door was slightly open, and he could see the corner of something thin and pale, with a familiar texture. It was canvas. A canvas panel, the kind Gad had sometimes painted on.

He bent and tugged hard at the ill-fitting door till it popped open. He paused, worried now that the sound was too big, that it would wake the whole house. But no one stirred. Gad sank to his knees. His mouth went slack. There was a whole stack of canvas panels, leaning against the wall in the darkness.

He slid the panels from their hiding place and huddled at the end of the pantry, bent over the paintings as if shielding them from view, though who he might need to hide them from, and why, was beyond him. One by one he looked at each: Landscapes, still lifes, the fields around Rexburg split by knifepoints of silver water, cattle taking shelter in the blue shade of some magnificent spreading tree. An old barn sagging on its foundation, and through the missing vertical slats of its walls, the bright slashes of sky, an impossible blue. Flowers gathered in a vase, the vase touched and rounded by delicate light, the petals at the limit of their fleeting vitality, just on the verge of falling. There was such a caged and melancholy feeling to every scene that at first Gad thought it must be Arletta's work. Then he recognized something in the collection, something that rang inside him, a lifelong reverberation. In the dull, muted colors and the monumental blocks of composition, Gad recognized the rigidity and confinement of a masculine mind. In that moment, he knew—felt the knowing the way he felt the fire of the Holy Ghost. Aran's absence from the shop, his secrecy, his reticence and silence. Everything made sense now.

Gad sank down to the pantry floor, collapsed with his back against the wall, opposite the open hungry mouth of the cupboard. He looked through Aran's paintings again, and then once more, lingering over them, noting the delicacy and skill of the brushwork, the intentional placement of each minute dab of color. Gad may have been secretive about his own art, but he'd been at it all his life, which was long enough to recognize a great inborn talent when he saw it. He felt queasy with amazement. All these years, all these years as Aran's father, and he'd never known; he'd never seen this side to his boy. He had never looked closely enough to see. The paintings were good, so damn good—a great hot flood of pride and love rose up to the level of Gad's heart.

He looked through the panels again. A moon rose over a ripe field, into a pale gray dusk. An old garden gate succumbed to the sweet, bright leaning of a lilac in bloom, and there were puddles in the track beside the gate, puddles reflecting a brightness and a light that existed somewhere outside the scene, somewhere beyond the confines of the composition. The well of awe and pride was still rising. It was almost enough to drown Gad's envy, the stabbing thing high in his breast that said it should have been he who'd painted so true. It should have been he who felt this freedom to see all the things that were beautiful and real.

Gad slid the panels back into their hiding place. He got up slowly from the pantry floor. His body ached—knees, back, heart. He was halfway across the house and almost to his bedroom door when he realized he'd forgotten to find something to eat, and his hunger was as sharp edged as ever.

21

Pioneer Day

Linda lay flat on the couch. She was sinking into the cushions, surrendering to their softness, and didn't care one bit that she was being lazy. It was a Thursday morning, so *Sesame Street* was playing on public broadcasting, which was the only station she could ever tune in clearly. The volume was just high enough for her to catch the sound of a piano, which a blonde-haired puppet was playing, flailing her fuzzy pink arms. Linda wasn't really paying attention.

Sandy came out of the bathroom, still unwinding the last few rollers from her hair. She stood over the couch coaxing the ends of her bob into place. The piano jangled on.

"Prairie Dawn," Sandy said. "Don't you think that's a great name for a girl? If my first baby is a girl, I'm going to call her Prairie Dawn."

"Gross," Linda said.

"Come on. It's not so bad."

"If you name your daughter after a puppet, she'll never forgive you."

"I've got to start thinking about baby names. Things are getting pretty serious with Joel."

Linda sat up quickly. "You aren't pregnant, are you?"

"Of course not! Gosh, Linda, we've been over this before. I'd never do *that*."

"You said—"

"I only meant that Joel might ask me to marry him soon. Very soon."

Linda laughed. She couldn't help it. "You've been seeing Joel for, what, two months? Not even that long."

Sandy looked down at her, neutral and waiting, as if she expected Linda to say something more, as if there ought to be a more compelling reason to delay marriage, other than *You hardly know the guy.*

When she realized Linda had nothing else to offer, Sandy said, "Joel has been home from his mission since early May." As if that explained everything.

"Well," Linda said dryly, "I guess it's time, then."

"It sure is. You know he's nice, and everyone at Singles Ward says he has a great chance of becoming a bishop like his dad." Sandy drifted toward the bathroom. "Gee, wouldn't it be something to be a bishop's wife?"

"It sure would be something," Linda said vaguely. She was still a little hazy when it came to the intricate male hierarchies that steered the church. She knew women could rise as high as president of the Relief Society, but no higher than that.

Sandy called from the bathroom, "Aren't you going to get ready?"

There was no need to ask what she ought to be getting ready for. It was the twenty-fourth of July: Pioneer Day, which was evidently the most important regional holiday on the calendar. Linda couldn't recall any of her Mormon friends caring one whit about Pioneer Day back in Seattle—not even the Jepsons. But out here, in the dry isolation of rural Idaho, the whole town buzzed as if it were Christmas. Almost every business in town had closed so no one would be left out of the celebration. There was going to be a big parade, followed by a picnic at the park, complete with bands playing on the outdoor stage and baking competitions—even a rodeo at the fairgrounds on the edge of town.

"I don't know if I should go," Linda said.

Sandy leaned out of the bathroom to stare at her. "Of course you're going. Everyone goes to Pioneer Day. All the girls from church will meet up at the park so we can dance together once the music starts. Come on, Linda. If you don't make an appearance, the girls are going to miss you something awful."

Linda made a noise, somewhere between a grunt and a groan.

"I'm serious, Lin. I think Joel might really pop the question soon. What better time to do it than Pioneer Day? I want you to be there if he asks me. You're my best friend."

"You have loads of better friends than me."

"I do not. Anyway, all the cutest guys in town will be at the park today. Lee will be there, I'm sure."

"So?"

"So maybe he'll ask you out again. Or maybe you'll meet someone else who's nice."

Linda supplied in imagination what Sandy had left unsaid. *Nice, which is the opposite of Aran Rigby.*

There was a knock at the door. "I'll get it," Linda said at once, grateful for a reason not to answer Sandy. She already knew it was Aran. She could see his warped silhouette through the pane of amber bubble glass beside the door. Aran's height and habitual stance were familiar by now—not quite slouching, but not exactly standing straight, either. The sight of him made her swallow hard, even dark and featureless and bent through the honey-colored glass.

She slipped out onto the front step and shut the door quickly so Sandy wouldn't see.

"Hi," she said.

Aran looked down. "You don't have any shoes on."

"Who needs shoes on a day like this?"

"Listen, I just wanted to see—"

"If I'll go to Pioneer Day with you?" She pulled a face. "Honestly, the whole thing sounds like a drag."

"It is kind of a drag, to be honest. But the parade isn't so bad, as far as parades go, and at least there's the barbecue after. Spare ribs make everything more bearable. Maybe if we're in it together, it could even be fun."

"I suppose neither of us can get away with skipping Pioneer Day altogether."

"You really don't want to go?" Aran sounded almost awestruck at the thought.

"I'm not sure I can avoid it. It seems the entire town is expected to drop everything and go watch this damn parade. I guess it can't be that bad. I'm probably being unfair. Big-city bias and all that. It's just that I can tell already, this will be another place where I won't fit in."

"Yeah, I know what you mean."

Aran glanced at the street. His Charger was parked at the curb, right behind Linda's Beetle. The Charger had once been a sleek gold, but the paint had faded under the harsh Idaho sun to a sickly greenish tan.

"Listen," Aran said, "why don't we skip it? Let's play hooky—get out of here, go for a drive on our own."

"Pioneer Day seems like a requirement around here. If I don't do what's expected, they might run me out with pitchforks and torches."

Aran's expression turned sober. "I think it'd be a real shame if you fit in, Linda."

She didn't know why that made her feel good, but it did. "Hang on a minute. Let me change my clothes. And stay away from the window—don't let Sandy know you're here." She was wearing the same old jeans and tight-fitting top she liked to wear at home, when no one but her roommate could see.

"Don't change," Aran said. "Not unless you really want to. You look perfect the way you are."

"I'll just get my shoes, then. It'll only take a second."

She dodged back inside. Linda could hear a hollow plastic clattering from the bathroom—Sandy pawing through the drawer where she kept her makeup compacts. She went into her bedroom, stuffed her feet into socks and her favorite old sneakers, and slid down the hall again, hoping Sandy wouldn't catch her. The bathroom door opened abruptly.

"Say, Linda, have you seen my Mary Quant blusher? I can't find it anywhere, and I—" She stopped, goggling at Linda, who was halfway to the door. "Where are you going?"

"Out."

"But we've got to get downtown for the parade. You aren't even dressed yet."

"I'm not going to the parade. I'm skipping Pioneer Day this year."

"You can't skip! It's your first!"

"Good luck with Joel." Linda picked up her pace. She had one hand on the doorknob now. A shiver went through her, some tight internal current of electricity. Maybe it was mischievous glee at defying the town's expectations, or maybe it was just excitement over going somewhere alone with Aran, out on the long, lonely roads between the fields. "Tell me all about it tonight, will you? I'll cross my fingers and hope you come home with a ring on your finger. Bye!" She dodged outside before Sandy could raise another objection.

"Let's get out of here," Linda said to Aran, and headed for his car while he was still fishing the keys from his pocket.

The sidewalks were packed with people making toward Main Street for the big parade. Mothers in tidy long-sleeved dresses shepherded flocks of children through a crosswalk. When they'd left the most crowded streets behind, she relaxed in her seat. She kicked off one of her sneakers and put her foot up on Aran's dash. She figured he wouldn't mind.

"So where are we going?" Linda said.

"Anywhere but Pioneer Day."

"Sandy just about choked to death when I told her I wouldn't be there. I can't believe what a big deal this is out here in Idaho."

"No one does Pioneer Day in Seattle?"

"Oh, I'm sure the nice Mormon families have barbecues in their backyards. But there's no parade, that's for sure. The whole city doesn't get in on the festivities."

He looked at her from the corner of his eye.

"Maybe I'm wrong," Linda said, suddenly afraid that she'd done something to upset him. "I wasn't all that tied into the church back in Seattle. I went to the meetings every Sunday and most of my friends were Mormon, but maybe I wasn't paying close enough attention. Maybe it all passed me by."

"You got me wrong," Aran said. "I was just thinking that city life sounds great. No one expects you to show up for some rinky-dink parade? You don't have to stand around at the park waiting for the bishop to come over and say hello and shake your dad's hand and bestow his approval on your family? Sounds like Heaven to me."

"Just think—if we'd gone after all, we could have knocked your bishop flat on his ass. You, the so-called Devil worshipper, with the dangerous city girl on your arm."

Aran huffed a little. It wasn't quite a laugh.

"No one has said a thing about you," Linda said. She could have kicked herself for hurting Aran's feelings. "Not to me, anyway. But not many people talk to me, except Sandy and some of the girls at Singles Ward. I'm almost as much a pariah as you are."

"That's a good word—'pariah.'"

He was smiling easily now. Linda let her foot fall down from the dash. "Hey, how come you don't go to Singles Ward? You aren't hiding a secret girlfriend, are you—or a wife? I mean, you're, what, twenty-five? That's ancient in Mormonville—way too old to be single."

"First of all," Aran said, "I'm twenty-three. And second, can you imagine anyone wanting to marry me?"

"Yes."

Linda realized she'd said that word much too quickly. She turned and watched the fields again. It was better than looking at Aran, better than letting him see her red face.

He said, "There's no way in hell I'm going to drag myself to Singles Ward. I can't think of a better way to humiliate myself than to get up on the auction block so every girl in Rexburg can turn me down."

"Is Singles Ward really that much of a meat market?"

"Of course it is. That's the whole point: Pair everyone up and marry them off as fast as possible. Put everyone to work making lots of Mormon babies." He looked at her again, that slow sideways glance. He said, "Why are you going to Singles Ward?"

"Because I'm single."

"And you want to get married?"

"Someday, when I find the right man."

Aran stared out at the very straight road. "Who's the right man?"

"God, I don't know. How does anyone know something like that?"

"People get married all the time, so someone must have figured it out."

"People end up miserable all the time, in marriages that never should have happened."

"You're right about that," Aran said quietly. "I don't think that'll happen to you, though. You know what you want out of life."

She wondered if it was true.

Aran seemed to sense that he'd skirted close to a sensitive topic. He said, a little too cheerfully, "You love art. You told me all about how you used to spend hours in museums. I have an idea: let's say our favorite artist's name on the count of three."

"Why?" she said, laughing.

"Just for fun. Ready?"

Aran counted. Linda said Mary Cassatt; his answer was Wyeth.

He said, "We can't possibly be compatible if you're an impressionist and I'm a regionalist."

"Guess we'd better give up now, then." She put her hand on his knee, which felt oddly formal to her, a stiff and awkward touch. But he looked down at her hand and smiled, then went red in the face, so she understood that he liked it.

He said, "Why do you like Cassatt so much? Why is she your favorite over all the other impressionists? I would have thought you'd pick someone more conventional like Monet or Van Gogh."

"You think I'm a conventional girl?"

Aran grinned.

"I don't know why I love Cassatt so much," Linda said. "I've never thought about that before. I guess because she always painted mothers and children together. You can tell how much those mothers loved their babies."

She had given something away in her voice or her words, shown more than she'd wanted to reveal. She withdrew her hand and looked out at the fields again, which had changed from potatoes to cattle pasture. She could feel Aran's eyes on her. They were sharper than the eyes of the passing drivers in town, or the housewives who muttered at her and Aran when they went out walking together. She didn't know whether to love or hate the clarity with which Aran saw.

After a time, he pulled off the road into a patch of bare dirt, a depression between two thick stands of roadside weeds and sun-faded flowers. Beyond the weeds ran an old wire fence and just there, where Aran had left the road, was a metal gate with rounded corners. Its four heavy bars were spotted with rust. The turnout didn't look distinct from any of a dozen others they'd passed—access points to fields and cattle pastures. But Aran seemed to know the place.

They got out of the car. He pulled an olive-drab army pack from the back seat, slung it over his shoulder. "Come on," he said, and ducked between the bars of the gate.

Linda followed. The sun was high, hot on her face and the top of her head. The warmth of the day raised a dense, lazy, vegetal smell from the field, which was a cow pasture, she now understood, with a faint two-rutted track running from the gate out to a bank of low, scrubby trees. Linda picked up her pace, caught up with Aran. There were no cattle nearby that she could see, but she had a vague fear of them. She didn't know how to behave around cattle. She barely knew how to behave around people. Sagebrush clawed at her jeans, but she liked the smell of the sage. It was both sharp and earthy, and it made her feel as if she were in a different world, as if the gate they'd crossed had admitted them both into another realm held apart from Rexburg.

"I come here to paint whenever I can," Aran said when Linda reached his side. "Once you get into those trees, nobody knows you're there."

She could hear a cow calling from somewhere far off. Then a meadowlark, a giddy, soft song with a trickle at the end. They reached the trees and Linda's anxiety diminished. The branches closed overhead, green shadows. She slowed to make the walk last longer. She wanted to savor all the small, quiet charms of the day—the droning insects, the easy feeling she had when she was close to Aran's side, the comfortable nature of their silence. She thought for a moment that time wasn't real. There was no such thing as years or days or ages, no past, not even a future to worry about. She was suspended in the honey light, the slowness, the smell of the sage. She took his hand and knew it would be okay to do it. She felt as if she had always been holding his hand, and would be holding it still for a hundred years to come.

When they came out on the other side of the trees, Linda was surprised by a bend of water glittering in the late-morning sun. It was a broad creek with a stony bed, and it moved just swiftly enough that she could hear the current chattering over stones. A green scent rose up forcefully around her, the smell of damp earth.

Several yards back from the creek, just under the low gnarled branches of the trees, Linda found an old farmhouse or barn—a simple structure, little more than a box with a peaked roof, obviously a skeleton. The siding had faded to gray, and chinks had broken apart between the planks, admitting light from the other side of the building, spilling shadows out to where Linda stood. She let go of Aran's hand and went to the old house. She held on to the frame of the door and peered inside—tentative, reluctant to disturb the ancient memories that still lingered, a general bustle around a long-gone hearth, a woman's voice singing, children laughing under the leaves. All vanished now, and yet not vanished. There was a window across from the door, no glass in it, of course, not even the frames for panes—nothing but a patch of sky with the old and unknown hanging in the darkness around it. She put her back against the door frame, lifted one foot and propped it on the wood behind her so she was leaning, one legged, like a shorebird dozing in the sun.

"It really is beautiful here in some ways," she said. "Idaho, I mean—this country. I didn't expect to find beauty, when I first came. But if you get out of town and look hard enough, it's a real nice place. Sometimes it's almost magical."

Aran didn't make any reply, though he was close by. She could feel his presence just a few yards away. She looked in his direction and found him standing, facing Linda and the old house. He had braced a sketch pad against his stomach. His other hand moved so rapidly the charcoal in his fingers blurred, and he kept looking from the pad up to Linda, back down again.

No one had ever drawn her before. She stood up squarely, shoved her hands in the pockets of her jeans.

"No," Aran said, distracted, "go back to what you were doing before. Put your leg up the way it was."

Slowly, Linda returned to her leaning pose. She looked away from him, out across the creek and the pasture. She had a strange sensation of exposure, felt suddenly vulnerable, uncertain, as she'd never felt in Aran's company before. But she also felt as if she were being seen more clearly than anyone had the power to see. She didn't know whether she liked it or not.

After a few minutes, Aran said, "Okay. I'm done. Do you want to see?"

Linda went to him. The world seemed to dilate around her, so she moved through a space that would never quite bring her to Aran's side. He had the sketch pad tucked under one arm now; he was bending to the old pack, getting out sandwiches and bottles of 7UP as if he'd done nothing worth remarking, but Linda could already see the sketch behind his arm, and it was extraordinary. She took the pad while he busied himself with setting out their lunch on a little scrap of faded blanket, which he'd also taken from the pack.

Linda stared at the drawing. It wasn't photo perfect, of course, but it didn't need to be. It was something more than realistic—a slice of time and emotion, a fragment of memory caught and recorded in the very moment it had been made. She saw herself, the wood and the doorway, the dark space around her. And beyond, the pure white square of the window, framing her face. Aran had jotted a few quick, dark specks with hard angles in the window beyond her profile—birds flying over the pasture.

"It's only a study," he said dismissively, "to get the values and composition down. I'll do a bigger piece from this—a painting. The blue sky in the window will be real nice against all that brown."

Linda looked at the sketch again. Her eyes filled with tears. It would have been one thing if Aran had drawn her portrait, a simple rendering of her face. This was something more, something that felt like a secret between them, a silent acknowledgment. Linda saw in the study—in the echoing memories of the old, faded home—all the longing and isolation she felt inside herself, the tight, ever-present melancholy, breathing in but never breathing out.

22

Fine the Way We Are

Aran kept his eyes on Arletta so he wouldn't have to look at Gad, who was staring at him down the length of the family table with his usual hard intensity. Arletta carried in the last serving dish from the kitchen and set it on a trivet. Tamsin followed with a pitcher of ice water and filled everyone's glasses. The pitcher was sweating heavily by the time she finished, scattering fat drops of water all over the tablecloth. Aran watched the damp spots spread through the fabric. Gad hadn't forgiven him for shirking Pioneer Day almost a week ago. Aran had already caught two lectures on the importance of showing up for family functions, the importance of doing his part to maintain the Rigby reputation. If he had to listen to another speech about his failings as a son, he would blow right through the roof. He would say something his father could never forgive.

Finally, Gad stopped glaring and started dishing up supper, filling everyone's plates for them, passing them back one by one. Arletta's chicken casserole and boiled vegetables and mashed potatoes smelled as good as ever, but Aran found he had little appetite. He could feel something coming, a sharp crackle in the air, a tension needing to burst like a jag of thunder.

Gad asked Ondi to say the blessing. They all bowed their heads while Ondi delivered a pitch-perfect prayer, thanking the Lord for the many blessings (not specified) that He had bestowed, asking Him to bless the food, that it would nourish and strengthen their bodies. When the prayer was finished, Brig and Ondi tucked into their supper like they'd been starving for weeks. Moving pipe out on the farms had made them lean and sun browned and hungry.

"Well," Gad said, in that tight, measured tone that always indicated he was struggling to control his temper, "how has everyone's day been?"

"Great," Tamsin said. "I helped Mom hem the new curtains this morning."

"Good girl."

"How's Grandpa?" Aran asked.

Gad shrugged as if it were a question of no real consequence, though Aran knew his father was haunted by his old man's sickness. The cancer had come on suddenly, sapping Grandpa Rigby of his big, effulgent presence, his jolly demeanor. Aran thought it must frighten Gad a little, to see how quickly and thoroughly a man could be reduced. It certainly grieved Aran.

"He had another test this morning," Gad said casually. "Your uncle Delyle called and told me all about it. No change. The treatments haven't been working like we all hoped."

"I'm sorry to hear that," Aran said. "I'm sure we'll all be praying for Grandpa tonight."

After a tense and brittle silence, Brig asked, "Have you heard anything from the bishop yet?"

"Not yet," Gad said. "But it hasn't been long since Bishop Kimball and I had our meeting. I let him know how important it is to you boys to receive your calls—how hard you've been working, how much you've been looking forward to serving your missions. I told him you're good, honest, respectable young men."

Once more, Aran felt Gad's eyes on him, judging, demanding. He kept his attention on the food.

"Jiminy," Ondi muttered, "it doesn't seem right, that we have to go begging like this."

Gad gave Ondi a bracing pat on the shoulder. "Now, don't get discouraged. You're still nineteen, so there's really no delay—not yet. Maybe the Lord is testing your obedience."

Brig said, "Me and Ondi aren't the ones who are being disobedient around here."

"What do you mean?" There was a note of danger in Gad's voice.

"In this town, is what I mean," Brig said. "Someone has been spray-painting a bunch of nonsense all over the post office and the library. Even up on the water tower. Haven't you noticed?"

Gad exhaled. "I've seen it."

Ondi said, "This weekend we're leading a bunch of the kids in Young Men's downtown with buckets and scrub brushes so we can clean the place up. Though I don't know how to get spray paint off brick."

"That's smart," Gad said. "I'm sure Bishop Kimball will take notice."

"Don't know if it'll do much good, in the long run. Am I crazy, or is there more of this graffiti all the time? At first it was only in a couple places, but lately—"

"It's everywhere," Brig said. "We've never had vandalism like this in Rexburg before. Who in the world could be doing it?"

Gad grunted, took a long draft from this water glass. "I have my suspicions."

From the corner of his eye, Aran watched Tamsin replace her fork on the table. She held herself very still.

"Who?" Ondi said. "I find it hard to believe any of the boys I know could—"

"Not a boy," Gad said. "I'd bet my life that it's that newcomer—the girl with the black hair. The one who hangs around with Sandy Jepson."

Aran reached with his foot to bump Tamsin's ankle. He knew, of course, that Linda and Tamsin had been spending time together. But Aran was dead certain that no one else in the family ought to know about Tamsin's secret association with the outsider. Nor should anyone other than Tamsin know that Aran had been dating Linda. If Gad learned of it, disaster would follow. Eager as he was to see Aran with a girlfriend, Linda wasn't the kind of girl Gad had in mind. If Gad knew not one but two of his kids were involved, Linda would become a hand grenade tossed in their midst. Aran wasn't ready to see his fragile new happiness blown apart—not yet.

Tamsin mistook Aran's warning, or maybe she didn't care. She spoke up at once. "You're thinking of Linda Duff. She just moved here this summer—going to Ricks in the fall."

"How do you know her?" Ondi said.

"We're friends."

Aran set down his water glass heavily, hard enough to catch Tamsin's attention. He gave her a tense, pleading look, silently begging her to keep her mouth shut. Tamsin flashed a small, determined smile.

"You're too young to have friends in college," Gad said.

"I'm seventeen. That's not too young."

"Don't talk back to your father." Arletta's voice was lilting, almost mocking.

Brig sat up straighter. "Wait a minute. Linda Duff?" He and Ondi shared a look. "We know her."

"You do not," Aran said mildly.

This was it, the detonation. There was no stopping it now.

"Everyone has heard all about her," Ondi said. "She works for the IEC."

Gad said, "The what?"

"The Idaho Environmental something or other. She's an environmentalist."

Gad set down his fork. Red faced, he stared at Tamsin.

"Linda isn't an environmentalist," Tamsin said. "She does survey work."

"For an organization that's trying to stop the dam," Brig said. "Same difference."

Aran shot another glance at his sister. Gad wasn't so much in favor of the dam's construction as he was opposed to the people who opposed it. He considered anyone involved in federal matters to be either enemies of Heaven—the government sought endlessly to destroy true religion, according to Gad—or no-good, freeloading hippies who wanted to ruin honest men's lives and fortunes by ushering communism into America.

Tamsin said, "The IEC is only trying to figure out how damming the river will affect the wildlife. Like trout, for example."

"Who cares about a bunch of dumb fish?" Brig said.

Ondi added, "We can't risk another big drought like the last one. It'll wreck the economy for the whole region. You shouldn't listen to that ecological nonsense, Tam. It'll rot your brain."

"Oh, stuff it," Tamsin said. "What do you know?"

Gad dropped his hand hard on the table. The dishes and silverware jumped. In the brief silence that followed, Aran could hear his mother humming lightly under her breath. She was looking at the tablecloth, watching the spots of dampness spread with a faraway expression, just as Aran had done.

"For one night," Gad said, "for one dad-gummed night, I would like this family to have a quiet, peaceful supper together."

No one spoke. No one moved.

"You're all either grown up or old enough to control yourselves," Gad went on. "You aren't a bunch of children anymore."

The silence stretched. One by one, they resumed their supper. Aran could feel a hot little halo of victory radiating from his sister. He didn't understand it, this need Tamsin had to kick the hornet's nest. It was so much easier to be quiet and complacent, as far as you were able. It was easier to get along.

After a few minutes, Gad said, "You aren't to see this Linda person anymore, Tamsin."

Tamsin looked up sharply from her plate. "Why not?"

"Because I'm your father and I said so."

"That's a rotten reason."

"Heck," Brig said, disgusted.

Gad was already right back into it, thrusting himself upward, a tower of offense and anger. "It's the best danged reason there is. It's your duty to obey your father."

Tamsin sagged back in her chair. Aran knew she was struggling not to roll her eyes.

Suddenly, Brig said, "What about Aran? Are you going to forbid him from seeing Linda, too?"

All eyes turned to Aran. He glanced up from his plate, then back down again. He could feel his face going red, red as his father's. He wanted to reach over and grab Brig by his throat, crush him, wring the life out of him. The urge to do violence—and against his own brother, no less—horrified Aran. He swallowed hard.

"What are you talking about, Brig?" Gad said.

It was Ondi who answered. "Aran and Linda Duff have been dating."

"We aren't dating," Aran said. "We've gone on a few dates, but we aren't steady. There's a difference."

He would like to be steady with Linda, though. And now he thought every good thing in his life, Linda foremost among them, was about to be swept beyond his reach. He felt dizzy and small and feeble, and hated himself for feeling that way, the way no man was supposed to feel, not ever.

"Where did this Linda girl come from?" Gad addressed the twins—who he thought, as ever, were the only ones in the family who would tell the truth.

"Some West Coast city," Ondi said.

"Is she a member of the church?"

"She goes to Singles Ward," Brig said. "But nobody knows if she's baptized or not."

"What difference does that make?" Tamsin said in the same moment Aran said, "She's baptized."

Gad and the twins ignored both of them.

"This stranger," Gad said, "this interloper, comes blowing into town from a coastal city, working to stop the dam, pretending to be a member of God's true church?" He rose again from his chair and pointed down the table, straight at Aran. "No son of mine is going to date a hussy."

"She isn't," Aran said. "You can't talk about her that way."

"And no daughter of mine is going to fall under the influence of a Satanic person."

"Satanic?" Tamsin said. "Get real."

"Go to your room, Tamsin. Right now."

Eagerly, she left the table.

Aran tried to keep his voice calm. He knew his face was burning. He knew the whole family could see his anger. "I'm twenty-three, too old for you to be telling me who I can and can't date."

Gad roared. "If you think you're a damn man, then act like one! Still living under my roof, too unreliable to work at the steady job I've given you!"

"I get my work done."

"Not the way it should be done!"

"You wonder why I won't work alongside you? Take a look at yourself right now, Dad."

"What, do you want me to treat you gentle? Treat you like a girl? Aren't you man enough to live a man's life?"

"I just want . . ." Aran didn't know what he wanted. Not from his father, not from anyone else. He couldn't say more than that.

"Maybe I'd give you what you want," Gad shouted, "if you'd give me what I want."

"And what is that, Dad? What, for the love of God?"

"A son I can be proud of."

Aran pushed himself up. He couldn't look at his brothers, and certainly not at Gad. He paused beside Arletta, laid a hand gently on her shoulder. She was trembling. "Good dinner, Mom." Then he headed for the door.

"Where are you going now?" Gad demanded.

"What do you care, old man? What have you ever cared?"

Aran walked through town till the sun set, heavy and red in the sky. He kept going, restless, as twilight settled over the valley. High up on the Bench, the windows of distant homes glowed. The stars came out, one and two at a time, three, a dozen, till the night sky was clamoring with them and the heavens felt crowded. He found himself at last under the trees on the Teton River, past the northern edge of Rexburg, where pavement gave way to the open plain. He sat under the trees, listening to the water as it flowed through the dark, the crickets singing a cold, metallic song. He tried to pray, but no prayer came to him. None ever did, unless he was painting or thinking about his paintings.

Since he couldn't pray for guidance, he simply wondered instead— what he ought to do about Linda. If he broke things off with her, it would certainly make Gad happy. And he wondered why Gad always seemed to arrange things so that whatever would make him happiest would make Aran the most miserable, and whatever would bring a little joy to Aran's life, or even a scrap of contentment, would set Gad to gnashing his teeth and wailing about how he'd been wronged.

When the night got chilly, Aran headed home. Gad had turned the shop light off, so Aran was obliged to come up the drive in the dark, with only the stars overhead to keep him from falling. He stood for a while, watching the family home, suspicious and not at all sure what was making him feel that way, like the house itself might open up a sudden, sharp mouth and bite him. The lights were burning in everyone's windows, even in his own. He thought Arletta must have slipped in and turned it on for him, maybe left a plate of cookies on his nightstand. Arletta did the best she could with what the Lord had given her.

As he stood there, staring, the green curtain moved in Tamsin's window. She looked down and saw him in the lightless drive. Aran wondered how she'd known to look just then, how she'd known Aran would be out there in the yard.

Tamsin unlatched her window, pushed it open. She leaned out into the night.

"Why did you do that?" Aran said, just loud enough for Tamsin to hear. "Why did you start that fight?"

"I don't know. Sometimes I can't help it. I have to set it all off that way, because watching everyone blow up is so much better."

"Than what?" Aran said, disbelieving.

"Better than everyone pretending we're all fine the way we are."

23

SMALL AND QUIET

Tamsin had meant what she'd said to Aran that night, but the next day, when Gad still hadn't let go of his anger, she regretted it more and more. There was an impulse inside her that she'd never understood—a quick-flitting, sly-eyed thing. It made her do things she knew were unwise, but sometimes a knowing took hold of her, bone deep, a certainty that none of this was right. Sometimes the feeling grew till Tamsin knew she would crack under the pressure.

She didn't like to hurt Aran, though. She always regretted it, whenever she blew off a little too much steam and Aran was the one who got scalded. There were times when Tamsin felt as if her brother was more a part of herself than her own spirit. And there were times when she hated Aran for yielding to Gad. She hated how easily he'd given up, surrendering himself to their father's will, agreeing to become whatever Gad wished to make of him. She hated herself for making it harder for Aran to find a little peace, to settle quietly into the role Gad had chosen for him.

She pulled off her headphones because she could hear them yelling at each other down by the shop. All those hard and hateful, indignant, offended words came up to her room and cut through the music.

Tamsin got up from the floor, went over to the window, and opened it by a crack so she could hear exactly what was going on, and figure out, maybe, some way to make it better.

"I saw you with that no-good hussy this morning," Gad was shouting.

Aran said, "You were spying on me?"

"I told you no one in this family is to associate with that girl anymore."

"Don't be such a creep, Dad."

"She's no good. No good for you, no good for Tamsin, no good to anyone in the world."

"I don't have to listen to this."

"You sure as hell do. I've met your little girlfriend already, Aran. I recognized her the moment I saw you with her. I could never forget her, after the way she treated me. I know she's an unnatural woman."

"Unnatural? What are you talking about?"

"I had an encounter with her in town. Weeks ago. She was rude. She has no respect for the proper order, no respect for authority. A person like that is dangerous. She'll lead you astray from the Lord."

"For heaven's sake, Dad, listen to yourself. What are you so afraid of?"

Gad roared at him. "I fear nothing, nothing in this world, do you hear me?"

"Nothing except a twenty-year-old girl. I'm a grown man. I can make my own decisions."

"Then act like it," Gad fired back. "You live under my roof because you can't support yourself—"

"Because you insist that I work at your business. Not my business; yours."

"A real man would make his own way in the world. By the time I was your age—"

Tamsin left her room then. She ran down the stairs and past her mother, who was humming over a dishpan full of soapy water even though she could surely hear the fight, too. Everyone in the neighborhood must have heard.

Tamsin bolted out the door. She was across the lawn to the shop, in the thick of their argument, before Aran or Gad saw her coming.

"You leave him alone," Tamsin shouted at her father.

Aran took her by the arm, tried gently to pull her away, but she jerked out of his grip.

"Don't get involved," Gad said to her. "This doesn't concern you."

"Yes, it does. Linda is my friend, whether you like it or not. And she's Aran's girlfriend, whether you like it or not. That isn't going to change, not for either one of us."

Gad went quiet then, and red. He turned the full force of his stare on Tamsin. She quailed inside, as she always did whenever he looked at her that way. There was something inborn in her, pressed forever into her spirit, that made her go small and quiet before the power of the patriarch. She guessed that same small and quiet thing lived inside Aran, too. Maybe everyone was born with it—everyone Tamsin knew, except Linda. But though she could feel her resolve quaking, Tamsin stood where she was and stared right back at her father. She didn't yield an inch to his rage.

"I can see," Gad said, coolly now, "that this Linda person has already worked her influence over you."

"So what if she has?"

Aran said, "Tamsin," his voice pitched low and cautious.

Gad said, "This is exactly what I hoped to avoid. Corruption. Of my own daughter, my only daughter."

Tamsin smiled. Or rather, the sly thing that lived inside her smiled, and Gad saw it. He was shaken by it, just for a moment.

She said, "I was corrupted a long time ago, long before I ever met Linda."

"Tamsin!" Aran said.

The next second, Gad grabbed her hard by the upper arm. He pulled her close, barking in her face. "I won't let you fall away. Not you. I won't lose you to sin, like I've lost Aran already."

Dimly, Tamsin was aware of Aran crying out, "Let go of her, Dad! You'll hurt her!" He pulled Tamsin by her hand, trying to rescue her from Gad's grip.

Gad said, "It's not too late for you, Tamsin. I can still keep you safe. You'll be old enough to marry soon."

"What?" Aran said.

"There are good boys in the church, good men. Fine young men just back from their missions. Any one of them would be happy to take a pretty girl like you as a wife. I'll talk to the bishop, talk to their fathers—"

Tamsin laughed. Right in his face, she laughed. "You're going to arrange a marriage for me? Good luck with that."

She felt his grip weaken and wrenched away at exactly the right moment, when she could do it without struggling.

"This is nineteen seventy-five, Dad, not the nineteenth century. You can't marry me off like I'm your property, like I'm your chattel. Go ahead and try. I'll call CPS. I'll call the news station. The media will be all over you. Your reputation will be shot. Your business will fail. Do it, if you think you can get away with it. You can't arrange a marriage for me, and you know it."

Tamsin turned then and headed back toward the house. She paused only a moment, to catch Aran's eye and hold him with her stare. He was wide eyed, pale with shock, but there was something else in his expression, too, like awe, like a revelation.

24

THE GLORIES THAT COME TO OTHER MEN

He couldn't and he knew it. Couldn't make his daughter marry a man of his choosing, couldn't make her into something she was not, a righteous and proper woman. He could never, no matter how he tried, interest Aran in the family business or trust his eldest son to carry on his legacy after he retired or died, whichever came first. Nor could he tear the twins away from their own futures. They were too brilliant, their minds agile and fine—they were made for bigger and better things than this town had to offer. They would be engineers someday, or lawyers, or politicians with grand futures. He couldn't keep the twins chained here to something as small—he was forced to admit—as small and insignificant as this business was. Aran had the right temperament for sign making, that simple contentment with the here and now, but he lacked appreciation for the work itself, and above all else, he lacked sufficient love for his father, a desire to follow in Gad's footsteps.

He couldn't and he knew it.

He saw it all now, clearly, every bitter truth to which he'd blinded himself before. Gad was an insignificant man in an insignificant town. Whatever glories the Lord had bestowed upon other men, He had withheld them all from Gad Rigby. His family was small, already breaking apart, sweeping itself beyond his strength to hold them together. The legacy he'd toiled for all his life would mean nothing in the end. And even the secret he kept from everyone, the sketches, the careful drawings, the panels he had painted in the few quiet hours he'd stolen for himself—even those were insignificant when compared with Aran's tremendous talent, the ease and responsiveness that were the hallmarks of his art. Gad could never make himself into what Aran was: a prism through which the light of the world bent itself and fractured. The fragments of light spilled out in wild disarray, but the reflections Aran threw were beautiful. Gad had been denied even that power, to see the Lord's Creation through the facets of a prismatic mind.

He couldn't be anything other than what he was, what the Lord in His infinite and careless whimsy had made of him.

Gad left the shop. He slammed the door behind him, but the sound wasn't enough to snuff out his rage. He went to the back of the lot, to the old metal oil drum where he burned the scraps from his sign making. He took the can of kerosene from the garden shed, poured a stream on the refuse in the barrel, and lit it with a match from his pocket. Then, calmly, he returned to the house. Everyone had fled by then, Arletta vanishing into the bedroom, Brig and Ondi walking away down the drive, Aran to the Devil knew where. Gad went to the pantry and tugged the cupboard open and took out all of Aran's paintings, every last one, tucking them under his arm like they were nothing more than a bundle of kindling or the old broken leg of a chair, useless.

But he didn't go straight back to the burning barrel—not yet. He went into the shop and took the key from his pocket and unlocked the lowest drawer of his filing cabinet, and there were his own paintings, the landscapes he had tried out so tentatively, hesitant still lifes, a portrait or two—not especially good but not bad, either. Gad had always suspected he had some small talent that could be nurtured along and shaped into something greater, if he was ever fool enough to try. He swept everything up, years' worth of secret paintings, a decade's worth or more. Only then did he return to the yard.

Gad began tossing the paintings into the flames one by one. He stood and watched as each one blistered in the fire, the paint scorching and bubbling like sugar, then flaring up, the flames licking higher the more Gad fed them. Heat pounded against his face. Noxious smoke brought tears to his eyes, and he blinked them away or wiped them quickly on his sleeve. A dozen or more of Aran's paintings. Then a few of his own. Aran's again. Somehow it seemed right that they should all be erased together, reduced to the same anonymous ash, the same colorless cinders.

He had no idea anyone in the family had seen him till Tamsin's voice came down from the second floor of the house, from her open bedroom window, "What are you doing, what is he doing, Aran, oh my God, Aran, what's he doing?"

Then his son was at his side, clinging to his arm, bellowing with such agony that Gad thought for a moment he had fed Aran himself to the fire.

When he dropped the last of Aran's paintings in the barrel, Aran made a sound like some big animal shot through the rib cage, a gruff, hurt final sound with a pain inside it, the kind of pain you can't recover from. Gad raised the last panel, held it out to the flames. The last was one of his, a portrait he'd made of Tamsin when she'd been gentle and small. Aran glanced at it. His wild, disbelieving eyes flashed up and caught Gad's, and deepened with understanding.

"Don't." Aran grabbed his wrist, trying to stop him. "Don't do this to yourself. Don't destroy it."

Gad wrenched away from his son and let the portrait fall.

25

WEIGHT

The twins, halfway to Main Street by the time Gad was finished, stopped walking and turned back to look in the direction of home. Maybe they'd heard Aran crying out. Maybe they'd felt it. Something made them pause and listen and shake their heads.

Quietly, Ondi said, "Why does he do this stuff?"

"I don't know." Brig waited, listening, but there was nothing more to hear except the mourning doves calling softly and the occasional car on the road. "Do you ever think . . . ?"

He didn't need to say what he was thinking. Ondi had thought it, too. Maybe the bishop was delaying their interviews for another reason. Maybe Aran wasn't the problem. Maybe the bishop wasn't even aware of why he hadn't called in the Rigby twins for the expected talk. Maybe it was all in the hands of a power higher than Bishop Kimball, and the Rigbys had been judged unworthy. They had all been found wanting.

"Sometimes I want to sock him," Brig said, "for the way he treats Aran."

"Don't do it. You know better than to get on his bad side. He'll only come down ten times worse on us."

"I know. But I can't help it. Sometimes I want to do it, anyway."

Ondi said, "Sometimes I do, too."

Upstairs in her bedroom, Tamsin tore her backpack open and dumped out all the spray cans. She was blinded by tears, but she found the drawers of her dresser and stuffed the pack full of clothing. She put it on her shoulders and stood in the middle of the room, panting, her fists locked around the straps, wondering where she would go. Where could she possibly go? Something heavy and dark and suffocating was rising in her chest. Gad had attacked Aran, but Tamsin had felt it, too, the thrust of a blade straight to her middle, the rending apart of her spirit. He couldn't have hurt Aran worse if he'd maimed him, if he'd taken a blade to his physical body or broken all his bones. And weren't she and Aran one? Weren't they united in all things, even in this pain?

She remembered the shack at the edge of the wheat field. Those paintings hadn't burned. They still existed, whole. So Tamsin could be sure that she was still intact, at least. Gad hadn't destroyed them both—not yet.

The tears dried. She let the pack slide from her shoulders and hit the floor behind her heels. She stood there, smelling kerosene and smoke, and she didn't cry, and didn't run. There was no place she could run to, anyway.

Aran had fallen to his knees in the short dry grass after Gad had dropped the last of the paintings into the barrel. He wasn't aware of his father leaving, walking away. All he could see was the fire and the panels warping, buckling, falling away to nothing, and even though he saw it, he couldn't comprehend it, how quickly and thoroughly a thing could be unmade. After a while, the flames didn't lick up quite so high, and Aran felt the hardness of the ground under his knees, the bruises beginning to form there. The physical pain couldn't eclipse the great searing agony inside, but it did sharpen his thoughts. It brought him something he'd never had before—resolve. He stood slowly, brushing flecks of grass from his knees. He never took his eyes off the fire till he turned and went for his car. Long before he slipped behind the wheel, he knew exactly where he was going: to Linda's place, and damn what Gad or anyone else thought about it.

Inside the house, Gad was holding his left hand under the tap, running cold water over a burn. He hadn't realized he'd touched the rim of the barrel till he'd left the fire with Aran kneeling mute and helpless before it. But now it hurt bad enough to make him cry. Through the kitchen window, he watched Aran get into his Charger and back down the long drive. Aran's face was calm, devoid of all pain, which only made Gad's burn throb all the worse.

Gradually, he became aware of Arletta standing beside him. He hadn't heard her approach. She had drifted over to him like a fog, like a ghost, and hung there, just in the periphery of his vision. He was afraid to look at her. Afraid she would look the way she did in his nightmares, when her grin was wide and ravenous. Instead, he looked at his hand. An ugly red slash marked the heel, right up onto his wrist. It was already starting to blister.

"Anger is a burden," Arletta said softly, her voice rather singsong, as always. "It only grows heavier the longer you carry it. And it only hurts you in the end."

Gad's jaw clenched. He couldn't clench his hand into a fist. The damn thing would hurt too much if he did.

"I'll get a compression bandage," Arletta said.

"You do that."

She left the kitchen. Only then could Gad bring himself to look at her, when her back was turned. She moved slowly, as if something old and heavy were yoked around her shoulders, as if she had carried that weight for a long, long time.

26

WRECKING BALL

"He destroyed everything?"

Linda's voice was small and pained. It only made the interior of the car more confining. Aran had been grateful to find her at home, glad she wasn't out working that day, unreachable in some distant field. She'd been able to tell right away that something was wrong, just by the look on his face. She closed the door to her duplex and got in his car, and then at last, Aran found he could talk. He told her everything while they headed out of town. He was driving the same road they'd taken on Pioneer Day, and maybe he had some vague idea of going to the old farmhouse again, where he'd made that study of her on an afternoon when he'd felt there was something good in this world. That day seemed so far off now, it might as well have been decades gone, a lifetime in the past.

But Aran didn't make it to the pullout and the old metal gate. He'd begun to cry while he recounted how Gad had burned his paintings. He had seen men cry plenty of times at testimony meetings—it was almost expected then. But Aran had never seen a man crying when he wasn't in thrall to the Holy Ghost, and his own pain baffled him, made him feel like he couldn't breathe, so he pulled off the road, onto the shoulder above a deep irrigation ditch, and stayed there in that place, which was just nowhere.

He couldn't look at Linda. The tears were still coming. He wiped his eyes and watched the blackbirds flying over the sage plain and said, "He didn't burn everything, thank God. Only the paintings I'd hidden at the house. I had no idea Dad had found them. He never said a thing about them, not to me. But I do have others. I have one place Dad will never find—no one will. Thank God, he didn't get them all. He didn't get the best of my work." Aran paused. He drew a long, shuddering breath. "There are some paintings Dad can never see. He *will* never see. I'd destroy those paintings myself before I'd let them fall into my father's hands. Or anyone else's."

"Jesus, Aran."

Linda said nothing more for a long spell. She cranked down the window. A fresh breeze came in, redolent with dry dust and the far-off sourness of cattle. The coolness and the smell calmed Aran, some.

Linda took his hand. He felt he had to look at her then.

"Listen," she said, "your father is an abusive man."

"He's not."

"Listen to me. He isn't a good person, Aran, and this thing he did to you . . . it's not okay."

"He is good. He tries to be good."

"Like hell. He tries to be God."

"He's just afraid. He's a frightened person. It's worse now that my grandpa is dying. I think I've known my whole life that my dad is afraid of . . . of everything, of the world, but I didn't really *know* how scared he is till today."

"What on earth does your father have to be scared of?"

"Himself," Aran said.

"What do you mean?"

"I think he treats me this way—as if he hates me—because he sees himself in me. I knew that when I saw his own paintings right there with mine, burning in the barrel. He can paint, Linda. Tamsin told me once that he can paint—she found Dad's art, all hidden away. But I didn't realize he was so good. He'd be even better if he'd practice, if he'd let himself do it without shame. But he won't. He's convinced himself to give up his art—or to hide it, anyway—in favor of this life that doesn't make him happy. And here I am, defying him, refusing to take up the same life he's chosen for himself. That's why I think he treats me this way. I remind him of what he might have been, if only he'd been brave enough."

Linda kept her eyes on the field, the sagebrush plain beyond. But she didn't let go of Aran's hand.

"I know I ought to hate him," Aran said. "For everything, but especially for this. I think I did hate him, once. I can't anymore, not now that I understand what's in his heart. All I can do is feel sorry for him."

"Do you love him?" Linda sounded more than a little incredulous.

"I don't know. I don't think I ever have. He isn't a man you can love. He won't allow you to do it."

"My parents had their share of problems," Linda said, "God knows they did. And *do*. But I've always loved them, flaws and all. Maybe I shouldn't love them—especially my dad, who abandoned me. Abandoned us, me and my mom. I can't help it, and I've never questioned it. I've known for years that I don't want a family like the one I was stuck with. But I've never doubted for a minute that I love my parents."

"Why do you think that is?" Aran felt he was drifting, lifting up out of himself. He was somewhere far from here, and that made it safe to question her, to examine these small and bitter mysteries with a curious eye.

"I don't know," she answered. "But our parents made us—with their bodies, with their habits, with their minds. We are who we are because of them. Maybe that means there will always be a part of us that needs their love. Like an instinct."

"Do you think I'm a terrible person? For not loving my dad?"

"No." She squeezed his hand. "I don't think that. I just don't understand."

"Love has never entered into my relationship with my father. He's always been this big, solid, immovable presence—a monolith or a mountain. I never had a choice but to put up with him. You don't love the fact that the sun rises in the east. It's a thing so constant, you never think about what it might be like if one day the sun rose somewhere else. That's what it's like, being my father's son." He laughed bitterly. "And yet, knowing all that, I still can't make myself stop caring about his approval. Isn't that crazy? Isn't it stupid? Like throwing yourself at a mountain, expecting it to flinch."

Linda said, "What is it you want? I mean what do you really want, more than anything else in the world, more than you want to make your father happy?"

Aran thought for a minute before he answered. He was surprised to find that the tears had dried on his cheeks. "I don't know."

"You do know. Be brave enough to say it."

"I want to paint for a living. Not signs—art."

She let go of his hand with a little sigh, barely more than a breath. It sounded like satisfaction. "Then that's what you should be doing."

"You can't make a living from art."

"Says who?"

"Everyone. Everyone knows you can't."

"Some people must. Why shouldn't you be one of them?"

He couldn't think of a good answer. "Tamsin said the same thing to me once."

"Your sister is a pretty smart kid."

Aran smiled. "I know. But my dad won't like it one bit, if I give up on the sign shop."

"Your dad will cope. He'll have to."

"I'll have to move out," Aran said, "if I hope to do it at all. I can't quit working for my father's business and still live under his roof."

"Good. It's past time."

"I suppose I can get a job moving pipe, like Brig and Ondi do. There are always plenty of farmers looking for that kind of work."

She waited, allowing him to puzzle it out for himself.

He said, "It'll take me a few weeks of working in the fields before I can afford a place of my own."

"I have a little extra money. I'll give it to you so you can find an apartment now. Don't wait. That'll only give your dad more time to get you back under his thumb."

"I can't take your money, Linda."

"Think of it as a loan if you want. You can pay me back later, whenever you can afford it."

She turned toward the breeze. He could hear her inhaling, smelling the wind and sage. When she let her breath out again, the sound was heavy and sad.

"What's wrong?" Aran asked.

"I can't help feeling a little guilty. This fight you had with your dad—this terrible, days-long fight—it's all because of me. Sometimes I wonder if I ought to leave this town. I'm something worse than an outsider. I'm a wrecking ball. Your dad isn't a good guy, and you don't deserve to be treated the way he treats you, so I'm glad you're going to leave. But I still feel like I came out of nowhere and smashed your family apart."

"I'm glad you came out of nowhere. As for my family, I guess some things need to be smashed apart." Aran was damn sure he wasn't strong enough to do the wrecking on his own. "Even if you hadn't broken a thing, I'd still be glad you came."

She looked at him then. "I came here to make a family. Instead, I destroyed one."

Aran leaned across the space between them and kissed her. She was quiet then.

He said, "You're my family now."

27

The Farthest Corner

Aran had taken all his clothing out of the dresser drawers and stacked everything in neat rows along his narrow bed. The folded shirts, the trousers, the socks matched and rolled into small white eggs, all waited expectantly. The duffel bag lay at his feet. His hands itched to pick the bag up and stuff it full of his few belongings. And he would do it—he would. But there would be a finality in the act. Once he left, he could never come back home again. This house would no longer be his home. It would only be his past.

A light tap sounded at his door. It was Arletta. She pushed the door open a few inches, peered inside. Her face was half in shadow.

"Mom. Hi."

She glanced at the bed, the folded clothes, the bag waiting at his feet. "You're leaving," she said.

Aran didn't know how to answer. "Yes" would be too short, accusatory. Any longer explanation would seem like justification, and he didn't want to make excuses or defend his independence.

"I've known for a long time," Arletta said, "that you'd be going."

"You have?"

She pushed the door open wider. She had never looked old to Aran before, but he could see the years stealing up on her now, the gravity of her long silence taking hold.

She said, "Let's go into town and get some ice cream. Doesn't that sound good?"

It did sound good. Soon Aran and his mother were seated across from one another in the little ice cream shop off Main Street, with the old-time cash register jangling and the stereo system playing syrupy music from decades past. Arletta had brought him to that same place, that same table in the corner, many times when he was a boy. When Gad had proved too much to handle, there had always been the ice cream shop and a scoop for each of them—peach melba for Arletta, Aran's rocky road.

"How did you know I was planning to leave?" Aran asked her. "I didn't know myself—not until yesterday."

"I'm your mother. I notice everything about you, even the things you can't see on your own."

He picked the marshmallows out of his ice cream with a spoon. He had always liked saving them for last.

"I see more than anyone thinks." Arletta was airy, almost amused. She never looked up from her dish. "I know what I seem to be—a fool. A complacent, obedient, quiet little fool."

"You're not," Aran said. "I've never thought that, not about you."

"What choice have I had in this life, except to smile and go along? But I'm not empty headed. I see. I see everything, when no one else is looking."

Aran laid his spoon on the napkin. He couldn't even think about another bite now. "What did you see in me that told you I was going?"

"Peace, which none of the rest of us have."

Aran laughed. "Peace? I don't think I've ever had peace."

"You have it now. It's easy to think you haven't got any such thing when the world around you is in chaos. But I've seen a confidence in you. My boy knows who he is and where he's going. It's more than your father has ever known about himself."

Aran wanted to believe it. He thought he might become a man who knew where he was going, with enough time and peace.

"What about Tamsin?" Aran said. "She knows where she's headed better than I do." *Much better.* "She's a whole person, and I've never felt like one."

It brought a lump to his throat, admitting such a thing, saying it out loud. He spooned up more of his ice cream to hide his feelings.

"Tamsin will get carried away someday by the force of her own personality."

Arletta spoke dreamily, as if reciting a prophecy. It made Aran shiver.

Candidly, she added, "No one can feel like a whole person around your father. He won't allow it. It frightens him. But that doesn't mean you aren't whole. You'll understand what I mean when you're out there, on your own."

"A lot of things seem to frighten Dad."

"You've noticed that, too?"

Aran nodded.

"You were always observant. My far-seeing, clear-eyed boy. You got that from me, you know."

"Grandpa's cancer seems to scare him out of his wits."

"It isn't your grandpa's cancer that has your dad so upset. It's the weakening, the slowness of it, the way it makes a man smaller. And there's nothing anyone can do about it—nothing but pray."

Arletta finished her ice cream, ran the spoon along the bottom of the dish, licked the last of the melted sweetness. She seemed entirely satisfied. Aran found he couldn't take his eyes off her, though she looked down at the tabletop or at the featureless wall, and her expression was distant, hazy, permanently detached. Not the kind of expression one would expect on a woman so keen and insightful.

After a minute, Arletta said, "Your father won't allow you to leave. Not easily." She still wasn't looking at Aran. "He'll be worse now than ever before."

"That's what I was afraid of."

"He's worst when you defy him. When you tell him no without any room for argument. That's when he becomes dangerous. That's when he takes what he wants, and if it hurts you more to give it, then so much the better."

Aran realized he was shaking. He said, "Has Dad ever hurt you?"

Arletta didn't answer. She acted as if she hadn't heard. But she heard everything—Aran knew that now. Her right hand had slipped below the tabletop. Aran realized it was resting low on her stomach.

She said, "You need time to get all your things out of the house, so he's none the wiser. Then he can't stop you or make you change your mind."

"I won't change my mind. Not anymore."

"Still—I know what he's like when you cross him."

"I've only tried to live my own life."

"Exactly," Arletta said. "Next Saturday, I'll find some excuse to make your father take me all the way out to Idaho Falls. You'll have time, then, to pack up all your things and go."

"Thank you," Aran said.

"Just be sure you're gone completely before we come home."

The following Saturday, it took Aran little more than an hour to pack his belongings at the family home. He stuffed most of his clothes into the duffel. The rest he tossed into cardboard boxes with his books, the handmade pochade box under his bed, his razor and toothbrush from the bathroom. He slid his record collection into a couple of old milk crates and carried his turntable down to the car. And when his childhood room was empty of everything except the bed and the night-stand and the hollowed-out dresser, Aran left a note on his mother's piano. It said simply, *Thank you.*

He had spent the previous week in preparation. It hadn't taken long to find a job moving pipe. He was set to begin working Monday morning at the biggest potato farm in the area, the two-thousand-acre holding of Russet Burbanks that carpeted the Bench with green. Aran was glad it wasn't the same farm that employed Brig and Ondi. He needed to make the cleanest break possible if he had any hope of shaking Gad's influence.

With a signed letter of employment from the farm's foreman to prove he would have money for rent, Aran picked up Linda from her duplex and took her out to the Mooseburger for fries and shakes. They scoured the classified listings in the *Standard Journal*, circling a few likely ads with a stick of charcoal from Aran's pochade. Before the day was out, Aran had secured his apartment. He could hardly believe it was so easy. If he'd known it was only a matter of putting one foot in front of the other, he would have moved his feet long ago. There was a sick, sinking feeling deep down in his guts, underneath all the elation. That sickness told him nothing could be so simple—not where Gad was concerned. He ignored it. A new life lay before him, and he was eager to explore.

The apartment was small—one cramped bedroom, a little open area with a shabby kitchenette, an oddly long and narrow bathroom that surely had been added as an afterthought. The whole arrangement was perched above an auto body shop on the western edge of town, close enough to hear the highway when there was any traffic on it, accessible by means of a long stairway with an iron railing that vibrated under his feet when he climbed. The landlord allowed Aran to keep the sofa and armchair that were already in the place, since it was a pain in the neck to wrestle furniture up and down those stairs. The apartment was run down and beat up and needed a good cleaning, but it was his, and he loved it from the second he stepped across the threshold.

Linda paid the first month's rent. Straight away, they drove into town to the Deseret Industries thrift store, where, for a few bucks, they rounded up a mattress with box spring, bedding, and towels—well used but clean—and a whole array of chipped, mismatched dishes and cookware. They tied the bed to the roof of Aran's car and drove slowly all the way back to his new place.

Aran figured he could set up one corner of the apartment for painting. The light that came in through the south-facing windows was pretty good, at least in summer. He figured by the time the fall came around and the days were growing shorter, he'd be able to afford enough lamps to work by. And he would work, every day—every evening when his labor at the farm was done. Time was his alone now—his to command.

"You don't have to go to church at all anymore, if you don't want to," Linda said in that sly tone she used sometimes, when Aran couldn't tell whether she was joking or not.

"I do want to."

She hesitated just long enough that Aran knew it hadn't been a joke. "Of course you do. Of course."

"In fact," he said, "I'm going tomorrow. Right back at it, no reason to wait."

"To Singles Ward?"

He took her hands, pulled her closer, kissed her briefly in that warm southern light. "Why should I? I'm not single."

"You aren't going to your family's ward." Linda pulled her hands out of his grip. "Aran, don't be crazy. Your dad will go ballistic."

"Not at church, he won't. I want him to see—I want the whole town to see—that I'm not under his thumb anymore. I'm a respectable man living a straight, honest life. Whatever my past sins may be, I'm moving forward now. Let everyone in the whole place see it—my dad especially."

"I haven't been to that ward since my first Sunday in Rexburg."

"You don't have to come with me if you don't want to. I'll understand."

"Are you sure I can't talk you out of this?"

"I need to do this, Linda. For Tamsin's sake, if not my own. I left her a note when I moved out—and one for my mom, too—but she'll be hurt if she doesn't get a chance to see me again."

"You've only moved across town, not to the surface of the moon."

"Tamsin won't see it that way. So if you don't want to come—"

"Oh, I'm coming," Linda said. "Whatever happens, good or bad, I'm going to be at your side."

Next afternoon, Aran and Linda entered the chapel together. Not even a full day had elapsed since Aran had struck out on his own, yet already the story was making its way around the congregation. Gad and Arletta, Tamsin, and the twins hadn't even arrived yet. Still, people looked at Aran with open surprise and then checked themselves and hid their shock behind smooth smiles. Almost no one would approach to shake his hand. A few of the older men, members of the senior priesthood who had known Gad all their lives, moved past Aran quickly with their eyes averted so he would have no chance to speak to them, making them choose between polite custom and provoking Gad's anger.

"Jiminy Christmas," Aran muttered. "Will you look at how they're all avoiding me?"

Linda breathed out. It wasn't quite a sigh.

"Don't say 'I told you so,'" Aran said.

"I wasn't going to."

"But you're thinking it."

She glanced at him, smiling. "Aren't you thinking it, too?"

"They all want to run away from me. It's as bad as it ever was with those rumors about worshipping the Devil. I expected my dad to be cold, but I didn't think the congregation would fall in line behind him."

"Should we sit with your family?"

"Heck no. The back pew is fine."

They sequestered themselves in the farthest corner of the chapel and kept very still. Everyone had begun filing to their usual places. Sister Perks settled on the piano bench; the opening chords of the convocation hymn filled the chapel. It made Aran feel dizzy, watching those familiar proceedings from this corner, from a distance, when he had spent every Sunday of his life, more or less, with his eyes fixed on the front of the chapel, listening to the rustle of assembly behind him. He had never seen the young mothers bouncing toddlers impatiently, fathers leaning in to silence restless children with a menacing look. He had never seen the covert scramble of siblings fidgeting, nudging, kicking one another where their parents couldn't see. It brought a funny little pang to his chest. He missed his sister already. In all the excitement and urgency of moving out, he hadn't stopped to ask what would become of that bond between himself and Tamsin. The secret paintings were surely out of the question. Linda was a presence in his life now—and not a presence he would wish away. He would have to make it clear to Tamsin that they couldn't do it anymore. It was all over now. It had to be. It was part of the life he'd lived before. With a new future before him, Aran didn't need the control, the rebellion.

At that moment, his family entered. They were almost late for the sacrament meeting, so there was no time for them to mingle in conversation. They filed quickly to their usual place, where Aran's uncle Delyle had held seats for them. Gad was moving with a strange, mechanical stiffness. The swinging of his thick arms was almost robotic. Aran watched his father with an intensity he couldn't understand. What was he looking for in Gad's darkened face? Weakness, he realized. Evidence of having been diminished. But he could read nothing in Gad's low brows and hard-pressed mouth—nothing except anger, which was always there.

Tamsin kept her face turned down as she hurried along the aisle. Aran caught a glimpse of her reddened eyes, the flush along her cheekbones. She had been crying—maybe for a long time. He felt rotten to the core. And soon he would have to tell her they'd never paint together again. He would break her heart, the poor kid.

But once Tamsin had sat in her usual place—at Gad's right hand now, since Aran wasn't there as buffer—one of her friends from school leaned close and tugged on her red-gold braid. Tamsin turned her face, listening as the girl whispered quickly in her ear. Then Gad silenced them both. But Aran knew what that girl must have said to his sister. Waiting, Aran kept his attention on Tamsin even while Bishop Kimball led the opening prayer. When the congregation repeated *Amen*, Tamsin looked over her shoulder. She knew exactly where to find Aran. Their eyes locked across the vast plane of the congregation. Despite the redness of her cheeks, Tamsin smiled.

Aran and Linda fled as soon as the sacrament meeting had ended. They drove home to Aran's apartment with the windows rolled up so they could yell the whole way—wordless howls of wild tension finally unleashed, and laughter, so much laughter they were both teary by the time Aran parked his Charger outside the body shop.

They ran up the quivering stairs, and Aran slammed the door behind them and fell onto the couch next to Linda, where they went on laughing for a few minutes more, though Aran felt sometimes as if he were crying.

When that frantic energy had expended itself, they both sat for a long time in silence. Now and then, a car hummed along the highway.

Calm now, Aran said, "It was like everyone in the whole congregation picked up on Dad's anger."

"They were all trying very hard not to step on his toes," Linda said. "They tried as hard not to piss him off as I've ever seen you try."

Aran gave her a sharp look. She knew he didn't like cursing. Linda only grinned in return.

"You know what I thought, watching my dad walk in?" Aran said.

"What?"

"How ordinary he looked. Like any other man in the place. But everyone is so cautious around him. They all think he's some great fixture of the town, just because he's a Rigby, I guess. But he has no power at all, not really."

"None," Linda agreed. "He can't hurt you. He can't ruin your life, unless you let him do it."

For supper, Linda heated a frozen pizza. The oven was scarcely big enough to fit the pizza inside, and the edges burned, but it was still the tastiest thing Aran had eaten in years. They sat close together on the old couch with plates on their laps because they hadn't thought to buy a coffee table at the thrift store.

"Well, here you are," Linda said.

"Here I am. I really don't know how I'm going to make this work. I have no idea how to make an art career happen."

"You have to market yourself, dummy. Market your work."

"That's the problem. How does a guy market his work? Where do I even begin?"

"Leave that to me. I'll handle it."

She took his empty plate to the sink, began washing the dishes.

"You know how to market art?" Aran said.

"I'll figure it out. I'm a pretty smart cookie, you know."

"But why?" he asked quietly. "Why would you do all that work for me? And the money you gave me for the first month's rent on this place . . ."

Linda shut off the water. She leaned against the counter, looking as bewildered as Aran felt, like she'd just realized something momentous. Like some invisible being had bent down to whisper in her ear.

Linda never answered the question. She didn't need to. Aran went to her and put his hands on her waist, the compelling slenderness of her body. His hands slid down to the curve of her hips. He knew they were about to do something, everything, that his father wouldn't approve of. He knew they would allow themselves to be carried away by sin. He didn't care just then. He thought he probably wouldn't care ever. He would let Linda take him to any place she wanted to go.

28

CATHEDRAL OF THE WORLD

Where she wanted to go was Jackson Hole, Wyoming.

For a couple of weeks, after her shifts with the IEC finished, Linda retreated to the town library, to the periodicals, where she pawed through old art collectors' magazines, searching for leads she could follow. Eventually, she recognized a pattern in the articles and ads in the back pages of *Artforum* and *Southwest Art*. The ski town of Jackson Hole—some two hours away, just over the Wyoming border—seemed to be emerging as a new destination for high-end collectors. What luck Aran had, to live so close to this fledgling hotspot of the art world. What luck Linda had. If they'd been forced to travel all the way to San Francisco or Santa Fe—or worse, New York—the whole thing might have been out of the question. They were only a couple of broke college-aged kids. They didn't have many resources, except for Linda's stubbornness and a little pocket change for gasoline.

She jotted down the names of the likeliest galleries, knowing all the while that Aran would resist putting himself forward. He didn't seem to believe he was worthy. He thought it laughable, this idea that his art could hang alongside the modern masters. He had argued for starting small—some of the shops in Rexburg might consent to display a local landscape or two, and maybe a handful would sell over the course of a year. Maybe, Aran said, they might expand to Idaho Falls. Possibly, they'd get as far as Salt Lake City. Linda had agreed to the local angle, just to soothe his nerves. But she had seen much more of his work by then. Aran was ready for the big time.

She said nothing about the galleries in Wyoming. She spoke only of a getaway, a weekend vacation, a cozy camping trip for two. Hadn't they both earned a break? Hadn't they worked hard all summer, suffered through so much chaos? They were due for a little peace and quiet. The season was rapidly fading, the high mountain fall coming on. The valley was depleted, a flat dunnish gray, the wheat fields cut and baled into straw, the potato vines dying back, almost ready for the harvest. If they didn't go now, Linda said, they might not get another chance till the following summer.

Aran agreed to the trip. Casually, Linda told him to pack some nice clothes, just in case they decided to treat themselves to a fancy dinner in Jackson Hole.

While Aran showered, Linda slipped some of her favorite paintings from the stacks of panels that lined his apartment walls. She crept down to Aran's car and tucked the paintings under a folded blanket in the trunk, right beside the tent and sleeping bags she'd borrowed from Sandy's cousin. There was a bag from Ben Franklin in the trunk, too, containing a few ready-made frames. She was back upstairs in Aran's apartment by the time he emerged from the bathroom with a towel around his waist.

They set out for the Tetons while the morning was still fresh. Rexburg shrank to nothing on the long, straight road behind them. The turning season had curled and bent the tall grasses along the verge; all the flowers had faded to ghosts. Everything was golden or russet where it wasn't bleached and dry—the stands of poplars and cottonwoods far across the fields, the hides of cattle, the light on the wings of the little dark birds who scattered in fear of Aran's car.

Soon even the Bench had sloped gently down to meet the valley floor. That was when Linda got her first clear view of the Teton Range. She had seen the mountains, of course, from the Bench above town, but from that vantage, they had been only distant blue chips of stone, a minor disturbance on an otherwise smooth horizon. Now, as each mile brought her closer, the mountains seemed to rise with ponderous and deliberate strength, a giant stretching its limbs, waking from the earth. They grew up out of the brown foothills, towering till she thought they would blot out the whole sky and swallow the world. Vertical, bare, sharp as temple spires, the peaks brooded over the landscape like vast and immovable gods.

"Wow," she whispered.

Aran only smiled.

She couldn't take her eyes off those mountains. She pressed her cheek against the glass to stare at them in worship and wonder. Then her ears popped, and the foothills were sudden walls, and the highway dropped down into the shadow and stone of Teton Pass.

Linda forgot all about the glory of the mountains in her terror of the descent. She had never imagined a road so steep, the earth so slanted, it felt like it was sliding away beneath her. Surely the car couldn't remain on the road. Gravity would take them at any moment, rip them from solid ground—they would fall through nothing to the valley floor, which was a thousand miles below, an endless drop. Her breath came short. She clung hard to the handle of the car door as if that could save her.

"Nothing to worry about," Aran said, but Linda could see the long black tracks where wheels had locked and tires skidded, the places where trucks had plowed off the road onto ramps built for just such a catastrophe. By the time they reached the punched-in valley below the pass, on the eastern side of the Tetons, the air stank of friction. It was a wonder Aran's brakes hadn't caught fire.

On the valley floor, they made their way through a friendly pine forest, reassuring and green. Linda regained her hold on her wits. By the time they paid their fee at the entrance to Grand Teton National Park, she was immersed again in the landscape, casting reverent eyes toward the heavens, to the stark majesty of the mountains. That view struck her with a quiet thrill—the best argument anyone had ever made for the existence of an almighty God. She thought, *No wonder Aran can paint with such expression and emotion. He grew up here, in the world's own cathedral.* The glory of nature was stamped forever on his soul. Beauty must be an instinct to anyone born and bred in this land.

They pulled into a campground at Jenny Lake. Aran backed to the campsite, a knoll with a clear view: the great diagonal thrust of the mountain, all summer-beaten granite, bare and pink flushed against a blue, blue sky.

Linda bounced out of the car before Aran had even cut the engine. "Pop the trunk," she said. "I'll get the tent out."

"Hold on a minute."

Linda wouldn't wait. She didn't want to risk Aran finding the paintings under that old blanket—not yet.

The tent was one of the new geodesic models, no breeze to set up with its crisscross of flexible poles. It took a solid hour to assemble the tent and stake it out against the wind.

"You look tired," Aran said.

"You look dirty," Linda shot back.

"I could use a nap. We can go hiking around the lake later this afternoon."

Not quite able to meet his eye, Linda agreed.

They rolled out their mats and sleeping bags inside the tent, then kicked off their shoes and lay down, side by side. Aran's hand found hers straightaway. She fit her fingers between his and brooded that small, quiet thrill in her stomach, the feeling she always got when he held her hand, a feeling that the world was set for the moment in a pleasant balance. Light came in through the tent fabric, blue and sub-dued. Dozens of insects had landed on the exterior and were walking in silhouette—long-bodied things with luminous, fine-veined wings like teardrops of glass. Ordinarily, she would have been disgusted by the creatures. Now they struck her as part of the magic of that place.

Linda watched the insects for a long time. Aran seemed to be watching them, too. She could sense that he was still awake, his attention held by the otherworldly shape and motion of the creatures. In the quiet pause, she knew the time had come to tell him about the real purpose of their trip. She had to tell him sometime.

Before she could speak, Aran said softly, "Tomorrow is Sunday."

Linda waited for him to say more.

He was staring up at the roof of the tent. His eyes were narrowed, as if in contemplation of some inner pain. "It'll be the first Sunday I haven't gone to church. Except for the time I had the flu."

Linda reached for him, put her arm around his body.

"I guess it's for the best," Aran said. "The past two weeks since I moved out, my dad hasn't spoken to me at all. Not even at church."

Linda had gone back to Singles Ward, pleading with Aran to accompany her. He wouldn't. Nor would he try out one of the other wards in town. He couldn't seem to tear himself from his family's congregation. He had insisted that Gad would come around, sooner or later. His anger would ebb, and he would accept the facts: Aran was his own man now.

"It's like I don't exist anymore for everyone except Tamsin," Aran said.

"You're twenty-three. Your dad had to know you'd move out some-time. That's what people do when they grow up."

"Dad wanted to be the one to tell me when to go. That's the prob-lem. *I* decided. I did it on my own. That's what he can't forgive: the fact that I made the choice, not him."

Linda moved closer. She pressed her face against his shoulder.

"I guess I'll have to figure out where to attend church now," Aran said. "I won't go to the family's old ward if everyone treats me like a ghost. The ward across town—they'll take me. But it won't be the same."

Linda paused, weighing her words with care. "You could leave the church altogether. If you wanted to."

"It's not the church I have a problem with—not really. It isn't God who's the problem. It's everyone else who has a problem with me."

She thought, *We could move here, to the mountains.* Her heart pounded with sudden longing. *We could live far away from Rexburg, far from any town where the people watch you and judge you and expect you to fit into all the places they've made for you. We could have our own lives, our own ways, our own gods to worship. We could sing our own hymns.*

She didn't understand why she couldn't make herself say it all aloud. But she could say this: "Aran, don't be mad at me."

He turned his face on the flat camping pillow, looked into her eyes.

"We can't go hiking this afternoon."

Aran looked disappointed. "You don't want to hike?"

"I do . . . tomorrow. This afternoon we have to go to Jackson."

"Why, did you forget to pack something?"

"No, I've made some appointments. With art galleries. To show your work."

He stared at her for an agonizing eternity. Finally, he said, "I didn't bring any of my work."

"I brought some. Your best—or my favorites, anyway. I picked them out while you were in the shower. I hope you're not mad at me for making these appointments. I guess I sort of tricked you into this. I feel rotten about that, but it was the only way to get you out here and get your work into the right hands. You wouldn't believe me before, that you were ready to show in the big venues, in real galleries."

Aran sat up, too. He seemed amused, as if Linda were being naive and girlish. That almost made her angry. She wanted to slug him on the shoulder.

"It's all right," he said. "I think we'll get laughed out of every single gallery in Jackson, but I'm not mad at you. Not one bit."

"You sure?"

"I'm sure."

Linda took his face in her hands and made him look at her.

She said, "You trust me, don't you."

It wasn't a question. Aran nodded.

When they'd approached the first gallery in downtown Jackson for their three o'clock appointment, Aran had balked on the Old West boardwalk. *Feldermann Associates*, the sign on the door had read—and below that, the gallery's motto: *Masters of Western Art.*

"I'm no master," Aran had whispered.

Linda had replied, more casually than she'd felt, "Pretend you are. They'll never know the difference."

The moment they'd stepped inside the gallery, her monumental resolve had slipped. They were surrounded by paintings of astonishing quality—most of them depicting Native American scenes, cowboys on the trail, or wildlife in dramatic poses—bull elk bugling in the frost, bison stampeding through the sage, bighorn sheep locked in combat on rocky ledges. The paintings were huge, much larger than any she had seen Aran create, and all of them were in carved, gilded frames.

But the gallery's owner, Tony Feldermann, had welcomed them warmly. Linda had fallen back on her own advice, and presented Aran's small paintings in their ready-made craft-store frames with all the gravity and dignity that should have been reserved for the masterpieces hanging on the walls.

Once they'd passed Aran's work across Feldermann's mahogany desk—every bit as ornate as his frames—there was nothing to do but wait while he examined each painting in minute detail. Feldermann's expression was painfully neutral, impossible for Linda to read.

Aran was dressed in his Sunday slacks, a sweater vest with a tie underneath—Lee Christiansen's favored style. He fidgeted in his leather chair. Linda had worn her best, most conservative dress, navy blue with lace at the collar. She hoped her hair didn't look too much like she'd been lounging around a campsite. She held herself staunchly upright, gazing at Mr. Feldermann with an easy, confident, patient expression, though her heart was pounding in her ears and she felt sick to her stomach, positively sick that she'd had such a harebrained idea and had dragged Aran through this crushing experience. What had she been thinking? She wanted to snap at Aran, tell him to pull himself together and stop all that shifting and shuffling. She wanted to scream from the tension of waiting.

When she knew she couldn't take another second of the silence, when she was ready to stand up and say, *Excuse me, Mr. Feldermann, we're sorry for wasting your time,* the man looked up from his perusal of Aran's work. He smiled.

"These will need better frames, of course," Feldermann said, "but I would like to show your work, Mr. Rigby. In fact, I believe my clients will take to your style. Let's start with these pieces, and I'll ask you to ship me six more of similar size that you'd like to show. If those sell, we can talk about a broader strategy. I'm thinking a featured show to highlight your work. You'll need to do some larger pieces, though—much larger. Three feet to a side, at least. How does that sound?"

Linda and Aran stared at one another. She knew her carefully constructed air, the facade of the poised, self-confident manager, had vanished in an instant. She was a wide-eyed kid, delighted and surprised, and she didn't care one bit if Feldermann knew it.

"That sounds wonderful," Aran stammered. "It sounds great."

They returned to their campsite by sunset, stuffed full from the expensive dinner they'd had in celebration. Linda had insisted they stop at a bakery in town just before the shop closed. She'd bought a small chocolate cake and asked the baker to ice "Master of Western Art" on top. When she opened the cake box at the campsite and showed it to Aran, he laughed so hard, a crow began to scold in reply. Then he kissed her, long and lingering, pulling her body against his.

"This is as much your victory as mine," Aran said.

"I know it."

She was warm with pride—glowing, and she knew that, too. She'd never before thought of herself as a marketer, a manager, but now she couldn't help feeling as if she had a knack for the work. She had taken a gamble and it had paid off, but it had been careful guesswork, the plan neatly laid and meticulously executed. Aran knew his talent. Now it seemed Linda had found a talent of her own.

"We make a pretty good team," she said.

Aran lit a fire in the small metal ring. They dragged a wooden bench closer to the flames as the chill of a mountain evening set in. They dug into the cake with tin camping forks and ate till they couldn't hold another bite. Then, as the red sunset faded and a dense blue night drew in, Linda took her guitar from its case and played.

At first, they sang happy songs, even funny ones, the kind you always sing at campfires. But the night spread itself around them, wide and lonely, and the ring of their firelight was very small. Linda thought of everything Aran had said that day in the tent. About his family not speaking to him—about Gad treating him like a ghost. Aran would have a real career now, or at least the start of one, and Linda would have a real career, too, if she stuck by Aran's side. She should have been thrilled. She wasn't—not entirely. She had ruined the family Aran loved. God knew she'd never meant to do it, and Aran was better off without his father, yet still . . .

Linda set her guitar aside and rose from the bench.

"You okay?" Aran said softly.

She didn't answer. She walked to the crest of the knoll, their quiet, isolated campsite. The great ancient slab of the mountain canted into the sky above, up into the pale and numberless stars. There, where Aran couldn't see her face, she allowed the tears to fall. She couldn't tell whether she wept from happiness or sorrow. With an inward throb of premonition, Linda thought she might never again be able to separate the two.

29

LOVE ONE ANOTHER

The day was already scorching by noon, the kind of heat you find sometimes at the end of summer, when the season seems to redouble its efforts out of sheer bitter will. The sun slapped down against the glaring walkways at the edge of the campus, rebounding into Tamsin's eyes. She would have given anything to stand on one of the smooth, manicured patches of lawn, where at least the sun wouldn't feel so vicious. But the honor code at Ricks College included a mandate that all students must keep off the grass, in addition to maintaining moral purity and grooming standards. Tamsin didn't attend the college, of course, but most of the twenty or so kids who'd turned out for the demonstration did. They were already sticking their necks out enough by openly supporting environmental policies. If anyone set foot on the grass, the entire group could be expelled for violating the honor code. So she screwed up her face against the glare and suffered the pounding heat as gracefully as she could manage, searching for Linda in the crowd.

Linda had been as good as her word. She had treated Tamsin like a real friend all summer long, even after she'd begun dating Aran. Linda was certainly the most exciting friend Tamsin had ever known, with her vexing job with the Environmental Council, her tight clothes, the aura of haughty self-possession she wore without knowing it. They had gone for burgers and shakes at least once a week and spent their Saturday mornings together at Porter Park, exchanging books and talking over what they'd read the week before. Linda had loaned a certain paperback to Tamsin. *Slouching Towards Bethlehem*, a collection of essays by a journalist from California—a woman who, Linda said, could see all the people she wrote about exposed for who they really were. Tamsin had read that book twice already, cover to cover. She had marveled at a secular world every bit as terrible and broken as the church had always claimed it was—and had marveled, too, that the world in its brokenness was far more beautiful than any rigid perfection. Tamsin and Linda had even climbed the water tower one more time, just for the heck of it, to look down on the whole town instead of feeling Rexburg watching them.

Aran was gone from the family home, and the two weeks Tamsin had spent without him had been bleak as the dead of winter. Even so, this had been the best summer she could remember. Linda's friendship had made her feel grown up and capable. Linda's ideas had left a permanent thrill of excitement in Tamsin's chest. Everything Tamsin had once thought immutable had become friable in Linda's hands. The city girl could crumble every edifice in her fist: the necessity of obeying authority, the default wisdom of men, the idea that some ideas were too dangerous to be entertained. Even the existence and nature of God Himself was something Linda shrugged at, and Tamsin was amazed that it could be so simple. That was all it took to break free: a shrug, and the willingness to turn your back on the life you'd always known.

With all of Linda's shocking ways, Tamsin had been dead certain she would turn up at the protest. But there was no sign of her among the college kids with their signs and their chanted slogans. Tamsin had a sinking feeling she knew exactly where Linda must be. The past two weeks hadn't only been grim because of Aran's absence. Linda had been harder to come by than ever before. Tamsin had seen her only briefly, and not as often as she would have liked, in the days since Aran had left.

Of course, Aran had invited Tamsin to his new apartment for pizza once, and Linda had been there—Linda was probably always there when she wasn't working out in the fields. Aran's place was small and run down, and the noise from the auto shop below had been alien, unsettling, but despite all that, an air of freedom and rightness had filled the place, sweetening the two hours Tamsin had spent on her visit. Aran had been tired from his work on the farm. That was why, he'd said, he hadn't seen Tamsin since moving out. Working all day moving pipe, then painting in the evenings till the light went bad—he didn't have much time for anything else.

It didn't seem fair that Tamsin should lose her brother and her new friend, both, in the same twist of fate, while she was forced to remain in the confines of her family. She was half tempted to give up on the protest and go . . . where? Not home. Home was too small and hostile now. To the park, maybe, to read a book like she'd done that first day when she'd met Linda.

Once the chanting and the sign waving really got underway, though, Tamsin forgot her frustration. Someone handed her a placard stapled to a long wooden stake. The sign read, *SAVE OUR RIVER*. It felt awkward in her hands, but she fell into the rhythm of the chants and bobbed and waved her placard in time to the words, and before long, she was hollering along with the rest.

At least an hour passed. Maybe another. Students who hadn't joined in the protest jeered as they went from class to class. Passing cars with lowered windows emitted strange disembodied shouts, which Tamsin could never hear clearly because the sound was warped and faded on one end by the motion. The shouts came more often than encouraging beeps from sympathetic drivers. Those were few and far between.

A group of boys walked up from the athletic field, carrying javelins from track practice. They paused at the corner of the square, laughing and pointing. Tamsin couldn't hear what they were saying, but their mocking expressions were clear enough. The protesters chanted even louder in response. *Hey-hey, ho-ho, the Teton Dam has got to go!* A wild surge of energy and power came over Tamsin. There was something delicious about standing up in front of her whole town, declaring, *I'm not like the rest of you.* She had wanted to do it much sooner than this. She ought to have done it years ago.

She was so carried away by that welling strength that she failed to notice the other demonstrators faltering around her, falling quiet, stirring with agitation. Someone nearby cried out, "Hey, what are you doing, mister?" Tamsin turned in time to see her father pushing through the crowd, making straight for her, red faced and furious.

Tamsin skittered back along the path. He was on her in a flash, though, seizing her by the arm, dragging her toward the street.

"Get your hands off her," one of the other girls yelled.

"She's my daughter," Gad shot back, because he thought that gave him the right.

Tamsin tried to pull away. Gad's grip only tightened, viselike, painful.

"Let go," she said. "You can't treat me this way!"

He went on hauling her toward the road, where his flatbed truck idled at the curb. "I can't believe you would shame me this way, Tamsin—shame our whole family. Hanging around with communistic trash—"

"God, Dad, McCarthyism is over!"

He jerked her closer. Tamsin could feel his hot breath, his barely bridled rage. "Don't take the Lord's name in vain."

Gad ripped the sign from her hand and threw it into the grass. The wood left a splinter in her palm. Far behind, the protest had broken down into helpless murmurs.

Gad opened the passenger door of the truck, said shortly, "Get in."

Tamsin got in and slammed the door hard. A moment later, Gad climbed into the driver's seat and pulled away from the curb.

"I can't believe you would do something like this." His voice was thick with offense. "My own daughter, humiliating me."

"This has nothing to do with you."

"It has everything to do with me! Do you know how I found out you were here? Bishop Kimball called me and told me he'd seen you. The bishop of our own church, Tamsin!"

"Bishop Kimball should mind his own business."

"Now you're asking for a smack."

Tamsin turned her face to the window so he couldn't see her rolling eyes. Gad hadn't paddled her since she'd been a little kid. He wasn't about to start again now.

"What on earth were you thinking?" Gad demanded. "And with your grandfather so sick? What if he finds out? The shame alone might be enough to kill him."

"Give me a break. I'm not going to kill Grandpa with a protest sign. For Pete's sake, someone in this town needs to stand up for what's right."

"What's right? You think the dam has anything to do with questions of morality?"

"I didn't mean morality—"

"I'll tell you what's not right, Tamsin DeLene: my daughter in the company of a bunch of long-haired, freeloading, sinful freaks."

She laughed bitterly. "Long haired? Those were all students at the college! Only girls can have long hair at that school, or they'll get kicked out for violating the honor code!"

"They won't be students for long. Word is going to spread and every one of those un-American bastards will be kicked out of that school for good, you mark my words."

"They can't be expelled for protesting. It's a constitutional right."

"In this town they can."

Tamsin refused to look at her father. She suspected he might be correct. She suspected that laws and rights were insubstantial things, more than half fantasy. She thought the only rules that mattered were the ones everyone agreed collectively to uphold. The town seemed to tighten around her. The air was thick inside the cab, and hot from her anger.

She said, "When I go to college—"

"You will not be attending college."

"It isn't your decision to make!"

"This family has limited resources. We aren't rich. Brig and Ondi will go to college once they've completed their missions. That's the most we can afford."

"Why didn't you send Aran to school?"

Gad cut her a dark look. No one had dared to mention Aran since he'd moved out. Tamsin held his eye, steady, waiting.

He ignored the question. "Higher education isn't necessary for a woman. You can learn everything you need to know about running a household from your mother, and from the women at church."

"Isn't necessary?" A sharp, half-strangled sound came from her throat. She thought it might have been a laugh. Maybe she was gagging. "Since when do you get to decide what's necessary for me and what isn't?"

"I'm your father. That's my job."

"I *am* going to college."

"You've got a hard wake-up call coming your way, young lady—"

"I don't want your money. I'll pay my own way."

He looked at her again, narrow eyed, suspicious. "How?"

"I'll get a job, like a normal person."

Gad's knuckles went white. He was gripping the steering wheel so tightly, Tamsin almost expected it to crumble in his hands. "Women do not work outside the home."

They were pulling into the driveway by then, so Tamsin judged it was safe enough to answer. "Linda works."

She threw the door open and bounced out of the truck before Gad could stop her, before he had even halted beside his workshop. Tamsin flew across the lawn, through the kitchen, up the stairs to her bedroom. Sweat ran down her back and stank under her arms. She tore off the sun hat, her blouse, kicked off her skirt, left everything in a pile on the floor. Her bedroom window was shaded by one of the poplars out in the yard, so the air was a little cooler there. Heat and moisture dissipated from her skin. She stood for a long moment in her bra and underpants, hands on hips, listening to the slight downstairs sound of her mother playing the piano. The opening bars of "Love One Another" played into the silence. Pause. Arletta didn't proceed into the rest of the music, but played the opening again, and again. The kitchen door banged open, then Gad's feet came heavy on the stairs.

"Tamsin," he said outside her door.

"Go away."

She heard the doorknob turn. Calmly, she faced the door and allowed it to open. Gad slammed it shut again immediately, the second he saw her bare skin.

"For heaven's sake," he said. "Why didn't you tell me you were undressed?"

"I told you to go away."

"I'm very disappointed," Gad said through the door, through the repeating music. "You've been willful and disobedient for too long now."

Tamsin took her backpack from her closet, removed the spray cans, and began packing a few things—clothes, her coin purse (not that it had any money in it), a couple of books. The air was crisp around her.

The sweat had almost dried. She felt cool, steady, certain of herself, the way she imagined Linda felt all the time.

"I'm going to call in some brothers from the church to give you a blessing," Gad said. "It'll help you get your head back on your shoulders. I pray it'll show you the right path for a young woman to walk. You aren't on the proper path now, that's for sure. You've fallen into sin, but . . ."

Whatever else he said made little impression on Tamsin. She no longer heard him. She looked regretfully at her record player and all the innocent church-approved sleeves with contraband rock music hidden inside. She wished there was some way to take her records along, but without a car of her own, it was out of the question. She might convince Aran or Linda to give her a ride back home on Sunday, when the family would be at church. She could sneak off with her turntable then.

Tamsin took her only pair of jeans from the dresser, which she was permitted to wear when she weeded the garden or helped her mother with the canning. She pulled the jeans on. Then a T-shirt, years old, tight enough now to cling to her body like one of Linda's tops.

Gad had talked himself out, it seemed. When he spoke her name again, he sounded tentative, almost frightened.

Tamsin slipped her feet into her sneakers, lifted the heavy pack to her shoulders, and opened the door. Gad flinched, dropping his eyes. Maybe he'd expected she would still be undressed. She pushed beyond her father without a word.

"Where do you think you're going?" Gad said.

Downstairs, the piano had stopped.

Tamsin hurried down the hall. The muscle of her bicep still ached where he'd grabbed her. She went down the stairs and past her mother. Arletta stood in the kitchen with her arms folded, looking at Tamsin directly, with a clear-eyed understanding.

Tamsin paused while Arletta surveyed her—jeans, tight shirt, the pack on her back. Tamsin's mouth opened, as if she wanted to say something, but she couldn't think of a single word, not one word of explanation. Arletta tilted her head toward the kitchen door, a sly, considering gesture.

"Stop her," Gad said. "Tamsin, you can't do this."

"Oh, leave her be," Arletta answered. "She'll be fine."

~

By the time Tamsin reached Aran's apartment out on the highway, she was covered in fresh sweat and her head was throbbing from the effort. Riding her bike with that damn heavy pack had been harder than she'd expected. She left her bike under the wrought-iron stairs and climbed up to Aran's door.

Every step she ascended made her feel sicker and smaller. So had each mile she'd ridden away from home. She'd thought that once she was free from Gad, she would be like a bird taken from its cage and tossed up into the air, dizzy and light with an abundance of new possibility. But Gad's influence seemed to follow her across the town. She knew her father was backward and frightened, knew he hated himself more than anyone else. Knowing it didn't make any difference. She had defied her father in a way that could never be forgiven. Something deep and inborn trembled at the knowledge—something that felt very much like terror. She had walked out into a howling wilderness. There was no going back again.

Aran answered the door the moment Tamsin knocked. He had a paintbrush in his hand. His radio was playing softly, the way it had always played in the shack out in the wheat field. At the sight of him, Tamsin sucked in a great, shuddering breath and began to cry.

Aran took her inside, sat her down on the old brown sofa. He rinsed his brush in a can of turpentine, then got her a glass of tepid water and made her drink the whole thing in slow sips before she could talk.

"I can't live with him anymore," Tamsin said—calm now, composed, but still astounded and disappointed over the bleak need inside her, the fear-love-turmoil where her father should have been.

"You'll be eighteen soon," Aran said. "You don't have to tough it out much longer."

"Don't I?" She stared at her brother pointedly. "How long did it take you to move out?"

Aran looked down, ashamed.

"I'm sorry," Tamsin said. "I didn't mean to hurt you."

"You've had a rough day. It's all right."

"No, it's not. I never want to hurt you." The tears came again. "You're the only person I love in all the world."

"Don't cry."

"Dad has been awful since you left, Aran, just awful. It's like the whole house is a bomb flying through the air and we're all waiting for it to hit the ground. He says I can't go to college. But I don't care what he says, I don't care. I'm going anyway."

She stood suddenly and took hold of her shirt, about to pull it over her head.

"Tamsin," Aran said.

She let her arms fall. Looked at him, waiting, knowing already what was coming.

"We can't. We can't do that . . . thing anymore."

"Painting?" she said. "It's just painting, Aran. It's not anything bad."

His eyes were still fixed on the floor. Like he was afraid to see her. "I don't know what to call it, painting or something else, but I know it can't happen here."

Quietly, she said, "The old shack, then."

"I don't think we should do it at all, not anywhere."

Tamsin sank back onto the couch. Somehow that felt like the day's hardest blow, knowing it was all over—the beautiful things she and Aran had made together out there in the solitude where no one could find them, no one could judge them. And it was worse, even worse, because Tamsin understood the source of this new and terrible loss. A friend wasn't supposed to hurt you. A friend wasn't supposed to take from you the only thing that mattered, the only thing that let you know you were real.

"It's because of Linda, isn't it?" Tamsin said.

"Yes." He sounded resolute now. "She's coming over soon—"

"Haven't you told her?"

"About what?"

"Don't give me that. You know what I'm talking about."

"God, no, Tamsin. I can't tell her about the paintings."

"*Our* paintings."

"She wouldn't understand. I don't understand. I don't know why I ever let you pose in the first place. I should have put a stop to it long ago."

Tears again. They'd been just below the surface, Tamsin realized, this day and every day of her life. She said, "You don't understand?"

"You do? What should we call it, this thing we've been doing together? There isn't a name for it. There isn't a name for what we are to each other. We aren't just brother and sister. You know we're something different, something more. And I can't even tell if it's a sin or not, if it's evil or not. I've asked myself a thousand times. I've prayed, but I never get any answer."

"How can you think that, Aran? Evil?" The paintings—the clear, unobstructed sight of herself—had been the only good and righteous thing Tamsin had ever known.

"I'm sorry," Aran said, awkward, guilty. "I just don't know what to make of this. I've never known what this is between us, why we do the things we do."

She forced herself to look up at him, though it cut her to see him in that moment, his doubt and his distance. "Those paintings of me are the best work you've ever done. You know that."

He sighed. "I know."

"Nothing else you've painted can touch them. Nothing even comes close."

Aran nodded.

"And you want to give it all up now, just because you have a girlfriend?"

"I want . . ." Aran ran his hands through his hair. Then he clutched his hair in his fists, as if he were trying to rip the thoughts right out of his head, pull them into the light where he could see them and sort them into some kind of order. "I wanted this to end long ago. I want it never to have happened. And I want to keep doing it forever, God help me, because nothing else I paint is the same. Nothing feels the same, nothing is so true."

"Then we can't stop," Tamsin said, weeping.

"This is sinful. It's wrong."

"Wouldn't it be a worse sin, to not bring something beautiful into the world?" This hard, ugly world; this dry, flat world; this red-faced, shouting world.

"How can those paintings be beautiful, how, when I'm so afraid of them, when I feel so ashamed of having made them? How can that be beauty?"

He crumpled onto the couch, at its opposite end, as far from Tamsin as he could get.

She said, "Maybe it isn't the paintings that are sinful. Maybe what's sinful is a world that tells you to turn your back on beauty."

"Those paintings are dangerous, Tamsin."

"I know." It was what she loved most about them.

"No one can ever see."

"You've said the same thing every time we've done it, every time we've painted together."

"It's true. They would destroy me—ruin any chance I might have for a career of my own."

"Beauty and truth can never destroy you. They come from you. They are you." She paused. A new realization had dawned. She wondered why she'd never seen it before. "The paintings would destroy Dad, though."

"I won't do it to him—ruin his life."

"Why not? He ruined our lives."

"Because I pity him," Aran said, and started to cry.

He tried to brush the tears away, but Tamsin saw, and was astonished. She leaned back into the dusty old couch, staring at the glare of sun through the window, the half-drawn blinds. How could anyone feel sorry for Gad?

"What happens if I really do make it—if I turn this all into a career?" He gestured vaguely toward his easel. "You think Dad will forgive me for proving him wrong, succeeding where he never had the guts to try? He'll hate me all the more, because he hates himself."

"All the better reason to show those paintings to the world. If Dad isn't going to forgive you anyway—if he's only going to get meaner and more hurtful—then why not let your best work out? Why not let our paintings do what they're going to do, and bring Dad to his knees? To hell with the consequences."

"I don't have vengeance in my heart."

"I have vengeance enough for both of us."

He smiled timidly, even laughed a little. But then he shook his head. "If we only had Dad to think about, I might agree. But there's Mom, and the twins. And Linda. I can't hurt her that way. She's everything to me."

Those words made a peculiar hollow in Tamsin's chest. She thought of what he'd said before, that they weren't just brother and sister, but something infinitely greater. She felt that fresh, new vacancy inside herself—the place where Aran once had been. The place where he would reside no longer, not now that he had Linda, who was everything. Now, at last, Tamsin could define them—herself and Aran. She could find the words for what they were: One soul torn apart by a cosmic mistake, the cruel impulse of a careless god. One soul in two bodies, opposite, male and female. A fractured thing that had somehow found a way to make itself entire.

And now they must break themselves again. For Linda's sake. Tamsin could have hated Linda for that, but she loved Linda just as much as Aran did. Aran's heart was Tamsin's own. Whatever he loved, Tamsin was compelled to love, too.

"Tell me this, at least." She was calm now with despair. "Are the paintings safe? You didn't destroy them. You didn't burn them up like Dad did to the others."

"They're safe. I left them in the shack. I didn't know what else to do with them. I couldn't bring them here, where Linda might find them, and I'll never be able to destroy them."

Tamsin nodded. She was grateful for that small mercy, if she was to have nothing else.

"Where can I go?" she finally said. "Where can I stay? I don't know if I'll ever be able to look at Dad again without wanting to burn the whole world to the ground."

"You can stay here till things cool off at home. It'll get better, I promise. You won't feel this way forever."

"Yes I will. But I might be able to put up with him a while longer, till my last year of school is finished and I can go away on my own."

"That's the spirit," Aran said. "I've only got this couch to sleep on. It's not especially comfortable, but it'll do. You can stay here with me till you feel strong enough to go back home."

Tamsin nodded mutely. She was unspeakably tired, as if her breath and blood had all drained away. She wanted to sleep for hours, for days. Slowly, she keeled over on the couch and curled her legs against her body. Aran stood and watched her for a long time. She could feel his eyes on her, protective yet baffled, helpless as Tamsin was helpless to cast off the weights they both dragged. At length, Aran returned to his easel and picked up his brush. The static crackled on the radio. Tamsin surrendered to sleep.

30

THE PATRIARCHAL GRIP

Leave her be. Leave her be.

Gad was standing on the open plain, among the sage and the long black scars of lava. The sun was high overhead and bright, and brighter still along the ground. Gad lifted his arm to shield his eyes. The glare bounced up from below. A wind moved, biting into his body. He looked down, saw that he wore nothing but his temple garments, stark white, bone white. That was when he knew for certain he was dreaming.

Far on the horizon—in a collision of light and sky where horizon should have been—he could see a girl's figure, a woman's figure, haloed by the glare. He remembered he'd been looking for Tamsin. He'd been desperate to find her, terrified by the feel of her slipping out of his hands, beyond his reach, where he couldn't protect her from the dangers of the world.

"Tamsin!" he cried.

He stumbled forward, into the cold and the light. The sound of water slapping around his ankles came to him first, then the slow, heavy impediment of trying to wade through a river, then a sensation of wetness. Gad realized the valley was drowning. Water had come from somewhere—from everywhere—and rushed in to cover the earth, and it was the flood that was responsible for all that blinding light, the water reflecting the sunlight from a low and sinister angle.

He called to Tamsin again. The woman on the horizon was too far to hear him, much too far. But squinting, he could see her turn to look back.

Leave her be.

Was it Tamsin's voice, or Arletta's? Was that Arletta out there in the drowning world? If so, where had their daughter gone?

He kept splashing forward, faster, faster. His arms thrashed the air for balance. The water was rushing all around him, rising to his knees, then higher, soaking the cuffs of his temple garment. Water gushed into the rents of the earth, filling black channels between the crags, running to the horizon, which was where Gad had to get to before it was too late, before Tamsin was gone forever.

He lurched upright in his bed. Gasping for breath, pressing a hand to his racing heart, he saw that Arletta was sitting up, too, staring around the dark room in confusion or alarm. The telephone was ringing.

Gad sprang from bed, hurried out into the living room. He didn't pause to turn on a light. He knew the way by feel, and there was no time, no time for anything. Tamsin had run off. He remembered that now. She had run away from home, and Arletta had done nothing to stop her, Arletta had said to let her go, and now the sheriff was calling with news no father could bear.

He took the phone from its hook and pressed it to his ear, but he couldn't speak a word. Whoever was on the other line had heard him pick up, all the same.

"Gad, is that you?"

He made himself answer. Forced out the word. "Yes."

"It's me—Delyle."

His brother. His eldest brother. What did Delyle have to do with Tamsin?

"Mother just called me," Delyle said. "Pop is pretty bad. She wants all us boys to head over to their place and give Pop a blessing."

A curious intermingling of relief and sadness moved through Gad's body. It left him weak, trembling. He propped himself up against the sideboard. "Now?"

"Mom sounded pretty urgent. I don't know for sure, Gad, but this could be it."

Gad craned his neck to see the clock in the kitchen. The radium hands glowed a faint green in the darkness. It was almost midnight.

"Of course I'll be there," Gad said. "If that's what Mother wants and what Pop needs."

He hung up the phone. Arletta had gotten out of bed and stood in the shadows of the hall, just outside their room, wrapped in an old, faded dressing gown.

"It's Pop," Gad told her. "Mother thinks he needs a blessing. Tonight—right now."

"I'll get some clothes for you," Arletta said, and turned away.

"I thought . . ."

Arletta paused when Gad spoke. His hesitation caught her up short. He said, "I thought someone was calling about Tamsin."

"There's no need to worry about her," Arletta said.

Gad dressed and ran a comb through his hair and took his old copy of the Scriptures from the bookshelf. In a daze, still reeling from his dream as much as Delyle's phone call, he drove to his parents' house—the small rambler halfway up the Bench, perched above the college campus. Gad's parents had moved there after his father retired. The family home on Ricks Avenue was too big for them, with all their children grown. Gad's father had given the Rigby homestead to him, out of all his sons. Gad had never understood why. It should have been Delyle who'd received it, being the eldest. Gad had always harbored a suspicion that the gift of the old family home had been meant as a sop or an apology—a trade-off for the dream Pop had demanded Gad place upon the altar of sacrifice, the career he'd yearned for as a painter or an illustrator. Gad had done his part, played the role that was expected of him. And he had been given his reward.

By the time he reached his parents' house, several cars were already parked in the driveway and along the starlit road. He recognized Delyle's, and his younger brother Jerry's. And there was the flashy new Triumph owned by his nephew Direlle, who was only one year older than Aran but already had a good little wife and two kids with another on the way, a proper career at the local newspaper—a proper life. As he pulled to the curb, he saw Bishop Kimball driving down from the Bench in the opposite direction. They both stepped out into the night at the same time.

Gad swallowed hard as the bishop approached.

"Brother Rigby. Gad."

"How are you, Bishop?"

"Blessed to be here with your family during such a difficult time."

Kimball reached out and took Gad's hand in greeting. The bishop's forefinger pressed into the underside of Gad's wrist. It was one of the tokens given in the temple. Gad knew the bishop had meant the gesture as a silent consolation. He had only intended to brace Gad up, remind him of the eternal nature of family, the surety of the Lord's grand design. Instead, Gad withered inside. His daughter had run off. His eldest son had abandoned the place Gad had made for him in the world, striking out in his own direction, without need or respect for his father. And this man standing before him, this man gripping his hand, had yet to grant his other two children the dignity and honor they deserved. It was all Gad's doing, his failure as a man. A righteous and worthy patriarch didn't just watch as his family fell apart. Yet Gad was helpless to put the pieces of his small eternity back together. The bishop knew it was all Gad's failing. Surely the Lord knew it, too.

"Let's go inside," Kimball said. "Your brothers must be there already."

A light was burning in the back room where Gad's father lay. He and Kimball moved toward it. The light made him blink and tear up, like the glare inside his dream had done, the sun reflecting on water. He felt as if he moved toward an impossibly far horizon.

In the lighted room, he found his mother, a timid, flitting creature, and his brothers and his nephew gathered at the bed. Gad scarcely saw any of them. Weeks had passed since he'd set eyes on his father. He couldn't reconcile that this small, white, wrinkled thing could be the man he had known and feared for his entire life. All the power had been drained from his father's body. The authority that had once felt as permanent as Scripture had blown away like dust. Gad's father lay on his side, half propped on pillows, curled into himself. He looked weightless and dry, like an artifact, like a mummy. The transformation and finality terrified Gad. He found all he could do was stare and breathe.

Delyle and Jerry had no such trouble. They were talking quietly to their mother, putting their arms around her shoulders, comforting her. And young Direlle was stroking Pop's white hair and his bony shoulder with a tenderness that made Gad hollow with longing.

Delyle crossed the small room. "Thanks for coming," he said quietly. "I only wish the rest of our brothers could be here, too."

Bishop Kimball took a small glass vial from his pocket. "Ordinarily, I'm happy to perform either the anointing or the sealing, but the Spirit has moved me to ask you fellows to do it. You're his two oldest boys—or the oldest who can be present, anyhow. Delyle, why don't you anoint your father for his blessing, and Gad, you give the sealing."

Delyle accepted the container of consecrated oil.

"I can't," Gad said quietly. "I can't do the sealing. I'm not worthy."

Bishop Kimball's brows lifted. "Of course you are."

"I have too much . . ." Gad couldn't force the word out. *Fear*. He shook his head, gestured for his brother Jerry, said, "You do the sealing."

All the men pressed in around the bed, Gad and his nephew to one side, his brothers and the bishop to the other. Their mother perched at the foot of the mattress, a gray and frightened bird.

Delyle dabbed his fingers in the oil, then touched them lightly to their father's brow. He placed his hands on Pop's head, recited his full name, asserted the authority of his priesthood. Gad felt none of that same authority within. He felt nothing but a void and a long black waiting, a certainty that this would be him someday, a curled skeletal thing half-conscious in a rumpled bed. Then Delyle was finishing the anointing prayer, and it was time for all the men to join together for the sealing.

They each placed their right hands on Pop's pallid brow, their left hands on the shoulder of the man next to them. Bishop Kimball reached across the bed, his fingers just brushing Direlle's arm. Gad was nearest the headboard, so he was obliged to lay both his hands on his father. As Jerry delivered the blessing, imploring Heavenly Father to grant strength and comfort to this man who had served Him so faithfully all his life, Gad could feel Pop stirring under his touch. A twitch, a small, thready pulse, an instinct toward life—not the life beyond in eternity but the one here and now, the one that was all any man could be sure of, if he looked deep in his heart, if he was honest with himself.

When it was over, Pop settled into sleep. His breathing was easier. Bishop Kimball had tears in his eyes. Gad and his brothers each kissed their mother on her cheek and Direlle wrapped her in his arms.

"I'll stay with Mom tonight," Delyle said to Gad. "But I'll walk you out to your truck."

On the sidewalk, Delyle caught Gad by his arm. "Are you all right? You looked so pale in there. And what was that business with the sealing—saying you weren't worthy?"

Gad exhaled raggedly. "I don't know, Delyle. Lately, I feel as if I've got nothing left inside of me."

"What the heck do you mean?"

"A man is supposed to be strong, not shrunken down to nothing."

"Pop is old," Delyle said. "He has cancer. It happens to the best of us, and he was always the best of us."

Gad stared out into the veil of night. He hadn't been talking about their father, but himself. He would end up like his own father someday, small and helpless, breakable, with no eternity to comfort him. Once more he longed to speak of it, the fear that lived inside of him. Fear of the End of Days, all the days Gad had ever known, the days he'd spent working toward righteousness and nothing else. To admit his own terror—of death, of life, of his father—was an insurmountable fear all its own. He could only shake his head and breathe in the night air and wonder what the difference was between them—himself and his brothers, and the bishop, and every other man he knew. What flaw in his character held him back from a perfect faith? All his life, Gad's faith had been colored by fear. How could he achieve immortality and conquer death if he lacked a perfect faith?

"You're worthier than you think," Delyle said.

"I wish I could believe that."

"Cut yourself some slack, Gad. You're only upset because Pop is so sick."

He almost said, *My children are gone, or will all be gone soon.* He didn't want Delyle to know about his shame.

Instead, he patted his brother on the shoulder, a hearty slap, as if he had already shaken off what troubled him. "You're right. I'll feel better once I've had some time to pray about it."

"That's the spirit," Delyle said. "Now go home and get some sleep."

Gad would go home. But he wouldn't try to sleep again that night. The dream about the flooded plain and Tamsin out there on the water was still too present, too clear. If he slept now, the nightmare would only return to him, and he wasn't sure he could wake himself before the waters rose.

31

A Tender Beast

Out by Aran's apartment, on the edge of town, there was no place to walk except along the highway. Linda led the way down the staircase to the parking lot, and from there, out to the dry margin of hard-packed earth between the road and the wasteland beyond. Tamsin followed, sniffling but otherwise quiet. There were no streetlights, but the sky was clear. A half moon rode high and remote among the stars, its silver light flattening everything, compressing distance, so there seemed no difference between far and near, between the town and foothills or the mountains way out there on the horizon where Linda and Aran had camped.

The night was chilly, autumn coming soon. Tamsin wore only her T-shirt, and when Linda glanced over, she noticed the poor kid was shivering, her thin, freckled arms wrapped around her body. Linda took off her jacket and draped it around Tamsin's shoulders.

"Why did you want to go for a walk tonight?" Tamsin said. "And here, of all places, along the highway?"

Linda ribbed her. "Why did you agree to come with me?"

The girl's smile had something fragile about it, something ready to break. To save Tamsin from crying again, Linda told her the truth.

"Sometimes it's easier to talk girl to girl. You know—without any guys around, even if the guy is your brother."

Tamsin put her arms through the jacket's sleeves. "All right. What do you want to talk about?"

"What happened at home. To you, I mean. You've been at Aran's place for two days now. What made you run away?"

Linda had come to Aran's apartment as planned—as she did most nights, nowadays, with half a tuna casserole for dinner. Sandy had frowned when she'd taken the leftovers from the fridge and said, "I'm off to Aran's. See you when I see you." Sandy didn't approve of Linda staying the night. It made Linda a little sick to her stomach, knowing she was such a disappointment to her friend, but she couldn't deny any longer what she knew in her heart to be true. When she was with Aran—when they were alone together, and in one another's arms—she felt cleaner and more sanctified than she'd ever felt at church. Sandy could think whatever she would. Someday, Linda would make her understand. For now, there was worship to be offered, and blessings to be received, and there was only one place where Linda had ever felt the Holy Ghost touch her heart with fire.

She had been startled, though, the previous evening, when she'd climbed the wrought-iron steps only to find Tamsin listless on Aran's couch. The girl's red eyes and miserable demeanor had told her it was trouble at home, even before Aran had tactfully said, "My sister is going to crash here for a little while. She needs a break. You know."

"I didn't run away," Tamsin said. Then she looked at Linda with some surprise. "Did I?"

"Kind of seems like you did. You can tell me about it. I won't go tattling to your dad. Whatever you say is safe with me, forever."

Tamsin's eyes narrowed in the moonlight. Far along the highway, a semitruck was approaching. Its headlights barely touched Tamsin's face, the faintest trace of golden color, which pulled her features from the flatness of the night, made her look cunning and feral, far older than she was.

Tamsin said, "Why didn't you show up at the protest?"

"I had to work."

"I haven't seen you lately, except when you brought Aran that casserole last night. You haven't spent any time with me for days."

"I know. I'm sorry. I've been so busy. Whenever I'm not out counting birds, I'm working on plans for Aran. He's told you, hasn't he, about the gallery in Jackson?"

"What gallery?"

"I helped him get representation at a gallery over in Jackson Hole," Linda said. "A good one—a big one, with lots of wealthy clients. He's going to have a solo show pretty soon. It'll be his big debut in the art world. I'm surprised he didn't say anything about it."

"I'm surprised, too." Tamsin spoke slowly, dazed by some emotion Linda could only guess at. Delight, she hoped. Maybe it was resentment. "I told him long ago he could make it in the art world, go professional, do it full time."

"You were right," Linda said.

Tamsin stared at her again, hard eyed. "I know I was right. But he didn't listen to me. He didn't believe me. He only listened to you."

Linda cringed inside. She didn't know how to respond to Tamsin's sudden anger, so she kept her eyes on the approaching truck, continued walking, and waited for Tamsin to speak.

"I went to the protest," Tamsin finally said, "and the bishop saw me and ratted me out, and my dad came and got me. Dragged me away in front of everyone, pitching a fit like I'd set a church on fire."

"Oh no. I'm sorry."

"That's all there was to it, really. I guess it doesn't sound like much, but I didn't run off because of what happened yesterday. I left because of everything—years and years of the same old thing. Dad has been this way my entire life. I finally decided I've had enough of being told who I am and what I should be. I thought, *If Aran could up and leave, then I can, too.* So I did. I thought it would be easy, right up until I was on my bike, riding away from the house. Then it got harder every second. It was like trying to pull a weight through deep water. It wore me out, and I thought, *I can never get away from him. I'll be tied to him forever. I'll never be strong enough to cut myself free, just like Aran can't cut himself free.*"

A jolt went through Linda's body, a strike of bleak knowing. Then the truck was on them. Headlights blinded her; she raised a hand to block the glare, and in that flash of light, the thunder of the truck's engine rattled her guts and shivered the ground. A second after the truck passed, a whack of wind struck them both, stealing Linda's breath and knocking something loose in Tamsin.

Tamsin was going to cry again. Linda could hear it in her voice. "Maybe if Aran and I had been as smart as the twins, and had sweetened Dad up instead of pissing him off, we wouldn't be what we are now."

"What do you mean?" Linda said. "What are you and Aran now?"

Tamsin shook her head. She wouldn't speak of that. She burst out with sudden fury: "I hate him. I hate my father. And I love him, too, Linda. I can't make myself stop loving him. I've tried. All I can do is hate myself for loving him, because I know he doesn't love me in return."

"Of course he loves you. You're his daughter."

"No." Tamsin was vehement, insistent. "That isn't love, it's control."

Cold struck right through Linda, ice in the pit of her stomach. She stared openly at Tamsin. The girl was only seventeen, but in those words, Linda heard all the wisdom of ages. A slick, treacherous certainty came over her then. It appeared, for no reason Linda could understand, in the memory of a painting she had seen as a girl—a unfinished study made by Cassatt: Stark red wall devoid of depth or nuance, pear tree climbing like a vine along the bricks. A woman on a ladder, stiff limbed, reaching to hand a pear to a child, but the child was half-formed, its face only a suggestion, a void in the paper, never really there in the first place. The starkness of the image was all around her, the uniform leaves of the pear tree vivid and hard as knives.

She thought, *What am I doing, tying myself to a family like this?*

She had come to Rexburg desperate to find or forge an ideal life, to make for herself a Mary Cassatt reality—the placid mother with a baby in her arms. Now she was sinking into this mire called the Rigbys, a monstrous and tender beast of Gad's creation, made in the warped image of his fear.

"It can't be as bad as it seems." Linda sounded more than a little desperate, even to herself. "Aran got away, set himself up to make his own life. He's even got a career ahead of him now."

Again, Tamsin shook her head. "Aran is different now."

"What do you mean?"

"He's changing. He isn't the person he used to be." Tamsin's eyes were distant and sad. She watched the highway, the long silver stretch of road, all the nothingness around it. "His head is barely above water. I don't know how much longer he can keep himself *himself.* One day, this whole town is going to pull him under. It'll swallow my brother whole."

Linda shivered in the cold.

"I can't lose him." Tamsin started to cry again. Her breath came in ragged sobs. Tears slid down her cheeks, white in the moonlight, one, then another. The tears kept coming. Linda had never seen anyone cry so much. "I can't lose Aran. I need him. I can't be *me* without him."

Linda put her hand on Tamsin's shoulder. It was a small, feeble gesture, but the girl's distress was so great, Linda felt she had to do something. She couldn't let the poor kid suffer alone.

They stopped walking.

"You and Aran will always be close," Linda said.

"Not like we were. I can't tell you—I can't explain. I promised Aran. I promised."

Linda shook her head helplessly. She had no idea what Tamsin meant. She couldn't make sense of a grief so vast, and over something so simple, so ordinary—a man growing up, moving on with his life, going forward into his future.

"Tamsin." Linda groped for any small platitude that might offer comfort. "Aran will always be your brother. No one can take that away. You can't lose him; it's impossible."

The girl drew one long, shaking breath, held it till Linda thought her lungs would burst. When she let it out, she was calmer, almost eerie in her self-control.

"I will lose him," Tamsin said, "someday. A time will come when I'll have to break away from all of this—my family, this town, the church. I'll have to go, if I want to survive. But Aran won't be able to do it. He won't be able to leave. His roots are already down too deep. He can't follow me out of this town. I'll have to leave him here, behind me. I'll have to go alone."

32

ASH AND KEROSENE

"Well, that is something else." Cloyd Orton dropped his bar towel and came out from behind the eatery's counter to admire Gad's work.

Gad held the new sign against his chest, facing out. It was no easy thing, to keep back a grin. Whenever anyone admired his work, it gave Gad such a rush of pride, he wondered if it wasn't sinful.

Cloyd shook his head slowly, then whistled long and low. "Everyone told me you were the best sign maker in the state, Brother Rigby, but I didn't expect an honest-to-goodness work of art."

Gad chuckled. "Heck, Brother Orton, it's only a small sign. Nothing to get worked up about."

"It's dad-gummed perfect, is what it is. And I fear you didn't charge me half enough for the work."

Gad turned the sign around again. He smiled down at his handiwork, humbled by Cloyd's lavish praise. *Orton's Café* arced over a deep-red field. The letters glimmering in gold leaf, rendered in a quaint, old-fashioned script. Below the eatery's name, Gad had painted *EST. 1942.* The sign was small enough to hang above Cloyd's door, but big or small, Gad put the same care and attention into everything he made.

"It's long past time I freshened up the outside of this place," Cloyd said. "This sure will make a good impression on the customers. And you know, there's more folks coming to town every day."

"College kids," Gad said, "getting set up for the fall semester. Seems they arrive sooner every year."

"It's the recession. Harder for families to pay tuition—more kids needing summer work if they want to make it through the school year. But college kids are pretty fond of burgers and fries, so the more the merrier, I say." Cloyd turned from cheerful to sober in an instant. "Say, Brother Rigby—I hear your dad's not doing so great."

A roaring sound filled Gad's head. Days had passed since the midnight blessing. And in that time, his father had recovered some of his strength, thank the Lord. Gad's mother had told him so. But despite his gratitude for that small mercy, Gad hadn't been able to drive the image of his ailing father from his head.

He cleared his throat. "My pop is pretty sick, all right, but Heavenly Father knows best. We're trusting in His plan, the whole family."

"Amen. What else can we do?"

Gad slid the new sign onto Cloyd's counter. "Do you need help hanging this beauty? I can send one of my sons down to lend a hand."

"Boy, your kid Aran is something else, isn't he?"

The wind went right out of Gad's sails. Quietly, he said, "What has he done this time?"

"Aran came in not long ago," Cloyd said, "with that girlfriend of his—what's her name, Lynn?"

"Linda." Gad wanted to spit.

"That girl is something else, too—a real fast talker. She can wheel and deal with the best of them. Anyway, Aran brought in a few of his paintings, and that girl of his talked me into hanging some on the walls where my customers can see. Said they'd give me a cut of the price if any sold. I was set to turn them down—paintings seemed a little too fancy for a place like mine—but then I really looked at them, and I have to tell you, Gad, I was moved. Honest truth, I was moved. They were just a bunch of barns and fields and gardens and whatnot—all scenes from around here, nothing I hadn't seen a hundred times before. But they made me feel like I was noticing the world around me for the first time. Really seeing everything, you know, like my eyes had been closed all my life and I only just now decided to open them. I can't explain it."

A strange vibration ran through Gad's body, a current of surprise and disbelief. As a kid, Gad had touched an electric cattle fence by accident, and the jolt had started down at the ground first, in the soles of his feet, and zipped up his spine into his arm; the force had grabbed him for a second, shaking him clean out of his senses. That was the way he felt in that moment, staring at Cloyd Orton.

Cloyd was still talking. "Well, of course I said yes right then and there, just for the pleasure of looking at Aran's paintings while I worked. I wasn't sure anyone would buy, but two of them have sold already. Folks are real interested when they come in. They spend some time oohing and aahing over the new paintings before they sit down to order. I've made ten percent on each sale, just for giving Aran the use of my walls! How do you like that?"

Gad looked cautiously around the diner. Sure enough, there were paintings hanging above every booth and along the hall that led to the washrooms. All were framed in simple dark-stained wood. A few of Cloyd's patrons had gathered near one of Aran's pieces. The customers pointed at the painting, tilting their heads as if the thing might take on a different shape if they looked from another angle. Even at a distance, Gad could tell the paintings each held a certain everyday melancholy. As Cloyd had said, the images tugged at the soul and filled the viewer with a sense of seeing this town, this countryside, for the first time in a lifetime.

Gad was standing in front of the nearest painting before he realized he'd left the counter. It depicted a dark-haired woman—Linda, he assumed—standing in a field with her back to the viewer. She was far away, small in the frame, almost lost in the ochre of the landscape. At once he remembered the dream, the nightmare—Tamsin or Arletta far across a flooded plane, walking on the water. The woman in the painting was staring at the horizon, but without a view of her face, her thoughts were a mystery. Everything was touched by a fine and delicate light—the girl's shoulders and hair, the trees blocky and small in the distance, the ragged tops of the grasses.

The painting was beautiful. And it was speaking, though Gad was fairly sure he wasn't clever enough to understand exactly what it said. It was, as Cloyd Orton would say, really something—a quiet achievement at small scale, a lifetime of emotion contained on a piece of Masonite, nine by twelve.

Gad felt something very like relief expanding inside, crowding against his shock and that slow, simmering sensation of offense—the constant twitch of betrayal that he never could be rid of, not even in sleep. Relief filled his chest till he felt as if his ribs would crack. Aran hadn't been crushed by Gad's rash reaction, burning all those paintings. He was glad to know it, and downright startled to realize just how happy he was.

For Gad was certain he had crushed the art right out of his own soul. He'd hurt after the fire. It had been a physical pain, a thick, heavy pressure in his throat, a persistent ache in his stomach. He ached all the worse for knowing he'd caused that same pain in his son, his firstborn. More than once, Gad had asked himself whether he was a monster or just a plain damn fool.

Looking at the painting on Cloyd's wall, at the light on the woman's turned back, Gad asked himself, *Why did I do such a thing, anyway?*

Why did he ever do these things?

～

When his work in the sign shop wasn't too demanding, Gad would fish an old sketch pad and a stick of charcoal from his filing cabinet and try to draw, but he couldn't even start, couldn't lay the tip of his charcoal against the paper. Pad and charcoal seemed to bounce away from each other, like magnets placed wrong ends together. He would sit for long stretches of time—silent, fruitless minutes—holding the charcoal between finger and thumb, as stunned and horrified as if he held a cigarette or a joint, and the paper would stare at him blankly, whitely, glaring in the shop's fluorescent buzzing lights.

It wasn't fair. It wasn't right that Aran had recovered from the loss of his paintings, had gone on seeing and making as if nothing had changed at all, while Gad had lost it entirely, whatever small talent he'd once possessed. He would never get it back. That was what the dreams meant, wasn't it? The blackness taking him, wringing from him all that was good and nourishing and sweet. And the flood that pushed everything out to an unreachable horizon.

He wanted to weep, but of course he couldn't.

He wanted to draw and paint again. He couldn't do that, either.

On the first Saturday in September, Gad heard the telltale sound of a car coming up the drive. He thought it would be Aran. It must be Aran, returning to ask his forgiveness for the bitter way they'd parted when last they'd seen one another. He pushed himself up from his desk. He was ready to grant whatever Aran required, whatever would free the bonds on his spirit and allow him to make art again.

But when he looked out the window, it wasn't Aran's Charger coming up the lane. It was that girl's car, the interloper. Linda. A strange metallic taste burned along Gad's tongue. He watched her drive slowly toward the house.

Gad left his shop just as Linda was getting out of her car. She held a store-bought bouquet in one hand, the flowers wrapped in green paper. She heard the shop door slam, looked around in alarm, saw Gad striding toward her. She glanced at the house, then at her car as if maybe she was thinking of getting back inside and driving away before Gad could reach her. She decided against it. The damnable girl stood her ground, watching Gad warily.

"What are you doing here?" he said.

"Aran told me your father is sick. I brought some flowers for Aran's mom—and for you, I suppose. I wanted you both to know how sorry I am for your troubles, and to know that Aran and I are happy to help if we can."

Gad looked down dismissively at her bouquet. "Aran and you? What have you got to do with him? You aren't worthy of my son."

She laughed. The vile creature actually laughed. "I'm glad Aran isn't like you."

"Keep my son's name out of your mouth."

"I'll say his name whenever I want. Aran, Aran, Aran! You can't stop me. I've got every right to say it. I love him."

A white flash of silence burst in the space between them, blinding Gad for a moment. He drew in a sharp breath. His vision cleared. The girl was even paler than she'd been before, and wide eyed, astonished by her own declaration.

"My family has enough trouble as it is," Gad said. "If I see you, or hear of you hanging around my daughter or my son anymore, I'll—"

"Gad Rigby, what in the sam hill are you doing?" Arletta was already halfway across the grass. The kitchen door banged shut behind her.

"Stay out of this, Arletta."

She ignored him. Not in the way she usually ignored him, with a distant, hazy stare and a vapid smile. Now she was disregarding Gad with a hard, incisive glare, a face like thunder. She looked at Linda for a long moment. Then, deliberately, she softened. "You must be Aran's girlfriend."

"Yes," Linda said. "I'm Linda Duff."

Arletta smiled, caressed the girl gently on one shoulder. "It's so very nice to meet you. I've been hoping I'd have the chance. How is Aran doing? Does he like his new place?"

"Yes," the girl stammered a little. "He's . . . he's been working hard and getting by. I think he's very happy."

"Thank Heavenly Father. That's good to hear. And how is Tamsin?"

"Very well. She's been helping me clean up Aran's apartment, get it all fixed up like a real home. I think she's getting tired of sleeping on his couch, though."

"We don't need to talk about this," Gad said.

Arletta went right on talking, all the same. "That's Tamsin for you. Such a helper. I see you've brought flowers."

Linda held up the bouquet. "They're for you. Aran told me his grandfather has been terribly sick."

"He is, the poor man. I fear it won't be much longer before the angels call him home."

Linda smiled, but it was shaky. "Aran has been pretty sad about it. I know he loves his grandpa. I just wanted to . . . offer any help. If we can help at all, we will."

"This is nonsense," Gad said. "All a lot of show, to rub it in our faces, how much Aran has—"

Arletta talked over him. Actually spoke right over him as if he weren't there. "That's so good of you. Aran was always a sweet boy, so considerate, so kindhearted. And I can see you're the same."

Arletta took the flowers, smelled them, gave a happy little sigh. "You tell Aran we're grateful for his offer. And tell him we love him."

Gad grunted in disgust.

Arletta fixed him with that unfamiliar look, the sudden clarity, a striking authority in her eyes.

"Tell him we love him," she said again. "We both do. Now I'm sure you're busy and have lots to do."

"Yes." Linda looked as stunned as Gad felt. "I guess I'd better get going. It was nice meeting you, Mrs. Rigby."

"Such a joy to meet you, too. Drive safely, now."

The girl got back into her car. Gad hoped Arletta would vanish back into the house where she belonged and leave him alone to resume his scolding of the black-haired hussy. But Arletta only stood there in the stark September sun, sniffing her damn fool flowers.

Linda locked eyes with Gad through the window of her car. With a solid barrier between them, most of her fear seemed to have dissipated. Where there had been uncertainty, now Gad could find only dispassionate observation. He felt as if the girl were flaying him with her eyes, stripping away all his armor, exposing the small and brittle pieces of his soul. She squinted. Frowned. Then she started her engine and backed slowly down the drive. Gad heard the kitchen door open softly, then close. He was left standing alone in the empty yard, under an empty sky.

33

To the Sage

Linda didn't go back to the duplex, nor did she drive to Aran's apartment. Instead, she ascended the Bench and parked her Beetle at the dry dun edge of a vacant lot. She rolled down her windows and got out but kept the keys in the ignition and left the battery on, with the radio cranked up loud enough that she could hear it from outside the car. Then she climbed up onto the hood and slouched back against the windshield and sat there in the afternoon light, in the hard, sideways heat of summer's end, looking down on Rexburg.

The car's hood was so warm from the sun, it was almost too much to bear. The backs of her thighs felt stung through her jeans. The confrontation with Aran's father had left her weary, and somehow that hard slap of realization—that she loved Aran—had wrung her out all the more. Linda felt like some old used rag, limp and threadbare, and vaguely, she was conscious of a certain absurdity, that it was all too much and in fact it was a scream that a twenty-year-old ought to feel this way, cynical and broken down. She sagged, closed her eyes, allowed her body to soak in the heat—the front of her warmed by the sun and the back of her by the metal and glass of her car. Like a lizard on a rock.

Like some small, instinct-driven thing with no real mind or will of its own.

She wondered: Did she really love Aran? Certainly, she was attracted to him. The things they'd already done together, before Tamsin had taken up residence on his couch, were proof enough of that. And she liked him a great deal, his gentle and thoughtful nature. There was no doubt that Linda loved his painting, his art, as much as she had ever loved those years-gone visions in the sanctity of the museums. But did she love him enough to make it matter, enough to wade through the mess of his family?

Flattened and immobilized by the warmth, she felt something give inside—an easy crumbling, a falling away of some high, hard, monumental thing. Curious, indolent with exhaustion, she realized it was her stubbornness and her pride buckling under all this weight. It was so much easier to give in, to let Gad Rigby claim his victory, let the whole damn town have its way. Gad had been right. She didn't belong here. It would be better for everyone if she left Rexburg forever. A bitter taste rose in her throat at the thought of leaving Aran—his easy laugh, his kind and honest eyes, and most of all, the great staggering brilliance of his art. But she was a wrecking ball. She would only hurt him if she stayed. She would hurt herself even more.

Between one radio song and the next, she could hear crickets in the lot around her and all the way down the steep slope of dry grass to Rexburg, small and self-involved on the valley floor. There were meadowlarks calling in the potato fields, too, with that trilling, falling, honey-bright sound she had come to love. She had never heard meadowlarks in Seattle. But there was no reason why she ought to go back there, to what scraps of family she still had. She could go anywhere, follow any road to a new life. Wherever she went next, it would have to be someplace that had good birds—birds that sang like they meant it.

Or maybe she would go to New York. The big city, the biggest city of all. Aran had talked endlessly about the museums he'd seen there.

Linda longed to stand in the presence of such greatness, passing hours in silent contemplation of composition and light, just as she'd done in her lonely childhood. Like a pilgrim, she would trek across the country and find herself at last, weary and dust covered, before a framed painting, Cassatt or Wyeth, and she would feel the trembling holy fire and know the terrible, long, desolate journey had been somehow worth it, and in a soft, mysterious, ill-defined way, right and good for her soul.

Yes. That was where she would go next: New York. She wondered whether the Beetle could make it that far—all the way across the continent. Her money certainly wouldn't last that long, but she could stop and live for a while in other towns, working at diners or shops till she'd saved enough to fix her car and move on again. Nebraska, Ohio, one Dakota or another. Out there, she could be anyone she wanted to be. She could be her true self, whoever that was—not an ideal woman, a good Mormon girl, but the kind of woman she could live with.

She could leave the next day if she wanted. Sandy would understand. Sandy would find another roommate in a snap, with fall semester just around the corner and more students coming to Rexburg every day. Besides, Sandy's wedding was only a few months off, and then she'd have a home of her own, a real home with Joel the bishop's son, and her bright, orderly future perfectly arrayed, already predetermined.

Aran was the only thing keeping Linda from leaving that very night. She would like to say goodbye to him before she left Rexburg for good. If she could only see him and talk to him once before she departed. That was all she wanted—to explain, if she could, why she had to go. She couldn't stay and pretend anymore that she belonged here, that she could survive in a place like this. And she wanted to tell him how much she loved him. That, most of all.

The music ended. News broke in—top of the hour. More talk about the dam, the flurry of lawsuits to try to stop it, warnings from environmental groups that it was too dangerous, the bureau couldn't be trusted.

Linda imagined the river choked in and penned, rising restless up the walls of its cage. Something fierce and wounded opened its eyes deep inside her and stretched and flexed a tense, feral body.

Do it, she said in her heart to the river. *Do it,* she said to the dam. *Come in and do your worst, or your best. Rush in and wipe this place off the map, off the face of the world. Wash all the shame and heartbreak away, scour it all down to dust, to basalt, to the old, dead, buried bones of pioneer women. Ruin this place like it ruined me, like it's ruining Aran and Tamsin and everyone good who comes into it. Let it be over and done with. Scatter it all to the sage.*

34

LOOKING FOR BROKEN THINGS

Evening. All the edges of the world, the edges of the day, brown and withered. Aran pulled out of the Mooseburger parking lot, back onto the highway. Tamsin, with her full backpack sitting between her feet, sucked pensively on the straw of her milkshake. Aran had put her bike in the trunk of his Charger. With the rear seats folded flat, the bike barely fit. He could hear the bike's front wheel revolving slowly behind him.

"School starts on Monday," he said with forced cheer. "Senior year."

"So what."

"So it's your last year before you turn eighteen. Then you can get away, go off by yourself, and start college. You should be happy about it."

"I'm never going to be happy about going back to live with Crabby Appleton."

"You couldn't stay with me forever, Tam."

"Why not?"

Aran thought of a perfectly good answer—*Because you've got your own life ahead of you, and I've got mine. And we can't be like this forever, so wrapped up in each other that we do things no one can ever know about, things no one will understand.*

She went on talking before he could speak. "Because of Linda, that's why."

"Hey," he said gently, "don't bring Linda into this. And don't be mad at her. It isn't her fault."

"Like hell it isn't. She was supposed to be my friend, but now she's your girlfriend instead, and I'm left out in the cold."

"No one is leaving you out in the cold. Linda and I both love you."

"Whoop-dee-dee."

"Come on. You're being a real pain. I'm trying to help, you know."

"I know." She sighed, let her head fall back against the car seat.

He said, "You should do everything I didn't do when I was your age. Keep lots of friends at school. Get involved with something: sports, cheerleading—"

"Cheerleading?" Tamsin said, astonished.

"Anything. Whatever will keep you busy and out of the house. Maybe it's time you really put some effort into the programs at church. The Young Women always have service projects going on."

"I don't ever want to go to church again," Tamsin said.

"It's not that bad."

"But there are a hundred things I'd rather do on a Sunday. I think there are a hundred things you'd rather do, too."

"Mom and Dad won't like it much if you stop going. It'll only make Dad crack down harder. He'll make your life a living hell."

"Big deal," Tamsin said. "He does that already."

"Take some advice from your big brother, who knows what he's talking about. For the sake of your own sanity, pretend you're happy with church till you're old enough to move out on your own. Then you can do whatever you like."

"Not if I stay in Rexburg, I can't. You know how people talk."

Aran felt a little lurch inside, like his heart was kicking him in the ribs. So Tamsin planned to leave town once she graduated, which was less than a year away. He had never before considered that she might leave. Families didn't do that. They didn't break themselves apart, not even when the going got rough, like it was now between Aran and Gad.

Their turnoff came. Aran paused with his signal clicking to let an approaching car pass. Beyond, at the foot of the dull, tired Bench, Rexburg was waiting for him. His throat went tight, looking at the town, an island among the wheat fields.

"Look," Tamsin said, "it's Linda. That's her car."

Aran focused on the approaching vehicle. There was no mistaking the orange Beetle, nor the dark shag hair of the girl behind its wheel. Linda was headed out of town. There wouldn't have been much surprising in that—the IEC head office was in Idaho Falls, more than an hour away, and Linda was often required to report to the office. But this was a Saturday evening. Why was she leaving Rexburg now? As Linda passed his Charger, Aran could see that her face was red and twisted. She'd been crying. And she didn't seem to see Aran at all, didn't recognize his car. Her attention was fixed on the road ahead, the world beyond Rexburg.

As soon as Linda had driven by, Aran cranked his wheel and stepped hard on the gas. He swerved into the dust of the shoulder, then back onto the highway.

"What are you doing?" Tamsin said.

He didn't know. Or he *did* know—a bright, hot bolt of certainty flared inside him all at once—but he didn't really believe he was doing it. The transmission chugged. The Charger accelerated faster now. He was gaining on Linda by the second.

Aran leaned on his horn. He could see Linda's face in her side mirror—brow furrowed, looking back at him, expecting a stranger but finding Aran instead. Her expression of annoyance shifted to wonder, then a pained resignation. She put on her blinker and pulled off the road. Her tires kicked up dust.

Aran cut his engine and got out. He went to Linda eagerly as she emerged from her car, but her arms were folded, her mouth pressed thin. She kept her distance.

"What are you doing here?" she said.

"Catching up with you."

Linda looked back at her car, the long stretch of highway beyond. Aran could see boxes in the rear of the Beetle, a suitcase and duffel bag on the passenger seat. She said nothing.

"I saw your face when you passed us back there. You looked like you were crying."

Linda glanced past him to the Charger. Her expression shifted subtly, impatience giving way to what might have been caution or suspicion, tightly controlled. Aran looked, too, and saw that Tamsin had rolled down her window. She was half out of the car, sitting on the door with her legs inside. She leaned one forearm on the roof of the Charger, sucking on the straw of her shake, watching Aran and Linda with intense curiosity.

Linda drew a deep breath. She faced Aran squarely. "The truth is, I was leaving town. For good."

There was a feeling under his feet like the ground pulling open, slow, inexorable. He was falling into a pit. He said, "Why? And . . . you were going to leave without saying goodbye?"

Linda's chin quivered. She turned away, rubbed one eye with the back of her hand. "I wanted to say goodbye. I wanted to wait and talk to you first. But then I just knew I couldn't wait, not one second longer. Your dad is crazy, Aran. He's *crazy*."

Aran shook his head.

"You can't keep on denying it," Linda said. "There's something broken in him, and it will break you, too." She took in another long breath. There was a shudder to it, like a sob. She said, "I thought I could make myself into the kind of girl who belongs in Rexburg. But I can't. There isn't any reason to stay."

"What about me?" How weak he felt asking that question. "I'm no reason to stay?"

"Your family is . . ." She tossed her hands feebly into the air. "Just as bad as mine ever was. Worse, in some ways. I came here looking for a new way to live—some way to be whole. I didn't come looking for broken things."

He stared at her like she was the only illuminated object in a vast expanse of darkness. There was nothing else to see, nothing in the world except her. He couldn't make any of this work without her strength, her mind—not his career, not this chaos with his father. He needed her like he needed the blood in his veins, or like he needed Tamsin, his reflection and his light. Needing, he thought, was a kind of love. Maybe it was the truest love of all.

He said, "Marry me."

She laughed, a small and bitter sound. "Are you kidding?"

"I'm not kidding. We can make something that isn't broken. We can do that together."

"I'm not the kind of girl anyone wants to marry. Not out here."

"Good. I don't want that kind of girl. I want you."

"Aran, I can't live in this place. I can't. It's like living in a cage. You don't know how weird it is, how unnatural, because it's all you've ever known."

"I know it's weird," he said impatiently. He didn't know. He knew that he had no point of reference, that he lacked Linda's sophistication. But he trusted her. Linda's judgment was always sound. "We'll move away. We'll leave."

"We don't have the money to leave."

"We'll have the money someday. With my show coming up at Feldermann's gallery, who knows what we'll be able to do, where we'll be able to go."

"We can't count on that. We can't count on anything." She pounded one palm with her fist, squeezed her eyes shut, refused to look at him. Aran had never seen her so distressed. "It's all too uncertain. It's all too crazy and unknowable, and I can't stay here, I can't, Aran, it'll poison me. It'll poison you."

Aran took her gently by the shoulders. Linda opened her eyes slowly. There were tears in the corners and along her lashes, small tears, points of light.

He said, "We need each other. I wouldn't have a career at all without you."

Linda's face hardened. "It's my career, too. Get that straight—it's mine. I put in just as much work as you do."

"You do," Aran agreed. He knew that was true, too. He didn't begrudge her the truth. "And so you need me, don't you? You need an artist to market if you're going to keep it up. If you're going to build a career of your own."

"It will be my own. If I say yes. If I agree to marry you. You won't control me, the way your dad tries to control your mom. The way all the men here control all the women. I won't be owned, Aran. I'll have my own life, my own ambitions."

"Yes," he said. "Yes, yes. I swear it. I don't want to own you. I want us both to have it all together, the lives we want, the futures we want. Damn what anyone else thinks. We can be black sheep together, our own little flock."

"And we'll leave, as soon as we have enough money to go. We'll get out of here and never look back."

"We'll never look back," Aran promised. "Not ever."

For a long time, Linda said nothing more. She watched him with her brows knit together, an expression of anger and confusion, exasperation. Aran never took his eyes off her. He could hear Tamsin fidgeting in the car, maybe climbing back inside—then a meadowlark calling out in the sage, the notes falling down sad and easy.

Finally, Linda let out the breath she'd been holding. "Okay," she said, "I'll marry you." But she wasn't smiling.

Just before Aran took her in his arms and kissed her, she shook her head like she'd surprised herself with those words.

35

Reasons to Celebrate

September was almost out when the calls came. But they did come, at last. Gad had been arranging his photographs on the big, solid work-table in his shop, setting out all the images he'd captured of Aran's work, the framed paintings from Cloyd's diner laid in a grid before him. He had just sought permission from Cloyd earlier that day to photograph Aran's paintings—as keepsakes for the family, Gad had said, because they were all so danged proud of Aran—and of course Cloyd had said yes. Gad had filled up the roll of film in his camera and taken it straight-away to the Fotomat booth in the Broulim's parking lot, and just after lunch, the film had been developed. As he'd spread the photos on his worktable, a little worm of guilt had gnawed its way into Gad's heart.

But the moment he heard his boys whooping and hollering down by the mailbox, he knew what they were so wound up about. He knew it in an instant. The Lord had finally called them both to service. Their missions would soon begin, and wasn't that all the sign Gad needed from the Lord? Wasn't that justification enough, and reason to put his guilt to rest?

He shuffled the photos into a hasty stack, slipped them into the paper envelope, dropped it in the drawer of his desk. Then he went outside to congratulate his boys.

Brig and Ondi were running toward him, running through the yellow leaves that spun down from the poplars. Each held a large envelope in one hand, the packets containing all their specifics and instructions, and each was waving aloft the letter itself, like banners raised to Heaven.

"We did it, Dad," Ondi shouted. "This is it—it's our calls!"

In that moment, Gad could see them as they had been, little russet-headed tykes chasing one another through a haze of sunlight, long faded. He laughed, gladdened and relieved, and threw his arms wide to catch them. They both embraced him at once. They were men now, and strong. They could almost squeeze the breath right out of Gad's body. He could hear the letters crinkling as they pounded him on the back and clung to him, the way boys hold to their fathers.

"I'm going to Uruguay," Ondi said. "Can you believe it?"

"And I'm going to Finland," Brig added, right on his heels, "like you, Dad—just like you did."

Gad blinked the tears from his eyes. "I'll be danged. I don't know when I've been so proud."

Arletta and Tamsin had come out of the house to see what the ruckus was about. Arletta had clasped her hands together under her chin. Even Tamsin, who had been surly and withdrawn since the start of the school year, was smiling.

"We're going to have a party," Gad said. "A real big bash. You hear that, girls? Start planning now. We're going to send these two missionaries off in proper order."

After the boys had shown their letters to their mother and gone into the house, Gad returned to his shop. He took the photos of Aran's paintings out of his desk and laid them out once more. There was no more hesitation. This thing he was about to do—it was what Heavenly Father wanted. It was what was required of Gad if he hoped to regain his status as patriarch of the family. After a few months, he would have Aran back and in the proper frame of mind, contrite and reverent, ready to resume his place. That Linda girl would be cast aside where she couldn't influence Tamsin or Arletta any longer. Everything would be under Gad's control. He only needed to do a little extra work to make it happen.

He looked down at all of Aran's paintings together, assessing them as a body, identifying the similarities. He went about this task the same way he handled all his work: with order and precision. Gad took the little notebook from his shirt pocket and began jotting a few words here and there, observations, guidelines. Before an hour had passed, he'd filled several pages with notes and had moved on to making sketches.

Then he took his drawing pad from the locked filing cabinet, and his good graphite pencils, his charcoal. He was pleased at how quickly the fundamentals of art came back to him after that long dry spell, after he'd burned his ability away. He figured that, too, must be a sign from the Lord that he was doing right. If Heavenly Father hadn't wanted Gad to copy Aran's work, the twins would still be waiting for their missions right now. And some invisible force would have stayed his hand.

Autumn withheld its usual bluster of rain and gray winds. The weekend of the twins' celebration was warm and blue as summer. The boys had helped Gad roll up the big bay door of his shop and push the long, solid worktable out to the edge of the grass. Arletta had draped it with a red-and-white checked tablecloth, which she and Tamsin had buried under an acre of food—green Jell-O squares with pineapple and whipped cream, funeral potatoes still hot from the oven, homemade rolls and boiled corn and a huge bowl of five-cup salad so sweet it was attracting flies. Gad was proudly manning the charcoal grill, flipping burgers and hot dogs and chicken wings marinated in Arletta's special sauce of horseradish and 7UP. The whole family had joined in the celebration—all of Gad's brothers and sisters who still lived in Rexburg, plus their children and their children's children. Bishop Kimball and his wife were there, the neighbors along Ricks Avenue, and of course, the pack of fine young men and women who were friends with the twins. Gad's lawn was packed with visitors. Kids chased each other in and out of his shop. The twins and their friends were lobbing water balloons at one another. Even Pop had managed to make an appearance, for a half hour anyway. It had cost him a good deal of strength to hobble from the car on Mother's arm and sit for a while in a cushioned chair, which the twins brought out from the house. But he'd placed his hands on their heads, Brig and Ondi each in turn, and offered them a grandfather's blessing. Gad hadn't felt such satisfaction in years.

Delyle and his son Direlle came wandering over from the house, each swigging from bottles of orange pop. Direlle's two small sons toddled past, pursued by their heavily pregnant mother.

"This is quite a bash," Delyle said.

Gad chuckled, flipping another burger. "We're all so glad to see the boys off on their missions. Did you hear Brig is going to Finland, just like his old man?"

"I remember how worried you got," Delyle said, "thinking of all the work you'd have to do to learn the Finnish language."

"I guess every fellow feels a bit intimidated at the prospect of learning a whole new tongue," Gad said. "But Brig's a smart boy. He'll have an easier time with the language than I ever did. And Ondi already knows a bit of Spanish from high school."

"They're two fine young men, all right," Delyle said.

"And Aran," Direlle added. "You know, we got a press release down at the paper about the art show he's having in Jackson Hole—since he's Rexburg born and bred, I guess, and if you're going to be a big star, the *Standard Journal* is the place to get the local word out. I looked into it.

That gallery that's hosting his work—it's a big one, Uncle Gad. A real big player in the art world."

Gad fussed with the chicken wings to cover his surprise. He hadn't known Aran was having any show—not anywhere, let alone at some muckety-muck gallery.

"The press release included a few pictures of his work." Direlle gave a low whistle. "He's some talent. I'm no kind of expert on the subject, but boy, I sure thought those paintings were something else. I felt real proud that he's my cousin."

"Yes," Gad said slowly. "Aran has been blessed."

"You know," Delyle said, "I didn't think Aran would ever get his act together. All those stories we've heard about him, these years gone by. But you whipped him into shape, Gad."

"He's a credit to the town now," Direlle agreed. "We never saw that coming."

Gad swallowed hard. Was Aran to take this from him, too? Rise to a place of honor within the community, rise up to replace Gad in everything, even simple respectability? *Steady,* Gad cautioned himself. *You've got a plan. Heavenly Father has shown you the way.*

"Say, where is Aran?" Direlle asked. "I was hoping to see him today and catch up with him. I wanted to hear all about his show."

"He gets busy and distracted," Gad said. "You know how those artsy types can be."

In fact, Gad hadn't told Aran about the party, though he had no doubt Tamsin or Arletta had leaked the news.

"Heck, there he is now." Delyle nodded down the drive.

Sure enough, Aran and that sharp-eyed jezebel were walking up from the avenue, both a little tense and wary.

"Excuse me," Direlle said. "Nice talking with you, Uncle Gad." He was off across the grass, already reaching out to shake Aran's hand, as if Aran were some kind of rock star.

Delyle shook his head fondly, watching their two boys out there at the end of the lawn. "Look at them, all grown up, with lives of their own now. It's some kind of miracle, isn't it?"

Gad grunted in response.

"You've done wonders turning that son of yours around, Gad. I have to say, I respect you for it. You're a real good father, a real good man."

Gad thought of the photos inside his shop, the sketches and plans he had made. He didn't know how to answer. He thought it was safer to keep his mouth shut. So he only shrugged and nodded a little, and flipped a few more burgers, making the grill hiss and spit.

Tamsin was carrying another bowl of boiled corn from the kitchen when she saw that Aran had arrived. She fixed a placid smile to her face and set the corn on the long table outside the shop. Gad, who was still talking to Uncle Delyle, gave her a sharp, critical look, the same peevish assessment of Tamsin's clothing he'd been dishing out since the summer. His attitude had grown even more possessive once Tamsin's senior year of high school had begun. And now that the twins would be leaving for their missions, the darkest days of all lay ahead. She would be the only child left in the Rigby home. There was nothing to shield her anymore, no one to deflect Gad and splinter his worst impulses. He would blame every perceived slight on Tamsin, make her responsible for all his failures. The certainty curdled her stomach. She couldn't stand the smell of the barbecue.

As soon as she'd delivered the corn to the table, Tamsin dodged away again, before Gad could call her back and send her off on some unnecessary errand concocted merely to assert his control. She hurried to where Aran and Linda were chatting with Direlle, down in the shade of the poplars.

"Is that my little cousin?" Direlle crowed. He pulled Tamsin into a sideways hug. "I swear, you're more grown up every time I see you. I can still remember when you were a tiny thing wearing pigtails. You'll be getting married before much longer. How about that?"

"Hi, Direlle," Tamsin said, with a long-suffering glance at Linda.

Linda gave her an ironic half smile.

A terrible pang of nostalgia welled up inside Tamsin. Everything had changed forever over the summer, in just a handful of weeks. She wanted to be friends with Linda again, the way they'd been before—reading together in the park, going for long walks where they could talk about anything they pleased with no men to overhear, climbing up the water tower to look down on the world. And she wanted her brother back. She wanted the Aran who had been hers alone, the Aran she had trusted to see her, really see her, and reveal the image of her true self to her desperate, longing eyes. She didn't understand how to *be* in this new world where Aran had a home of his own, a fiancée—even if no one knew they were engaged except for Tamsin, who had witnessed the whole awkward scene. She felt the only reality left was the one Gad controlled, and Tamsin had no power to rebel against him anymore, not now that Aran had left her and taken the magic of his painting with him.

Soon enough, Direlle was pulled away by Ondi, who had a hundred questions about the mission field in South America—Direlle had served in Chile. There was a loud metallic crash from inside the kitchen, as if Arletta had knocked over a whole stack of pots and pans.

"I think Mom needs some help," Tamsin said, turning toward the house.

"Wait." Linda caught her by the wrist. "I'll go give her a hand."

"Are you sure?" Aran said.

"Of course. I like your mom. She stuck up for me once, against your dad."

With that, she was off, walking rather stiffly into the crowd of neighbors and relations. She looked like she was striding into battle, braced for an attack from any angle.

"I didn't know Linda had met Mom already," Tamsin said.

"Neither did I," Aran answered.

"Is she okay? She looks a little sick."

Aran sighed. "Linda called her mom this morning to tell her we're engaged. It didn't go well. Her mom wants to drive out to Idaho and rescue her. Linda had a fun time convincing her not to do it."

"The cat's out of the bag," Tamsin said. "It's nice not to be the only one who knows the big secret. When are you going to tell Mom and Dad?"

"I don't know," Aran said. "When the time is right."

"The time will never be right. Anyway, Linda's mom is welcome to rescue me, if she wants to get someone out of Rexburg."

"Her mother thinks I'm going to subjugate Linda, turn her into some sort of household appliance."

Tamsin watched Direlle's two little boys go running past their father, who was absorbed in conversation with Ondi. Direlle's young wife was lumbering after her children, the great stark roundness of her pregnancy making her look too tired and frail.

"Can you blame her?" Tamsin said pointedly. "When's the wedding?"

"End of this month."

"Are you two getting sealed in the temple?"

Aran shook his head.

"Why not?" Tamsin said.

"It isn't what either one of us wants."

"Linda said so?"

"I didn't ask. I didn't need to. I know she wants it this way, and I do, too."

Frowning, Tamsin looked at her brother more closely. A rapid flow of shadow moved across his face. He and Tamsin both looked up in the same instant. A cloud of blackbirds had risen up out of the poplars, twisting above the neighborhood. Aran smiled at the sight. Such a weight had lifted from his spirit. Tamsin had rarely seen him like this before: peaceful, satisfied. That sick feeling from before was back again, tightening her stomach. She realized it was envy. She wanted what he had—distance, separation from their father. A chance to define herself on her own terms.

She said, "Are you still going to church?"

"Sure. Why not?"

He hadn't changed that much, then.

Tamsin said, "Dad isn't going to like it one bit—you not being sealed in the temple."

"One more reason for Dad to be disappointed in me," Aran said. "Add it to the heap."

"Easy for you to say. You don't have to live with him anymore." An idea struck Tamsin suddenly, such a bright flash of inspiration that it left her blinking. "Linda said she wanted to move away. I heard her, when you proposed. Why don't you do it, Aran? Take off to some other town. You can take me with you. Please."

"You've only got one more year left of high school. Besides, even if we did move away, I don't know if I could convince Linda that we ought to bring you along."

"I wouldn't get in your way. Neither of you would know I was there."

"It might be years before Linda and I can afford any home better than that apartment. What would you do, sleep on our couch all that time?"

"No," Tamsin said, clutching her hands together. "Only till I'm eighteen."

"Tam," Aran said gently, "don't be silly. You know that would never work out. Besides, I don't think I can leave Rexburg yet."

Tamsin's mouth fell open. Aran looked up at the birds again, the whole great shifting flock twisting and flexing in the sky. He seemed unaware of her dismay.

"Are you crazy?" she demanded. "You promised Linda you would. And why would you choose to stay here, Aran, where *he* is?"

He put a hand on Tamsin's shoulder, squeezed it gently. "I have to believe that Dad can be saved. I have to believe our family can be saved. It might take time, but God will give us mercy and change Dad's heart."

"Oh, spare me," Tamsin said. "You aren't going to have a temple wedding, but you're still trying to make nice with God? You don't need this church, Aran. You don't need this town, where everyone thinks the same and acts the same and expects you to be someone you can never be. There's a whole world out there, waiting for us—waiting for you and your paintings. Get out there and find it. And take me with you. I'm begging you."

Aran closed his eyes. "I need to try it my way first, before I pull up stakes and leave. If there's any way for this family to reconcile—"

"By appeasing the tyrant?"

"—I have to give us that chance."

"You're crazy. And it'll drive Linda crazy, too, all this bending over backward to make Dad happy. To *try* to make him happy."

"People can change, Tamsin, under the right circumstances. I've changed."

"He'll never accept what you've done, taking your life into your own hands. It makes it harder—don't you get it?—harder for him to go on pretending we're only reflections in his mirror. He'll try all the more to destroy you. This time, he might actually do it."

Aran breathed deeply. It wasn't exactly a sigh. But Tamsin could tell he'd listened. He was thinking carefully about what she'd said.

"You know," Tamsin ventured, "we can destroy Dad first, before he can hurt either one of us again. Before he hurts Linda, too."

"No," Aran said at once. "The paintings will stay hidden."

"They're my paintings, just as much as yours."

"How do you figure?" he said, wryly.

"My body. My image. Those paintings wouldn't be anything without me."

Aran bit the inside of his cheek. He agreed with her—Tamsin could tell.

He said, "Don't use art for evil purposes. This isn't what art is meant for—to manipulate and control. If you turn those paintings we made together into a tool for sin, it'll break your heart, and mine."

Tamsin didn't answer. But she thought, *Evil is in the eye of the beholder, and so is sin, when all's said and done.* It wouldn't be an evil purpose, to put Gad in his place.

A shout rang from the direction of the grill. "You what?"

Tamsin and Aran both looked around. Linda was there, with Arletta beside her, both of them setting dishes on the table. It was Gad who had hollered. Linda and Arletta were looking at each other, and even across the lawn, Tamsin could see how pale Linda looked, how startled. Without a word, she and Aran hurried to Linda's side.

They arrived just in time to hear what Linda was saying, quietly, hesitating. "—Of course we planned to tell you, Gad. We didn't want to take anything away from Brig and Ondi."

Arletta said, "I saw her ring when she came into the kitchen to help me out. I asked her about it."

"A secret engagement—" Gad said.

Aran put his arm around Linda's shoulders. "There's nothing secret about it. You weren't the first person we decided to tell, that's all."

"It's my fault," Arletta said. "Linda told me in the kitchen, and I blurted it out to Gad without thinking."

Tamsin assessed her father, his red face, his tight-pressed mouth. The news that Aran and Linda would soon be married had stripped something from Gad, taken him down a peg. Tamsin seized the moment. She clapped her hands once, sharply, and yelled for all the guests to hear, "Wow! What great news! Did you hear, everyone? Aran is getting married!"

"How about that?" Uncle Delyle said. "Congratulations, Aran. Congratulations to both of you."

A crowd began to assemble around the grill—around the happy couple. The twins pushed in, both of them reaching out to shake Aran's hand. "We've got all kinds of reasons to celebrate today," Brig said.

Gad's anger subsided. The tension was dispelled. Better still, Tamsin had stolen the power of the moment right out of her father's hands. Gad cast a hard glare at Tamsin while the cousins and aunts and uncles called out good wishes to Aran and Linda. Tamsin knew she would catch hell later for spreading the word like that. Her father would be rottener than ever before. But it felt so good to pluck out his fangs, if only for a moment, she couldn't help but smile.

36

BETTER THAN NONE

It was the end of October. Even in the afternoon, the air was cold enough to see your breath. Most of the trees along the riverbanks had shed their leaves, but patches of orange and gold still remained, and in the irrigation canals, the water ran high and fast, smelling of rain in the Teton peaks, mineral, granite cold.

Linda waited at the bay window of her duplex. Sandy wasn't home. The previous night, Linda had confessed that she and Aran would tie the knot at the courthouse, before a justice of the peace, and Sandy had been stunned to silence at the news. When Linda had emerged from her bedroom that morning, Sandy's bed had been empty—neatly made as always—and the duplex was still. She had passed the day packing her things into bags and cardboard boxes, wondering where her friend had gone. No doubt she'd been so disturbed by Linda's choice to have a civil marriage rather than a temple sealing that she couldn't stand to remain in Linda's company. Or maybe Sandy just couldn't stomach the fact that Linda was really going to marry Aran Rigby. It must have felt like an indictment of Sandy's beliefs, Linda had mused—a rejection of the morality that had made Sandy who she was, the steel at the core of her spirit.

After today, the duplex would be Linda's home no longer. She would live with Aran in his cramped, noisy apartment. She had put on her nicest dress, the navy blue with the lace collar, which she'd worn that day in Jackson Hole when Aran's career had begun—when her own career had begun. She didn't have the money for a proper wedding gown, but the navy dress seemed the next best thing, a proven charm for luck. She felt a little chilly, though, which she attributed to the change in weather and not the stunned, final feeling deep in her stomach. She wrapped her arms around her body, waiting for Aran to arrive. It was her wedding day. This was it. No going back, only forward.

A car pulled to the curb, but it wasn't Aran's Charger. In fact, it was Joel Kimball's car, and Sandy came bouncing out the passenger side, arms full of a large garment bag and several bunches of grocery-store flowers wrapped in cellophane sleeves. She struggled up the walk, trying not to step on the trailing garment bag.

Linda opened the door.

"Thank goodness," Sandy panted, "you haven't left yet. I was afraid I wouldn't catch you in time."

She dropped everything in a heap on the sofa.

"What's all this?" Linda said.

"Your wedding dress. You don't think I'm going to let you run off and get married in that old secretary's getup, do you?"

Sandy wrestled the garment bag out from under the flowers and drew down the zipper. The gown inside was stylish and modern, with a lace bodice and a high pearl-buttoned collar, long flowing sleeves that billowed around the tight chiffon cuffs, and a gauzy ruffle at the hem.

"It's incredible," Linda said. "Where did you get it?"

"Rodella insisted you should borrow it. She bought it for her wedding, which will be next April."

"She's letting me wear her wedding gown before she has a chance to wear it herself?"

"I guess your decision to butcher all those ABBA songs really paid off."

Tears came to Linda's eyes. She tipped her face up toward the ceiling so her mascara wouldn't be ruined. "I don't deserve this. You. And all the girls at Singles Ward."

"Come on." Sandy lifted the gown carefully in her spread arms, then headed for the bathroom. "Take that old thing off, and I'll help you get into your real dress. We don't have much time. You said you've got an appointment with the justice of the peace at five thirty, so we'd better get a move on."

Rodella's gown was a little loose around the bust, but Linda didn't mind. She watched her friend's face in the mirror while Sandy fussed over Linda's hair, playing with the dark curls, trying to get them to fall just so over Linda's shoulders.

"You were gone all day," Linda said. "I thought you were angry. I thought, when I told you I was marrying Aran Rigby, you'd made up your mind never to speak to me again."

Sandy caught Linda's eye in the reflection. "To tell you the truth, I was mad at first. I thought you were plain crazy. I thought you were ruining your life. After all, we both came here to Rexburg so we could go to college, but you never enrolled once fall semester started."

Linda bit her lip. It was true. She'd become so invested in the art business, so fascinated by the intricacies of her negotiations with dealers—and so thrilled by her success—that she hadn't bothered to enroll.

"Big deal," Linda said. "You'll probably drop out once you marry Joel."

"No I won't. I intend to get my two-year degree. You never know when it'll come in handy, and after all, we're living in the age of women's liberation. Why shouldn't I have a degree? And I thought, *Why shouldn't Linda have a degree, too? What the heck was the point of Linda coming all this way to Idaho if she isn't going to get an education after all?* But now I understand. Heavenly Father put you right where He wanted you to be."

She turned Linda around by the shoulders, looked earnestly into her face. "I still don't know what to think of Aran. He's so different from all the other men in town. I still suspect those rumors about him were true—or partly true, at least. But I can tell you're wild about him. If you love the guy, then you love him, and that's all there is to it."

"Thank you, Sandy."

"As for being gone all day," Sandy said, "it's no easy task to find a loaner wedding dress on short notice. Now you'd better go see if you can put together a bouquet from all those flowers I bought. I've got to change into a dress of my own. I can't be your bridesmaid in this old denim skirt."

Linda gathered mums and yellow roses into simple posies while Sandy rummaged through her closet. "I'm glad you're going to be my bridesmaid," Linda called. "I wanted to ask you if you'd do it, but after I told you last night that we were going to the courthouse instead of the temple, you looked disappointed—"

Sandy came out of her room in a simple pink dress with a ruffled hem. "Don't say anything else. Just zip me up. I was a real toad, Linda, and I'm sorry."

"Does Joel know you're going to be the bridesmaid at the wedding of the infamous Aran Rigby?"

"No, and I wouldn't care what he thinks, even if he did know. You're my best friend and you've made your decision. That's all that matters to me. If Joel doesn't like it, he can go stuff his head, and so can anyone else who doesn't approve. Oh—I almost forgot. I found a blue ribbon in my closet. We can use it to tie up your bouquet. That has you covered for something blue, and the dress is something borrowed."

"That'll have to be good enough," Linda said. "It's only half the luck, but half is better than none."

Aran arrived a few minutes later.

"This is it," Linda said. She'd begun to shake.

"I'll be with you the whole time."

"Come to dinner with us after the marriage certificate is signed. Aran got his first check from the gallery a few days ago. We're driving out to Idaho Falls, to that nice Italian restaurant, to celebrate."

Linda and Sandy went side by side to meet the groom, carrying their hasty bouquets. Aran scrambled out of his car with Tamsin right behind him.

"Surprise," Linda said. "How do I look?"

Aran gestured rather weakly at his Sunday slacks, his simple white shirt and black tie. "I'm afraid I'm a little underdressed by comparison." He came to her and pulled her into a lingering kiss. "You look beautiful. Absolutely beautiful. Are you ready?"

Linda smiled up at him, and for a moment she didn't notice the chill of the fall day or the tight, cautious feeling in her stomach. She forgot she was wearing another woman's gown, and that she had only half the luck she was due. She thought she had ended up, after all, exactly where she was meant to be.

She said, "Ready as I'll ever be."

37

SUNSET

That same October night, after Gad had finished his work and gone inside to wash up and wait for his supper, he received a visitation. It was preceded by a knowing—the still small voice in his heart, speaking without words. That was the way revelation happened. That was how a man knew the truth and recognized the pattern of the Lord's working.

He was washing his hands at the kitchen sink. One moment, an ordinary operation—the same thing he did every day when his labors were finished. The bar of soap with its darkened cracks, the lather sliding over his knuckles, the hiss of water running. Next moment, the most familiar and innocuous act was weighted with a sudden, bewildering significance. Gad shut off the water, stared unseeing out the window at the purple twilight below the poplars, a last autumnal flare of sunset lingering in the sky. There was still soap on his hands. He groped for a towel. He couldn't take his eyes off the vanishing light.

Then he was aware of movement and color down at the end of the drive—his nephew's flashy car turning onto the gravel, creeping toward the house at a reluctant pace. Gad stopped breathing for a spell. He thought it likely he might never breathe again.

He went outside to meet Direlle. His nephew parked rather haphazardly beside the shop and came toward Gad with his hands shoved deep in his pockets, his shoulders a little hunched.

Gad and his nephew looked at one another silently in the gathering dusk. Gad wanted him to speak and break the tension, yet he feared the inevitable message, both at the same time.

"I went with Dad up to see Grandpa tonight," Direlle finally said. "He took a sudden turn right after we got there. I'm sorry, Uncle Gad. Grandpa Rigby is gone."

Gad exhaled.

"I'm glad my father was there with him," Direlle said, "and with Grandma, too. I'm glad I was there. But I wish there'd been time to tell you first—you and Jerry and all your sisters. I wish you could have been at his side, like we were."

Gad nodded. He looked away. His hands still felt damp at the palms and between the fingers.

"I've got to go tell Jerry now," Direlle said, "and everyone else."

"Yes. I know. You go and do that, son."

"Are you all right, Uncle Gad?"

Gad nodded again, took his nephew by the hand and shook it firmly, as if to prove to Direlle and to himself that he was still present, still as real and undaunted as a man ought to be. Gad surprised himself by pulling Direlle into a rough hug. The young man tensed at first—no doubt he was startled, too—but then he pounded Gad on the back, held him tightly, muttered something stoic and religious as a form of comfort.

Gad let him go. He watched Direlle walking through the twilight, upright, strong, willing to do the work laid before him no matter how difficult it might be. And when Direlle had driven away, Gad remained outside with the crickets singing in the empty lot behind the house and the low moan of passing cars a few blocks away. Strange, that a town so small ought to feel so widely spread from the place where Gad now stood. Everything he loved, everything he had hoped to love, was far away. Aran had picked up Tamsin for some reason or other, some get-together, and the twins were down in Provo training for their missions. Soon they would be on other continents, in other hemispheres, and when they returned, they would be transformed from boys into men. Arletta was inside the house, but she was as far from Gad as she had ever been.

A stark, pressing vision came to him then, brief as a heartbeat but no less haunting for its fleeting nature. He saw himself in place of his father, a small creature abated to helplessness, in a dark room with death and eternity standing near. And no one at his bedside, no one at all.

He thought, *If I die alone someday, it'll be my own doing.*

That, too, was a revelation, a certainty conveyed by a still small voice within. He considered the photos he'd taken at Cloyd's, the sketches and value studies, the corner of his shop where he'd made folding screens to shield from view—from his own view—the easel in the corner, the canvas on the easel, a painting just like one of Aran's taking steady shape. Exactly like Aran's work.

He pushed the guilt away. Heavenly Father had sent a sign. Gad had divine approval. He was meant to do this, meant to reclaim the future and the dream his father—his dead father—had stolen and his son had claimed despite Gad's natural right and precedence.

But he wished—for the sake of that fleeting vision—that he had been made a kinder man. He wished he'd been a gentler father and had learned somewhere along life's hard, lonely road how to fix what had been broken inside.

38

VEILS

The day of the funeral, a rain set in. It was a heavy, persistent rain, noisy and gray, the kind that falls on Rexburg only once or twice a year. The clouds had snagged themselves on the Bench and their bleeding bellies obscured all sight of the valley with shifting curtains of silver. The parking lot outside the funeral home smelled ozonic and sharp. Up in the high elevations, the black volcanic soil turned to knee-deep mud, but the potatoes had all been harvested so no one was concerned.

The funeral director, who had lived in Rexburg all his life, knew there would be crowds and congregations filing in to pay their last respects. The deceased had been the patriarch of a pioneer family; the Rigbys had called this valley home for almost a century straight. The custom was to allow immediate family time alone with the departed after the congregation had paid their last respects. But Hyrum Rigby would draw a crowd. The director had arranged for the departed's children to view his body first and in privacy, each son or daughter accompanied only by their spouses, their children, and their grandchildren.

Gad and his nearest kin were scheduled for eleven in the morning, when the rain was at its worst. He and Arletta held newspapers above their heads as they walked through the parking lot to the funeral chapel's door. Tamsin ran ahead. Aran and Linda were already waiting, just outside the chapel, pressed close together under a black umbrella. On their left hands, they wore simple rings of white gold, no diamond for Linda. Aran and his father nodded to one another. Then Aran opened the door and held it so Gad would be the first inside, so he could lead the family.

As they passed together into the parlor, Linda and Arletta found themselves walking side by side. Arletta lowered the newspaper she had held up to protect her hair. Linda retracted the umbrella, shook white drops of rain from its folds. Arletta extended a hand, silently, and Linda took it and squeezed. Arletta still remembered the smell of the flowers Linda had brought that day when she'd argued with Gad. Arletta had cut the stems and put them in water, humming to herself all the while, and the bouquet had lasted two weeks before it faded.

Linda kept hold of Arletta's hand. There was no rush to drop it. She watched Arletta watching Gad—Arletta marking the reluctance with which Gad approached the casket, the distance he kept between himself and Aran. Linda thought, *She's quiet, Arletta. But she still speaks, if you know how to listen.* The minute tension around Arletta's eyes whenever she looked at her husband—that was a way of speaking. And standing there with Linda, holding her hand, instead of going with her husband—that was a volume, a roar. Linda thought, *It's better, though, to speak with your voice. It's better not to be mistaken, or to keep so quiet you can be ignored.*

Arletta did watch Gad—it had become an old habit, to tally and catalog her secret knowledge of the man. But she gave her husband only a fraction of her keen attention. She was more interested by far in the young woman who kept that tight hold on her hand. Her daughter-in-law. It seemed so strange to think it, so alien, exciting. Linda had chosen this family. It was a choice, not like most marriages that happened out here, which were more incidental than intentional, more convenience than love. This bright-burning girl from the city had seen Gad Rigby's clan for what they were and had stepped willingly into their circle. Linda alone, of all the family, was unimpressed by Gad's bluster, unmoved by his rage. Arletta would have given everything in her possession—which wasn't much to speak of—if she could learn how Linda managed it. How she remained her own woman.

There were still a few drops of rain on Arletta's hands, running down to drip from her knuckles. There was something in Linda, Arletta mused, that was like the rain. There were layers and veils behind which Linda obscured herself, like the curtains of silver out there in the valley, hiding everything from sight. Linda didn't allow you to see her true self unless she wanted you to see it. There was a certain strength in that, an inborn wisdom. Arletta had tried to do it all her life. She didn't believe she had ever succeeded.

Arletta remembered being naked, being a girl, and throwing herself into the river with those other girls, how their voices unleashed had cut the night and sounded bright as music. She remembered how the water had shocked her with its coldness, jolting her out of time and place. The coldness had been the river's secret power. And Linda, Arletta thought, was very much like water, like water sweeping in.

Down near the foot of the casket, far from her dad and her brother, Tamsin looked at the body and did not shiver. That surprised her. She had expected the sight of her grandpa dead in his casket would give her some kind of turn. But the thing that struck her with more significance even than death was the sight of his sacred temple clothing, the white garments in which all priesthood holders were interred. Someone had dressed Grandpa Rigby in a simple white robe, a white cap that almost looked like a cartoon baker's hat, and a square apron of green satin. The satin was wrinkled across one corner. All the mysticism of the temple had boiled down to this.

Death to Tamsin seemed in that moment a friendlier thing than she had expected. She didn't feel the need to cry. This was natural, inevitable. Death was something that couldn't be stopped—a leveling of the ground, a scouring away of the edifices of power. More than the urge to cry, she felt the tickle and itch of raindrops sliding down her scalp. She didn't want to scratch, because it would have been disrespectful to the dead, a mockery of the fact of death. You can't feel anything like an itch after you've died.

Gad and Aran said nothing, but there was nothing to say. Aran kept his hands folded, the right covering the left, hiding his wedding band. He knew there would come a time when he was the only one left standing. Gad wasn't as permanent or as powerful as Aran had thought him to be. He was already a bit like Grandpa Rigby, in fact, if Aran looked at him the right way. Aran had taken himself just far enough beyond his father to create a new life, and that life was beginning. Gad was inert, constrained in his place. Gad had built his own reality like the walls of a coffin, and he had chosen to lie inside it. Gad couldn't take anything from him, Aran realized. He never could.

And Gad—his thoughts were all for immortality, as he looked down at his fallen father. For all Gad could say, his pop might never achieve an eternal life—who really knew what waited beyond, if he was honest? But Gad could still secure an eternity of sorts. He would go on living through the art he was making now. It might hurt Aran. It surely would, if Aran ever came to know the truth. But Gad would be hurt far worse, to go into death the way his father had done it, without a thing to outlast him here in the earthly realm.

39

HOUSEWARMING

Linda pulled the roasting pan from the oven and set it on a trivet. Beef à la mode, allegedly. The roast smelled good enough to eat, yet the whole thing terrified her, the way the heavy slab of meat had shrunk in the hot oven, the newness of the pan—of the kitchen, of everything. Outside, it had begun to snow again, and the flakes spun and lifted and blew back up into a dim periwinkle sky as if to emphasize the great height of the Bench, how far above the town Linda lived now, so high that gravity worked differently here. The view from her new home always made her dizzy. She was glad the snow had returned and obscured, with its dusky haze, Rexburg on the valley floor. The new copy of *Joy of Cooking* lay open on the countertop. The book had been a wedding gift from Arletta—mailed to Aran and Linda rather than hand delivered, with a card that had read only, *Love, Mom*.

Linda hadn't been able to find any wine or brandy for her beef à la mode—not a drop of alcohol in the whole town—so she had used cranberry juice instead. That terrified her most of all.

Aran came into the kitchen, pale, looking a little sick to his stomach. He had trimmed his beard short and put on a nice shirt, which Linda had ironed for him—not one of the paisley prints he preferred, but something subdued and conservative, something his dad would approve of. "Smells good," he said.

"God knows what it'll taste like. Cranberry juice instead of wine."

Aran put his hand on the small of her back, which Linda assumed was meant to comfort her. She could feel him trembling. Neither Linda nor Aran had spoken much to his family since their wedding in October and the funeral right after—though Aran and Tamsin were still close as ever. It was January now. The Rigbys hadn't even spent Christmas together. When Linda had understood that Gad wouldn't include Aran in the family traditions, she had tactfully suggested they go to Scottsdale for the holiday, a sort of delayed honeymoon.

The distance and change of climate had done Aran good. He had painted prolifically, desert scenes, and Linda had taken the panels still wet and sharp with the smell of linseed oil to all the galleries in town. Before they'd headed back to Idaho, she had secured two new contracts with the Scottsdale dealers.

The time had come, though, to put Gad's pettiness behind. Linda didn't like it one bit, but they would be stuck in Rexburg for a couple more years at least. The money had come pouring in, a cascade of fortune Linda had never thought to see—but she had found herself pregnant, too. It hadn't been planned. The timing couldn't have been worse. Just when she and Aran finally had enough cash to escape Rexburg and set up anywhere they pleased, Linda's own body had betrayed her. As a new mother, half-terrified and entirely uncertain, she would need Arletta's help. She would need Sandy's help, too. She understood with a deep instinctive chill that other women were a necessity now. And so she and Aran were forced to make nice with Gad, smooth things over just long enough that their baby could be born and raised up a year or two.

The house on the Bench had been Aran's doing. He had purchased it as a surprise for Linda—and a way to make her as comfortable as he could, Linda assumed, while they waited out the next few years and planned their exodus from Rexburg. The house was certainly beautiful, though not nearly as extravagant as its neighbors. Linda would have preferred any simple, humble home on the valley floor. Gad would feel Aran's new height as a slap in the face. It would make him even more difficult to reconcile with, and further endanger Linda's necessary alliance with Arletta.

All these thoughts she kept to herself. Nothing about their situation could be altered. Day by day, she reminded herself to stay focused on the few things within her control: the sales of Aran's paintings, arrangements with new galleries, whatever tenuous plans she could make for a hazy, distant future.

Aran opened the refrigerator to peer at the tomato aspic, which Linda still couldn't believe she had coaxed from its mold without the damn thing falling apart. He went to the sink, ran the tap, stared at the snowfall. Only then did he recall what he was doing and take a glass from the cupboard and fill it with water. But he set it on the counter without drinking.

"If you want to make yourself useful," Linda said, "you can take out the scalloped potatoes."

When he opened the oven door, a wave of heat struck Linda's back. She didn't turn around, just stood there watching the bubbles subside in the marinade.

"Do you think my folks will like our new place?" Aran sounded so boyish—hopeful, yet frightened.

Linda thought in that moment she couldn't possibly love him more. No one had ever loved anyone as much as she loved Aran, and yet she knew that was ridiculous. Just about everybody was in love with somebody, and love, she reasoned, must feel more or less the same to everyone. But because she loved him, she understood what Aran was really asking and why he was so afraid. He hoped the house on the Bench, and the marriage that had survived three months already, and his flourishing career, and the baby on the way, and his wife who could puzzle out how to cook a fancy supper, would prove evidence enough that he had put his life together without Gad's rigid guidance. He hoped his father would finally respect him, man to man.

For her part, Linda merely hoped Gad Rigby would behave like a normal father—for one night, at least.

"Of course," Linda said. "What's not to like?"

Their home was a humble one—two stories, red brick built into the hillside, with a daylight basement they'd converted to a spacious studio. Aran spent a good ten hours a day down there, working to meet the demand of an ever-growing list of galleries and dealers, which Linda managed from the kitchen table upstairs. Linda had been able to decorate the house well, but her taste was earthy and restrained. She doubted whether anyone would notice the money she'd spent on setting up her home. She had never tended toward ostentation.

Though surely a time would come when everyone in the town realized that she and Aran had come into money. They had already replaced both of their old cars with a brand-new Cutlass Supreme—Linda had given the Beetle to Tamsin, much to Gad's disapproval. Their shared career wasn't merely on an upward swing. It was on a rocket, blasting into space at a speed that shocked even Linda, exceeding her rosiest projections.

"I can't wait to see the look on your mom's face when we give her the big news," Linda said.

Aran smiled, but Linda noted more anxiety in his expression than anticipation. "I wonder what my dad will say."

Linda had discovered her complication a few weeks after the wedding. She hadn't told anyone else but Aran, not even Sandy, who was wrapped up anyhow with plans for her own imminent wedding—a sealing in the temple, of course. And after tonight, the pregnancy would be a thing known—a fact of the world, irrevocable. Linda was filled with a curious dread. She had thought this was exactly what she'd wanted—to step into the soothing color of all those paintings she had loved, a mother adoring her child, the child smiling up at its mother. But once she'd been certain a baby was on its way, she had found herself grieving. Her career had only just begun, and now she must give up all that excitement and passion—for a few years, at least. She must fall in line, do the one thing everyone expected her to do: have a baby, sacrifice her body, be a mother first and a businesswoman last, if ever again, if at all.

Linda wavered between resenting the little life to come and feeling an instinctive, gripping protection of that same fragile creature. She loved it, fiercely, stubbornly, angrily. She knew the baby would steal something vital from her life, a tiny thief making off with Linda's future right at the moment when she'd discovered who she really was. Yet she couldn't help longing to see its face. Someday, sooner than she would like, she would hold that child in her arms for the first time, and the baby, a real and permanent thing, would close like a shackle around her life, and Linda would be forced to confront what she had made.

She thought, *I'm younger than I ever suspected. Much too young to be married, too young to be a mother. Too inexperienced to handle what the Rigbys have thrown at me—at us.*

"They'll be here any minute," Linda said, shoving all her grim thoughts aside. "Get that nice platter from the pantry, would you? I have to make our beef à la mode situation look halfway presentable."

Aran helped her arrange all the serving dishes on their new dining room table. The aspic was still quivering when a knock sounded.

"That's them," Linda said. "Are you ready?"

Aran didn't look ready. He led the way down their short hall to the front door.

It was Tamsin whom Linda saw first when the door opened, thank goodness. The girl was already beaming, standing in front of her parents on the snow-dusted steps.

"Man, oh, man," Tamsin said, "this place is great." Tamsin had already seen the house, of course, but she was evidently putting on a show of awe for her parents' benefit.

Aran welcomed them in. He and Linda pressed against the wall, making way while the family shuffled in and hung their coats on the rack beside the door. Gad's eyes flicked down the short hall. He wouldn't look at Linda directly, only grunted in what might have been a greeting.

Arletta carried a potted amaryllis. One angular bud had already opened in a burst of white-veined pink. "Happy New Year," she said, passing the plant to Linda. "A little housewarming gift."

Arletta wandered into the dining room. Her eyes were clearer than Linda had ever known them to be, her face radiant with something that looked very much like triumph. Arletta went to the bay window and took in the view of Rexburg, a small pallid glow on the valley floor, half-concealed by falling snow.

"You've certainly done well for yourselves," Arletta said.

"We've been very blessed." Wryly, Linda thought, *A few platitudes ought to make Gad happy.*

She and Aran had continued attending church—now at the ward on top of the Bench. But something had gone out of the experience for both of them. They were doing it for show. Linda knew that much without having to ask Aran whether his faith still remained. In their new church, Linda no longer felt the warmth that had existed at Singles Ward. But then, she no longer felt a desperate, driving need to belong, either. God was a distant, uninvolved being, and Linda was content to leave Him far away where she had initially found Him. Aran, for his part, attended dutifully but never mentioned church when they weren't there. And sometimes they would laugh together over something the bishop had said, or over a line in a hymn taken out of context. Alone, they were irreverent. Linda loved Aran best of all then, when he could laugh about the divine mysteries. The new freeness of his spirit made Linda feel a little less constrained. More than once, she'd wanted to tell Aran she thought they ought to give up on church altogether. But the time wasn't right for that conversation—not yet.

Linda could feel Gad somewhere nearby, lurking in her periphery. She was just as determined to avoid looking at Gad as he was at her. Tamsin laughed at something Aran had said. The sound made Linda jump. She realized Arletta was no longer beside her. Arletta had crossed the room to the sideboard. One of Aran's largest still lifes hung above it in an ornate gilded frame. Arletta was gazing up at it, warm and proud.

"It's a good one," Linda said. "I wanted him to sell it. I was sure it would go for a lot of money—maybe the most we'd ever made on a sale. But Aran said no. He wanted to keep it. He said he wanted me to have the best of his work."

"I always knew my boy had something special inside him," Arletta said quietly. "Something too bright to be snuffed out."

Linda set the amaryllis on the sideboard, right under Aran's painting.

Aran showed his family around the house while Linda put the finishing touches on the table, filling glasses with water, straightening napkins, tucking serving spoons into all the dishes. Her heart was fluttering and so was the baby—scarcely large enough now for Linda to feel its first tentative movements. According to the book she'd read, that should have been impossible. Second and third pregnancies might be felt by the fourteenth week, but never a first. Linda was certain, however. Something was stirring inside her.

"Well," Gad said when the family came to the table, "you've managed to climb the ladder. I never would have thought you could get so far—not by selling a few paintings."

Linda spoke up before anyone else could. "Aran, honey, why don't you give the blessing?" There was something quick and calculating in Gad's demeanor. He was looking for a chance to reassert himself, Linda knew—any slim opportunity to gain the upper hand and remind them all who was in control. Well, this was Aran's home—his and Linda's. They would remain masters of their own domain, and if Gad didn't like it, he could choke on it.

When the blessing was finished, Aran served, carving the beef into tender slices, loading all the plates with scalloped potatoes and aspic salad.

"I can't get over your house," Tamsin said. "It's so far-out."

Arletta smiled benignly at Tamsin. Her habitual vague, unfocused expression had returned. "Don't use slang, dear. You know your father doesn't approve."

"Folks must be buying your paintings like they're going out of style," Gad said.

Aran kept his eyes on the plate he was filling, humble, almost contrite. "I'm doing all right. Linda and I are just so grateful for our blessings. It's hard to make it as an artist, especially in this economy."

Blessings, my ass, Linda thought. It wasn't God who managed the steady stream of inquiries, ran ads in collectors' magazines, or called the galleries when checks didn't arrive on time. It was her work, as much as Aran's, that had brought them to this place.

Of course, once the baby came, Aran would have to handle his own affairs while Linda handled diapering and nursing and potty training and endless hours of screaming fits, and lost sleep, and gained stretch marks. Aran wasn't cut out for business. She tried not to dwell on what that might mean for their bottom line. The very thought made her queasy.

Mary Cassatt never painted anything like that, she thought. *What a vision that would make: Mother Subsuming Entire Self for Sake of Child She Only Thought She Wanted.*

When everyone's plate had been filled, Aran cast a nervous glance at Linda. She swallowed hard, then nodded. Might as well get it over with.

"Listen, everyone," Aran said. "We didn't only ask you to come over tonight so you could see our new house."

Gad huffed a quiet laugh. Linda ignored him.

"We also have some news." Aran took Linda's hand. "Big news. We're expecting our first baby—due at the end of June or the first week of July."

"No way," Tamsin said, grinning, while Arletta pressed her hands together and let out a very uncharacteristic squeal.

Gad cleared his throat and lifted his glass in salute. He raised his voice to cut through the celebration. "That's fine news, Aran—fine news. You know, I just received word this afternoon that your brothers have left Provo, and they've both arrived at their missions."

Silence fell like a brick into the room. In that momentary beat, Linda saw Tamsin turn away from her father, rolling her eyes. She saw the light dim to nothing in Arletta's face. She felt Aran's hand go limp in her own.

Aran said, "That's great. Fantastic."

"It sure is," Gad said. "We should all celebrate, now that we're finally together as a family. I call your brothers' success something worth celebrating."

Linda locked eyes with Gad. She refused to look away, refused even to blink.

Gad gave her an infuriating wink. Then he shoveled up some of his food. "Good pot roast."

"It's beef à la mode."

"Looks like pot roast to me. Tastes like it, too."

"So," Tamsin said, "are you hoping for a boy or a girl?"

Gad intercepted the conversation immediately. "You know, it's terribly cold this time of year in Finland, where Brig is now. I remember that cold from my own mission. I bet poor Brig is thinking he'll never get himself thawed out again."

"It doesn't matter whether it's a boy or a girl," Arletta said. "It will be precious and loved."

"And down in Uruguay," Gad went on, "it's summer right now. Can you imagine? That has to be a shock to the system, to get on a plane in

Utah where the snow is three feet deep and get off in a whole new place where it's a hundred degrees by day."

Linda left Gad to his own devices for the rest of the meal. There was no point in trying to turn the conversation back to the baby. Gad would persist, and no one in the family would find strength to defy him. She and Aran had already asserted themselves too far in buying a home on the Bench. Gad wouldn't allow them to steal any more attention—not tonight. In a way, Linda was almost happy she didn't have to talk about the baby. She'd been terrified all night that she might break into tears once the announcement was made. Then everyone would see—Aran especially—that she wasn't as hopeful as a new mother ought to be.

For the better part of an hour, Linda listened while Arletta and Aran followed meekly wherever Gad led. They talked about the twins, the difficulties they must have faced in learning their new languages, how many wayward souls Gad expected them to save. Only Tamsin refused to participate. She ate steadily and didn't look at her father, not once. Tamsin didn't respond to the least word that issued from Gad's mouth. Linda could have hugged her for that.

When supper was finished, Linda went to the kitchen. She had baked an apple pie early that morning, and stood for a long time with the knife in her hand, staring down at the crust. It was perfect, golden brown, the edge neatly braided. She had even managed to position the five vent holes precisely in the center.

Gad will never change, she realized. Then, with a terrible, slow awakening, *Neither will Aran. He hasn't changed, not at all. He only thinks he has. He's still Gad's boy, still Gad's to control. He always will be. And I'm stuck here now, with a baby on the way.*

She looked up, blinking back tears. Outside, the snow was spinning into a black night.

Stupid, Linda thought. *Stupid to rush into this so fast, to marry a man without really thinking it over, without knowing his family at all.* Never in her life had she felt so young, so shamefully aware of her naivete.

"Hey."

Linda whirled, still clutching the knife.

It was only Tamsin, lingering on the threshold of the kitchen. She put her hands up. "I come in peace."

"You scared me," Linda said.

"I'm sorry. About scaring you, and I'm sorry about my dad."

"It's okay."

"No, it isn't. He's an ass."

"I know he is."

"I don't understand," Tamsin said, "why no one else will stand up to him. And sometimes I can't make myself do it, even when I know I should. Sometimes I can't resist him. It gets harder all the time to tell him to go shove it."

The tears came again. Linda wiped them with her wrist. She didn't even put the knife down to do it.

"I'm really happy for you," Tamsin said. "You and Aran—about the baby."

There was something sad and old in Tamsin's eyes, a long, reticent sorrow, jarring in a teenage girl. Linda wondered whether Tamsin really was happy about the baby. Maybe it was only Gad's shadow dimming every smallest light.

Linda said, "I hope it'll be a boy." She didn't know how she could raise a daughter in this place, this family, this world.

40

An Incantation

The drive from Aran's new house back to the family home felt as if it were taking years—down into the valley, where the lowly lived. But at last, Gad turned up the gravel drive with the birches bare and stark against a half-seen winter, and the headlights crossed into the falling snow and made the house and the shop seem both near and impossibly distant. Gad shut off the car, and silently, his small family got out and tramped through the foot-high snow to the kitchen door. Gad hung back, watching.

Arletta went inside, but Tamsin paused at the kitchen door. The light above the concrete steps made a sallow ring. The girl stood, haloed and attended by the flakes that came whirling into the light, and looked back at Gad. "Aren't you coming?"

"In a minute."

Gad went into the shop instead. There, sheltered at last from scrutiny, he hissed out a long breath and looked desperately around the space, but all he could see was Aran's new house—how fine it had been, how expensive, the red-brick facade and the Oldsmobile in the driveway, the two young crab apple trees in the yard, sgraffito lines through the snow.

Everything Aran had now—all of it—belonged to Gad by rights. He felt in some obscure, inevitable way that Aran's talent was really his. Aran's success was Gad's doing, too, since Aran had come from him. He had sired that boy; he was the genesis of everything his son could claim. And there was that harlot Linda, sinking such a hook into Aran—a baby, his first child. She had Aran for good now. She would never let him go.

At the thought of the baby—his first grandchild—a flutter rose in Gad's chest. He crushed it out ruthlessly. He told himself he didn't care that he would be a granddad soon. The very word "granddad" seemed an incantation, a spell to transmogrify Gad into something warm and weak and cooing, something he couldn't allow himself to be—something for which his treacherous heart yearned with a sudden, fatal force.

Gad paced from one end of the shop to another, past the screens that hid his easel and the latest painting he'd copied from Aran's body of work. He crossed again, glanced at the calendar on his desk. He had circled today's date in black marker. Why? Surely not for the supper at Aran's house. That was the kind of engagement Arletta kept track of, not Gad. Then he remembered. The gallery in Boise owed Gad a letter—and, if he was blessed, a check.

He shut off the lights in the shop and stepped out into the snow. Winter slapped his cheeks as he made the long walk down the drive to the mailbox. The night smelled of smoke and ice, which were almost the same smell. The mailbox, when he touched it, stuck to his fingers for a moment, frozen there by the cold, which was the first Gad knew that his hands had been sweating in the pockets of his jacket. He was anxious to learn what his future might hold, if it held anything at all.

There was an envelope from the Boise gallery among the circulars and coupon books, but it was too dark to read, so Gad prayed as he walked back up to the house: *Heavenly Father, let my faith be justified. I've done as You directed. Give to me what's mine.*

Inside, he kicked off his boots and left them to dampen the kitchen floor. The house was silent—Tamsin up in her bedroom, where she barricaded herself most of the time, Arletta rustling faintly in the upstairs bath.

Gad went into the den and settled in his reclining chair. He dropped the rest of the mail on the side table and tore open the letter from Boise Fine Art. His hands shook as he slid the letter free. A check fluttered out and he grabbed for it, missed, bent from his recliner to snatch it up off the floor. He held the check up to the light. Two thousand three hundred dollars. For a moment, Gad could only stare at the figure. It was more money than he'd ever made from a single sign-painting gig. It was more money than he'd made in two or three months of work put together.

He unfolded the letter.

> *Dear Mr. Rigby,*
>
> *We are pleased to inform you that the patrons of Boise Fine Art responded favorably to our recent showing of your works. Six of the ten paintings displayed have sold. You will find your check enclosed along with an accounting of sold works by title, final price, and gallery commission.*
>
> *We look forward to hosting another show whenever you are ready. We would love to include your son Aran's work in our next show, as well! Many attendees asked about the availability of Aran's paintings and seemed eager to add him to their collections.*
>
> *With sincere gratitude,*
> *Paul Wheeler, owner*

Gad tucked the letter back inside its envelope and stared at the check again. A few more shows like the last one, and he'd be close to

Aran's level of success. Maybe he would buy a place right next to Aran's, and it would be bigger and more richly made—just to show that kid who was high and mighty after all.

He could feel a new potency flowing through him, confidence like none he'd known before. He rose from his chair and slipped the check into the breast pocket of his shirt. He called up the stairs, "Tamsin, come down here a minute. I want to talk to you."

The girl would be eighteen in May. It was time to start thinking seriously about her future. And now, with easy money in his pocket—proof from the Lord that strength would be rewarded—Gad knew the time was ripe to assert his will over his headstrong daughter. Tamsin had gotten the better of him the last time they'd discussed the matter. Gad was still raw over the memory. She wouldn't defy him again.

Tamsin came rather heavily down the stairs, stomping on every step. Her expression was sulky. She stood at the entry to the den, shifting from one foot to another. She wouldn't come closer than that.

"You'll be eighteen in a few months," Gad said.

"So?"

"So I think it's best that you start attending Singles Ward after your birthday."

Tamsin squinted. "Why?"

"So you can find a suitable husband, obviously. I want you married by your nineteenth birthday, or shortly after, and settled into a good, secure life."

Tamsin drew herself up. She sucked in a long, slow breath—for a moment Gad's firmness wavered. He had the impression she would pull him right in, the way a trout snaps down a fly, into some vast and mysterious greatness inside of her. He thought she would scream, and didn't know how he would react if she did.

Instead, the girl answered levelly. "I am not getting married when I'm nineteen."

"Yes you are, Tamsin."

"Like hell."

Gad took a step toward her. "Don't use that kind of language—not around me, not around anyone. It isn't right for a young lady."

"You can't tell me what to do," Tamsin said.

"I'm your father. It's my job to tell you what to do."

"How convenient for you."

Gad stuffed his right hand into the pocket of his trousers so Tamsin couldn't see him clenching his fist. It wasn't that he was itching to hit the girl—he wasn't that kind of man. He just didn't want to frighten her, and he couldn't think of any other way to maintain a tenuous hold on his temper than squeezing his fist so tightly his knuckles wanted to split. He wouldn't get angry now, not when the Lord had restored him to this place of rightful mastery.

Calmly, Gad said, "I only want what's best for you."

"How come you've never asked me what's best for me? Why do you think you know my mind better than I do?"

"Girls your age don't know—"

"That's bullshit, Dad."

"Watch your language." It was harder every moment to maintain a perfect calm. "You're my daughter, my only daughter, and I love you. It's a father's most important work to see that all his children have good, happy lives. Especially his daughters. This world can be cruel to women."

Tamsin snorted. "Tell me about it."

"You need to find a nice, sensible young man to settle down with. Going to Singles Ward will signal to the whole town that you're ready for marriage."

"Well, I'm not ready."

"You will be, by the time you're nineteen."

"Look, Dad, I don't know if I want a husband *ever*, let alone next year."

Gad was struck silent, light headed with surprise. It took him far too long to command his speech again, and while he groped for some response, he could feel Tamsin growing, expanding in her strength and fury.

"What are you talking about?" Gad finally said. "Of course you want to get married, you want to become a mother. All girls do."

"I've already told you I want to go to college."

"I thought you gave that silly idea up. I thought you'd become more sensible."

"Surprise: I haven't." She was all acid. "I will go to college, and that's that. End of story."

"But why? Why would any girl want to spend more time in school than she has to?"

"To learn things." Tamsin practically howled those words at him.

"I'm not having this argument with you again, Tamsin. We won't have the money to send you to college, so it's out of the question." That wasn't entirely true anymore. A few more art shows and Gad could send all his children to college if he chose to do it. Tamsin didn't need to know that.

"I'll send myself," she said. "I'll work to earn the money."

"You will not work. No daughter of mine will do something so undignified."

"Jeez, Dad, this isn't the Dark Ages. You know what I think is undignified? Trying to control your children like they're puppets on strings."

"Tamsin—"

"Even when they've grown up and moved out and have careers now of their own, and marriages of their own, and soon, children of their own, even though you didn't want to talk about that at dinner."

"Leave Aran out of this."

"Why wouldn't you talk about the baby, Dad? Does it scare you, to realize that Aran will be a father, too? Once he's a father, he'll be in charge of his own family. And then he'll be on even footing with you. You won't be able to lord it over him anymore."

"I've had enough of your back talk."

"You know what I think you're so afraid of? That Aran will realize, when he's a father himself, what real fathers are supposed to be like. Then he'll see you for what you are."

Gad shuddered. He almost said—almost pleaded with her—to tell him what he was, to name it. Instead, he clenched his fist again. He said, "You're pushing me."

She crumpled a little, and the anger in her eyes melted to despair. "Please," she said. "I'll go to a Mormon school. I'll go to BYU. I'll go to Ricks, if you want, so I'm still here in town."

"I'm sorry, Tamsin. College is out of the question. You don't need it, and it's a luxury we can't afford. But once you meet the right man— the man the Lord intends for you to marry—you'll see I was right all along. You'll be ready then to accept your place in the divine plan. It'll all make sense. You'll be glad I was firm with you and didn't allow you to run off to some college campus, to ruin your life and your one shot at happiness."

She breathed in raggedly, not quite a sob. "I should have stayed with Aran." Then she left the den without Gad telling her she could go.

As she climbed the stairs, Gad called, "I love you."

Tamsin didn't answer.

After she'd gone, Gad crossed back through the snow to his shop. He rolled away the partitions that hid his easel. His latest painting was there, waiting for him—a large, colorful still life, springtime lilacs spilling from a purple vase. The painting had been wrestling with Gad for weeks. All of his paintings wrestled. None had ever come easily—he'd been forced to dredge each one out of himself, and always found himself finishing a painting before it felt complete. Every work left him with a certain blunt dissatisfaction, a sense that nothing was right.

Gad picked up a brush and mixed the right shade of violet on his palette and stood back to see where he could make improvements. His attention strayed. He thought of the word "granddad," and it opened something wide and longing in his soul. He wondered what Aran's child would look like and saw, with a kind of slow and shameful guilt, Aran as a tiny boy, two or three years old, wearing his little denim overalls, playing in the garden. The lilacs had been blooming that day. Twenty years ago or more, yet every vivid moment came back to Gad with a deep throb of pain. The sweetness of the flowers hanging in the air. And Aran's funny gait as he'd run, hands held up as if in perpetual astonishment at the world. Gad remembered he had told himself then, a young and smitten father, that nothing in this life could ever be so perfect as the sound of his little boy laughing.

Gad pushed the memory away. Gently, he shut it behind that wall in his heart where all betraying things were penned—his agonies and weaknesses, his memories and doubts. Like shutting a tiger in its cage.

Gad stepped toward the canvas, touched his brush here and there, dotting in the color. He didn't like a thing about that painting. As with all the rest, the still life was skewed somehow and shadowed, despite its forceful color, the innocence of the subject. A small, sinister voice whispered, *This isn't art. It never can be. Art isn't a tool for harm, a thing made for vengeance.*

Gad tried again, daubing in a soft edge, then a hard one. No matter how he worked at the damn thing, the painting resisted. He was still fighting it, and still losing, when midnight came.

41

DON'T DARE

It was May, early May, and the lilacs were blooming. When Aran stood in the backyard and looked down into the valley, he could see specks of pale violet among the brief and hectic green. Astonishing, that he should be able to see lilacs from so far away. He had just cut the grass, even though he'd done the same job earlier that week. He needed the mindless, mechanical nature of the task, a distraction from his thoughts. Somehow the sharp green sappy smell of fresh lawn clippings mingled in his mind with the sound of a crop duster moaning low over the potato fields, and it all seemed the same to him, the steady rise and fall of the plane's engine and the thickets of lilac on the valley floor and the weeping cut-grass smell, all one dead-end banality, a wall with which he had collided.

Linda came out into the yard, huge and magnificent in a billowing blouse. She held two glasses of lemonade so their bottoms rested on her seven-month belly and left damp rings on the goddess-white cotton of her maternity shirt. She was always doing that now, carrying things on top of the baby as if it were a shelf or a sacrament tray. She handed a glass to Aran.

"What's on your mind?" Linda said. "If you keep mowing the lawn every few days, there won't be any lawn left."

There was no real need to ask what was on Aran's mind. He was haunted by the same worries that plagued Linda. After those first months of precipitous rise, the sales of Aran's paintings had plateaued. Now they were trending downward, crashing as swiftly as they'd risen.

"The usual," he said.

Linda exhaled, a weary sound, not exactly a sigh. They'd had this conversation dozens of times already. "It's like I always say, Aran: There will be ups and downs. It's something we have to expect. Demand for your work will ebb and flow. It's the overall trends we need to watch, not the numbers from one week to the next."

That was the problem. Back in March and April, his anxieties had revolved around "one week to the next." By now, the steadily decreasing sales *were* an overall trend. What was more, Linda—for all her intelligence, all her instinct—was only twenty-one, with no real experience in business. Maybe she didn't know what she was talking about. Maybe they had gambled everything on luck. Their luck had held for a while, but it would hold no more.

"I just can't understand," Aran said. "It doesn't seem right, it doesn't seem logical, for demand to rise so steeply and then . . ." He shrugged. How could he describe this present situation, the state of affairs since the end of winter? Plummet? Shatter? Like being sucked into a black hole—nothing, a void where there was no money, no interest, despite raving articles in all the best magazines.

"It doesn't make much sense," Linda admitted, looking down past her belly. She never looked down, never gave an impression of defeat. It was more concession than Linda had ever made to Aran's fears. He knew she was terrified, too.

"What am I going to do," Aran said, "if I can't provide for you and the baby?"

"We can sell the house, if we need to, and everything in it."

"No." Forcefully. He wouldn't give up this life he'd made, everything he'd built at such terrible cost.

"We might not have a choice. I don't like it any more than you do, but in a few more weeks, we'll have a baby to think of. We'll have to do what's right."

"I can go back to the fields—move pipe again. Maybe I can work my way up to foreman."

Linda didn't say anything. There wasn't enough money in moving pipe. They both knew that. Besides, it was seasonal work. But if he could only sell a few paintings here and there . . . he didn't even need to sell as many as he'd moved through the fall and winter. Two or three a month would do the trick and allow him to stretch a farmhand's pay far enough that they could get by.

"I can work, too," Linda said.

"Not with a baby to look after."

"Sure I can. Women do it all the time." She didn't sound enthusiastic about the idea.

Aran tried to imagine it, the strain of them both working—breaking his back in the fields, Linda at the Blocks department store or behind a register at Broulim's. Both of them coming home dull eyed and surly, their child crying for attention they were too worn out to give.

Slowly, he said, "Maybe what I should do is go down and have a talk with my dad."

"No, Aran—"

"I could go back to painting signs. If I really put some effort into it, I can take the whole business over when he's ready to retire. He's got clients everywhere, and I know sign making is steady enough work to support a family."

"Don't you dare—not after all we've been through, how hard I've worked to get you away from that man."

"That man is my father."

"Which doesn't mean he has a right to control you."

Aran's head hurt. His head hurt all the time, these days. He hadn't touched his lemonade and the glass was sweating in the sun. Drops of water ran down over his fingers, fell into the grass.

He said, "Sometimes I wonder if God is punishing me."

"For what?" Linda said, loud, disbelieving.

More and more often, she struck him that way—not a believer in anything, unless it was in Aran's talent and her own limitless potential.

He said, "Maybe I'm being punished for disobedience—defying the head of my family."

"Oh, for God's sake." She gestured to herself, the imminent swell of her body. "This is your family now, Aran, and you are the head of it. Together with me. We're both the heads."

"I was raised to obey my father."

"There has to be a limit. There has to be a line you won't allow him to cross. When are you going to become your own patriarch? You'll be a father at the end of June. You can't allow your dad to manipulate you forever."

The glass trembled in his hand. He could feel the ice cubes rattling. He said, "That's what I'm most afraid of, out of everything else."

"What, the baby?"

"I don't know how to be a father. My dad is the only example I've ever known. What if I can't do it? I'm not just talking about the money. What if I make a mess of it, Linda? What if I'm cold and controlling and angry and scared and this baby grows up to hate me?"

All the impatience and anger fell away from her then. She moved closer, as near as her belly would allow, and rubbed his back in little circles, intimate, comforting.

She said, "You won't be like him, not one bit. You already know how to be a good dad. Do the opposite of everything your father did to you."

42

REVELATION

Tamsin was the first to learn the truth of what Gad had done. Later, much later, when distance had granted some mercy and she could bear to look back on her family, she wouldn't be surprised by that fact—that she'd been first to understand. Who else should have seen the plot clearly, but the lone Rigby whose eyes had always been open?

On the last day of May, Tamsin lingered on a blanket at the end of the drive in dapples of light and shade. She had cracked the spine of a paperback so it would stay open, but the pages were riffling in the wind. She hadn't read a word. All her thoughts were on the future. Her eighteenth birthday had come. In a few more days, she would graduate from high school, and then she would be gone. Tamsin still had no idea how she would make her escape, but she wasn't without hope. She had her own car now, thanks to Linda. She might get in the Beetle and head out of town that very summer and never come back, except she had no money for gas or hotels, and no way to get it. Tamsin hadn't even tried to find a secret job. Even if the ice cream shop or the Mooseburger agreed to hire her, word would make its way back to Gad in a matter of hours, and she would be forced to quit again.

The mail truck appeared around the corner and crept down Ricks Avenue, pausing at every box. Tamsin jumped up from her blanket, nudged the book closed with her toe. She went and stood beside the mailbox and smiled at the postman when he reached through the window with a bundle of flyers and letters.

"You must be waiting for something special," the postman said.

Tamsin took the mail, pressing the whole bundle against her chest.

"Got a missionary out there somewhere," the postman guessed, "sending you love letters—is that it?"

Tamsin laughed. "Sure."

When the mail truck moved on, she returned to her blanket and tore open a large brown envelope without pausing to look at the front side. The envelope was big enough to hold a course catalog and informational pamphlets from one of the colleges she'd written to. Big enough to hold an application. She reached in and felt the slickness of glossy paper—a pamphlet for sure. Eagerly, Tamsin drew out the contents, then sat blinking down at the strange things in her hands, which weren't catalogs or brochures for the University of Montana or Adams State in Colorado, but rather a booklet of paintings.

It was a promotional device for an art gallery—featured works in an upcoming show, a show highly anticipated by collectors, according to the text on the cover. Tamsin swallowed hard. Something about the brochure made her feel queasy. "The Rigby Vision of the American West," the title read, and the paintings on the cover looked like Aran's. And yet they weren't Aran's paintings. Tamsin thought she recognized every piece, yet something was skewed and misaligned in the compositions. Something was missing. Her thoughts treaded water through the warm summer air. Only very slowly did Tamsin come to wonder why Gad had received a brochure from one of Aran's galleries.

Then she understood.

Tamsin flipped through the booklet again, studying every painting. The copies were good, in a technical way—a soulless way. The skill should have surprised her, and yet it didn't, not at all. Hadn't she found her father's secret cache of paintings long ago, when she'd gone snooping through his shop? She'd thought Gad had given up painting after he'd burned Aran's work. He hadn't, though. He'd kept on going.

A folded, typewritten letter accompanied the brochure. Tamsin opened it and read, though she already knew what the letter would say.

~

Tamsin stormed into her father's shop, threw the brochure down on his workbench. It made a satisfying slap against the table. Gad looked up from his desk, dropped his pencil in the crease of his accounting book.

"Did you think I wouldn't find out?"

"Tamsin, what are you doing in here?"

He sprang up from his chair, moved toward a plywood partition on wheels. The partition was only halfway closed across the corner of his shop. Tamsin could see the suggestion of an easel and a half-painted canvas blurred by shadow. So that was where Gad had done his dirty work.

She pointed to the brochure, stabbed it with her finger like maybe she could reach Gad's heart through its pages. "You've been copying Aran's paintings. Selling knockoffs of his work."

Gad smiled coolly. "You're overreacting. I've been selling my own work."

"Like hell you have."

"Look more closely. It's my name on the paintings, my name on the exhibit—"

"Rigby. That's the only name that matters. I know what you're doing. You changed small details here and there so you can claim all these paintings are original. But you aren't really trying to sell originals, are you, Dad? You're trying to undercut Aran's market. You're stealing his customers—his vision—his money."

Gad settled back into his chair. There was no point now in trying to hide his easel. He picked up his pencil, returned to the accounts. "Aran has nothing to complain about. That's the nature of the business."

"He might lose his house." Tamsin couldn't keep her voice down, couldn't maintain control over anything, it seemed. "He told me all about it the last time I saw him."

"When did you see him?"

"I went up to visit Aran and Linda just last weekend. I was helping Linda make some clothes for the baby. Not that it's any of your business, not that you have a right to know. Aran was upset. I could tell by how quiet he was. When Linda went to the kitchen to fix us all some lunch, I finally got Aran to admit what was eating him. His sales have dried up. He couldn't figure out why. I guess we know the reason now, don't we? He could lose everything, Dad. His career might be destroyed forever!"

"Good. Let him lose his house, his high-and-mighty lifestyle. Let him lose it all. He never deserved it in the first place. A faithless, disobedient man, the shame of our family—why does Aran deserve what I never had?"

"You're a sinner. Your soul is black with sin."

Tamsin didn't so much speak those words as allow them to burn through her. They seemed to come from somewhere beyond herself, from a great crackling fire of rage that had charred the air around her. Gad flinched. One small corner of Tamsin's mind was sequestered beyond that madness, observing the whole scene with detachment. She wondered with calm curiosity whether the fiery voice—and the terrible electricity all around her—was the Holy Ghost after all. Maybe the Spirit had visited her, an unbeliever, in her hour of need.

She said, "Alma prayed for his son when he did wickedness and was led astray."

"Don't quote holy Scripture at me, as if I don't know the word of God."

"What have you done for Aran? Nothing but cause him pain."

"Enough of this!"

Gad had hold of himself now. Whatever superstitious dread Tamsin had evoked with her unearthly self-possession had already snuffed itself out. He was nothing but fury now. He left his desk and swept down on her, but she didn't move. Tamsin gave no ground to the man who had once been her father. He gripped her arm, began hauling her to the door.

"This nonsense is over," Gad said. "All of it. You've got no place meddling in a man's affairs."

He shoved her out of the shop. Tamsin stumbled in the grass but righted herself before she fell. Gad tried to slam the shop door in her face. Tamsin lifted her foot just in time to stop the door from closing. It rebounded from the sole of her shoe, and Gad jumped back. She could see him shaking.

"You fix this," Tamsin said. "You undo what you've done to Aran, or I'll make you regret it. I know a secret, Dad—one that will ruin the whole family. It'll destroy your business, your standing in the church. It'll wreck Mom's life, take down Brig and Ondi, too, before they're even back from their missions."

"You're lying," Gad said.

"Look at me. You know I'm not."

"Get out of here. I'm sick of looking at you. More trouble than you're worth, just like your brother."

"Make amends to Aran, and then leave him alone. Stop trying to control him."

"I'll lead this family as I see fit."

"Then I'll destroy this family—every single person in it. And I'll start with you. It'll be exactly what you deserve."

43

HALFWAY THERE

Aran wasn't home when Tamsin came knocking. Linda, with one hand on her swollen belly, told her Aran had gone out painting.

"Where?" Tamsin asked. "Did he give you any idea where he'd be? I have to tell him something important. It can't wait."

Linda was pale. The baby or the steep decline in Aran's sales was draining her. The old cutting look had faded from her eyes. She was haunted now, and quiet. Tamsin couldn't believe she was the same girl who had once climbed the water tower to look down on Rexburg, the same girl whose hair had tangled in the wind.

"Is everything all right?" Linda said. "You seem upset."

"I am. And nothing is all right, but Aran needs to know about it first. He'll tell you everything once he knows, but he needs to hear it before I can tell you. I'm sorry, Linda. I hope you understand."

Her hand moved in tight circles over the baby. "It's about your father, isn't it?"

Tamsin nodded.

"Aran went south along the Bench," Linda said. "Somewhere down past Poleline Road. I don't know any more than that."

Tamsin drove for half an hour, wandering up and down the dirt tracks and service roads between the potato fields, bumping along dusty ruts, fearful she would pick up a nail or drive over an old twist of barbed wire and be stranded out there, miles from the nearest house. Finally, Tamsin spotted her brother, small in a vast green field, the crops knee high around him. He was standing still before his French easel—not painting, but staring at the horizon where the tops of the Tetons melted into the glare.

Tamsin left her car right there in the middle of the service road. She set out down a long furrow of earth. The soil was dry and water cracked, breaking and shifting underfoot. She felt as if she walked for hours, for miles. When she was close enough to call his name, Aran turned slowly, almost as if he'd expected to find her out there in the stillness of the field. Tamsin was panting from the long walk, and from grim anticipation of what she must say. Aran watched her with an expression of desolation. The panel on his easel was white, untouched. He waited for Tamsin to speak.

"I know what happened to the money," she said. "Your sales. Dad has been undercutting you. He's been selling copies of your work, making money off your name."

Aran stared at the low white glare again, the unreachable horizon. His mouth fell open, as if he wanted to speak, but what words, what words could anyone find for something like this?

"You have to believe me, Aran. It's true. I confronted him. He didn't deny it."

"I believe you," Aran said, softly.

"He seemed pleased about it—glad I'd found out. Like he was rubbing my face in it, the sick old bastard."

"It makes sense. Of course. Perfect sense."

Aran spoke as if in a dream. Tamsin couldn't have said whether he was aware of her presence, whether he was conscious of anything at all, save for the thunder of her news. She took hold of his arm. Through the rough plaid of his shirt, she felt his sinews jump, startled by her touch.

"What are you going to do about it?" Tamsin demanded.

"Do?"

"You can't let this slide. You have to put your foot down, make him see—"

He flared up suddenly. "What can I make him see? That he has the power to ruin my life? He knows that already. He's already done it."

"No, he hasn't."

"The money is gone. Or near enough that it might as well be gone."

"You can get it all back: the sales, your career—"

"No, I can't. It's over. It's been over for months now."

Tamsin shoved him hard. Aran stumbled backward over the potato vines and almost fell. Guilt stabbed her, but she didn't let up. Someone had to knock some sense into her brother, and she was the only one close enough to do it.

"Will you shut up," Tamsin yelled. "For God's sake, listen to yourself! You've let Dad push you around all your life, and you've never stood up to him, never, not once!"

Aran staggered upright, affronted and disbelieving, while Tamsin went on shouting at him, beating her fists against the empty air.

"God, I'm so sick of this town and this pointless life, and I'm so sick of this family! Everyone gives Dad whatever he wants without even trying to fight!"

"Tamsin—"

"He's a tyrant. He thinks he's a god! He can snap his fingers and everyone does his bidding. I'm the only one who ever says no to him! The only one!"

Aran was stepping over the rows of plants now, reaching for her. Tamsin moved back. Her throat was raw, and her ears hurt from the sound of her own screaming, but she couldn't stop. She didn't want to.

"I can't keep saying no to him," she cried. "I can't. It's harder all the time. He's going to win someday, Aran. He's going to turn me into the same thing he made of you, and Mom, and Brig and Ondi."

Aran caught her in his arms, pulled her against his chest, held her till she stopped sobbing and shaking and she was breathing easier, breathing in the smell of turpentine from his shirt.

"It's okay." He rocked her gently from side to side, murmuring close to her ear. "Tamsin, it's going to be okay. You aren't like me. You're strong. He can't break you like he did me."

She pushed away from Aran. "Yes, he can break me. He's already halfway there."

"What do you mean?"

"He's been threatening to marry me off for a long time."

"I don't get it," Aran said. "To who?"

"I don't know. Anyone, I guess. It doesn't matter to him, as long as I'm somebody's wife, as long as I'm having babies and obeying my patriarch like a good girl. That night we all came to your house for dinner, after we got home, he told me I couldn't go to college and I had to be married by the time I turned nineteen and I . . . I couldn't stand up to him the way I used to. I was slipping, Aran—don't you get it? Slipping away from myself."

Aran kept his hands on her shoulders. He watched her face till Tamsin drew a long, ragged breath. Then he let go of her. She could stand on her own.

"Why?" Aran said. "What's different now? He could never rattle you before."

Tamsin looked at the blank panel on his easel. She said, "It's the paintings. How long has it been since we've painted together?"

Aran shifted, dragging his feet in the soil. "Almost a year."

"I can't see myself without your eyes," Tamsin said. "Without you, I don't know who I am."

"But Linda—"

"I know," Tamsin said shortly. "I don't want to hurt Linda, either. She's the best friend I've ever had. But I can't let Dad win. And you can't let him win, Aran. You can't let him get away with what he's done to you."

"I don't see what I can do about it," Aran said. "If I had enough money to hire a lawyer, then maybe—"

"We have something better than a lawyer. We can ruin him, take him apart, destroy his standing in this town, this church—"

"No, Tamsin. I don't want to ruin our father. That would make me no different from him. He's the one who ruins people, not me."

"We've already let Dad have his way for too long—for all our lives. I won't let him take my soul. Not when I have a way to fight back."

"You can't show the paintings to anyone, Tam."

"Those paintings will sell." Tamsin knew it was cruel to use Aran's desperation against him. She was her father's daughter, after all. "Those nudes are your very best work. There's nothing else like them in all the world. Collectors will pay good money for them. All your money troubles could be over—"

"My marriage, too."

"If you won't sell the paintings and take the money—and give half of it to me—then I'll make sure the whole town sees them. I'll do it."

"It'll ruin you in this town."

"Good. It'll be worth it. Dad will be finished here, too—church, business, everything."

"And I'll be finished. Are you so eager to destroy me?"

"I guess you have a tough choice to make, then." Tamsin hated herself for being so ruthless, leaving him no way out. But this was what it had all come down to—what Gad had engineered. She must break Aran's heart or allow herself to be broken. "Sell the paintings and give me half, or everyone will see what we've done together."

Aran looked at her for a long moment. The color was high in his cheeks, furious red. Tamsin knew he was weighing her, trying to decide how serious she was. Tamsin knew she'd won a bitter victory when Aran exhaled suddenly, pinching the bridge of his nose. He closed his eyes.

"I'll destroy those paintings, Tam, before I hurt Linda that way. I'll burn them up like Dad did to my old work."

"You won't," she said. "You love those paintings too much to burn them. You love me too much. Besides, you aren't like Dad. You can't destroy beautiful things."

He couldn't speak now. He could only whisper. He couldn't look at Tamsin, either. "You have to give me time. If the paintings must be sold, it'll be Linda who arranges it. She's the only one who has the right contacts and knows how to bargain."

"Fine," Tamsin said.

"I need to tell her first." Aran faltered, swallowing hard. "What we did together, you and me. I need to explain what those paintings *are*—though I don't know yet, myself. It'll take some time to figure it out. I have to do it gently if I'm going to have any hope of keeping Linda."

"You have two days," Tamsin said.

"I need longer."

"You don't have longer. Two days. After that, the paintings are mine, and I'll do with them whatever I like."

44

Obedient Son

Aran spent those two days sequestered in his studio, rising from bed before dawn, while Linda was still sleeping. There seemed little purpose in staying beside Linda now, no point in lying still. He didn't sleep by night. He didn't really sleep at all during those two long days. Aran remained in the basement studio till well after dark, too. Sometimes when the weight of anxiety and helpless despair became too great a burden, he would collapse for a few minutes on the broken-down old couch he kept near his easel, with one arm thrown across his face to block out the light. The dull surrender to a gray half consciousness couldn't really be called sleep, but it restored enough energy that he could keep on working, keep on thinking through his dilemma. He never found a solution, though. There was no way to reveal the truth to Linda without hurting her terribly. There was no sure way that Aran could see to save his marriage.

At first, when he and Tamsin had parted ways and he'd returned from the field, Aran had spent several hours digging through boxes of his old books and sketch pads and stray records—all the things he'd taken from his family home but never unpacked. He'd come across the sketch pad from the previous summer, the summer when he'd met

Linda, and had sat on the cold floor of his studio turning page after page. The images were like glimpses of someone else's memories. Shaded blocks of cattle under the trees, his mother at the kitchen window, looking out from the dim and private confines of her interior. And there was Tamsin, of course, standing astride her bicycle in the middle of the driveway. His brothers playing catch at the end of the yard, their symmetry, the ball like a moon in the sky, perfectly white, perfectly round. Gad was there, too, more often than Aran liked to see. It surprised him, how frequently he'd drawn his father, but in every sketch, Gad was looking away. Always turned away from Aran.

When he found the sketch he'd made on Pioneer Day—Linda lounging in the door of the abandoned house, the window bright behind her—he'd been seized by an urge to paint. The need came upon him with such ferocity that he didn't realize till that moment how little he had wanted to paint those past several months since the money had vanished. He'd only been putting himself through the paces, doing what was necessary to pay his bills. He had lost all sense of inspiration. Yet now here it was again, the sweet and sudden fall of lightning, the bolt that burned from a distant heaven, straight down into his heart. Inspiration was never a thing Aran had been able to predict or control. It came when it came, and all he could do—all he'd ever been able to do in its trembling presence—was respond, the obedient son.

He took the old canvas off his easel, though the painting was still wet and only partly finished. He fixed a new one in its place and set to work that very hour, blocking in the forms, drawing the rough shape of her in shining lines of ultramarine and alizarine. The hours passed, the brush kept moving in his hand, and the painting became a prayer. *Give me hope,* the pigments said to his canvas. *Leave me some way to save my marriage, my future.* And whether he was painting or slumping on the couch, everything he saw and everything he made had a deep umbral cast of shadow, a darkness surrounding the isolated figure of his wife—his heart—and a single, hard-edged square of blue sky beyond.

Both nights, he ate supper with Linda at the table upstairs and she asked him what was wrong. Aran could only answer, "The usual," but she looked at him for a long time. He could feel Linda's eyes on his downcast face like a touch, like the pressure of some insistent hand.

By the end of the second day, the painting was complete, but Aran still had no answers. He rinsed his brush, set it aside, stepped back wearily to look at what he'd made. The image was perfect and true. And the time had come to confess everything, and spoil a fragile beauty.

Aran drove to the shack at the edge of the wheat field. The evening was hot, the summer rising to its full and short-lived power. The heat had put all the birds to sleep early, so the slamming of his car door was almost the only sound, a hard, harsh clap of finality that went on echoing inside his head. Aran moved slowly through knee-high grass and clouds of lazy gnats toward the place that had once been his and Tamsin's alone. This was the last time he would set foot inside the old studio. Once he'd confessed to Linda, once he'd put everything in her hands, the shack would be a space holding nothing, a lacuna in a dry, brown world, and everything he and Tamsin had shared—everything, even the simple, innocent bond of brother and sister—would be finished forever.

Inside, the light was low, the shadows dense. The shack still smelled faintly of linseed oil and turpentine, and the space was still ghostly full of Tamsin's presence, her stark, unbending stature in a sideways light. The chair in which she had so often posed was empty by the window. But all the panels were there, leaning against the wall in stacks of ten or more, each bearing the image of a strength Aran had never possessed in himself.

"I'll miss you," he said aloud to Tamsin's lingering presence. It was clear to him now that once this was over—when the terrible fallout of this day had settled, and whatever life remained to Aran crept in its new direction—he must leave Rexburg forever. With or without Linda, he would have to go, and Tamsin must go, too. Somewhere, beyond the reach of that town, a fresh and separate world waited for his sister. Tamsin still had a future, and a world she might shape to her will. Aran couldn't say the same for himself. He couldn't see clearly enough to know.

He gathered up all the paintings of Tamsin, every last one, and found himself back home in his studio without recalling the drive. He went around the perimeter of the room, leaning each panel against the wall, facing into the center where he stood, sick and shivering before his easel. He looked at the freshly painted canvas one last time—his prayer, his inspiration—and then he called Linda downstairs.

She came down into the basement. The swell of her pregnant body was thrust out before her like a barrier.

"What is it?" Linda said.

Then she said nothing. Her eyes went to the floor—to the wall around the floor, the ring of dark portraits closing in around her. Linda turned in a slow circle. Aran could only watch, gutted and helpless, as she took in the sight. Bleak understanding flashed in her eyes. There were thirty-nine paintings in all. Aran had counted them as he'd set them out for Linda to see. And there was no mistaking the figure, the unclothed body, in each and every one. That copper hair. There was no mistaking.

"What is this?" Linda said, breathless.

"Some . . . some paintings I've done. In the past. Before I met you."

"Oh my God."

"Linda—"

Her shock evaporated, or at least it was eclipsed by rage. She rounded on Aran, drew herself up like a snake ready to strike. "I don't want to hear it. Whatever you've got to say, I don't care. I don't want to hear it, it doesn't matter, nothing matters anymore. This is over. It has to be over, all of it—this marriage and this life and this thing you've been doing for God knows how long."

"It isn't what you think," Aran said, knowing how weak and commonplace his denial sounded—and knowing how untrue.

The paintings both were and were not what Linda thought them to be. Aran himself had never been able to sort out the tight wrap and weave of Tamsin's influence, his need for her. He only knew that she struck him with the same bolt of fire he'd felt two days before, when he'd begun the painting of Linda. Tamsin—with her power of defiance, her wholeness of self—was inspiration. She was the very embodiment of Aran's drive to paint. That was the most sense he'd ever made of this wreck, this ruin. Tamsin was a constriction of compulsion all around him, and Aran was like some small creature caught in a spider's web, shrouded in white silk till you could no longer see the animal inside. All that had ever existed of him was the cotton bulk of the web, the shapelessness, the wrapping.

"What is it, then?" Linda closed on him. "What exactly is this, Aran, what is going on? Because I know what it looks like. You know what it looks like. What else can it possibly be?" She recoiled again, before Aran could answer. Her hands went around the unseen child. "Oh, God. You have to stay away. You can't come near my baby."

Nothing had ever hurt him so badly before. He'd never known such hurt was possible, a fast, erosive agony. It flung him entirely out of his body. He felt as if he were a hundred miles away, watching this terrible scene unfold through a pinhole of pain.

"Linda, please. Just listen to me."

"I will not listen, you pervert, you freak!"

"I've never touched Tamsin. I never would—I've never wanted to. The paintings were never about *that*, Linda, not at all."

"Then what? What is it about?" She spread her arms, thrust them toward the walls, the ring of images she couldn't escape. Aran didn't know whether she was crying or laughing. He suspected Linda herself couldn't tell the difference. "What is this thing you've been doing, and why have you been doing it when you know it's wrong?"

"It isn't wrong."

She let out a ragged breath, closed her eyes so she couldn't see the paintings or him.

"It's just art, Linda. That's all it's ever been."

For a long moment, she said nothing. That was the worst of it, Aran thought—the way he could feel her gathering her wits, evaluating what was right there before her, seeing it all in a way Aran never could.

When she spoke again, her voice was low and dull. "This isn't just art. It's not your usual work. It's better, Aran—even better than you usually do. There's feeling in these things, these . . . portraits. Real emotion. I can see it. This is something more than art, something *more*." She pressed the heel of her hand against one eye, trying to hold back tears by force. "Just tell me what this is, what she is to you. I have to know. I have to make this make sense somehow, somehow, or I can't keep going, I can't hold it together for another day."

What name could he put to the strange force that had haunted him for so long? He said, "She's my muse."

Now at last Linda took note of the new painting, the canvas on the easel. Her back was turned to Aran but he saw her shoulders go tense, her neck stiffen. A guttural scream ripped from her throat and filled the studio, battered its walls. Linda lurched at the easel. Her ungainly body moved faster than Aran could believe. She grabbed the box knife from his taboret, the razors he used to scrape his palette clean, and with a flick, extended the blade.

It was only a heartbeat of time. In that terrible, suspended moment, Aran knew she would destroy the painting—the first fire of inspiration that had burned in him for months. This was the only image he had wanted to paint in all this long, dry, difficult time. Aran would let her destroy it. He had no choice. Linda controlled everything—his life, his future. It was all in her hands.

She stopped just before the razor sliced the canvas. She opened her hand. The box cutter clattered on the floor.

"Why?" She was too level when she spoke, too calm.

Aran moved cautiously to stand beside her. He didn't try to touch her.

"I didn't tell you about those paintings," he said, "because I knew you wouldn't understand. I knew you'd assume something terrible was going on—"

"No," Linda said. "Your muse. Why? Why wasn't it me?"

There was no answer to that question—nothing Aran could make sense of, nothing any reasonable person could understand. What fans a spark into a flame? What divides that which ought to be whole, and hides the better half of a heart in another person's body?

When it was clear that Aran would give no response, Linda staggered away from him, toward the sliding door that let out into their backyard. Aran followed her outside. It seemed the best thing to do.

She was leaning against the side of the house, sucking air as if the muggy evening could give her some relief.

"What else?" she demanded. "What else haven't you told me? I'm stuck here, Aran. I can't leave with this baby till I find some way to support myself and this kid." She rasped out those final words as if they had stirred a greater rage. "I'm stuck with you and your awful family, at least for a few months. So tell me right now: What else don't I know about you? What have you been hiding?"

He almost answered, *Nothing*. But that would have been a lie. There were things Linda didn't know about him—things no one knew, not even Tamsin. He owed Linda the truth now. All of it. Aran steeled himself, took a deep breath, looked at Linda directly, even though she still refused to look at him.

"Those rumors," Aran said, "about me. They weren't all lies—not entirely."

"Oh my God."

"There was a time, years ago, when I was desperate for money."

"No."

"Joel Kimball set me up to sell . . . something . . . for his friend."

"Joel Kimball? Sandy's husband?"

Aran nodded.

"Oh my God!" Linda shouted.

"It was years ago, and only one time. I've never done it again. I never would."

"This whole town," Linda said, staggering away from the house, out into the grass. She glared down at Rexburg on the valley floor. "This entire place is nuts. I wish I'd never come here. I wish this town had never existed at all. I wish it could be wiped off the face of the earth."

"Linda—"

"I don't want to hear it, your justifications, your stupid excuses. It's true. This town is crazy and your family is even crazier. I've always known it. But I never knew till now how deep the madness ran."

"We aren't crazy," Aran said, weakly, knowing it was pointless to deny it.

She laughed, unamused. "You don't think so? You've been painting your teenage sister nude, and your dad has been copying your work to try to steal your career. What isn't crazy about that?" She stormed back into the studio, talking all the while. "Your mother is a space cadet and your brothers—I'm sure there's something wrong with them, too. We just haven't learned their secrets yet."

She was turning slowly again, glaring at the paintings of Tamsin with one hand pressed to her chin, a calculating expression.

"We need the money," Linda said after she'd examined the whole collection again.

"I know."

"Desperately."

"I know."

"If I'm going to get out of this town and take care of this baby, I've got to have the money."

Aran nodded, held his breath.

"I can sell these paintings," Linda said quietly.

"They're only studies."

"It doesn't matter. They're still . . ." She paused, swallowed, fought to speak on. "They're still your finest work. They're a cut above, Aran—they're almost unreal. I'm taking them to Jackson Hole, to Feldermann's gallery."

"No. If the art world knows I painted my sister like this, my career—"

"*You* didn't paint Tamsin." She almost spat those words at him. "Make up a fake name. I don't care what it is. Sign that name to every single one of these portraits. I'll tell Feldermann it's a new client—that I've expanded to represent other artists besides the great Aran Rigby."

Such mockery in her tone. It made his stomach churn. But she was right. It was a way out of this mess—the only way out, if they hoped to preserve what little they still had.

"I'll do it," Aran said. "Whatever you think is best."

"Here's what I think is best." Linda spun to face him. "We're leaving Rexburg as soon as we have enough money to go. That was the deal we made when I agreed to marry you."

"It was," Aran admitted.

"You didn't take me seriously then. You'll take me seriously now."

"Yes," he said, "I will." He meant it.

"The moment these paintings are all sold, as soon as the money is in the bank, we're leaving this town and your family forever. That includes Tamsin. Her most of all."

He had no choice but to agree—not if he hoped to hold on to Linda, and their child. His career, too, if that could still be salvaged.

"Tamsin needs to leave Rexburg, as well," Aran said.

"I don't care where she goes. Straight to Hell, for all I'm concerned."

"You don't really mean that."

Linda choked on her tears. She still loved Tamsin, however she might deny it.

"Linda, she needs help."

"I'll say she does."

"She needs a little of this money—whatever money we can get—so she can put some distance between herself and our dad. If she can't get away from him, he'll . . . ruin her. The way he ruined me."

Linda shrugged, turned away.

"Please," Aran said. "I'll do what you ask. We'll leave as soon as we have the resources, I swear. We'll sell the house and take the baby and go wherever you like, anywhere you like, and I won't have a thing to do with my family ever again. But let me do this one kind thing for Tamsin. Let me give her a way out of this town, before I say goodbye to her forever."

Linda breathed in once, sharply. Then slowly, she exhaled. "Fine."

"Thank you," he said.

"I'm going to call Feldermann first thing in the morning," Linda said. "I'll take everything over to Jackson on Friday morning. With any luck, the deal will be done before the weekend, and I'll never have to think about this mess again."

"I'll go with you," Aran said. "I don't want you driving alone in your state, with the baby, and how upset you are."

"Like hell you'll go with me. I need the time alone to think."

A chill swept over Aran. She would spend the drive thinking about him—whether she could still stomach being married to a man of his sort. He might lose Linda and the baby after all.

He said, "Whatever you want. Whatever you need."

There was nothing else he could do.

45

THE VERY SKY

Tamsin was helping her mother wash the dishes after supper when the phone rang. She heard Gad's recliner creaking in the den. He was pushing himself up to answer the call.

"I'll get it," Tamsin said, grabbing for a dish towel to dry her hands.

She spun away before Arletta could stop her. This had become a routine for Tamsin—answering calls the moment they came, fetching the mail, opening the door whenever a neighbor or one of her aunts came knocking. Anything she could do to outmaneuver Gad, to make herself the face and voice of the Rigby home. Those opened doors and sorted letters were very small victories, but even the slightest authority over her father was well worth the trouble.

She reached the phone moments before Gad did.

"I got it," Tamsin said, and picked up the receiver. "Rigby residence."

"Tamsin. This is Linda."

Tamsin turned her back on Gad, though he was already returning to the den. Aran had phoned a couple days prior to let her know the deed was done, the cat was out of its bag and wasn't going back in again. "You won," Aran had said. "I showed her everything, God help me." When Tamsin had asked him if Linda was all right, Aran couldn't answer.

"Hi." A terrible deep quaking settled in Tamsin's stomach.

"I'm calling from the pay phone at Porter Park. I want you to come down here and meet me."

"Why are you at the park? What's going on?"

"Just get here fast. I won't wait all night."

The line clicked, then hummed in Tamsin's ear.

She returned the phone to its hook but found she couldn't move. Linda wasn't at home. Had she decided to leave Aran, then? That wasn't what Tamsin had wanted. Aran's warning returned to her, bubbling up from memory in disjointed pieces. *This isn't what art is meant for. Manipulate, control. Those paintings we made together—a tool for sin. Break your heart, and mine.*

"Are you all right, dear?" Arletta said from the kitchen. "Who was calling?"

"I have to go." Tamsin started for the door.

"At this hour? It'll be dark soon."

Tamsin didn't answer. She hurried through the kitchen door, out into the mellow light of sunset. She could have taken the Beetle. It would have been faster. Instead, she pulled her bike from the long grass beside the shop. Somehow that seemed right—as right as she could make things, now. The first time she'd met Linda, it had been at that park, and Tamsin had ridden the bicycle there. She would do the same tonight, bring this hard, grim drama full circle.

Tamsin had thought to ride to the corner of the park where she knew the pay phones stood. But when she arrived on the path that encircled the wide green field, she spotted Linda at once. Linda was unmistakable in her flowing red maternity shirt, her body wide and swollen. She was standing more or less in the same place where Tamsin had met her, that afternoon a year before when they'd talked about books and other harmless things.

Tamsin left her bike leaning up against an aspen tree. She walked out into the field, dizzy, almost breathless. Barn swallows were strafing the grass, chasing the insects that rose in the evening light. The birds dodged and wove around her legs. Their wild flight made Tamsin feel as if she were about to walk off the earth.

She approached Linda slowly, stood mute and trembling a few paces away.

Linda reached into her purse. She produced a roll of cash, handed it to Tamsin. Tamsin took the money without a word.

"Make the most of it," Linda said. "It's all you'll get from me."

Tamsin looked down at the roll. She wouldn't count it in front of Linda, but she supposed there must be a few hundred dollars in her hand, at least.

"It's an advance from Feldermann," Linda said.

"From whom?"

"Aran's gallery, over in Jackson Hole. One of his galleries—his first. My first. Feldermann was kind enough to give me an advance against some of our projected sales. He didn't need to do that. But he could tell the paintings will all sell, every one. They're works of genius."

"They are," Tamsin said. "You went to Jackson?"

"I took all the paintings with me. They're gone now. They're in Feldermann's hands. No one knows Aran painted them. No one will ever know."

"But they were his best," Tamsin said.

"He never should have made them."

There was no response Tamsin could give that wouldn't upset Linda more. She stuffed the roll of cash in the pocket of her skirt. It hung there, heavy on her hip.

"When the paintings sell," Linda said, "when the rest of the money comes in, you won't get a penny."

Tamsin chewed her lip. She had wanted half. She was entitled to half. But she didn't argue. She said, "I made him do it, you know. I made him do all of it—painting me that way, even when he didn't want to, even when he said we should stop. And then I made him tell you. I . . . threatened him. I was going to expose him, and us, and everything, every bad thing about our family. He didn't have a choice. He had to tell you first."

Linda looked away, up to the Bench where her house was, and her husband. "You made him tell me?"

"He didn't want to do it. He knew it would hurt you. I knew it would hurt you, too, Linda, but I was trapped. I didn't have a choice."

They both fell quiet. The swallows flitted around them, rapid and dark as spirits.

Finally, when she could stand the silence and the chill no longer, Tamsin said, "It never meant what you think it meant."

"What did it mean, then?"

"It was control," Tamsin said. "The only thing I could control."

"Look at me," Linda said.

Tamsin couldn't do it.

"Look at me," she said again.

Tamsin forced herself to meet Linda's eye. She expected Linda to unleash all her fury then, and God knew, Tamsin would have deserved it. Instead, they only stared at one another while the sun went on sinking and the light turned redder around them, then violet blue, then dusk. There was anger in Linda's expression, and pain. But Tamsin also saw something she might have called sympathy.

"We stopped," Tamsin said, "after you came into the picture. Once Aran fell for you, we never did it again. He wouldn't. He said it wasn't right. I gave it up for you, Linda. I gave up having control over my life because I didn't want to hurt you. You were my friend. I loved you."

"Are you sure," Linda said, "it never happened again? Once I was here?"

Tamsin nodded.

"Are you lying?"

She shook her head.

Another long silence.

Tamsin asked, "Are you going to stay with Aran?"

"I don't know. Not tonight, that's for sure. I'm going to sleep at Sandy's place. I've already called her—and Aran. I'll decide about the rest in the morning. Or later than that. Maybe I'll never decide. I don't know yet, I just don't know."

"Linda, I—"

"You should go now," Linda said.

Tamsin hesitated.

"Go. I can't look at you anymore."

"Aran is a good person. He never did anything wrong. It was my fault—all of it."

"Goodbye, Tamsin."

There was nothing left to say. Tamsin walked back toward her bike, but everything around her was a blur in the twilight. The dim swallows flung themselves across her path, wheeling into the heat and blindness of her tears.

Tamsin never knew how she managed to sleep that night. But morning light woke her, watery and pale in her eyes. She sat up slowly in her bed. It was Saturday. Her body ached. She felt old, worn out, like a rag that had been used and wrung too many times and was threadbare now, ready to rip in two.

She slid out of bed and opened her sock drawer, found the roll of money Linda had given her. She counted it, then counted again. Four hundred and fifty dollars. Not a fortune, by any means, but it would be enough to get her out of Rexburg. It had to be enough. She stuffed the cash in her pocket.

Tamsin wouldn't be able to take much with her—only a few changes of clothes, a book or two, perhaps a photo of her family. She could only carry whatever she could fit in her backpack. Anything more would be noticed. Gad would see and grow suspicious. Even Arletta might try to stop her. She packed quickly, choosing what to take and what to leave behind with a dashing speed, not giving herself any time to succumb to sentiment. When she had all the necessities in her pack, Tamsin glanced at the clock on her nightstand. It was half past eleven already. Why had Arletta allowed her to sleep so late?

Downstairs, in the great final emptiness of the house, Arletta began to play the piano. Tamsin paused on the threshold of her door, listening as the chords rang up through the bones of the old family homestead. It wasn't a religious song. That fact struck Tamsin and held her in her place. It was "Bridge over Troubled Water." Tamsin hadn't even known her mother knew the song, let alone that she could play it. She had never heard Arletta play any piece of music that wasn't a hymn or a song from the church's primary school for very young children.

Tamsin lifted the pack to her shoulders and went downstairs, into the den. She leaned against the wall, watching her mother's hands on the keys, her mother's face in profile. She could imagine Arletta as a girl, naked and wild in the river. She must have looked very much like Tamsin did, back then.

The song ended. Arletta looked over at Tamsin, smiling in her usual way, distant, hazy.

"I like that song," Tamsin said.

"So do I."

"You've always been so good at the piano."

"You'll find the things you're good at, too, dear."

Tamsin tightened her hand on the strap of her pack. It was heavy, laden with her future. She said, "I love you, Mom."

Arletta smiled again. Then she began to play the same song over. Tamsin left the den. She left the house. She took the keys to the Beetle from the pocket of her jeans, almost pulling out her roll of cash in the process, and started the engine, but she was crying too hard to see anything in the side mirrors as she backed down the drive onto Ricks Avenue.

Tamsin couldn't seem to stop herself from crying as she headed through town. She tried to distract herself with thoughts of where she might go next. Idaho Falls was the obvious answer. It was the closest city. But where after that? She wondered how long the old Beetle could last before it broke down. Boise? Spokane? Maybe she would go south instead, all the way out to California.

She felt something thinning inside her, something attenuating to the width of a thread. It was her connection to Rexburg, she realized—small and delicate, ready to snap.

She passed the wheat field at the edge of town, the turnout that led to the old painting shack. Tamsin hit the brakes. By sheer luck, there was no one on the road behind her. She put the Beetle in reverse, backed up to the turnout, headed down the long, dusty track she knew so well.

She left her pack inside the Beetle. There was nothing in the shack anyway, nothing for Tamsin to bring with her out of Rexburg, except the memories. It was past noon now and the day was hot, the insects churring in the grass. The low metallic drone made Tamsin feel sleepy. She hadn't gotten much rest the night before. Far across the wheat field, in the cottonwoods along the river, she could hear a chorus of birds, their singing almost frantic. Strange, Tamsin thought, that the birds should be so lively on a sweltering day like this.

She stepped inside the old shack. Her foot on the threshold made a hollow sound. There was the corner where Aran once had been, his easel, his palette, his bright eyes that saw all the beauty in a hard, flat world. But the corner was empty. Aran was missing, missing from everything. Tamsin knew in that moment she wouldn't see her brother again.

Slowly, Tamsin sank into the old ladder-back chair where she had posed so many times before. She looked at the empty corner, tried to force some reconciliation, an acceptance that Aran was gone—or would be gone soon. Linda would take him away where no one in the family could find him. And that was if Aran was lucky, if he and Linda remained together at all.

Tamsin could feel the warmth of the sun streaming in through the glassless window, striking on the side of her face. How Aran had loved that light. How he had loved the sight of Tamsin in it. And how Tamsin had thrived in the light, in the act of being seen.

Little by little, a prickling awareness worked its way past her musing. Tamsin sat up, rubbed her eyes, stared out the window to the wheat field. What had caught her attention?

The birds, Tamsin thought.

They were louder now. It wasn't her imagination. The birds in the cottonwoods were screaming, scolding; the sky was in turmoil. Magpies and jays and clouds of starlings erupted over the distant line of cottonwoods. They twisted in the air above the river, shrieking and crying till the very sky seemed to heave and contort. Tamsin had never seen birds behave that way, not even at sunset when they argued over their roosts.

She thought, *All the world feels what I feel now.*

Tamsin stumbled out of the shack. The unnatural clamor raised another chill up her spine. In a dim, peripheral awareness, Tamsin heard another sound—car horns honking back in the town, more than a mile away. Then the eerie howl of a siren. She stared along the highway, breath frozen in her chest. The noise from town rose to a frantic pitch. Had there been some terrible accident—a fire?

With a slow, sinking dread, Tamsin understood that the sound from Rexburg and the sound in the sky held the same urgency. She squinted up into the bright summer glare, at the specks of birds wheeling and screaming overhead.

Something lean and wild leaped from the grass and shot past Tamsin. She jumped, then whirled to stare after the animal. It was a coyote, bolting down the dusty path to the highway. The coyote sprang up the verge, onto the pavement, then vanished in the tall grass on the opposite side of the road.

She had never seen a coyote so early in the day. Stupefied by the strangeness, Tamsin stared again at the field, and saw more animals running—coyotes leaping through the wheat, deer bounding in white-eyed terror. Tender stalks bent and broke where the animals cleaved their paths. All those creatures were running toward her, to the road and the town—to the higher ground beyond, where the Bench stooped down to touch the valley. A farmer's dog veered out of the wheat and shot past the shack, a black Lab with eyes white rimmed, its tongue dripping froth. A pack of coyotes streamed around her, paws cutting into dry earth. A horse galloped by, lather on its sides, breath a harsh rumble.

And then, beyond the wheat, where the cottonwoods marked the river, Tamsin saw a shudder and jerk—trees falling. And over the tops of the trees, something high and brown and churning, something moving faster than Tamsin could run.

46

EVERY BIRD IN THE SKY

Aran never slept Friday night. He didn't even try. Just before sunset, Linda had called him from a pay phone at the park to tell him she'd returned from Jackson Hole. Feldermann was enthusiastic about her new client, Linda had said, and felt certain he could sell the nudes quickly and well. They weren't the kind of thing most of his clients went for, but he'd found the style and mood so expressive, so unique and compelling, he was willing to branch out beyond his established collectors and present this brilliant new painter to an entirely different clientele.

"I'm sorry," Aran had said. "I'm sorry you had to lie to him."

Linda had answered in the same flat monotone. "I'm not coming home tonight. I'm staying at Sandy's place."

"All right." He had half expected that already. "Do what you need to do. I understand."

He'd found he couldn't sleep in his bed. It had been too empty and cold without Linda beside him. He'd gone downstairs instead, to the couch beside his easel, and lain there through the long, dark hours staring up at the low ceiling, feeling the weight of the house pressing down on his chest, on his heart. He'd asked himself how something as empty as a broken home could weigh so much.

The next he knew, there was daylight at the sliding glass door, beyond, out along the valley. High, yellow light—the sun had reached its meridian. He must have slept after all, and now it was noon or later. Thank God, he hadn't dreamed.

Aran sat up slowly. His back ached. Every part of him ached. His mouth was dry and fuzzy, and his eyes burned. The hollowness all around him was worse, though, worse than any physical discomfort. These minor pains would be forgotten. But the loss of everything else— Linda and the baby in particular—Aran would go on feeling forever.

The front door opened. The sound of it sent a jolt through Aran's body. She was back. It had to be Linda. Only she had a key to the house, and in her city-girl way, she had always insisted they lock their doors, in defiance of Rexburg's conventions. Aran wondered if he should call out, let her know he was downstairs. Maybe she'd only come home to gather up a few things. Maybe she didn't want to stay. But no footsteps sounded across the floor. She was up there, standing still, dazed or stunned in the entryway.

Aran forced himself to rise. He climbed the stairs, knees creaking like those of an old man. There she was, waiting for him in the modest foyer with her hands on her belly, the keys dangling from their ring, which she had looped around one finger. Aran's eyes darted to the other hand. Her wedding band was still in place. That was something, at least. The door stood open behind her. He could see the crab apples swaying in the wind, scattering the last of their white flowers.

"You came back," he said.

"For now."

"All the paintings are gone?"

"I'll never have to look at them again," Linda said, "and you won't see them, either."

Aran nodded.

"I got an advance from Feldermann," Linda told him. "Not a big one, but it's something. That's how much he believes in those paintings, how eager he is to get them out in front of collectors. Feldermann is a good dealer. He knows the business well. I think we can expect those pieces to bring in enough money that we can move away. The only question is how long it'll take. A couple of months at the most, I hope. I can't take much more than that."

Aran let out a grateful breath. Linda had said "we." That was more than he'd expected, better than he'd prayed for.

"I gave most of the advance to Tamsin," Linda said, "but it's all she'll get from me. I won't give her a penny more, not even after the paintings start to sell."

"You saw her?"

"Last night, after I came back from Jackson. I met her at the park. I gave her enough money to get out of here and stay far away from me. And you."

Aran said, "Was she . . . okay?"

Linda didn't answer the question. She only looked at him.

After a pause, she said, "If we're lucky, we'll be able to start moving by the fall. Sell this house. Buy another one in some other town. Denver, maybe, or Santa Fe. I'd thought Jackson Hole might work, but it's too close. I won't live anywhere near your family—not after this. But we're going someplace where I can open a business of my own. I'm going to have my own gallery. I'm going to be like Feldermann."

"That's a great idea," Aran said, rather timidly. It wasn't that he was opposed to Linda running her own gallery. No doubt she would do it well. But he could sense that there was more coming, more waiting to be said, and he knew he didn't want to hear it.

"I won't be tied to you," she went on. "I'm going to make my own way in the world. You'll have your career and I'll have mine, and if . . . if anything else goes wrong between us . . ."

Quietly, resigned, Aran finished the sentence for her. "You can take care of yourself."

"And our baby."

He nodded again. He understood.

"It might take us that long," Linda said, "till I've founded a business of my own, before we have enough money to sue your father."

Aran blinked rapidly. "Sue him?"

"Of course. He isn't going to get away with this, Aran. He stole from you—from us. He tried to destroy both our livelihoods, everything we've worked so hard to build."

Aran had considered suing Gad once. When Tamsin had first given him the news, a lawsuit had sprung instantly to mind, his first and most sensible reaction. Now it seemed like too much. It wasn't that Aran wished to spare Gad. Rather, he wanted it all to end. Legal proceedings would keep him entangled with his father for months or years. Now all Aran wanted was a clean break.

"A lawsuit will be kinder than what your dad deserves," Linda said. "Look, you may not like it, but these are my terms. This is the way it's going to be." She turned from him suddenly, pressing her eyes with the heel of her hand. "My mother was right. I never should have come to Rexburg. And I damn sure shouldn't have married you."

"I'm glad you did," Aran said. "I'm glad you're giving me another chance."

She looked at him with sudden venom, gestured at the swell of her body. "I don't have a choice. Either I stick with you for a few more years, or I go off on my own as a single mother and try to support this baby and myself without a job or an education. You've got me trapped, Aran—right where you wanted me."

"I never wanted to trap you."

"It's what every man in this place wants. Every last one."

"You'll feel differently, once we've left. You know I've never been like the other men in Rexburg."

Linda sniffled, lowered her eyes. She knew that much was true. And Aran's acceptance of her terms—his acknowledgment that they would leave after all—seemed to have taken the edge off her anger.

"Thank you," Aran said, "for giving me another chance. I will still swear to my dying day that nothing ever happened between Tamsin and me—nothing except for what you saw, just posing, only art. But I should have told you."

"I know nothing else happened."

He took one hopeful step toward her. "You do?"

"Tamsin told me why she did it—what it meant to her. And I understood. It all made sense to me then. She's the only reason why I'm giving you another chance, Aran. There was truth in her eyes. I may never want to see her again, but she was my friend once, and I loved her. I trusted her. And I knew Tamsin was telling me the truth."

She turned away from him, dropped the house keys on the little table beside the door. "I need air."

Linda went out into the front yard with that slow, yawing gait—the reluctant heaviness of her body. He watched her through the open door. She stopped under one of the young crab apples and looked up into its branches. The ragged, wind-torn blossoms dragged along her brow. How beautiful she was, how firm and upright, even in this state, with her heart broken and all her dreams trampled underfoot. Another gust of wind sighed across the Bench, scattering the white petals out across the lawn. Linda turned to watch them flying. Aran smiled to see her, there in the luminous sun, in a moment of peace and wonder.

The smile froze on his face. Then it faded. Linda had gone very still. Aran could sense an awful tension in her, a hot and calamitous waiting. His immediate thought was for the baby. Had something gone wrong? Had all the stress of these last few days done some damage to their child?

He hurried outside. Linda was staring over the crest of the Bench to the town below. He followed her gaze to the north and east, where something dark had lifted into the air far beyond the boundaries of Rexburg. The wind moved hot and dry around them—he thought it must be smoke out there on the sage plain, maybe from a brush fire. But the dark cloud roiled and twisted in ways no smoke could move. Aran realized he was looking at birds—flocks of birds, all the birds that had ever existed, every bird in the sky. Something had frightened them into the air. The vast flock grew larger by the moment. It was moving toward the town. His heart began to beat with a curious thickness. Something wasn't right.

Car horns began to honk down on the valley floor—dozens of horns, a small tin sound. The streets of Rexburg filled with cars. All the cars were headed for the slope, for the Bench.

"What's going on?" Aran whispered.

"It's the dam," Linda said. "It can only be the dam. It's broken, Aran. There's a flood coming for the town."

"We've got to do something. Call the family—"

Linda wailed suddenly, "Sandy! Tamsin! Oh my God, I didn't want this to happen, Aran, not to Tamsin!"

He pulled Linda as close as the baby would allow. Shuddering, she pressed her face against his neck. He could feel Linda's tears soaking through his shirt, sliding down his skin. Aran went on holding her, shielding her from the sight, as a line of cars climbed the flank of the Bench and sirens blared out belated warnings. But Aran couldn't look away. The flood rushed into the valley, relentless as God's judgment, a beast of brown that inhaled trees and swallowed the land and left a uniform nothing where the world had been. He could see the pale patch beyond town, the wheat field where his old shack stood. And beyond the wheat field, the cottonwoods along the river, which were vanishing five and ten at a time, winking out of existence, subsiding under a featureless churn of water.

Moments later, the flood slammed into the town itself. Houses and shops along the highway's edge vanished, but still the waters came, surging into the heart of Rexburg. He thought of his mother. Even Gad. And Tamsin, most of all—Tamsin, who was half of him and more.

A hot, desperate, clawing thing rose up inside. It came out as a hoarse and helpless cry, like the screaming of the birds in their wretched circles.

47

A Baptism

It struck Gad as particularly strange—and continued to strike him that way for many years after—that when he heard the great wild thunder of the flood, he didn't think of Arletta first, nor Tamsin, nor even his life's work, everything he'd toiled so many years to build. The moment the feral roar of the water shook him, Gad was overcome by a wrenching desperation to get to Aran, wherever he was, and protect him.

All Gad knew at first was that sound. It sounded initially like a roll of distant thunder—nothing unusual in that—but it went on and on and seemed to be coming closer. He knew, with a deep and primal certainty, that the sound meant danger. He froze in his place, halfway between the shop and the house. A small, bright specter seemed to stand on the lawn before him, looking up into his face—Aran as the child he once had been, in his little overalls with something clutched in his fist, a grasshopper or a leaf. Gad saw Aran toddling through the grass, and himself chasing after. He could feel himself as he'd been back then, when he was still young, trembling under the warm, soft weight of responsibility the Lord had given him. But the boy was running faster all the time. Gad couldn't reach Aran, couldn't protect him at all, and the approaching sound was loud as the shame inside him, an endless bellow, and Gad knew that whatever was making that hellish noise was about to do to him what he had already done to Aran's life. This was justice, this ending. Gad had no one to blame but himself.

A siren screamed from somewhere close by. Gad jolted out of his stupor. He ran toward the house. As he crossed the yard, he could hear another howl rising above that churning, awful din—the cries of helpless animals caught up in some calamity, and car horns blaring as people fled from the valley up to the Bench. Up to higher ground. That was when he knew.

"Arletta," Gad shouted.

She was there in the kitchen with the radio on. Stunned and glassy eyed, she stared at him. "There's a flood coming," she said vaguely. "The man on the radio said so. What should we do?"

Gad grabbed her hand. He pulled her up the stairs to the second floor. Arletta stumbled on the steps, but Gad didn't slow—he went on dragging her, pulling with all his strength, till she regained her feet and kept running. Even when he reached the second floor, Gad knew at once, by some God-given instinct, that he hadn't climbed high enough for safety.

"The attic," he said. "Come on, Arletta, move!"

She helped him pull the hinged ladder down from the ceiling. Gad went first so he could push the heavy trapdoor out of the way, but Arletta was quicker now, coming out of her haze to face the urgency of the moment. Once he was inside the hot attic, Gad reached down and took her under the arms and hauled her bodily into the darkness.

"We need to get up higher," Gad said. "To the roof. How?"

"There's a hatchet up here somewhere—my father's. My family used it to cut down our Christmas trees."

Arletta ducked behind the boxes of holiday ornaments and other things Gad hadn't thought of in years, the children's baby clothes, Arletta's wedding dress, albums of photos and reels of film. She emerged with something heavy, pressed it into Gad's hand—he felt smooth wood polished by age, the reassuring heft of an ax-head's weight.

"Stand back." Gad swung the hatchet with all his strength, aiming at the planks between two beams, which he could make out faintly in the light of the open trap door.

The ax was blunt. It bit into the wood and stuck there, so Gad had to wrench it free and swing again, five, six times before the planks and outer shingles splintered and daylight came knifing in. Gad beat at the opening with the butt of the hatchet till the hole was just large enough to pass through. Then he took Arletta around the waist and lifted her again. She clawed frantically at the roof. Gad was afraid she would find no purchase, but finally, she pulled herself up.

He shoved boxes across the attic floor till he could climb up himself. Old, dry cardboard and the family's keepsakes buckled under his weight. Gad kicked and grappled his way up into the unforgiving light.

He and Arletta scrambled to the peak of the roof. It was the best they could do at making for higher ground. *Please*, Gad prayed, *let it be high enough.*

He looked out across the rooftops of Rexburg in time to see the flood overtake the town—a wall of brown water at least fifteen feet high. That churning, muddy demon swallowed running cattle and farm dogs; its hard face was lashed with massive logs from the lumberyard upstream, and whole cottonwoods torn up by their roots. The barrage of logs smashed against the city. The sound of it was worse than any Hell Gad had imagined: Animals screaming, people screaming, the sustained blare of horns. Worst of all, the ceaseless growling of the water, the moan of a town coming apart. Houses torn whole from their foundations raced half-submerged up the streets. One colossal white farmhouse spun in the water where North Second East should have been. Gad could see people clinging to its roof and chimney, crying out for help.

Arletta gripped his arm. "Gad! The gas tanks!"

He stared toward the massive gasoline storage tanks at the western edge of town. The tanks were mostly submerged; only their upper edges were visible now, slim nail parings of white above the water. As Gad watched in helpless horror, a raft of logs smashed into the tanks. A fireball billowed above the flood, rocketing into the sky, so hot that even at a distance, Gad had to throw up an arm to shield his face. When he looked again, burning logs were careening through the streets, battering into the houses that hadn't been swept from their foundations, setting treetops ablaze.

A heartbeat later, the water charged up Ricks Avenue. Gad's street lay on the slightest rise, just enough that some of the momentum had dissipated from the flood. But still the water came faster than Gad had thought possible. In seconds, a brown morass had swallowed the shop. The steel walls fell away as if melting; the water ate the shop and climbed, unsated, up the sides of the house, reaching greedily for Gad, for his wife, whom he threw his arms around as if he'd ever had the strength to save her.

Gad was sure his home would be tossed off its foundation, carried away like the others he'd seen, or sucked under, vanishing as his shop had done. Water slapped along the eaves, then up above the edge of the roof, creeping another foot higher.

Gad held Arletta more tightly, because she was screaming now, wailing and tearing at him, fighting to get away. He had never seen Arletta in the grip of such emotion. He hadn't known this force could exist inside her, this terrible, furious strength and need.

He pinned Arletta's arms to her sides, trying to keep her there at the peak of the roof, above the water's reach. He prayed for readiness, prayed for the strength to meet his death bravely. He would surely be consumed. He would slide down into a familiar weight of darkness, the suffocating thing that had hunted him in nightmares. Now that the moment had come, Gad almost welcomed it—an end to this mess, the terrible ruin he'd made of his family. This would be a final baptism to wash away his sins. But before he could leave this world, he had to find Aran again, tell him he was sorry. He had to tell Aran what he knew in his heart was true: that he, Gad, was a harsh and half-made man—but in his stilted, broken way, he loved Aran, and always had.

The water ate one line of shingles, then another. Arletta was still thrashing against him. Where did she think they could go now, Gad wondered dully. There was no place higher than this—no place they could get to. Soon even the roof would be gone.

The waters ascended another foot. And then they didn't. Gad stared hard at the place where the flood rippled around the skirt of his roof. It wasn't his imagination. The flood had stopped rising. It was holding steady, and the old Rigby homestead still clung to its foundation.

Gad squinted across a blinding sweep of water and sunlight. The worst of the flood had passed them by. He and Arletta would survive—thank God, thank God.

He gave Arletta a gentle shake. "Get hold of yourself. The water isn't rising anymore."

But she went on screaming and shoving, fighting to break free.

Only then did he realize what Arletta had been shouting all along. "Tamsin!"

Gad went numb. His arms fell loose around his wife. She dropped to a crouch at the peak of the roof. Wailing, Arletta tore at her hair, she clawed her own face. The sound of her grief mingled with the blaring of horns and the cries of the stranded. It throbbed with a terrible pulse inside Gad's heart.

48

GONE

As soon as she understood that it was water coming toward her, a high wall of water, Tamsin moved by instinct for the highest ground in her vicinity, which was the roof of the old empty shack. She circled the outside of the building till she found an unglazed window, then scrambled up into its frame, set her feet against the sill, and straightened as best she could. Her hands pawed and scrabbled at the faded wood. She was quaking and disoriented and almost fell, but she managed to find the edge of the roof with her hands, and then she was clawing, working her fingers into the cracks between shingles. Her nails bent and broke. She kept on digging till she found some purchase and could hang there by her hands. She kicked up with one leg. It wasn't any different from climbing up the water tower. She told herself so in a strangely calm and distant voice. *Like climbing the water tower, easy, that's it.*

She got her foot up to the roof, strained and levered—then she was crawling up the shallow slope to the peak, gasping, weakened by the effort. The shack wouldn't be high enough to save her. She knew it even when she reached the top.

By then, the water had surged up out of the riverbed. The wheat field was more than halfway gone. The flood closed on Tamsin, the water's surface buckling and heaving with black logs and the ravaged bones of cottonwoods. She cowered against the shingles, cried out in wordless fear as logs collided with the shack and a great lifting, heaving sensation overtook her, a wild disintegration of everything solid and real.

She was moving very fast. The dun ridge of the Bench to one side and the distant mountains to the other whipped by. Tamsin realized she was still crouched on all fours, that her limbs were shaking violently with shock. And then she understood that she was on the roof of the old shack, or what remained of the roof—a flat patch of shingles and beams, scarcely big enough to hold Tamsin above the water. The fragment of roof had wedged itself in a tangle of cottonwood branches. She held very still on her precarious raft, terrified the smallest twitch might dislodge the shingles from the tree and drop her in the water.

The flood dragged Tamsin into town. Everything was a churn of mud and froth and the blocky shapes of drowned cattle rolling to fling stiff legs into the sky. One end of her raft hit the angle of a house's roof and Tamsin was spun about, the clouds and the sun and the screaming birds a great spiral overhead. The raft shuddered, sank on one end; a few chunks of debris broke away and vanished under the surface. She would be pulled under, too, unless she did something, unless she tried to find solid ground. She thought she might be able to leap from where she crouched to the roof of the house, but she couldn't force herself to stand. The next moment, what remained of her cottonwood raft tore itself away from the eaves and Tamsin moved swiftly down Main Street, or the place where Main Street had been.

Something vast and orange and roaring ripped into the sky, just to Tamsin's right. She huddled down against the wood as a blast of heat pummeled her back, her hands, which she had thrown by instinct over her face. When she looked up, there was fire all around—logs burning, a reek of gasoline, zigzags of flame licking along the surface of the water. Some of the leaves of her cottonwood had caught ablaze. Tamsin crawled to the edge of her raft and scooped up the brown angry water, splashed and dug and cursed and wept and threw weak handfuls of the flood onto the flames till the fire was extinguished.

Then she sat back on her heels and stared. What else could she do? The scrap of the old shack's roof was wet, rocking in the turbulence, scraping and splintering against the cottonwood. But she seemed to be slowing now. The burning logs had spread away, fanning out in a slackened current. Tamsin turned carefully. Rexburg, what little she could see of it, was already far behind. The flood had carried her all the way out to the basin west of town, where the highway cut straight and true toward Idaho Falls and beyond, to a world that was bigger than this.

Little by little, the current slowed. The cottonwood began to bump and drag its branches against the earth. Here and there, a jagged shine of basalt broke the surface. Tamsin had ridden the flood all the way into the sage lands beyond the town.

She pulled her knees to her chest and held herself that way, huddled and waiting, till the raft began to rotate under a lazy sun. It came to rest among the old dark fissures of basalt. Still she didn't move. There was nothing around her now except the sound of water, a gentle slap against stone. Even the birds were no longer crying. They had all flown away. She hid her face against her drawn-up knees till her breathing slowed and some of her shaking stilled, and she knew her heart was still beating in a sure, steady rhythm.

Only then did Tamsin try to stand. The patch of shingles had lodged on solid ground. The fragment of roof did not rock beneath her. The cottonwood had subsided into the mud. Her legs still felt insubstantial, but she made herself step to the edge of the raft and off it, into the waiting world.

Tamsin clambered up a sharp thrust of stone that rose several feet above the valley. There she remained, looking out across the glare while her body solidified and the pieces of herself came emphatically back together. To the west, the water had sunk down into the fissures of the earth. It lay tame and glittering in narrow channels, all the fury of the flood gone now, out beyond the narrowness of Rexburg and its valley. A ridge of basalt ran from the place where Tamsin stood to a slope above the highway. She could get there if she were careful and took her time.

Tamsin's hand strayed to the pocket of her jeans. The denim was wet and chafed her skin, but she could feel the roll of money. She still had that, at least. She looked back, one last time, to the place where the town had been. The Bench stood clear of the ruin. The valley was flat, uncolored devastation—the flood had swallowed it all, the family home and Aran's shame, all of Gad's control. Nothing held her to Rexburg anymore. She was beyond everything that had once constrained her.

"I'm sorry," she said, to Linda and Aran and her mother, to everyone, though no one could hear. It didn't seem right, that she ought to leave without telling them how sorry she was.

Tamsin set off along the ridge of black stone. The basalt was sharp and crumbling. Several times, her wet shoes slipped, and she fell, cutting her shins and knees and the palms of her hands, but she always got up again. She kept pressing on.

A still small voice inside her said, *What do you think you're doing? You can't get by without your family. What will become of you, where will you go?*

Silently, Tamsin answered: *Hollywood. Redwood. Anywhere but here.*

She kept walking till she reached the highway. She kept on walking still.

49

Fast and Testimony

When the sheriff began patrolling along the top of the Bench, blaring through his loudspeaker that the flood was no longer rising, Aran left Linda at home and hurried past the long line of parked cars, down the slope to where the water touched the swell of the land. Crowds had gathered there—people who had fled on foot, who'd had no time to reach their vehicles—and all of them were clamoring for rides in the handful of small aluminum fishing boats that were nosing into the shallows. Over the cough of the outboard motors, Aran could hear people shouting for gasoline to fuel the boats. "Bring gas cans from the houses on the Bench, whatever you can find!" Women were crying hysterically, children screaming in terror—the only reality they'd known had been swept away in an instant. One of the men in a boat shouted, "I've just been over to the college campus. Most of the buildings there are perfectly dry on the upper floors. It'll do for a shelter, for now." Another called from the crowd, "Just got off the radio with a friend in Idaho Falls. They're sending supplies by helicopter."

One of the women shouted, "What about our homes? We need to get back and check on them. I need to know if my house is still standing!"

A tri-hull edged around the group of boats, maneuvered sideways toward the Bench and the crowd. Aran flinched. Joel Kimball was in the stern, handling the little outboard motor with unthinking ease.

"Let's get organized," Joel shouted. "Every boat should take a different street. We can carry you toward your homes, so at least you'll know if there's anything left. We can pick up anyone who might be stuck on roofs or in the trees and take them to the campus. That's the best we can do for now." Joel noted Aran in the press of people. He pressed his lips together for a moment, then said, "I'll take Ricks Avenue and the area around the hospital. Come on, Aran—get in."

Joel was the last person Aran wanted to ride with, but he'd do it, for his family's sake. He scrambled down to the edge of the water, which was scummy with debris, and got into the boat. "Thanks," he said shortly.

Joel turned the tri-hull around and juiced the motor. They sped away from the crowd.

"Is Linda all right?" Joel said.

"She's fine. We were already up on the Bench, but my family . . . I appreciate you giving me a ride. How's Sandy?"

"Right as rain. Our house is just high enough that we only got our basement flooded and the carpets got a little wet, but no serious harm done. We're the lucky ones. I took Sandy over to the campus. She's helping the Relief Society put a shelter together, for everyone who lost their homes. The minute we knew we weren't going to be washed away, she said, 'Get me in your fishing boat and take me wherever there's work to be done.'"

"She's got a good heart," Aran said.

Joel was quiet for a while. The boat cut rapidly through the bright water, straight down the place where Main Street should have been, its boundaries barely defined by the flat roofs of shops and businesses nosing out of the water.

Joel said, "I was awful sore at Sandy, you know, when she stood as bridesmaid at your wedding. But she didn't roll over and take it. She stood up to me. Pointed out what a real low guy I've been to you, Aran, all these years. I'm sorry about it. I'm sorry about everything—all the trouble I caused for you and the sins I committed along the way. I've repented. I want you to know that. But I never apologized to you, till now. I should have done it long ago. I'm not asking you to forgive me. I'm not sure I can ever be forgiven, except by Heavenly Father, and even then, I guess it'll be a real long time before I've proved myself worthy of forgiveness. But I wanted you to know I'm sorry for it all."

Aran ventured a glance at Joel. He was watching the water ahead, eyes narrowed against the fierce glare, but there was a certain stillness to him that made Aran believe he was sincere.

"Thanks," Aran said.

The boat turned, then turned again, and Aran realized he was on Ricks Avenue. The first few houses on the street were gone—fully submerged or ripped from their foundations; Aran couldn't say which. The huddled mass of leaves just ahead must be the poplars at the end of the drive. There was debris lodged in their branches—planks of wood, a twist of barbed wire, a red cushion from somebody's sofa. And a piece of the green metal siding from his father's shop.

"Here," Aran said. "Turn here."

The tri-hull maneuvered around the poplars. Aran's heart pressed forcefully against his ribs. But when they cleared the poplars, he could see the peak of the homestead roof riding stoic as the Ark atop the flood. His mother and father were sitting at the apex, Gad looking with dull surprise at the boat, Arletta weeping in her hands.

Aran stood carefully. "Mom! Dad!"

Gad lurched to his feet. "Aran, is that you? Thank God! My boy is safe."

Moments later, Aran was helping his parents into the boat while Joel kept the tri-hull more or less still. Arletta was shaking violently, eyes wide, more vacant than they'd ever been. Gad was pale. He kept an arm around Arletta's shoulders.

"Where's Tamsin?" Aran said.

His mother gave a terrible groan. Gad lowered his face, and at first, Aran thought he was laughing—his shoulders were heaving, heaving, with a short, hard rhythm. Then, Aran understood that Gad was crying.

"No," he said.

Joel put a hand gently on Aran's back. "Let's get them to the shelter—first things first. Then we can go tell the sheriff we've got a missing person to search for."

"Not the shelter," Aran said. "Take us back to the Bench—the place where you picked me up. My parents will stay with Linda and me till this is all over."

~

Given the circumstances, Linda didn't object to her in-laws staying in the house on the Bench, no matter her suspicion of Gad. She understood as soon as she saw them approaching—Aran and his parents, with no one else beside them—that the family had more troubling concerns.

She went out to meet them, wrapped Arletta in her arms, though the baby made it difficult. "Don't say anything," she murmured. "Just come inside, all of you."

For six days, the family held out hope while the floodwaters receded, and Rexburg turned to the daunting task of putting itself back together. Once-pristine homes were stained with mud inside and out, clear up to their ceilings. Silt and fouler things had to be shoveled away from doors and windows. Felled trees were cut with chain saws and hauled away by tractors, commandeered from the farms on the other side of the valley where the flood hadn't reached. Sandy and Joel, who'd thought their troubles small in comparison to the rest of the town, noticed a terrible stench in their home on the third day after the flood. Joel ventured into his basement to find a dead, bloated cow. He'd been obliged to tear a hole in the floor and the outer wall just to get the thing out again. No one could imagine how a cow's carcass came to be wedged in such an unusual place.

As cleaning and reconstruction proceeded, and the families who'd taken shelter at the campus returned to salvage what was left of their homes, the search went on for all those who couldn't be accounted for.

Whenever another body was found, the names of the dead made their way around Rexburg. Some of the dead had come from smaller communities upstream, closer to the dam—the villages of Wilford and Sugar City had been washed away entirely. Eleven souls were lost in all. But Tamsin was never found.

Aran embarked on a private search for his sister's remains. He was determined to find her himself. He owed Tamsin that. He couldn't protect her, couldn't even be there with her at the moment of her death, but he could find her and bring her home.

He began the search at the wheat field where the old shack had stood, though of course there was no wheat field now, only mud, and the shack hadn't even left a footprint to mark its place. But he did find the orange Beetle tipped on its side in the irrigation ditch that ran along the highway. Tamsin was not inside, however, but her backpack was. Somehow Aran had known even before he'd approached the car that he wouldn't find his sister there. He didn't feel her in that place. Since he'd taken all the paintings from the shack, he'd known he would never find Tamsin there again.

Aran searched alone through the devastated valley for one more day. Where there had been pasture and farmland, all the familiar scenes he had painted, now there was only a stinking wrack of waste. He waded through countless acres of mud. The wet got inside his shoes and soaked into his jeans, and his feet and legs began to blister. Still he kept searching, watching the sky for signs of carrion birds, following their small, echoing voices over an anonymous land. He found cattle, horses, wildlife, all destroyed by the flood. But he didn't find his sister.

The following morning, when Aran left his house at dawn to continue looking for Tamsin, Gad was already waiting at the door. They looked at one another in neutral silence. Aran decided he wouldn't say a word, wouldn't try to stop him. Gad, for his part, decided the time had come to say everything he should have said months and years before.

They got into Aran's car. The light at the eastern edge of the Bench was tentative and pale.

"Where are you going to look today?" Gad asked.

"I don't know," Aran said. "I haven't had much of a plan on any day. Just went wherever I could think to look."

"Are the roads clear enough that you can get out to the lava heaves?"

"I think so," Aran said.

"Go there. We'll look for her there."

Aran pulled out onto the road. He glanced at his father from the corner of his eye. "Why the lava heaves?"

Gad hesitated before he answered. It wasn't a pause, but it wasn't the petulant silence Aran so often received. "I had a dream once," Gad finally answered. "A dream about *her*, out there, walking on water. I tried to get to her, and I couldn't. She was already too far away."

They drove on in silence, over the crest of the Bench, descending to the bedraggled town.

Gad said, "I thought it was a nightmare at the time, just an ordinary bad dream. Now I believe it was something else. I think it was a revelation, but I was too stubborn to recognize it." He choked. He covered his eyes with his hand. Weeping, Gad said, "I was too unworthy to understand the truth when the Lord put it right in front of my face."

Neither of them said another word till they'd crossed what was left of Rexburg and headed southwest out of town. Aran kept glancing at his father, waiting for Gad to give some signal, to recognize the place he'd seen in that revelatory dream. But nothing was familiar here.

Gad did gesture, though, raising his hand almost unconsciously, for he'd felt something pull at him, a greater tightness in his throat than the one that had been strangling him for days now, while he'd lain awake in the guest bed of Aran's home.

Aran pulled at once off the road. There was no turnout and little shoulder—only the same rotting mud that was everywhere, but he and Gad got out of the car together. They slipped and floundered away from the highway, onto the barren plain.

They found the place where basalt buckled up out of the earth. They found the gullies where Aran and his brothers had once played army, filled now with mud and the debris of ruined lives, with standing water that reflected the gray skies of dawn. A cottonwood was wedged between two crags of stone, a patch of shingles caught in its branches—the fragment of a roof. There was nothing else to see, nothing to see for miles.

Gad and Aran stood looking down at the tree, the sodden shingles. A feeling came over Gad then, a stirring in his heart. He hadn't eaten for well over a day—he had no appetite to speak of—and he felt light headed, detached from everything he had been before. He shrank at the work that lay ahead of him—the words he must finally say—but he said them anyway. It was long past time.

"I was never a good father."

Aran looked up in surprise. "Dad—"

Gad lifted a hand to stop him. "Don't argue. Please, don't argue—just let me say it. I was a bad father to you and to Tamsin. And to the boys, I guess. I could have done better by your mother, too. But I regret all the terrible things I did to you most of all, Aran. Because I've always been proud of you. Even when I told myself I wasn't, when I told myself you were a shame to this family—"

Gad began to cry again. Once more, he ducked his face, hiding his eyes behind a rough hand. Aran had seen plenty of men weeping as they stood before the congregation. He thought, *He's bearing a testimony now.*

When Gad could speak again, his voice was high and thin. He almost sounded like a child, which annoyed him as much as it amazed him. He still couldn't look at Aran. He was afraid he might see disgust and rejection in his son's expression. He knew he deserved them both.

"I don't know why," Gad said, "I treated you that way. Why I let envy control me, and why I went after your livelihood. I was proud of that, too—so much in awe of what you accomplished. I guess I thought I deserved it more, because the dream was taken from me and I never had the guts to take it back. You had the guts. I've got none at all. And it seems so silly and pointless now, that I didn't set aside all my jealousy and bitterness and love you more, love all of you. It was such a waste of a life, to act the way I did."

Aran put his hand on Gad's shoulder. He could feel his father quaking, like the very substance of his body wanted to fall apart from shame.

"Why did you do it?" Aran asked gently.

Gad cleared his throat, wiped his eyes, did his best to put himself back in order. Businesslike, he asked, "What do you mean? Why did I interfere with your livelihood, or—"

"Why did you treat us all the way you did?"

Gad looked out over the wasted land, to the morning light spilling into the valley. "I wanted to protect you," he said at length. "All you kids and your mother. There's always been this fear in me, I guess you could say—this waiting for the End of Days. I thought the world was going to be destroyed by, well, all the prophetic stuff that's in the Bible. Wars and plagues and fire from the sky. I thought about it all the time. It was even in my dreams, and all I wanted, all I cared about, was saving each and every one of you. Protecting you all from destruction."

Aran gave a small, helpless laugh. It wasn't funny, yet he couldn't do anything else just then. It was either laugh or scream. He said, "You feared destruction, so you destroyed us all."

Gad accepted the rebuke. It was the least of what he deserved. He said, "As much as I feared all that prophecy stuff, I feared you even more."

"Me?"

"From the time I first held you in my arms. I looked down at you, a little baby, so fragile and new—and the purest terror I've ever known came into me, right there alongside the love and worship. I think that was the first time I ever really understood that nothing in this world, nothing at all, is under my control. You'll understand what I mean someday. You'll be a father, too, soon enough."

"I know."

Aran drew a shaky breath. He hoped Gad hadn't heard the unreadiness in his voice, but he did hear. He patted Aran on the shoulder, squeezed him roughly—the most affection he ever showed, the greatest measure of comfort.

Gad said, "You never truly understand how big and wild and dangerous the world is till you hold your baby in your arms. Then you can feel how far man is beyond the reach of God. You're the only thing standing between that precious little life and . . . well, a hundred dangers. A thousand. And suddenly, in that all-powerful desire to protect your baby, you can see how weak and helpless you are, and always have been—how little you can control. We're taught that men are to be masters of their households, but the moment you become a father, you realize mastery is an illusion and manhood is a lie. I could have torn out my own tongue more easily than I could have accepted that my house, like every house, was built on sand. And now Tamsin is gone. We've lost her forever because I couldn't do what the Lord expected of me. He took Tamsin because I refused to be a worthy father."

Aran put his arms around Gad. He held his father tightly while he wept.

In time, Gad composed himself. He sniffed and straightened, cleared his throat, put his hands in his pockets, and looked down again at the scrap of roofing stuck in the branches of the tree. He pried at one of the shingles with the toe of his boot.

Aran said, "All this suffering because of a fear of destruction. Because of prophecy. Dad, I'm not sure I believe anything about this religion anymore—this one, or any other. I was already halfway there by the time I met Linda. But these past few days, as I've been looking for Tamsin . . . Well, I still believe in something, but I'm not sure it bears any resemblance to what you've taught me to believe. This mess is too much—our family, our lives."

Gad nodded. "I can understand that."

Aran said, "We're going to move away—Linda and me. I don't see how we can stay here anyway. Not after this."

"Don't go," Gad said.

"It won't be any time soon. Linda and I will help you and Mom put your lives back together, fix up the house, get your business rolling again. And anyway, the baby is almost here. Linda will need Mom to help her, for a few months at least. But I can't promise anything past that. I already swore to Linda we would leave. I'm going to keep my word to her—always."

"That's good," Gad said brusquely. "A man should always honor his wife—especially one of Linda's kind. She's a good woman, Aran, a real smart and capable woman. Brave, too—nothing can intimidate her, not even a sad old sinner like me. You're lucky to have her."

"I know," Aran said, "I am."

Gad said, "I think it will be good for your mother, to be with the baby for a while. To have another child to love again, now that . . . now that Tamsin is gone for good."

Aran put his arms around his father again. They grieved together till the sun was high enough to pull a mist from the sodden ground. Then they went back to Aran's car and headed for the town. Behind, in the spaces between the jagged stones, where the sage was bent and broken, the white mist moved like ghosts across the valley.

50

GREEN

Linda carefully pinned the pattern for another baby dress to a spread of soft fabric, which Arletta had brought from Idaho Falls. The fabric store in Rexburg still hadn't reopened, three weeks after the flood, but the baby wasn't about to delay its schedule over something as insignificant as an environmental catastrophe. There were still plenty of tiny clothes to be made, provisions to be stored in the pantry of the red-brick house on the Bench. A new reality was rapidly approaching.

Across the dining room table from where Linda worked, Arletta was running the sewing machine. The presser foot chugged tirelessly. In Arletta's capable hands, the fabric Linda had cut transformed into shirts, onesies, bloomers, tiny bib overalls. It was a good thing Arletta had plenty of experience with sewing. If it had all been placed in Linda's hands, her baby would have been left naked as a jaybird.

There was one week left, maybe two at most. Linda felt dizzy at the thought. She leaned back in her chair, breathing deep. Fresh air flowed in through the open windows. July was almost here, and the world outside smelled hot and growing. It wasn't the dry sage smell Linda remembered from last year, her first summer in Rexburg. Once the town had been cleaned up properly and the stench of rotting things had abated, the lush perfume of a second spring had overtaken the valley. All that water had filled the ground; the plants had seemed to take up the duty of recolonizing the stripped-bare earth with special vigor. The breeze coming in off the valley was warm and green and hopeful. It soothed some of Linda's persistent anxiety.

Someone knocked at the front door. Arletta looked up, allowing the sewing machine to stop for the first time that morning.

"I'll get it," Linda said.

"Are you sure?"

"It's good for me to get up and walk around. The doctor said so."

Linda pushed herself up from the chair. It still astonished her, how wide and unbalanced her own body could be. She moved heavily through the house and opened the door.

Sandy and Joel were on the other side. Each carried a stack of casserole dishes with tinfoil sealing the tops.

"What's all this?" Linda said.

"Dinner," Sandy answered. "And lunch. Breakfast, too, I bet—I remember all us kids used to eat whatever was in the freezer for breakfast when Mom was busy with the new babies."

"You cooked for me?"

Sandy grinned. "Of course I did. Joel even helped a little."

Linda had to back down the entry hall so Sandy and Joel could come inside. Her belly took up too much space. But she did take a few of the dishes from the top of Sandy's stack. It felt good to carry something. Aran and her in-laws had been so protective in the three weeks since the flood, Linda was hardly allowed to brush her own teeth anymore.

She led the way to the kitchen.

"Hi, Sister Rigby," Sandy called to Arletta as they passed.

Arletta didn't seem to hear over the noise of the sewing machine.

They arranged all the dishes on the counter.

"Cheesy broccoli," Sandy said, pointing, "and tuna surprise, and I think that one's chicken and mushroom. And there are three whole dishes of funeral potatoes. You can never have enough of those. Everything came right from my refrigerator, all wrapped up tight, ready to go into the freezer, so you don't need to worry about a thing. You've got enough here for two weeks of lunches and dinners, and Relief Society is already assigning more people to cook for you, so you'll have plenty of food coming in for three months after the baby arrives."

"Wow." Linda shook her head in amazement. "This is really nice, Sandy. It's a huge help."

Joel said, "Is Aran here?" In that very moment, Aran came jogging up the stairs from his basement studio. He was wrestling with one of his plaid shirts, buttoning it up to cover the simple sleeveless undershirt he wore now in place of his temple garments.

Aran and Joel shook hands. There was still the slightest tension between them. Perhaps there always would be, Linda thought. But they were trying their level best to get along, to leave the darkest moments of their respective pasts behind them.

"My dad's down at his house," Aran said. "I was just about to go and meet him. He and I have been working hard to put the old homestead back together. It's pretty well cleaned up and aired out now—almost ready for my folks to move back in. But there's still some work left to be done."

"I'll come along and help you," Joel said, "if that's all right."

Aran smiled. "Sure. We can always use extra hands."

Joel kissed Sandy on the cheek. "I'll pick you up this afternoon."

"Like heck you will," Sandy said. "Leave the keys with me. Linda and I are going to go for a joyride together."

Once Aran and Joel had gone, Sandy helped Linda pack all the dishes into the freezer. They remained in the kitchen, talking quietly while the sewing machine purred.

"How are you doing?" Sandy said.

Linda knew she was really asking about her emotional state. *How are you holding up, considering your eighteen-year-old sister-in-law was lost in the flood?* Linda couldn't face that subject yet. She still felt responsible for Tamsin's death. She had been cold to her, and had pushed her away, even after she'd looked into Tamsin's eyes and understood the truth of what she and Aran had done together—why Tamsin had done it. Jealousy and mistrust had dictated Linda's response. She ought to have found more empathy for her friend, her husband's sister. If she hadn't been so unyielding, so determined to push Tamsin away, perhaps the girl wouldn't have been wandering alone when the flood had struck. Tamsin might have made it to the roof with her parents. She would still be alive today.

Linda said, "I'm tired. Everything exhausts me. I wish this baby would hurry up and get here, and I'm also . . . a little afraid, I guess."

"That's only natural. It's a big change, and a big responsibility. But you'll have me to help you, as often as you need. Arletta, too, by the looks of it. Did she sew that entire pile of baby clothes? You've got enough there to keep your baby dressed for a year."

"She has been a big help with the sewing." Linda lowered her voice even more. "I'm not sure how much I'll be able to count on Arletta for anything else."

"What do you mean?"

Linda sighed. She looked out the kitchen window to the green valley, the long tracts of mud that were shrinking a little more each day as the earth healed and the plants closed in.

"She doesn't seem to understand what's going on," Linda said. "You know?"

Sandy glanced at Arletta, who was still bent contentedly over her work.

"She's worse than ever since we lost Tamsin," Linda said. "Everyone has tried to talk to her about holding a funeral—or a memorial service, I suppose we should call it. Aran has tried, and Gad, and Bishop Kimball as well as the bishop of our ward. Even I have tried to convince her. I think we could all use the closure. But Arletta refuses to do it. She won't hear a word about it, not from anyone. She told me she doesn't believe Tamsin is dead. She thinks her daughter will come back someday—just wander back into Rexburg like nothing ever happened."

"I feel so sorry for her," Sandy said. "I feel sorry for your whole family."

"So do I. Even Gad has accepted the truth. He's a changed man now. He's trying really hard to be a good dad—which might be too little, too late, if you ask me, but at least he's trying. I can see the effort he's making to be a better father to Aran. I still don't like Gad—not exactly—but I dislike him less now. The effort goes a long way."

"These are hard times," Sandy said, "but you have so much to look forward to."

Linda smiled, but she could already feel her smile breaking, the tears stinging her eyes. She gasped one little sob, then admitted, "I don't really want to be a mother, Sandy. I always thought I did. It was all I could think about sometimes, when I was younger, how badly I wanted a family like yours—a family that knew how to take care of each other. I didn't want to be alone and I didn't want to feel so broken. I thought being a mother someday would fix me. I thought it would fix everything that had gone wrong with my life. But as soon as I found out I was pregnant . . ."

Linda could say no more. Her admission already felt like a betrayal of the small life inside her—a creature she hadn't met yet, but which she knew already she would love with a blinding, forceful power, regardless of her present reluctance. In one week, maybe two, she would be dragged into a new reality of fear and strength and sacrifice and a towering, all-encompassing love.

"You don't want to be a mother?" Sandy looked down at Linda's belly, then fixed Linda with an ironic smile. "I think it's a little late to reconsider."

Linda laughed helplessly, dashing the tears from her eyes. "I know. I know! If I could go back in time, I would have done everything differently. I would have waited till I felt a little more . . ."

"Prepared?" Sandy suggested.

"Sure of myself. Sure I could really do it. But I can only go forward. And motherhood is coming for me, ready or not."

She glanced again at Arletta. The sewing machine went on rattling, industrial and steadfast. Arletta never looked up from her work.

"My mother didn't want me to join the church, or come out here to Rexburg. She told me once . . ."

Linda stopped herself. Sandy was still a true believer—she believed with every beat of her heart. And Sandy was the last person Linda wanted to hurt with her doubts and criticism. So she kept it to herself, all her fears about the way mothers were expected to behave in this town, this culture. At least the town wasn't a permanent restriction. They'd already discussed the merits of other cities, other places. Sandy didn't know anything about that yet.

Someday we'll get out, Linda promised herself, *Aran and the baby and me. We'll go to a place where we can be who we truly are. Then it won't matter anymore, that I'm not a perfect woman and Aran isn't a perfect man. We'll just do our jobs as well as we can, and nothing else will matter then.*

Sandy said, "You may not want to be a mom anymore, but you're going to do it anyway. I told you once how much I admire you for all your drive and brains. And for your stubbornness."

"Just like a mule."

"You'll be a good mother," Sandy said. "You're good at everything you do."

"I don't know if I'm strong enough for this." She looked pointedly at Arletta. "Sometimes I feel sure all the pressure to be perfect will break me."

"Not you," Sandy said. "Not even this town could break you."

She reached across the broad swell of Linda's belly and hugged her. They held each other for a long time, Sandy rubbing Linda's back and Linda pressing her cheek against Sandy's bright golden hair, letting the grateful tears well up and slide down her cheeks. Another breeze came in through the window, warm and gentle, sweet with the promise of a world made new.

51

AFTER THE FLOOD

July 9, 1976

Brig had driven the rental car all the way from the airport at Idaho Falls, and he was still wrung out from the strain of the past few weeks—first learning from his mission president in Helsinki that a flood had devastated his hometown, then waiting to hear if his family had survived— and finally, the agonizing blow, the news that Tamsin was gone. He had a headache and a sour stomach and the jetlag was getting to him. It was night in Helsinki, yet it was high noon in Rexburg, and Brig couldn't keep anything straight except the fact that his sister didn't exist anymore—not here in the earthly realm, at least.

"I'm telling you," Ondi said, holding up the scrap of paper as if Brig could read it while driving, "that's the address Aran gave me on the phone."

Ondi was more alert, having come from the southern hemisphere, where the worst he had to contend with was a sudden change from winter to summer. Brig reflected that he should have let Ondi drive.

"That address is up on the Bench," Brig said.

"Apparently, that's where Aran lives now."

They ascended the Bench and moved steadily toward the new address. The homes in the town proper still bore traces of the flood—staining and water lines along their walls, flattened patches of mud where once lawns and gardens had been. But here in the heights above Rexburg, the houses were stately and untouched, proud and secure against the sky.

It seemed inevitable, Brig mused, that one of the Rigbys should have ended up here. After all, their family had been among the original settlers. This was the place they deserved. And there was a kind of harmony to the fact that it was Aran who had made it, he who had risen above the town in the end. Something in that fact felt poetic to Brig, almost to the point of sanctity.

Ondi, for his part, found himself struck by the smallness of Rexburg. The disaster had left the town looking feeble, insignificant, even a month later. Not even the finest homes on the Bench could impress him the way they used to. He had lived half a year now in Montevideo, a city of more than a million souls. Why had he ever thought Rexburg so important—so powerful that its expectations must never be challenged, all its taboos kept inviolate?

Ondi kept looking down at the address and watching the house numbers as they passed, but his mind was on other places. He and Brig had been granted leave from their missions to mourn the loss of their sister, but soon enough, they'd be back at their work, and then, before Ondi knew it, his mission would be over. He was already wondering about the future. He thought he might settle in Salt Lake City—for a short time, anyway—then move on to some other place, a university in a secular town, a place at least as big as Montevideo. He would study engineering—civil engineering. He would learn how to build dams, or how to build cities so that floods couldn't unmake them. There was more to the world than this small town, and the world was waiting, waiting.

They found the red-brick house and Aran met them at the door with a long embrace for each of them.

"I'm sorry you were pulled away from your missions," Aran said. "I know how much you were both looking forward to serving."

"That doesn't matter," Ondi said, and Brig added, "We'll go back when things are more settled here."

By which he meant—all three of the Rigby boys understood—after they'd convinced Arletta to accept Tamsin's loss and agree to hold a service in her memory.

Despite Tamsin's absence from the family, the twins' homecoming wasn't entirely a sorrowful affair. There was a baby to meet—their niece, Genevieve, only two weeks old.

Linda called from the kitchen, where she was stirring gravy for a pot roast, "Good luck prying the baby out of Grandpop's and Nana's arms."

She watched through the kitchen's pass-through bar while the twins met Genevieve for the first time. Gad and Arletta had been taking turns rocking and cooing to the baby on the sofa that faced the bay window and the view of the valley below. Arletta was first to stand up and greet her sons, but she was eager to take Genevieve back from Gad and leave him to conversation with Brig and Ondi. Linda saw the way Arletta tucked the baby close to her breast, the gentleness and distant pain as she brushed Genevieve's soft cheek with her fingers. Now that Linda was a mother herself, she felt closer to Arletta than she ever had before. A new bond had grown between them, a tight and necessary alliance. No one but Linda could truly understand Arletta's pain, her reluctance to let Tamsin go. Only a mother could know the ferocity and permanence of that kind of love.

Linda thought, *We can stay in Rexburg another year if we have to. Maybe two. However long it takes for Arletta to let go. However long it takes for her to stop needing the baby so much, and for me to stop needing Arletta.*

Aran stood with one arm around each of his brothers, listening to their talk about the missions, the countries they'd been living in, how difficult the journey home had been. When a lull came, he said gently to his mother, "Why don't we introduce the little lady to her uncles?"

Arletta looked up reluctantly.

"Come help me with the gravy, Mom," Linda called from the kitchen. "I can never get it right. You've got to teach me the family secret."

Arletta passed Genevieve to Gad, then wandered into the kitchen, one hand toying with the ruby necklace Gad had recently given her. But Gad seemed in no hurry, either, to hand the baby to his sons. He cooed and tapped a finger on her tiny chin. Genevieve wrinkled up her face and squeaked at him.

"She loves her grandpop," Aran said. "These two have been inseparable. Mom and Dad officially moved back to their place last week— Dad, Joel Kimball, and I got it all cleaned up and dried out for them and replaced whatever furniture we couldn't save. But they've been permanent fixtures here since Genevieve came along."

"It's nice to see you all getting along so well," Ondi said.

Aran smiled. "We're doing all right. You know, Dad has been painting with me down in my studio. Did you boys know your old man is a pretty good artist?"

"Oh," Gad said, "I'm not as good as Aran."

"Like heck you aren't. Once things are back on track around here and the baby is a little older, Linda is going to take some of Dad's work out to the galleries, see if she can't land him a solo show. He's been developing a pretty good style. A style all his own," Aran added with a significant look at his father.

Gad didn't really hear what Aran had said. As usual, he was too enraptured by the baby. He petted her silky hair. Tamsin's hair had looked just that way as a newborn, cornsilk curls, copper red. In the midst of that bleak, barren summer, his granddaughter had come to remind him of the promise of salvation, an endless certainty of renewal. The baby had ushered something warm and soft and permanent into

Gad's heart—a gentleness, a willingness to accept what he had been given.

"All right," Brig said, stretching out his arms, "you've hogged the baby long enough. Hand her over."

They all laughed as Gad passed the baby to her uncle. Aran left them there, content with the sound of their happiness, and went to kiss Linda in the kitchen.

"Did you get the mail yesterday?" Linda said. "Feldermann called me last week and said he was sending a check, but I haven't seen it yet."

"I forgot," Aran said. "I'll go get it now."

He left by the kitchen door, stepped out into the warmth and flush of the summer day. A thick, languorous smell of growing things rose up from the valley. Aran looked down at the silver curves of the river, innocent and tame now between its banks. He could no longer tell where the wheat field had been, or the old, abandoned shack where he and Tamsin had so often painted together. The whole valley was a tangle of new growth, a wilderness yet to be reclaimed by man.

Aran reached his mailbox, took out a bundle of letters and a catalog, flipped through the stack with idle curiosity. There was the expected envelope from Feldermann Associates—Linda would be relieved. He sorted through the circulars and postcard advertisements from the local businesses. Then he came across another envelope, addressed to him— unremarkable except for the handwriting. The look of it, the distinctive shape of the letters, pulled Aran out of himself, left him stunned and unaware on the side of the road. It took him several frantic heartbeats to understand why that envelope had shocked him so, and just what he had recognized on its face.

The letter was addressed in Tamsin's handwriting.

Aran tore open the envelope so desperately that he dropped the rest of his mail. Everything went scattering in the wind. He managed to pin down Feldermann's check with his foot, but he let the rest of it go, let it all blow off across the street and into the potato fields beyond.

Shivering, Aran turned his back to the house and hunched his shoulders, guarding the letter from view, though he was alone out there by the road. He unfolded the paper and read.

> *Dear Aran,*
> *I'm safe. I'm in San Francisco. Can you believe it? I'm starting at City College in the fall, and after that I'll go to a university. I don't know which one yet. I guess any one I want.*
>
> *Don't tell Mom and Dad where I am. Or Brig and Ondi, if you hear from them. Maybe not Linda, either. I think she's mad at me. You can tell her someday, and Mom and everyone else, too, but not till I say so. I'm going to stay away for a long time. I won't be gone forever. I'll come back someday, when I'm all myself again. But I can't come back to you till I know how to be me, all alone.*
>
> *I guess Linda has had the baby by now. I hope he's good and healthy. I wish I could see him, and you.*
>
> *I miss you. I love you. Write to me and tell me how you are.*
>
> *I love you all, forever.*
> *Tamsin*

Aran sank down to the ground and sat there, cross-legged on the side of the road, with the gravel biting into him and the sun bouncing hot off the pavement. It seemed he wasn't capable of anything else just then, not even breathing. After a few minutes, a car passed and honked its horn. Aran climbed to his feet and picked up the envelope from Feldermann, but even as he did, he was reading Tamsin's letter again, which he realized he'd read through six, seven times already, maybe more. He stayed outside with his back turned to the house and the town till all the shock had fled and a quiet, cool acceptance had taken its place. This was real—this was true. His mother had been right all along. Arletta saw more than anyone suspected; she had told Aran as much, once. Somehow, she had seen even this.

He folded the letter and put it in his pocket, where he could feel the paper crackling and pressing against him. He paced across the front yard between the two young apple trees. Somewhere out in the furrows of the field, he could hear a meadowlark calling, a bright golden fall of song.

When Aran had composed himself, certain he could face his family without betraying Tamsin's secret, he went back inside. Linda was gathering everyone to the table. Aran took his place at its head. Brig pulled Arletta's chair out for her, but he was talking quietly to her even as she sat and spread her napkin on her lap.

"Once we've had a service for Tamsin," Brig was saying, "they'll call us back to our missions. There's no rush, but we should—"

"It's all right," Aran said. "We don't need to have a service for Tamsin if Mom doesn't want to."

Everyone turned to Aran, surprised.

He would tell them all that Tamsin was still alive. Just as soon as he figured out the right way to do it. They didn't need to know about San Francisco. He could keep that secret, for Tamsin's sake.

He said, "All we need to do right now is focus on the blessings we still have. And we have plenty."

Linda took her seat at Aran's side. She leaned in to kiss his cheek. "Gad," she said, "why don't you give the prayer?"

The Rigbys joined hands around the table. It wasn't the way they were accustomed to praying, but it seemed natural now, to reach for one another and take hold of everything that was precious and real. Aran brushed the letter in his pocket one last time before he took his father's hand. As Gad began to speak, Aran bowed his head in thanks.

ACKNOWLEDGMENTS

My novels, though fiction, are often based on real stories I've discovered in my family's history via genealogy and other research activities. This one is no different. It is based on real events that occurred within my family. I know that many of my readers look forward to lengthy notes at the end of my books describing the true stories behind my novels. I'm sorry to disappoint those readers here. Although this novel was based on true events, I'm going to keep all the hows and whens and whos under my hat for reasons of my own. Once in a while, authors ought to be able to cloak themselves in mystery.

I will tell you that I was born in Rexburg, Idaho, in 1980 to a family that followed a strict and traditional version of the Latter-Day Saint (Mormon) faith. My childhood and adolescence were mostly spent in Seattle during the school year. Summers were spent in rural places outside Rexburg, like the character Sandy in this novel.

The flood depicted in this book really did happen on June 5, 1976. Curious readers can learn about the disaster by searching for articles about the Teton Dam.

My sincerest thanks to Chris Werner, my acquisitions editor at Lake Union, and Danielle Marshall, the editorial director of the press, for letting me take another crack at this. Thanks to my developmental editor, Jenna Free, and my copyeditor, Valerie Paquin, for their hard work on this book.

Huge appreciation to the readers who have responded so enthusiastically to my previous books, *The Ragged Edge of Night* and *One for the Blackbird, One for the Crow*. I know I am not the world's most conventional novelist. So many readers have embraced my style and have asked for more of my books, and this support has been wonderful and life changing beyond my ability to express. I am grateful to every one of you.

Thanks, as always, to my wonderful and supportive husband, Paul, for being exactly who he is and filling my life with happiness.

ABOUT THE AUTHOR

Photo © 2018 Paul Harnden

Olivia Hawker is the *Washington Post* bestselling author of *One for the Blackbird, One for the Crow*, a finalist for the Washington State Book Award, and *The Ragged Edge of Night*. Olivia resides in the San Juan Islands of Washington State with her husband and several naughty cats. For more information, visit www.hawkerbooks.com.